I0760974

The Discontent of Mary Wenger

Paper Dolls, Book 1

Robert Tucker

The Discontent of Mary Wenger, Robert Tucker

Tell-Tale Publishing Group
Swartz Creek, MI 48473

Printed in the United States of America

Dedicated to Grammy and Poppa

Preface

Born and raised in 1922 in a coal mining town in the Alleghany Mountains of eastern Pennsylvania, Mary Wenger struggles to escape the influences and stigma of her impoverished immigrant childhood and the presence of death in the recesses of her mind. Her goal is to become a middle-class housewife and mother in pursuit of the American dream.

Emotionally torn between the conflicting historical social forces of feminism and the traditional roles of women in post-World War II society, she is plagued with a deep sense of despair, as she encounters one disappointment after another.

Spanning the continent during the decades of the 1930s, '40s and '50s to the turn of the century, her pathological, compulsive lifelong odyssey in search of an 'acceptable house' in which to realize her personal and economic goals throws her out of balance with her family and her siblings. She is blind to the fact a particular house is not necessarily a home and that her neurotic obsession undermines her ability to find happiness.

An ensemble of oppressed neighbor women and the published feminist writings of a wartime friend, Gwen Gebhardt, ratchet up her intense psychological conflicts and challenge her mental stability in confronting change.

Told with a subtle touch of humor, her memoir of discovery and fear of separation from her children expresses how her personal discontent, obsessions, internal demons, and depression affect her husband and children, as they mature and independently react to her attempts to mold them to her vision of how they all should be as a family.

The life of every character is determined by his or her delusions and how they clash with each other.

This woman's story resonates with novels by such authors as Meg Wolitzer, Anne Tyler, Ann Patchett, Jodi Picoult, Jane Smiley, and Joyce Carol Oates.

1

My Discontent

Since I was a young girl, I have always believed that death is stalking me. It lurks and hovers in the dark recesses of my mind like a virus waiting to strike and destroy when I least expect it.

When I was eight years old, I wrote a poem about myself and death.

My name is Mary
Sounds airy
Death is scary
It makes me wary
Being wary makes me carey

All my life, I have developed defenses and tried to be a protector of the people I love. They often didn't see things the way I did and they didn't agree with me. But I knew what was best for all of us.

I always have.

Chapter 1

Colver

My mother told me the first night when she and Dad moved in, the wail of an infant floated up to their bedroom. Eyes wide open with fear, she lay listening as the weak cry faded to silence.

"Mike, did you hear that?" she whispered and poked Dad in the ribs. "It came from the cellar."

"Just a cat. I'll chase it out in the morning."

Shaking his arm, she insisted. "It sounded like a baby. You must go down and look."

"I'm tired. I look in the morning."

"Please, Mike, I scared."

"Aah! All right." He touched a lighted match to their bedside candle. The electricity had not yet been connected. He went down the creaking stairs into the cellar.

Unseen by him, a woman's bare foot and leg were pulled out through the window. The glow of the candlelight was reflected by the wet shine of an object in one corner. Dad approached it and his blood chilled.

A newborn infant lay curled, the blood and mucous of the afterbirth still clinging to its blue body.

In horror, he fumbled his way back up the stairs to the bedroom where he blew out the candle and set it on the dresser.

Mother pulled the blankets close around herself. "What was it?"

Dad quickly climbed into bed. "Nothing but cat. I get rid of it in the morning."

Before Mother awoke, Dad buried the infant in the back part of the yard farthest from the house in a corner of what would be a vegetable garden.

Many years later, when I was a young woman, Mother told me she knew Dad had lied to her to shield her from the grotesque reality of what he had found in the basement. She knew the difference between the wail of a newborn infant and the wail of a cat.

She never asked him where he had buried the infant. She suspected she knew from the unusual growth and size of tomatoes she had planted in that section of the garden. The thought of the child as fertilizer sickened her. Believing the soul of the infant existed in the ripe red fruit, she buried the tomatoes in a field far from the house and dug up and destroyed the plants.

Refusing to explain why, she avoided planting any other vegetables in that part of the garden. The spot of untilled soil was a silent message to Dad that she knew what had lain buried there.

During the first twelve years of their marriage, my parents had four children, and Mum was again pregnant. The baby was expected sometime within the next month. I noticed that Dad appeared old and worn from the worry and labor of raising a family under poor conditions.

Day after day, he had driven coal cars into the mines. With only a bandana to mask his nose and mouth, he had breathed great amounts of coal dust which caused him violent fits of coughing from his lungs. He was a changed man from the father I had known as a small child. His youthful exuberance had faded away. The routine and unhealthy hazardous conditions at the mines had beaten him down. Weighted with weariness, he returned home each evening and sat in his easy chair and read the paper. His failing health never diminished his love for his family, especially his son.

John, the oldest, had been named after Dad's grandfather back in Czechoslovakia, the old country. Showing a softness of flesh from the indulgence bestowed upon him, he was a handsome, tall, fun-loving boy of twelve years with curly blonde hair and a sense of maturity required of elder siblings. Dad saw to it that John always received the best pieces of meat at the dinner table. His preferential treatment did not go unnoticed by his three sisters.

He was never allowed to play rough games, such as football or basketball with other boys at school. Mike constantly warned him to take precautions concerning the care of his fingers. John was a virtuoso violinist in the eyes of his father and of his teacher.

The one time a group of boys ganged up on John while he was walking home from school and threatened to break his fingers, my sisters and I jumped in front of him. Screaming and snarling and scratching like alley cats, we beat the snot out of the leaders and sent them running. They never bothered John again.

He was never required to do any of the household chores. We girls were even responsible for splitting kindling for the wood-burning stove, while our brother would come home from school each day and practice the violin until supper. We were accustomed to hearing the sensuous, vibrant, glassy sounds of his playing that filled the house and danced through open windows out to us on the veranda porch.

I was sitting between Ruth and Nina clinking ice in our glasses of lemonade. I slowly turned the pages of the latest Sears & Roebuck catalog while they chatted about the clothes and merchandise they would buy if they had the money. We all did a lot of wishing in those days. Wishing didn't cost anything but left us with an aching malaise and a shared emptiness that our imaginations could not fill.

Since we had little in the way of personal possessions, we shared everything. If one of us even bought a candy bar, we wouldn't think of eating it all. We would divide it up so each of us had a taste.

Dad rose from the swing and entered the house with a clipping from the catalog, opened a small desk drawer, and took out a sheet of paper, pen, and an envelope. Further deliberating over the advertisement, he walked into the kitchen and stiffly eased his tired body onto a chair.

As he explained later to us, the business sounded promising. It could mean a great deal more money. During his fourteen years with the mining company, his wage had increased by only a small amount.

Our meals consisted mostly of soup and noodles with chunks of boiled roast or chicken taken from the bone. Our diet was dependent on Mum's ability to bake, garden, harvest, and preserve fruits and vegetables. Crusty homemade bread was always in abundance on which we would spread tongue tingling strawberry, blackberry, and grape jams. Jars of peaches, pears, and vegetables canned during late summer and fall to carry us through the winter filled the cupboard shelves Dad had built in the cellar.

But now, the spring warmth no longer infused him with the relief and freshness of seasonal change. The harshness of his cough had increased, and one morning, he was startled to discover he had coughed up blood with his phlegm.

He hadn't told Mum for fear she would insist he see the doctor and he couldn't spare the money for himself, not with the birth of another child at hand.

I noticed the wrinkles around his eyes had deepened. At thirty-three years, he was an old man. The money from chicken farming would help and he would continue to work in the mines.

He finished the letter and sealed it in the envelope. Mum kept a few stamps in the cupboard above the stove. He licked and stuck one on, double checked the address, and walked back to the front porch.

My sisters and I were still telling each other our wishes and daydreams in terms of what struck our fancy in the catalog and what we would never own. Dad nudged me with the toe of his boot.

"You girls want something to do?"

A chorus of "Yes, but not work," answered him.

"Here, take this to post office."

My hand shot up and grabbed the letter. "I'll carry it."

As I set the catalog aside, I noticed the sound of the violin had stopped. Dad turned to re-enter the house and met John at the screen door.

"Is it all right if I stop now?" John asked.

"How long you practice?"

"Three hours."

"Do one more. Four a day. That what your teacher say. He say you are a genius, so you practice like one."

John returned to his bedroom.

Dad stepped past us and walked around the side of the house to the garden in back and picked up a hoe from the lawn.

Ruth and Nina and I jostled each other off the porch and along the walk into the main section of town.

The garden was badly in need of weeding. Mum hadn't been able to do it lately, so we girls would occasionally help out after school. Green beans hung heavily on their vines and the tomatoes growing in the front section of the plot were large and red. I didn't mind chopping the dull edge of the hoe into the dirt, but I didn't like to pull up weeds with my hands. I didn't have my Mother's green thumb. I was never meant to be a farmer and I never planted a garden.

When we returned from the post office, Dad was still out in the garden and we heard Mum calling to us. John didn't hear her because of his violin playing, which was quite loud.

When my sisters and I entered our mother's stale stuffy room, her eyes fluttered open. She felt warm to the touch. Her head lolled in a groggy manner. Her sallow Slavic features were drained of their usual rosy flush. She didn't have the will to move. Ruth opened the window to let in some fresh air. The three of us eased her out of bed and changed her from her nightgown into a loose-fitting maternity dress which she had made for herself. Then, barefoot, and with both hands on the banister railing and two of us balancing her, she made her way out onto the front porch.

She clutched her abdomen and doubled over, complaining, "I feel sick. Need to go in."

We helped her back inside and lowered her onto the couch.

"Where is father?" she asked.

"Out in the garden," I said. "Shall we get him?"

"No, I just feel dizzy for a moment."

We let her doze undisturbed on the couch. Ruth and I prepared dinner.

Late that night, Mum's water broke and the first sharp stab of labor passed through her. I heard her calling, "Mike, wake up! Mike!" I leaped out of bed and ran to their room as Mum was telling him, "Go for doctor. Hurry." We did not have a telephone.

"I'll go," I shouted and ran back to the room I shared with Ruth and Nina. They had awakened at the noise but were still in bed.

"What happened?" Ruth asked.

"Go help Mum. She's about to have the baby. I'm getting the doctor." As they ran out of the room and down the hall, I hastily pulled on a dress over my nightgown and jammed my feet into my shoes.

Running down the street, I saw myself as an angel of mercy on winged feet bent on saving my Mother and her baby.

As soon as Doctor Langfelder opened the door at my loud insistent knocking, I could smell on his breath he had been drinking. He was still wearing his shoes and trousers and a sleeveless undershirt. I could see from a bunched blanket he had been sleeping on the couch. The fights and arguments he had with his wife were no secret. He blinked and stared at me through his wire-rim bifocals as though he were having trouble seeing. His balding dark hair was askew and gave him the appearance of a rudely awakened rodent.

"Wha' you want?"

"Doctor Langfelder, my mother is giving birth. Could you come to our house right away."

He rubbed his bewhiskered jowls. "Your Woijcek's daughter, or at least one of 'em."

"I'm Mary. Please hurry."

"Can't you bring her in to the clinic?"

"There isn't any time. She's started labor."

"Have to get my bag. Wait here." Leaving the door open, he shuffled back through the living room. I watched him struggle into his shirt, pull up his suspenders over his paunch, and weave unsteadily into an adjoining room. As the minutes passed, I fidgeted impatiently and wondered where he had gone. I called out.

"Doctor Langfelder! Doctor Langfelder!"

He finally reappeared and walked unsteadily toward me. Sorry about the wait. Had to use the toilet. How far do you live from here?"

"On First Street at the corner of Main."

"Close enough we don't have to drive." He had his black bag in hand. "All right, lead the way. Let's go."

I ran down his mansion front steps and started to hurry on ahead until I realized he wasn't right behind me. I waited for him to catch up. Globe streetlamps cast their erratic shifting disjointed shadows like two dark spirits gliding along over the yards and fronts of houses.

When we reached our house, I urged him up the stairs ahead of me to my parents' room. Under the dim ceiling light, Mum lay pale and moaning on her back on the double bed. Sweat soaked her nightgown. Her hair hung in damp ringlets; her arm thrown across her forehead.

Dad and my brother and sisters stood crowded around the bed.

"Everybody out," Doctor Langfelder ordered. "Someone bring me towels and a pan of hot water. You stay. You can help," he said to me. He leaned over Mum. "Mrs. Woijcek, I'm Doctor Langfelder. Can you hear me?"

Mum nodded but did not open her eyes.

"I want you to raise and bend your knees and spread your legs so I can examine you."

I watched him peer and probe at Mum's private parts. "She's dilated, but she hasn't crowned yet," he said. He rolled up his sleeves and removed a pair of forceps and long scissors and some kind of thread from his bag. "I'm hoping we don't have to use these. Everything looks normal so far." He put the non-sterile forceps on the bedside table and adjusted the shade to provide more light.

Ruth and Nina returned with a large pot of steaming hot water and an armload of towels, which Doctor Langfelder motioned to leave on the bed. Ruth placed the pot of hot water on the side table and she and Nina left the room.

"Close the door," Doctor Langfelder ordered me. His speech was slurred. "Are you able to hear me?" He spoke to Mum. She nodded. "You've done this before," he told her, as he tucked two towels under her and spread another on the bed where the baby would emerge. "As you feel pain, breathe deeply and let it out in short breaths. You're dilated and your contractions have started. The baby will start to appear soon." He glanced over at me. I suppose I looked bug-eyed. "Are you sure you want to stay for this? Have you seen a delivery before?"

"I'll stay. I haven't." I had a hard time staring at my mother's exposed vagina and had to look away out of respect and embarrassment. "Is there anything you want me to do?"

He shook his head. "Not yet. Can you handle the sight of blood?"

"I'm not sure. I think so. Is there going to be blood?" At the time, I wasn't sure. I didn't even like to see bloody cuts of meat at the butcher. Three years before, I had seen a pig's carcass hanging in Dad's smokehouse. I had run away and vomited and sworn off meat. Much to my parents' distress, I had refused to eat meat after that, ever. I became a vegetarian, which distressed Mum, since she always cooked beef or pork or chicken. I couldn't help it if I was squeamish.

"Yes, this is going to be bloody. You can bring more towels and wipe her clean. It gets messy."

As the contractions increased, Mum grunted and moaned and howled at the pain. I sat on a chair next to the bed and held her hand. I thought her grip would crunch my bones. Doctor Langfelder handed me a damp washcloth to place across Mum's forehead.

Two hours passed. Doctor Langfelder asked me to bring him a glass of water. I went to the door, out into the hall and shouted down the stairs where the others were waiting in the kitchen. "Bring me up a glass of water for Doctor Langfelder!"

John came clumping up the stairs and handed it to me. Spilling water, I rushed back to the bedroom at my mother's scream.

"It's coming," said Doctor Langfelder without looking up. "Starting to crown. I can see the top of its head."

I handed him the water, which he drank in three gulps and handed back the glass.

I watched fascinated as the grayish colored fetus coated with blood and amniotic fluid pushed out. Doctor Langfelder assisted it onto the towels.

"It's stillborn," he muttered. "It's stillborn."

After a minute, he picked up the baby by its chubby tiny feet and ankles with his left hand, held it high, and spanked it on its bottom three times to get it breathing. The baby didn't start breathing.

Doctor Langfelder lost his grip on the slick surface of the newborn's skin. The baby slipped from his grasp and fell headfirst onto the bed between my mother's legs. The startled cry from the infant brought tears to my eyes. Mum's eyes were closed from exhaustion and she didn't see the grotesque position of her child, as it wailed.

Shaking and fumbling, Doctor Langfelder severed and tied off the umbilical cord. Moments later, Mum's bloody placenta leaked out of her vagina onto the towels. He arranged the baby so she could hold it next to her.

The rest of the family had rushed up the stairs at the sound of the first cry and were huddled at the open door. Doctor Langfelder avoided looking at Dad, as they entered the room.

"It's a girl. Everything went fine. She's all right. They're both all right. Now, best to leave 'em alone, except Mary. You and your sisters can clean all this up. Wipe down the baby. Help your mother get started nursing. Now that it's breathing, the blood's flowing and it's showing some color. I'm done here." He washed and dried his hands and dropped the bloody scissors into his bag. With a final look at me, he said, "The baby's fine. Thanks for your help." The rest of the family parted, as he walked out through the open door and stumbled down the stairs.

Mum named the child Margaret. Not until the baby was three months old, did she realize that something was wrong. Despite coaxing and handling and encouraging her little body, Margaret never attempted to sit up or roll over and reacted only to the touch of a hand. Her eyes didn't track movement and she didn't smile in response to our voices.

When we took her to see Doctor Langfelder, he told us there was nothing he could do. "You should take her to the hospital in Philadelphia. You would have to leave her there. Maybe they can diagnose her symptoms."

"No," I spoke angrily. "You were drunk. I saw you drop her."

"You drop her?" Mum was shocked. I had not mentioned anything to her about the birth.

"I did not drop her. Your daughter doesn't understand the delivery process."

"I know what I saw," I snapped back, my face a mask of fury that he was belittling me to cover up his incompetence.

"This conversation is over. If you want professional help, you need to take Margaret to the baby hospital in Philadelphia. That's all I have to say. Now, I have other patients waiting. We're done here."

As we left the clinic, I argued, "We can't leave her at the hospital. Who will show her love. They can't give her love."

"She get special care," said Dad.

"Mum, Dad, you can't send her away to die there," I insisted. "They'll put her in a room with freaks and we'll never see her again."

Tears streamed down Mum's face. Neither she nor Dad responded. I couldn't believe they were giving up just because of that drunken bastard who called himself a doctor.

The morning my parents were going to leave, I insisted they take me with them. Their understanding of spoken English was somewhat limited and I wanted to hear firsthand what any doctor would tell them.

A friend of Dad's had loaned him his car, a standard Chevrolet, to make the trip.

Except for when Margaret was taking her bottle, I held her for most of the way. Believing I could protect my little sister and restore her to health, I had assumed responsibility for her care, changing her and carrying her and attempting to get her to respond to my voice and touch.

Mum had wrapped Margaret in a soft cotton blanket with a pink and blue pattern and had tucked her feet into little booties I had knitted for her. The baby mostly slept during the ride, but from time to time, I noticed her eyes open looking up at my face in what I believed was an expression of trust while I was holding her.

When we pulled into the hospital parking lot, I wanted to tell Dad to turn around and go back home; but we had come this far and he and Mum decided they should at least hear what some other doctor, a specialist, who knew more than Doctor Langfelder, might have to say.

Reminding me of a Medieval fortress, the monolithic size of the six story concrete building intimidated us as we entered through the wide wooden front doors.

A slender middle-aged nurse with dark hair tucked up in a bun behind her white and blue wing hat rose with a smile of concern from behind a check-in counter to greet us.

"Hello, may I help you?" Her manner was kindly but did not allay my suspicions that anyone there could do more for Margaret than I could at home.

Mum spoke first. "Doctor say we should see doctor here about daughter, Margaret."

"I'm Mrs. Neeson," she pointed to her name tag on the blouse of her navy blue uniform. "Can you tell me something about Margaret?"

At that point, I couldn't contain myself. "Something happened when she was born. She doesn't do things a baby should be doing. It's because the doctor dropped her. He was drunk when he came to our house to deliver her."

Mrs. Neeson looked at me, not believing what I was telling her. "Inebriated doctors don't deliver babies."

"I was standing right there when it happened. He had whiskey on his breath. He smelled like a still."

"I see. Well, let me get Margaret signed in and then we'll have a doctor examine her."

Since my parents' writing skills were limited, I filled out the medical admittance form, They laboriously signed their names. Then Mrs. Neeson led us down a long hallway to an examination room. As we hovered at the open door, she said, "Doctor Gaddis may ask two of you to leave for the sake of privacy. It's pretty tight and crowded in here. He'll let you know. He'll be with you in several minutes."

Mum sat on a chair with Margaret next to the examination table. Dad and I stood over by a sink and plastic containers of medical supplies on the counter. I tried not to inhale the strong odor of disinfectant alcohol in a glass beaker holding three thermometers.

The several minutes became fifteen. I fidgeted with anxiety until I heard a brief firm knock and the door slowly opened. A tall young doctor with straight dark hair severely combed back from his brow stood there in his white lab coat and looked us over with a gentle smile.

"Mr. and Mrs. Woijcek, I'm Doctor Gaddis. It's nice to meet you. I apologize for keeping you waiting. Thank you for bringing your daughter in. Nurse Neeson told me you filled out the medical history form for your parents," he spoke to me in a kindly tone. Everything about him, including his boyish features, was pleasant, but firm. In a respectful way, he clearly established he was in charge. "The space in here is small, so I'm going to ask you and your father to sit in the waiting room. I'll come out and talk to you afterwards."

"I want to stay," I protested. "My parents' English is limited and I take care of Margaret at home. I want to see what you do and hear what you have to say."

"All right, ah, Mr. Woijcek, perhaps you wouldn't mind waiting in the waiting room."

"It's okay, Dad," I encouraged him. "I'll be here with Mum."

Dad nodded and left the room. Doctor Gaddis closed the door, then turned to Mum. "Mrs. Woijcek, would you place Margaret on the examination table, please."

"I'll do it," I said. "Here, Mum, I'll take her." I lifted the baby from Mum's arms and, supporting her fragile head just beginning to sprout silky blonde hair, gently lay her on the cushion covered with white paper Nurse Neeson had reeled from a roller under the head of the table.

Using a pocket pen flashlight, Doctor Gaddis checked Margaret's eyes. They did not track when he slowly moved his finger from side to side. When he tickled the bottoms of her feet, her toes did not curl and she did not grip his finger when he placed it against the palms of her hands.

"She shows symptoms of a neurological disorder," he said.

"What does that mean?" I asked.

"It could be caused by a spinal injury or may have occurred during her prenatal phase."

"The other doctor dropped her."

"Nurse Neeson told me you mentioned that."

"What we want to know is can you fix Margaret?"

"I'll have to take some X-rays to assess the condition of her spine. Until I have that result, I won't be able to advise you."

"Can you do the X-rays now while we're here?"

"There may be a short wait, but, yes, I'll schedule it. Her chart says you live in Colver. You came a long way."

"We have to go back home today, with Margaret."

Doctor Gaddis nodded. "I understand. But depending on the severity of damage to her spinal cord, Margaret may have to remain here for optimal care."

"You can put that out of your mind right now," I retorted. "Margaret will be coming home with us."

"I understand your concern, Miss. Let's wait and see what the X-rays show us."

I turned to Mum. "Do you understand what he's saying, Mum?"

She nodded.

Doctor Gaddis opened the door. "Will you bring Margaret and follow me."

Barely able to hold back tears, I scooped Margaret into my arms.

Even though the nursery on the third floor was staffed with attendant nurses and doctors, I didn't believe they could do more to sustain Margaret's life and make her comfortable in that sterile environment than I could at home. Despite X-rays showing Margaret's damaged spinal cord, I did not want to accept Doctor Gaddis's explanation of the medical facts and his "prognosis" of her "condition." My parents and I were sitting in his office.

"She has what is called spina bifida," he told us. "This is a condition where the vertebrae do not completely enclose the raw nerves of the spine and there is an opening in the spinal column. The nerves of the spine are at risk of injury from blunt trauma in the cervical region of the spine. That's the neck area. Or the cause could have been her position passing through the birth canal at delivery. Margaret has no touch sensations, which is why she doesn't respond to any physical touching or stimulation. She also doesn't have the ability to move by herself. She may experience spasms and have difficulty breathing, in addition to her overall weakness. She won't develop language. Although she's still too young to recognize the difference, she cannot control her bowel and bladder functions. As hard to accept as it sounds, her chances of survival are minimal."

I wanted to leap out of my chair and choke him. "I don't want to leave her here!" I shouted. "I can keep her alive! I want to take her home!"

"Miss, I know how traumatic this is for you and I know how much you love your little sister. But the decision is up to your mother and father."

I looked over at them. "It's also up to me!" I shouted. "I can take care of her. I already do!" They didn't want to leave Margaret in the hospital to live out her final days any more than I did, but, as I came to learn, notwithstanding their religious superstitions, they had a keener sense and acceptance of reality than I did or would ever have for my entire life.

We went to the infant care nursery to see Margaret one last time. I could barely restrain myself from snatching her up and racing out of the hospital with her.

We told Margaret how much we loved her. Our words sounded empty and banal ringing off the sterile walls. Then we left her behind.

With tears of remorse streaming down her face, Mum clutched Margaret's empty baby blanket to her breasts. Dad wiped away tears with the back of his hand, as he started up the car and pulled out of the hospital parking lot.

My uncontrolled tears at deserting my little sister were also tears of rage at the unfairness of life for Margaret and for the rest of the family. Time and again, I would experience forces over which I had no influence, but I fought just the same.

I was a young girl running. I ran everywhere. I ran with my schoolwork. With running / with argumentation, a young girl running to catch up with youth.

We returned home to find the chicks Dad had ordered from the Sears & Roebuck Company all huddled together dead. Mum and Dad took this as an ominous sign.

We never saw Margaret alive again. She withered and died that summer. After she was buried, despair moved in to replace our memory of her. A sense of death and foreboding pervaded the household. Superstition weighed heavily on the minds of our parents. To combat it, they immersed themselves within the security of a small sectarian religion that preached a utopian philosophy in an afterlife, for those who were strong in faith and good works, following a prophesied Armageddon.

Members of the religion called themselves Jehovah's Witnesses. The largely Catholic and Lutheran townspeople ostracized them and their children. Being scorned became our lot and reinforced for me the desire to escape to a better life.

John and my sisters shared my wish, but we were trapped and could do nothing. We were forever condemned to sitting on the porch steps wishing and dreaming. Our fantasies and imagination were not enough to fill the emptiness of our lives.

Chapter 2

Crushed

As graduation approached, I should have felt elated, but wasn't. I internally writhed with frustration and depression. Even though I had straight 'A's in English, Science, and Math, and would graduate at the top of my class, there would be no college in my future.

I had always considered school my second home. More than anything, I loved to read and study and participate in classes that dealt with concepts and ideas. I liked to use my brain. I was the first to raise my hand. Any question on any subject, I had the answer ready. My best and only friend, Violet Karpinsky, was amazed at how I did it. I read and studied ahead in the regular curriculum and made up questions I thought the teachers would ask.

Now, during my senior year, I was mired in accounting, shorthand, and typing classes to "prepare" me for the working world. Since the country was sunk in the middle of an economic depression, work was hard to find. My primary textbooks were Gregg Shorthand and an Underwood typing manual.

My friendship with Violet was limited to our time in class together and during lunch period. Since Violet lived in Wilkes-Barre and I lived in Colver, we didn't see one another outside of school. I would never embarrass myself by inviting Violet to my house, and always claimed I had no way of coming to visit her. Violet's parents weren't wealthy, but much better off than my family. Her father was a supervisor in a Pittsburgh steel mill and came home on weekends.

Colver, Pennsylvania is in the Alleghany Mountains. Located on the gradual rise of a plateau, the town provides a physical symbol of the community's social and economic hierarchy. An aerial view moving left to right reveals at the outskirts dairy farms and forests of spruce, birch, fir, ash, maple, and beech. Noticing and remembering these varieties was unusual for me, since even though we lived in a rural area, I was never an outdoor person.

Following the macadam road in from the farms, the streets are numbered one through six and cross the main road so houses stand in rows on either side. Our family lived a half block in on street number one. All houses on streets one through six were four and one-half rooms, white frame, and two story. Between each stood a half-acre open lot used by children for small, private baseball diamonds and general play areas. This first quarter of the town was laid out in a neat section of quadrangles.

The business district began at the end of sixth street and consisted of establishments along only one side of the main street: a hotel with a barbershop and tavern on the first floor. Next followed a dentist's office, soda fountain and grill, grocery store, and the post office. A public park with a bandstand and playground facilities was directly across the street.

Behind the business district stood the three blocks of King's Row. Constructed of brick, those houses had six rooms. They were the homes of the doctor, the dentist, storekeeper, postmaster, barber, tavern owner, and the mine bosses.

The elementary school, my favorite place as a child, sat across from King's Row.

Sidewalks lined all the streets. The town was kept clean in most areas. Continuing to the right, two more side roads crossed the main street. The one to the left led to the company owner's estate and his sprawling three story brick mansion. The mine superintendent's house was located across from the estate and was only slightly more elaborate than those on King's Row. The hospital was on the same road, only to the right.

The Italian sector was further along Main. Continuing down the winding mountain road past the hospital for one mile, sprawled a shanty town where the Polish miners lived just above the shaft area. Railroad tracks ran through this lower section of the plateau to the mines.

Violet said she wanted to introduce me to her older brother who played on the high school football team, but I would have none of it. If he would ask me out on a date, I would have to turn him down. I would have never let him come to my house to pick me up. Besides, even though he was handsome with snapping brown eyes and dark curly hair, he looked brutish, and I didn't care for brutish men.

Violet once told me she envied my blonde hair and movie star beauty. She hated her plain features and dark curly hair, a family characteristic. I never thought I looked like a movie star. I thought I looked like a frump with my straight cut pinned-back hair. Violet said, because I was so beautiful, I should be chosen for prom queen our senior year. But I didn't go to any dances or belong to any social clubs and I didn't go to the prom. My parents could not have afforded to buy me a dress anyway.

Not even Ruth had gone to the prom and she was a flirt. Boys were drawn to her laughing hazel eyes and physical athletic vitality. She could jitterbug like the professional dancers with all their flips and slides and twirls. We sisters weren't allowed to date, but that didn't stop Ruth and Nina from conspiring to disobey our parents.

I refused when Ruth tried to persuade me to secretly double date to a Saturday night dance being held at the high school. What Ruth really wanted was to neck with her boyfriend, Ned Robertson, a dashing football player with a reputation. Her scheme required us to lie to our mother and father about attending the dance after a football game. They permitted us to attend games, as long as we had a ride home with one of their JW friends.

"None of the boys like me anyway," I insisted while walking home from the bus stop one afternoon with Ruth, Nina, and John. "They think I'm snooty, because I'm smarter than they are. I don't want to sit around watching everybody make fools of themselves anyway."

"You're too hostile," said Ruth. "You need to give the boys a chance."

"Aren't you forgetting what Dad told us? They just want to have us for sex."

"That's what he told you, because he was probably like that when he was our age," John bitterly interjected. Mum and Dad had yelled at him one morning about wet spots on his sheets. Afterward, there had been daily morning inspections to catch John if he had been "having sinful thoughts," as they put it. "We're trying to protect all of you from getting into trouble."

"You could have any girlfriend you want, if you were interested enough," said Nina to John, who was eighteen years old. He had inherited Dad's small nose, deeply cleft chin, a crown of blonde curls, and blue eyes twinkling with mischief.

"Oh, I'm interested all right, but Mum and Dad aren't going to let me go out on a date any more than you. They think some girl will seduce me and then I'll have to get married."

"Talk about the flip side," said Nina. She had boys constantly ogling her exciting figure that exuded an overabundance of natural sex appeal. She moved with an easy fluid grace and unconscious sway of her hips that Mum criticized whenever she saw her walk down the street. To Nina's embarrassment, she would shout at her to "walk straight. Boys will think you are bad girl!"

All through her teenage years, Nina was infuriated with Mum for singling her out and admonishing her for just being a normal girl.

I excused Mum for her old country opinions, because she was not educated and had been forced to be subservient to her father and brothers. She was as much a victim of her times as we were.

Before she met and married our father, our mother's name was Eva Kohlarik. As she related the story of her life in a Bohemian mountain village, she seemed like some other person we didn't know; but her vivid descriptions were burned into my mind.

She lived with her father and three brothers in a timbered and stone cottage.

She said she had feared her father's dark-bearded face and scathing splintered eyes. She had to split kindling each morning for the fire while he waited impatiently for her to make his breakfast.

She used a large flat stump as a base to split kindling. His calloused hand often pushed her from behind and sent her stumbling. To demonstrate their respect and loyalty for their father, her three brothers did not immediately move their boots and legs from blocking her way, forcing her to step over them into the cottage.

She limped across the room to the fireplace where blackened pots hung from iron hooks over flickering coals. She pushed back unkept long brown hair that fell in rough wild tatters over her trembling shoulders. She stirred the thick grain and cornmeal mush in one of the pots, then poured it into five wooden bowls next to a loaf of dark bread. She poured five large porcelain cups of strong black coffee.

Her father and brothers jostled like an unruly herd into the cottage. She listened to the loud scraping of wooden chair legs on the wood floor as they slouched onto their seats. She set a bowl and a spoon on the table for each of them and one aside for herself. She hurriedly ate her own mush, snatched the remaining chunk of bread, jammed a wedge of cheese and two apples from the cold cellar into her side pack, and left the cottage.

She stopped at the outhouse to relieve herself, then walked up the dirt road toward the cow paddocks and the barn. Remnant chunks of melting snow clung to the steep pitch of the roof. The hard soles of her leather boots crunched frozen mud as she trudged along the road. Passing through the vaporous ghosts of her exhaled breath, she pulled down the ear flaps of her fur-lined hat.

As she entered the barn, the acrid odor of urine and cow dung in straw and bovine animal warmth filled her nostrils displacing the chill mountain air. Her brothers had finished their predawn milking of the herd and turned them out to pasture. Five tall metal cans of fresh raw milk waited in the neighboring milk and cheese shed for the cream to rise and be skimmed to produce cheese and butter. Her father, Jerome Kohlarik, was the village *Kase Herrsteller*, the cheese maker. Her brothers would transport the milk and ripened waxed cheese by horse drawn cart to the market, then return to muck out the barn and sterilize empty cans with boiling water in preparation for the evening milking.

Three cows roamed about loose in the runway. They stared frightened and swayed from side to side. Their noses dripped mucous, ragged ears flicked. Then they stumbled away with a clumsy attempt at speed. She shooed them outside into the paddock at the opposite end of the long barn. One brown and white spotted cow did not run. Eva walked to her and fondled her fuzzy ears. She had bottle fed and raised her pet from the time it was born and its mother had died giving birth. Eva talked to the cow as though she understood, as a friend.

"I think I'm going to run away, Dusa. I'm sixteen years old and a woman. Father has no right to treat me the way he does. I was tired this morning and didn't wake up. He said he's going to marry me to the *burgermeister's* son in Dusnik to join their lands. I'm sure I will run away soon. Will you be lonely without me? I will miss you."

She walked Dusa to the paddock and looked up toward the foothills. Scattered patches of snow survived encroaching swathes of long green grass and yellow, red, and blue wildflowers on the north facing slopes of the *Krkonose* Mountains. The sun's emerging eye crept from behind the mountain peaks and bathed the granite slopes and green spring valleys surrounding the Bohemian village tucked among rolling hills.

Eva shielded her eyes against the brilliant light. With Dusa close at her side, she drove the herd slowly away from the barn past the growing mound of straw and manure that would be spread to fertilize the spring vegetable garden. Following the dull metallic clangor of the lead cow bell, the herd wound its way into the mountains through dense forests, over shallow crossings of rushing cascading streams, and out into a large woodland meadow.

Eva removed her mud encrusted boots and flopped down in the long soft grass on a rise slightly above where the cows were grazing. Brushing away a fly, she took out her whittling knife and gazed out over the valley below. She spoke softly, more to herself than to Dusa, whose undulating jaws pulled up and chewed the fresh green growth close by.

"I can't let him beat me again. I'm not strong enough to fight him. He will just have my brothers hold me down. I don't want to do anything for him, for any of them. And I will never marry Gerd Hauser. His nose is too large and he has that awful habit of cleaning out his ears with his little finger and sucking it. I wish you could talk, Dusa. I'd like to know what you think about it all. I wish mother was still alive."

At noon, she washed her hands and face and dipped her bare feet in the tingling cold waters of a mountain stream, then ate her meager lunch of bread and cheese. As the day waned, the gentle warmth of the late afternoon sun and the softness of the grass lulled her to sleep.

The cows grew restless in their grazing and meandered back to the trail, except Dusa, who remained by the sleeping Eva while the others plodded down the steep terrain to return to the barn for milking. As the sun began to set and cast a dusky orange alpenglow, the sudden coolness woke Eva with a start. She looked around wildly.

"The cows, Dusa! They've gone home without us! Why didn't you wake me?" She pulled on her boots and jumped to her feet. "Come on! We have to hurry!"

The cows arrived at the barn and paddocks just as the last quarter of the crescent sun dissolved behind the spiral peaks. Unable to get in, they milled around restlessly, mooing to be milked and fed.

On his way home, Jerome Kohlarik nodded brusquely to villagers he passed along the central street of the town where he had been *burgermeister* for ten years since 1898. The walk from the *rathaus* town hall was not a long one but depressing.

His wife's death from heart failure eight years ago had left him wallowing in resentment that her kind loving nature had been wrenched away from him. He blamed the world. He blamed life. He blamed anything and everything he couldn't understand, anything that hinted at deprivation of his own well-being, especially material deprivation. The emotional and spiritual influence of his wife were gone forever.

Upon entering the cottage, he found his three sons fidgeting, because supper had not been prepared.

"Eva hasn't come home yet. There isn't any supper," said Franz, the eldest. "We fed the cows and did the milking. She wasn't there."

"Well, don't just fatten your ass. Go up to the barn and get her."

"She didn't come home. Her cow, Dusa, didn't come home either. They're still up in the hills."

"Then go find her."

Franz concentrated on scratching his elbow. "But it isn't often that she's late."

Jerome lunged at Franz, who dodged away from his father's raised hand and ran around the table and out the door. The other two brothers snickered. Jerome whirled on them. "Shut up!" They immediately fell silent.

Franz ran a short distance from the cottage. Glancing back to see if Jerome were following, he slowed to a walk. Suddenly he noticed Eva and Dusa coming down the last slant of the hill behind the barn. He turned and jogged back to the cottage, stopping at the open door. Jerome leaped up from the table and rushed him. Staying out of reach, Franz danced nimbly away onto the road.

"Have you no respect? I'll teach you to disobey me!" Jerome roared.

"I saw her coming. She's coming down the hill, just now!"

Jerome halted his charge and looked up. "Where?" Upon seeing his daughter and her cow, he strode quickly to the barn to meet her when she would arrive. Gloating, Franz returned to the cottage.

As Eva approached the paddock, she saw her father waiting for her.

"You're late and we're hungry," he glowered.

"I'm sorry. I was tired and I fell asleep."

Jerome grabbed her by the scruff of her neck and pushed her to the ground. "Is that all you can do is sleep? You'll come home first and prepare supper. Then you can come back and milk your damn cow. Your brothers took care of the rest of it."

Eva spit dirt from the tip of her tongue, then rose stiffly to her feet. Jerome hovered behind her, cursing her all the way to the cottage. They arrived to find her brothers stuffing themselves with bread and cheese from the larder.

"Supper, now!" Jerome barked.

Eva took a large crock of stew and potato soup from a naturally refrigerated rock cellar and poured it into a blackened iron pot hanging over the coals. She stirred it briefly with a ladle.

She removed the bowls and spoons streaked with rings and lines of dried mush from breakfast, washed them in cold water, and returned the spoons to the wooden plank table. She stacked five large bowls on a bench near the fireplace, then again stirred the stew, tumbling the savory pork and carrots, cabbage, and potatoes. The glowing heat from the coals warmed her hands and face.

Jerome lit the lantern candles hung along the walls casting flickering shadows. Eva's three brothers sat at the table with Jerome. The stew bubbled and exploded with orange and brown blisters. Jerome watched Eva closely, as she ladled the stew into the bowls. She placed the first before him, then set one before each of her brothers. As she returned to the pot to fill a bowl for herself, her father's voice snapped at her.

"You can eat later. Go milk your cow first."

She took one hot mouthful from the ladle and replaced it on the hook. Jerome and her brothers ate noisily, as she removed one of the candle lanterns and went out into the night.

In the barn, she found Dusa at the stalls among the other cows. The rustling of straw and the steady overlapping munching of hay increased her own hunger. She pulled harder and faster at Dusa's teats.

The lantern cast a small glowing arc around her boots and black wool skirt, as she plodded wearily back to the cottage. Upon entering, she found Jerome and her brothers had gone to bed. The hour was late. The candles flickered. The coals in the fireplace barely glowed.

Eva set down her lantern and picked up her wooden bowl. She reached for the stew ladle. The pot was empty. She repressed a flash of anger, then went to the cellar for a chunk of bread and cheese. She dejectedly crossed the room to her cot. A loud snore drifted down from the loft. She pulled out a small satchel from under her bed and quietly packed her few belongings.

The ladder to the loft creaked under a heavy weight. Eva whirled in fear of being discovered. Franz paused on the center rung and stared at her. She broke the silence. "What are you doing awake?"

"I have to take a shit." Franz continued down the ladder.

Eva pushed the satchel under the bed with the heel of her foot and Franz went outside to the small shed that served as their toilet. She pulled out the satchel again and stuffed the last few articles into it, then pushed it back under the bed and lay down. After a short while, Franz returned. She watched him enter with a suspicious look.

"What were you doing before?"

"I'm hungry. I was looking for something to eat."

His thin, uneven smile at her discomfort pushed into the side of his face. "We were extra hungry. The stew was good. Father said you could eat bread and cheese when you came back. We worked hard repairing the road today where it washed out." Franz belched. "I'll sleep better now. The potatoes were heavy. And the cabbage. You know what cabbage does. Oh, by the way, you better put some more shit paper out in the shed. I used the last of it." He climbed the ladder and disappeared over the edge of the loft.

Eva listened to him settle into bed. Then she quietly got up, pulled out her satchel, and crossed the room to the cupboards. She stuffed a small loaf of bread into one large pocket of her heavy coat and a wedge of cheese into the other.

She then reached into a small crock where she had seen her father hide the dowry money paid to him for her marriage and removed the leather pouch containing five-hundred krone she would use to pay for her passage to America. Shouldering her side pack, she walked to the door and took a final look around the room and up at the loft. The snoring increased.

She eased out into the night and walked quickly down the road into the village along the cobbled stone street, dark but for an occasional oil-burning lamp. She moved on through the sparsely populated town and paused a moment to look back from a rise at the outskirts before descending into the valley below.

A noisy stream rushing over the rocks at the roadside accompanied her for a few miles. She hiked on under a vast night sky filled with stars.

At dawn, she came to the Elbe River, found a secluded spot in a wooded grove along the water's edge, and sank down exhausted in a soft layer of leaves.

Keeping her eyelids open required too great an effort. She fell into a heavy sleep, as the sun rose above the trees on the opposite bank.

Her coming alone to America to escape from her father and the arranged marriage influenced me for my entire life. I respected the sacrifices she had to make to survive, including trading one condition of servitude for another.

Chapter 3

The Dance

John arrived at the house first and checked the mailbox. Excitement dawned on his face as he read the return address on one of the envelopes. Asking if there were any mail for us, we followed him up onto the porch. He handed over the stack and we flipped through it commenting here and there for no reason about inanities.

Rushing into the kitchen where Mum was preparing supper, he announced loudly, "Mum, Mum, I've been offered a scholarship to Ohio State."

We clustered around him, as he read the letter out loud, then stopped at a paragraph that stated he had to enroll in ROTC to accept the scholarship. The excitement drained from his face like a deflated balloon. He wouldn't be able to accept because of that requirement.

"What is ROTC?" asked Mum.

"Reserve Officer Training Corps for the Army. What does the Army have to do with music?"

Our pacifist religion forbade us from supporting the war effort and even pledging allegiance to the American flag as a false god. We were conscientious objectors.

"Since you got this offer, you could try other colleges," I suggested.

"It's too late to make the application deadlines."

We heard the mine whistle blow from far across town. Dad would be disappointed when he arrived home. I could picture him coughing from inhaled coal dust and sand dust that swirled up from the track bed where it was used to kill sparks from the engine and steel wheels on the rails. He joined other miners coming up out of the mine shafts and pits, then walking to their homes in their ghettoes. As a child, I had watched them completely black-smudged, wearing helmets and carrying picks and shovels.

While Ruth, Nina, and John went off to their rooms, I stayed to help Mum with dinner.

Dad was counting on John to be offered the scholarship. I heard him trudging up the porch steps and met him at the door before Mum could say anything. "Hi, Dad, we've got some good news and bad news."

His bleary bloodshot eyes stared at me from his soot begrimed face as I took his black metal lunch pail. "What is good news?"

"John will tell you after you get changed and washed up."

"About college?"

"It's about Ohio State." I moved aside to make room for him to step through the open door.

"I like good news."

"He has to explain it to you."

Dad's lips parted in a grin revealing two crooked teeth. "They like him?"

"Well, yes, they like him. But he has to explain something." I doubted an exception could be made so he could at least attend the University and get his degree. He could declare he was a pacifist later. The U.S. Government would force him to do two years of prison time, but that would be the trade-off. If he were to be drafted, declaring he was a conscientious objector would land him in prison.

Dad quickly washed at the laundry sink and went upstairs to change. He noticed that John's bedroom door was closed and his violin was silent. Wearing a clean shirt and trousers, he rumbled down the creaking wooden stairs and came into the living room where I was reading.

"John not here?" he asked me.

"He's in his room but let me explain about the letter."

"Why he not come down and tell me?"

"Letter not good," Mum called out from the kitchen.

"What you mean not good?" Dad shouted back.

I stood up from where I was sitting on the couch. "Mum, Dad, let me explain, then I'll get John to come down and talk about it."

"What she mean not good?"

"He was accepted, but with conditions," I said.

"What that mean?"

"They'll give him a scholarship, but he has to join ROTC."

"What is ROTC?"

"It's training for the Army, to be an officer in the Army."

"You mean fight and kill people in old country?"

"He would have to be trained to fight, but he might just be able to work at a desk."

"Army is about fighting and killing. I know from old country. Bible tells us we not kill."

"I know, Dad. That's the point of the letter that isn't good. He has to train for the Army to get the scholarship."

"I no like."

"None of us do. Most of all John. He's very upset."

"We find 'nother way."

"It's too late for him to apply to other colleges. He had his heart set on going to Ohio State. They have one of the best music schools."

"Maybe he not need school. He is genius."

"Dad, there is a lot about music he doesn't know."

"He have teacher."

"But Mister Fleming can take him only so far."

"John say his teacher tell him to try out for Cleveland orchestra."

"Does he really think John's ready for that?"

"John play on radio," said Dad.

"Well, if he wants to audition, he should give it a try."

"I tell him. I take him to Cleveland."

"When?" I asked. "I want to go with you, to be supportive."

"You miss school."

"That's okay," I said. "I'm ahead in every class." I turned to Mum. "It's all right if I go, isn't it?"

"You go. It is okay."

"Do you know what day?" I asked Dad.

"John know. You ask him."

"I will. Mum, you need some help with dinner?"

"Set table. That good."

I pulled open the cabinet drawer containing utensils and laid them out along with napkins at the family's designated places around the table. Mum served from the stove, so she left the plates and soup bowls stacked on the sideboard.

"How soon we eat?" Dad asked.

"Few minutes. Soup ready."

"I take," he said.

Mum ladled a steaming bowl of chicken and vegetable noodle soup with streaks of oily fat floating on the surface. I carried the bowl to the table and set it in front of Dad. Sensing the rising heat against his face, he carefully slurped from a large spoon.

That night after supper, his feet soothed in soft slippers, Dad settled into his easy chair with the evening paper. His steel-rim glasses gave his face a benign scholarly appearance, like a college professor. He still retained his handsome features but showed the wrinkles and aging of an outdoor laborer. Thanks to Mum's rich meals, his expanding belly displaced his once solid frame.

He paused to listen to the strains of a Vienna waltz from John's bedroom. The family had all avoided talk of the scholarship at the dinner table. But John still held out hope for the Cleveland orchestra audition.

Later that evening, Ruth, Nina, and I were readying ourselves for the one high school dance we were being allowed to attend. Our parents had grudgingly given in to insistent pressure from Ruth and Nina. I stayed out of their arguments, because I didn't care about going to a high school dance. Permission came with conditions. One was that I accompany Ruth and Nina to act as a chaperon, keep them out of trouble, since Mum and Dad trusted me and were suspicious of them. Secondly, John had to drive us to and from the dance and have us all home by eleven.

While Ruth and Nina devoted time in front of their mirrors, unnecessarily beautifying themselves with shared cosmetic resources, I only brushed my hair into glossy blonde waves and declined the application of rouge and lipstick and eye shadow, which, in my opinion, made them look like slatterns.

They completed their preparations, snatched up their small purses that I would be expected to guard whenever they might be asked out onto the dance floor. Although I didn't expect to be asked, I was a little miffed that they expected me to be the purse guard. They all could have left their purses out in the car with John, who would not come into the gymnasium anyway. He would wait out in the parking lot until it was time to drive us home.

The high school jazz band up on the stage played jitter bug and swing numbers and slow two-step waltzes. Ned Robertson, the football team captain, and his buddy, Russ Tyrone, grabbed Ruth and Nina as soon as they walked through the door and pulled them into the gyrating, hip shaking, jumping, and whirling mass of wall to wall students.

Clutching two purses, I managed to find an empty metal folding chair off to the side where I could be a spectator. A few minutes passed when I felt a swing skirt rustle against my leg as my friend, Violet Karpinsky, plunked down beside me.

"Mary, I'm surprised to see you here. I thought your parents didn't let you come to dances."

"Hi, Violet, I guess they think we're old enough. They made an exception."

"How did you get here?"

"My brother drove us. We have to be home by curfew."

"What's that?"

"Eleven o'clock."

"That only gives you two hours."

"Two hours of sitting here."

"Are you kidding? You're the most beautiful girl here."

"Haven't you heard what boys call me?"

"No."

"Cold fish and ice box."

"That's ridiculous. Someone will ask you to dance. Do you know swing?"

"I'm not good at the jitter bug. My sisters practice secretly at home."

"Do you have a record player?"

"We have a victrola, but we can listen only to my Dad's records of Strauss waltzes and other composers whose work my brother plays on the violin. We secretly listen to radio broadcasts on the Philco and hum the tunes."

"Hum?"

"We scat and hum the rhythm."

"Look at your sisters go out there. They're really smooth."

"Yeah, they were born to it."

"I don't know why I even bother to come to these dances," said Violet. "No one ever asks me to dance."

I felt no sympathy for Violet's bemoaning complaint. "You've got everything else."

"I'm not pretty and no dance partner."

"We all don't get everything we want," I said with an edge of bitterness. "We have to work for it."

"I'd trade places with you in a heartbeat," said Violet.

"No you wouldn't. Be grateful for what you have."

"At least you're my friend."

I looked at her kindly.

***

Almost tangible electric tension and high hopes rustled and stirred among the young musicians waiting for a callback to the concert hall stage. Dad and I were seated among other family members toward the rear of the auditorium. We could see John's blonde curls where he anxiously waited in the front row next to other young men and women violinists, violists, two cellists, and players of woodwind and brass instruments.

The conductor's assistant stepped to the microphone and read off the names of twelve finalists. John was among them. The first, a thin ascetic woman with dark hair severely pulled back into a tight bun, was called to the stage and asked to play a segment from the score of the Brahm's violin concerto. The exquisite flawless tones sailed out over the small audience. I admired her for her skill. She was clearly an accomplished violinist, at least ten years older than John. I suspected this audition was not her first.

Although John's performance of the same piece was competent, even I could discern the difference in expressiveness and interpretation. The conductor complimented him, but I didn't hear the rest of what he said. We watched John leave the stage by the side access steps and return to his front row chair to retrieve his violin case. As he walked up the aisle toward the exit, Dad and I rose from our seats and followed him out into the lobby. He avoided looking at us. His face, a mask of dejection, told us what we already knew, but Dad wanted to hear it from John.

"What he say? What he tell you?"

"He said I lacked maturity in my style and technique. He said I should try again in two years after more study. The truth is I'm just not good enough. You heard that woman before I played. She'll get a chair. I'm done with it. Let's go home."

"Two more years isn't so bad," I said.

"I'm done with it." He pushed open the exit door and walked quickly out into the parking lot to our car.

We made the long drive home in silence.

***

With a tug at his starched white collar, the high school principal rose from his chair on the gymnasium stage and walked to the podium. The moment in the school assembly had come that John, my sisters, and I dreaded. "Will everyone please rise for the pledge to the flag," Mr. Harding's demanding voice reverberated from the loudspeakers.

We had agreed among ourselves that we would only stand for the pledge and not utter the words or salute the flag in any way, such as placing our right hands over our hearts. One tenet of our religion was to follow to the letter the commandment: Thou shall not have any other gods before me.

The Bascom twins, Sarah and Emily, who attended the Kingdom Hall with our parents, refused to even stand. Their plain dresses and freshly scrubbed innocent faces did not go unnoticed. Despite their position below the mass of students standing around them, their bushy red hair was hard to miss.

Mr. Harding looked out over the auditorium. He governed a small high school and knew most of the students by name, or at least by their last names. With the Depression, he feared the Government might resort to socialistic measures to regain economic balance. He had stated in a past assembly his determination to remind his students that they lived in America and were Americans. He discouraged any deviation from the norm and instructed his teaching staff to conduct their classes in a like manner. His hawk eyes spotted the two Bascom girls and he spoke into the microphone.

"It appears we have two young communists among us this morning. Will the Bascom girls please see me in my office after the assembly. That is an order."

Blushing with embarrassment as all eyes turned on them, some in sympathy, some in disgust, and some emotionally neutral, Sarah and Emily bowed their heads.

"I pledge allegiance to the flag . . ." the assembled chorus of voices droned on like a current of mumbling water washing over meaningless words worn smooth.

At the close of the assembly, I saw the Bascom sisters report to Mr. Harding's office. The door stood open for anyone passing by to see and to hear. He glared at them from behind his desk to make them feel uncomfortable. "Well, what have you to say for yourselves?"

Not wanting to be noticed and called in, Ruth, Nina, and John moved on down the hall to their classes, but I remained listening near the door.

"You do realize, don't you," Mr. Harding continued, "that your refusal to conform and participate in the pledge to the flag is sufficient reason for me to expel you from school."

Eyes downcast, they did not respond.

"I'll give you one more chance. If you'll pledge to my office flag here, I'll let you stay in school. If not, you will clean out your lockers and leave school today."

The girls began to cry.

"Crying will do you no good. There's no room for pity when it comes to maintaining a free country. You must conform or else suffer the consequences."

"We're not the only ones," Emily sniffled. "The Woijceks never say the pledge either."

"I have never observed that they remained seated when I ask everyone to stand for the pledge to the flag."

"Oh, they stand up all right," whined Sarah, "but they don't put their hands over their hearts and they don't say the words."

"Mmh, I'm glad you informed me. You can return to school whenever you're ready to follow the rules. Goodbye."

As the girls left the office, I moved on slightly ahead of them, but overheard Mr. Harding's order to his secretary. "Miss Morrison, will you send a hall monitor to bring the Woijceks to my office. Check their class schedule cards to see where they are at this hour."

A few minutes later, a hall monitor went to the various classrooms where my brother and sisters and I were located and handed a note signed by the principal to each of our teachers. We all met in the hallway and filed into Mr. Harding's office where we lined up in front of his desk.

Mr. Harding cleared his throat. "You first ought to know that I expelled the Bascom girls a few minutes ago for their refusal to say the pledge to the flag. I am well aware that you and your mother and father are also members of the Jehovah's Witnesses. Before the Bascom sisters left, they informed me that you only stand up for the flag oath in assembly and do not actually salute it and say the words of the pledge. Is this true? I want to be fair about the whole matter and give you a chance to speak for yourselves."

We tensed in awkward and fearful silence.

"Well, have you nothing to say?"

I finally spoke. "Mr. Harding, our religion requires us to obey the commandment 'Thou shalt have no other gods before me.' By standing up, we feel that at least we're compromising."

"When it comes to pledging to the flag, there is no compromise. Either you do or you don't. The American flag represents everything for us and you must never forget that. Now, I'm going to give you a fair chance like I did the Bascom girls, only they chose to go their own way. If you will properly repeat the pledge of allegiance to my office flag here right now, and if you will promise to say the pledge in future assemblies, this incident will be overlooked. If you choose not to conform, however, I have no other alternative than to expel all of you from school. That is the law. So what is your decision?"

John, Ruth, and Nina looked at me. They expected me to speak for all of us.

"We cannot say the pledge, Mr. Harding."

"Cannot or will not?"

"Will not."

"Then as of this moment, you are all expelled. Clean out your lockers and leave the school. You may not return. And I'll see to it you can't enroll in any other school in this county. Damn religious fanatics, communists, the whole lot of you."

As we left the office and walked to our lockers, John said, "I'm supposed to graduate in June."

"We can enroll at Wilkes-Barre, can't we?" ventured Nina. "It's not all that far and we'd be riding the bus everyday anyway."

"That's what we'll have to do," said John. "I'm going to graduate in June even if it means leaving this state and finishing somewhere else."

A flush of shame and anger consumed me. Hot tears of remorse streamed down my face. Being barred from attending school devastated me. Next to my baby sister, Margaret, dying, I had never known such despair.

I choked on our mother's response when we told her what had happened.

"Mr. Harding is a disciple of Satan. We want no part of him. We will pray to Jehovah," she said. "He will take care of us. Too much education is not good. It will make you turn against Jehovah and The Bible. That is what the deacons tell us."

I shunned the Jehovah's Witnesses' dogma that education wasted our young lives that should be devoted to His service as missionaries. We were also expected to believe in the fear-mongering propaganda of Armageddon, the violent destruction of the "wicked system" of government and wars and financial gain and that, after we died and were resurrected, we would be chosen for a utopian existence of heaven on earth. I really didn't want to wait around for that to happen. Actually, I didn't believe it.

Wilkes-Barre High School wouldn't accept us, and the principal didn't mince words in telling us why. Two other high schools in the county also rejected us. We had been black-listed.

John didn't attempt anything further and Ruth and Nina gave up on the idea of ever finishing their high school education. They lolled around the house in a listless manner with nothing to do. I vowed that someday I would get my diploma.

I was a young girl running.

Chapter 4

Breaking Away

During the first few weeks of summer, my sisters and I existed in a constant state of boredom. I tried to fill the emptiness by spending hours at the library reading all kinds of books just as I had done as a young girl. Now that I was seventeen, *Far From The Madding Crowd* by Thomas Hardy and *Madame Bovary* by Gustave Flaubert were among my favorites. *Pride and Prejudice* and other novels by Jane Austen depicting the dependence of women on marriage to secure social standing and economic security also influenced me. I identified with the women leading suffocating lives with limited choices in repressive male-dominated societies.

Despite his threat to give up playing the violin, John still practiced every day.

How we were treated by our parents became a town joke. One day, teen-age boys gathered in a group on the road in front of our house and shouted jeers and catcalls at our "warden mother," who sat on the front porch ready to beat them back with her broom if they should venture further.

Sometimes, Ruth and Nina accompanied me to the library to read magazines. But before long, she and Nina were meeting boys in the town park. I never said anything to Mum about what they were doing. She learned from another woman who was a member of the Kingdom Hall congregation and she had seen Ruth and Nina drinking orange sodas with two boys from the Italian sector. Nina had gone off alone with one of them. When we walked home from the library late that afternoon, we saw our mother waiting behind the screen door.

As we entered, with a savage cry, Mum leaped at Nina, beating her about the head and slapping her face. Nina tried desperately to ward off the blows. "Mum, stop it! You're hurting me!"

I shouted, "Mum! Mum! Stop! Stop! What are you doing?"

"You go off alone with boy!" she shouted at Nina. "I know! Mrs. Pulaski see you! She tell me!" A smash across Nina's mouth lined her teeth with blood.

With some effort, Ruth and I pulled our mother away. "Mum! Stop this! Just stop! Nina didn't do anything! She was just talking to a boy!"

"Mrs. Pulaski say she saw you kissing and he had his hand in your dress!"

"It's all right, Mum," said Ruth. "I was with her. Nothing happened."

"Who was boy?"

Touching her bleeding mouth with the back of her hand, Nina spit out his name. "Nicolo Bonardi."

"He Italian! I no like Italians! They rape girl like you!"

"Mum, calm down," I positioned myself between Nina and my mother.

Ruth held Mum's arm. "Nicolo is just a nice kid."

"And what you do? Why you not stop?"

"Mum, it's okay for us to talk to boys."

"I see them come to house. I know what they want."

"They just want to talk to us," said Ruth.

"No, no talk. I know."

Ruth looked at me. I understood what was going through her mind without her saying anything. The conflict we were having with our mother related to being expelled from school and the repressive life in our town.

A few days ago, we had learned that one of the young mine workers, who was also a JW, had been taken out into the woods and castrated for refusing to say the pledge and sing the national anthem at a town meeting. That was when John told us he had been threatened by members of the varsity football team. He said he could no longer remain living in Colver. He was planning to leave and any of us could go with him.

From the sagging wooden front porch in need of repair that was never done, I watched my older brother and two sisters brush past, bumping me with their battered suitcases, as they stomped down the steps and walked with relentless strides out to the dust layered 1940 Oldsmobile parked in the dirt. Their grim expressions conveyed their intent that they would not be turning back.

We had no future in Colver. None of us did. I had sat with them at the kitchen table and listened to their talk and reasons and justification for leaving to create lives of their own. I had not participated in their plans out of respect for our mother, who, surprisingly, did not attempt to interfere. At sixteen, she had left her mountain village home in Austria- Hungary to escape an arranged marriage, traveled across Europe, and come to America on a freighter. Her fortitude was a model for me.

As much as I hated and despised life in the coal mining town where we lived, I could not bring myself to desert our mother and father. If I were to go with my brother and sisters, I would want our parents to follow. Once their children were gone, there would be no compelling reason for them to stay. The vacuum of loneliness would sadden them. Given my sensitivity for my parents and siblings, I could detect the unease in mother's daily cooking and cleaning routines and the dread in her eyes. The departure of her children would disrupt her strong maternal instinct. The family centered love she and Dad had nurtured for the past twenty years would be gone, wispy tendrils in the wind of memories.

The dilemma of separation distressed me. Our close-knit family coming apart pulled me in two directions. Our childhood home had been a sanctuary where we laughed and played together and supported and fended for each other. I belonged with them. Our physical similarities as brother and sisters were unmistakable.

My brother, John, had inherited Dad's tall strong body, gentle fun-loving expression, twinkling hazel eyes, and golden curls.

My older sister, Ruth, mirrored our mother's Slavic high cheekbones, wide jaw, light brown hair, and daring blue-green eyes. She enjoyed living on a farm. She would even go out and help the men cut hay and she would pick berries anywhere and wasn't afraid of snakes. I, on the other hand, was terrified of snakes. I didn't feel comfortable in the country. I feared to go out in the woods and fields to pick blackberries with my sisters because of the snakes. While picking blackberries, one of our friends had been bitten by a copperhead and had nearly died. As a small girl, I would break out in a severe rash and my legs would swell while just walking through tall grass.

Nina, the youngest, graced with cascading strawberry blonde tresses, projected the stunning features renown of Czechoslovakian women.

A blend of both my parents, I was told I possessed the delicate, imperious beauty of a Viennese princess, a description I did not take seriously.

I looked out across the yard while they loaded their suitcases into the trunk, then stood waiting. They expected me to come with them. I walked out to the car.

I thought of our father returning home that evening from the mine to find that all his children were gone, without even saying goodbye. Although he knew my brother and sisters planned to leave, they had been ambivalent and had not committed to a date and time, as though they were circling their decision and putting off the event. Like Mum, he would not interfere. Still, he would be distraught. I just wasn't comfortable doing that to him. I had argued that the others should at least wait until he was there to say goodbye. “Leaving without saying goodbye is disrespectful. We shouldn’t do that. It will hurt him terribly,” I told them.

John, the oldest, said, “Ruth and I talked with him last night. We said our goodbyes. It will be easier this way. He knows we’re leaving. He gave us the car. He even gave me a little money for gas and food.”

“Mum understands,” said Ruth. “They both understand. They went through this themselves when they were our age. It was even harder for them.”

“We told Mum that once we’re settled in Rockford, we’ll send for them,” said John. “Dad can find work there, healthy work. Working in the mine is killing him.”

“I want to say goodbye to Mum.”

“We already said our goodbyes,” said John. “If you’re going with us, throw some clothes in a suitcase and get in the car. We won’t wait long.”

“What about you Nina? Aren’t you going to say goodbye?”

She shook her head with a petulant scowl. “I’m not saying goodbye. Not after what she did to me.”

I looked back at our mother watching from the porch. My shoes scuffed the dirt, as I slowly walked to the white frame house wafting aromas of garlic, paprika, and freshly baked bread and cinnamon brown sugar apple pie through the screen door like a living creature beckoning us to stay. I trudged up the steps to mother wiping at tears with a corner of her flour and tomato-stained apron. Understanding our need did not quell the rush of sadness at seeing her children about to leave. I took her hands, gnarled with purple veins, hands that kneaded raw dough into loaves of crusted bread and biscuits and muffins and twisted pastries coated with powdered sugar. I gently put my arms around her.

“It’s okay, Mum. I don’t want to go but I have to.”

“I gonna miss all of you,” she spoke in broken English.

“We love you. We’ll miss you too. I’ll write. Give Dad our love.”

Mother nodded. I kissed her tears and looked into her distressed dark eyes and kind peasant face. “They’re waiting for me. I need to pack.”

“You go pack,” she said. “I stay here. I remember when I was your age and come to America. I don’t like you leave home, but that day come for all of us. We all do.”

Chapter 5

Sweatshop

Twice each day in steerage on board the freighter, as a teenage girl, my mother had stood in the food line with her fellow passengers making the ten day Atlantic crossing. Unaccustomed to the rising falling toss of the ship, she made frequent trips to the rail and lost what she had eaten. By the time she reached New York, sea sickness had left her weakened, listless and pale, and she had a stye in her right eye.

Warned by fellow immigrants not to exhibit any signs of illness at the risk of being quarantined, she fastened on a necklace with an amulet placed strategically at her exposed cleavage to draw and divert the attention of the male inspectors so that they would not notice her eye. After she passed through customs on Ellis Island, a ferry crowded with immigrants brought her to the city wharf where she disembarked. Managing to elude a hotel runner who demanded she hand over her steamship ticket and tried to grab away her satchel, she followed the shuffling mob into the streets.

Weak, frightened, and alone, she found herself standing at the entrance alcove of a building. Clutching her satchel, she watched pedestrians and vehicles flash by oblivious to her confused dark-eyed expression and *babushka*, a plain head scarf, and country clothes that marked her as an immigrant.

The acrid odor of urine and steaming manure rose to join a dirty bronze haze staining the sky. A fortress of tall brownstone buildings lined the tumultuous streets teeming with the movement of horse-drawn carts and cabs, their whip-cracking drivers vying for the right of way with newly invented automobiles and clanging motorized delivery wagons spewing black clouds of exhaust. An open market of produce vendors and butchers and bakers commingled with the clothing racks of haberdashery store fronts in a chaotic whorl of foreign faces and chugging motors punctuated by the clop of hoofs on cobblestones.

She paused at a fruit and vegetable stand to buy a pear and an apple with the last of her money. She did not know to whom to turn for directions or assistance. Everywhere she looked, people from all the countries of Europe seemed to have a place and a purpose, going to and coming from destinations, assimilated and established.

She moved timidly into the stream of humanity. Avoiding piles of fresh horse droppings and scuttling out of the path of delivery wagons bearing down on her, she was carried along block after block with no purposeful destination. At length, she wandered into a park with a tree-lined walk. Seating herself on the grassy knoll of a pond, she watched the ducks and swans.

The hard, black toe of a policeman's boot nudged her awake. "Sorry, miss. There's no sleeping here. You have to move on."

Eva stumbled to her feet, picked up her satchel and continued walking back to the mobbed streets.

As the fluid darkness of night filled the metropolitan spaces, she paused to look through the front window of a small restaurant she recognized as Bohemian from the posted sign and menus written in English and in her Czech language and from the aroma of ethnic food, goulash, stuffed cabbage, potato soup, *pierogi*, and *jaluski*, being served along with loaves of dark bread and steins of beer.

She discovered an alley at the side of the building that lead to an open kitchen door. Drawn by the intoxicating savory smells of garlic and paprika, she entered unnoticed by the busy chef, a large Czech woman, her face flushed from the heat of the oven and stove and her white apron stained with tomato sauce. Carrying platters and bowls of food, her two daughters, slightly older than Eva, rushed back and forth between the kitchen and the dining area. Wearing a full white apron, a Czech sous chef, looking vaguely like her father without a beard, sliced vegetables on a chopping block.

A hand's grasp away, a loaf of black bread and plate of sliced meat and cheese lay at the end of the counter near the door. A knot of hunger ached like a cyst in her stomach. Eva began stuffing her mouth.

Ignak, the sous chef glanced up and saw her. He walked quickly from behind the kitchen counter. Eva watched him approach. Too hungry and tired to be afraid, she did not run and she did not stop eating.

"Excuse me, miss," he spoke in a surprisingly deep, soft staccato voice. "Come and sit down." He guided her to a small table and chair in one corner. The Czech woman watched, then filled a plate with stuffed cabbage and *pierogi* and handed it over the counter to the *sous chef.* He placed the meal and a knife and fork and a glass of water on the table, then returned to his preparations.

Eva ate voraciously, barely stopping to breathe. When she was finished, she asked to use the water closet to relieve herself.

She didn't want to leave the familiarity of the family. Lenka, the Czech woman, told her to again sit at the small table and wait. "I will talk to you. You are new here and lost. We have friends who can help you. We all help each other. That is our way."

Eva gratefully watched the kitchen and service proceedings and listened to the exchange in her own language between the daughters, Aneta and Irena, and their parents behind the counter.

After a while, with her belly full of food and lulled by the warmth and chatter, her head nodded, and she dozed.

***

The clacking, rattle, and hum of one hundred sewing machines filled the factory like a gigantic beehive, the sound of her new life.

Eva adjusted a needle and replaced an empty bobbin on her Singer 66. Pumping the rectangular black metal foot pedal, she increased the rotational speed of the wheel and guided the cloth to create a narrow hem on the shirt following the cut pattern the roving inventory clerk had dropped into her in box.

Eva now wore a dark floral print dress and women's plain low-heeled shoes in place of her peasant clothing and farm boots. Two months had passed since she had been brought to the Sedlak household. A middle-aged Lukas Sedlak managed the factory and his wife, Renata, supervised the small army of immigrant women making clothing for men, women, and children.

Learning how to operate the machine had taken Eva only a few hours on her first day. Renata had duly noticed her progress and had promoted her to sewing more complex patterns.

The friendship between Lenka, the restaurant chef, and Renata had opened the door for Eva to have a place to live. The three Sedlak daughters and two sons had all married and moved out. Renata made one of her daughter's bedrooms available to Eva, who was indebted to the tall, lean, intimidating woman.

Renata's demanding work standards on the factory floor pervaded her established household rules for a young woman's behavior and etiquette. Her own dresses, shoes, jewelry, hats and hair emulated the *nouveau* empire columnar silhouette fashions of upper class New York women. Her smoldering dark eyes and fine facial features drew admiring glances.

Eva tried her best to please her, but learning English came slowly and she did not sufficiently shed deeply ingrained country mannerisms to Renata's satisfaction. Slurping her soup and coffee and chewing with her mouth open were habits difficult for Eva to break. At home, she felt awkward and uncomfortable in

Renata's presence, and except for breakfast and dinner, secluded herself in her room.

Working six ten hour days a week left Eva little time for a social life. She was too tired to do much more than go directly to bed after supper. Renata would wake her at dawn to grind through another day.

She rarely saw Renata's husband, since he would go to a pub with friends.

On occasional Sunday evenings, a few of the young women who worked at the factory with Eva would invite her to join them at a local dance hall. Even though Renata disapproved of her going, she did not interfere. She warned her to not drink alcohol and to beware of advances and propositions from strange men.

She joined the four girls wearing the most expensive dresses and shoes they could afford. Although they had rouged their lips and cheeks, Eva's natural complexion did not require any highlights. Chattering excitedly like a gaggle of geese, they walked along the dark streets spotted by splashes of yellow light from corner lamps.

The dance hall catered to young working class men and women who paid a nickel admission at the door. A Negro male ensemble of brass, clarinet, and drums provided popular ragtime music for the dancers to step out and shake and shimmy doing the turkey trot, grizzly bear, and bunny hug. Even though the swoops and glides of a tango were denounced by religious leaders and conservative citizens to be too suggestive of a sexual act, the band would occasionally throw in the iconic Brazilian rhythm.

Knowing polkas and folk dances from her Bohemian village festivals, Eva easily learned and adapted to the new style and was never at a loss for a partner. One night, she met the man she would eventually marry.

Chapter 6

Dance Hall Dandy

As a young man, my Dad did not expect Tereza Woijcek to answer his knock at the door of his father's brownstone townhouse. He also did not expect he would have to explain himself and what he was doing there. He wore a typical short coat over a wool sweater, trousers, thick-heeled boots, and a slouch hat. His leather satchel and backpack should have been obvious to the woman that he was an immigrant.

"Yes, what is it you want?" she spoke in English.

"I'm Michael Woijcek, Karel's son," he said in broken English.

"I'm Tereza, his wife," she switched to Czech. "He never told me he had a son by another marriage."

"He never told me and my mother he had remarried."

"I'm sure he must have written your mother."

"She never said anything about a letter. I didn't see much of her. She owns a dress shop and lives in Vienna. I lived on a farm with my friend and his family."

"Is that why she sent you here, to get rid of you?"

"My father invited me to come."

"He is remiss in telling people things," Tereza scowled.

"He told me I could stay here and that I could find work."

Even though Mike looked very much like his father, Tereza had no intention of letting him come into the house. "You will have to come back when he is home from work. You are a stranger to me."

"I'm going to be living here."

"Karel and I have to talk about that."

"This is his house. I came to the address he sent me and my mother."

"You're not setting foot in here until Karel and I have a talk. I have two children of my own. I am not going to make you meals and clean up after you."

"You don't have to cook and clean for me. I just need a place to sleep."

"There are boarding houses in the city."

Mike gauged the tense viciousness of this woman. Slender and tall enough to look him straight in the face, she had the characteristic high cheekbones and wide mesmerizing eyes typical of Czech women that could exert control merely by the effect of their beauty. She was many years younger than his mother, who was also imperious, but not so confrontational and combative as this immovable bitch. "How old are your children?" he tried a soft approach.

"That is none of your business. They are young. Karel has put us into his will. You are no longer in the will."

"So you do know about me. That was your concern."

"We are his family now. You are not."

"I know nothing of his will and I'm not here about that."

"You should take a room in a boarding house. I don't want you here."

"You are clear on that. However, I will talk with my father before making any decision."

"I told you. You have to come back later."

"All right, I'll come back. When will he be here?"

"Six o'clock. He will be having dinner. You are not invited to eat with us. You will have to talk with him afterwards."

"I'll be waiting to meet him right here on the doorstep," said Mike.

"You may not keep him from having his dinner," Tereza intoned. "His food will get cold."

"I won't keep him from having his dinner, but he will know I'm here to see him."

"Do not detain him," she commanded.

"We don't have to be enemies. I want nothing of yours."

"You're his son. You're poor. I don't trust you. He's a parsimonious man. He will not give you money."

"You've said enough," said Mike. "I'll be here at five: thirty, before he has to be served dinner."

"Be forewarned. You will have to eat elsewhere."

"I will. I don't want to sit at the same table with you."

Tereza slammed the door shut.

Mike stomped down the brick steps from the porch to the pavement. He had five hours until his father would return and very little money, not enough to afford a room and meals at a boarding house. He hoped his father had the balls to override his offensive wife. He wondered how his father could endure her, if she acted like this with him. What did he even see in her in the first place, other than, admittedly, she was beautiful? He depended on his father to help him for at least a short time. They would have to make an arrangement without his wife's knowledge, if that were possible. She probably poked her nose into all of his affairs. He probably had no privacy, no peace from such a harridan. He vowed he would never marry a woman like that.

He hiked along the sidewalk back in the direction from which he had come. The horse-drawn cab from the waterfront dock had taken him through a nearby section of the city where he had seen boarding houses and saloons about a mile from this upper class neighborhood. He had a strong premonition he would not be staying at his father's house.

After being processed through Ellis Island and upon his arrival at the waterfront battery, he had avoided the onslaught of immigrant hotel and boarding house runners demanding to take his steamship ticket and baggage so he would have to go to a particular lodging.

Surging throngs of people consumed him, as he roamed the traffic-clogged city streets filling the foul air with droning *oogah* horns and the chug of motorcars cascading with the clopping of horses' hoofs on manure-streaked cobblestones. He passed a row of tenement boarding houses, keeping their location in mind in the event he had to return to find lodging. If his father didn't subsidize him, he would end up in a flophouse occupied by vagrants and derelicts.

On another street near a textile district of clothing factories, he noticed a dance hall at the corner of a busy intersection and went to peer through the front windows of the establishment, closed during the day. After he was settled, he would return to this place.

He spent an hour nursing a beer in a saloon crowded with raucous men, elevator operators, file clerks, restaurant dishwashers, security watchmen in office buildings, furniture and building painters, waiters, seamen, electricians, porters, wholesalers, butchers, bakers, and cooks.

Manufacturing and assembly laborers were coming off their shifts in local factories. He wondered if he should apply for work in one of them. Whatever he did would depend on his father's generosity or absence of it.

Toward evening, he retraced his steps back to the town home and planted himself sitting on the front porch stoop to wait for his father's return. He saw him approaching out of the encroaching evening shadows. His face was familiar, features a reflection of his son, but with the drawn, wrinkled imprint of time and age by twenty years. He wore a dark business suit and pale blue four-in-hand tie snugged at the throat of a high collar. Gold studs winked from white shirt cuffs extending slightly beyond the coat sleeves. Soft gray mutton chop sideburns crept down his cheeks like squirrel's tails from beneath the bowled crown of a Homburg. As he drew near and recognized Mike, he shifted his briefcase from his right to his left hand.

Not expecting an embrace, Mike came down the steps and was surprised when his father's right arm encircled his shoulders and their bodies gently collided.

"Mikeime, Jak se máš? How are you? It is good to see you. Welcome to America."

Mike smiled, "De^{v}kuji dobr^{v}e, a vy?" and placed his left arm around Karel's shoulders.

Karel stepped back. "Let me look at you. You know some English."

"Enough to get by."

"You have become quite a strapping young man."

"I grew up on a farm. I worked hard and we ate well."

"Why are you waiting outside on the porch? Isn't my wife home?"

"She would not let me in."

"You told her you're my son."

"That's why. She doesn't want me to stay here."

"I'll take that up with her."

"I don't want to cause any trouble for you. I can stay in a boarding house, but I need money."

"I don't know what her problem is," said Karel.

"She said she persuaded you to write me out of your will."

"I'm sorry for that. Your mother plans to remarry and I have a new family. You're an adult now and can make a life of your own. I will help you get started. I promise. As I'm sure you realize, Tereza can be difficult."

"I don't envy you."

"Let me talk to her and see if I can get her to change her mind about you staying here for a short time."

As Karel started up the steps, the front door partially opened and Tereza looked out to intercept her husband. "Before you say anything to your son, I need to talk to you."

"There was no reason to be rude and impolite to him."

"Once you get inside, we'll talk."

Mike watched the door close and returned to the porch stoop to sit beside his satchel. He heard their voices shouting inside.

Fifteen minutes later, Karel came back out and Mike stood to speak with him.

"As you already know, Tereza says she doesn't want you living here."

"Even though you asked me to come," said Mike.

"I know. I know. I wanted to see you and help you out any way I can."

"You talked about finding work, but I need a place to stay."

"Here's what I'm going to do. I'm going to give you this sum of money, five hundred dollars, more than you'll need to pay for a room and meals at a boarding house while you look for work."

"That will be better than having to put up with your wife. She's a real bitch."

"Careful what you say. She is my wife."

"I'm not being ungrateful. I am insulted at how she treated me when I arrived."

"She's strong-minded, I'll admit. She doesn't easily apologize."

"How did you meet her?"

"She was a bank customer. She had an inheritance. She was not knowledgeable about her financial options. I helped her and gave her advice. She trusted me. We were drawn to each other and I began courting her."

"I'm not asking for her apology. I'm grateful that you'll help me with my expenses."

"It's the best I can do, under the circumstances."

"Mother said she wrote to you about me."

"She did. She did. I feel obligated to help you."

Mike's good-natured grin became a twinkle in his blue eyes. "I'm glad to hear that. I thought after you left when I was five, I'd never see you again."

"I always intended to bring you and your mother to America, but things changed. Gerda didn't really want to live in New York.

She had her business in Vienna. It was her decision to stay. I didn't want to live alone year after year. You can understand. I'm not a priest."

"You have a nice house. You're living well."

"I'm a senior accountant at the bank," said Karel. "I started as a clerk."

"I'm not good with numbers or money," said Mike. "I like to work with my hands."

"A bank is not the place for you."

"You said in your letter about coal mines."

"The Alleghany Company has an office here in the city. The mines are in Pennsylvania. I know about the jobs, because the company banks with us."

"Maybe I could find something here in the city."

"There are factory jobs," said Karel. "Hard and dirty work."

"I'm used to that. The farm was hard and dirty work."

"Not the same. You were outside in the open air and sunshine."

"Working in a coal mine must be worse," said Mike.

"You do what you have to do to make a living."

"Can I see you again?" Mike asked.

"Of course, just not here. Here is my business card. You can come to the bank."

Mike read the card, then stuffed it into a coat pocket. "I'm glad we met each other again."

Karel nodded. "I'm glad also. Good luck."

Mike turned and walked away.

The boarding house apartments were divided into a front room with access to two windows in the front of the building with a view of the street. A small bedroom on the third floor next to a long narrow hallway and a staircase lead to the ground floor. Mike took his meals in the kitchen dining room on the main floor with eight other male boarders.

A repetitive job on the assembly line of a Johnson & Johnson bandage factory in New Brunswick provided him a small weekly wage to pay his room and board. Two hundred dollars remained of the five hundred given to him by his father. He gave little thought to saving his money but preferred to indulge in drinking beer in saloons and frequenting the dance hall near the boarding house.

I enjoyed hearing him describe what a dashing young man he had been when he met mother.

"Yes, I was only sixteen, a young man, young and handsome. I walk in front of all the girls, you know? I was the best dancer. I walk up and down at the dance hall and twirled an umbrella and the girls all watch me. That was in 1916. I see Eva and I say to myself I know I want to marry her. She doesn't even look at me. She goes off and dance with some other fellow, not so good, not so handsome. That make me want her more than ever. We keep seeing each other at the dance hall and one day I ask her to marry me. She say no. I don't have enough money to take care of her and a family. She say I'm too young. We both work in factory. When we marry, she would stop, so I need to make more money.

"I want to marry her more than anything else in world. She had run away from home when she was only sixteen and come to this country. Her father was burgermeister and wanted her to marry some man she didn't like so he could have more land. She went all the way across Europe alone, a young girl. Then she travel on ship from Germany across ocean and come to New York."

He always smiled a little, remembering. "My father give us enough money to marry. We have a big wedding, eat, drink, dance for three days, like in old country. But after, I have to get better job and make more money."

He chuckled. "She chase me from house with broom and tell me not to come back 'til I have better job. I did not work in factory anymore. She tell me, if I want to be married, I have to act like husband, not dance hall dandy.

"I could not get good job and make lot of money, see. So we move here to Colver where I can get work in mines. Make more money as motorman. I drive train with empty cars into mine and bring out coal. There is always dust and it hard to breath. I wear handkerchief over nose and mouth."

Chapter 7

Leaving Home

John, Ruth, and Nina had climbed into the car, sealing themselves off from our house. I emerged ten minutes later with my suitcase, embraced mother one last time, then walked quickly down the porch steps and out to the car. I jammed the suitcase into the open trunk and shut the lid. With a final glance, I took the back seat on the side where I could see mother waving from the porch. I blew her a kiss and extended an arm to wildly wave through the rolled-down window. As the car pulled away, I continued to look back until the brown shingled roof passed from sight in the skein of gray coal dust that hovered over the town.

The initial enthusiasm and excitement of our departure quickly faded. We rode in silence into a shared unknown future. The farther we traveled west through the Pennsylvania forests and dairy farms slipping past the car windows, the memories of the life I loved and the life I hated pulled me back.

Even though we hadn't much money, we did have good times together, sitting around the warm stove, telling stories and helping Mum can food in enormous jars. In the winter, we went sliding down the surrounding hills on flattened cardboard boxes. I remembered one time when we had been sliding a long distance from the house and I had diarrhea and had to go right there in the snow. Having nothing to wipe with, I had borrowed the belt from my sister Ruth's coat and used it for that purpose. I thought it was a very sisterly thing for her to lend it to me.

Driving with the windows wide open gave the four of us little relief from the stifling summer heat and humidity and the odor of our bodies compressed in the automobile. Being wind-blown reinforced our sense of escape to freedom in search of new identities but leant nothing to a future that eluded us and to how we would support ourselves.

For the moment, our individual thoughts absorbed us. Our struggles and unknown realities of what lay ahead would be far different than sitting on the porch back home paging through a Sears & Roebuck catalog and proclaiming our wishes.

To the extent we would not be left completely up to our own devices, John had written a letter to a Jehovah's Witnesses family in Rockford, Illinois referred to him by the deacon from the Colver Kingdom Hall. As much as I detested the idea that we were dependent on assistance from another Jehovah's Witness family, despite the prejudice against him, John continued to be devout. I, on the other hand, wanted to separate myself completely from the religious propaganda and beliefs and influence of poverty on my life. I wanted to become an independent woman.

After a full day of travel, we spent one night in a dingy motel in Cleveland, Ohio. Too exhausted to care, I slept next to my brother on one of the two double beds. Ruth and Nina shared the other. Before leaving in the morning, we all took quick showers and washed our hair.

Ruth and Nina dozed except when we passed through towns and cities. Then they stared out the car windows to see the differences between Colver and where we were going.

Not having enough money for a second stay in a motel, we drove across northern Indiana and through Chicago far into the night and arrived at the home of Emmett Lyford in Rockford, Illinois at two in the morning. We lugged our suitcases from the car trunk to the front porch and stood huddled in the darkness until an overhead light snapped on in response to John ringing the doorbell.

Wearing pajamas, bathrobes and slippers, hair askew, Emmett and his wife, Doris, welcomed us with a mumbled sleepy greeting. John introduced us as we entered the living room.

"You look exhausted," said Doris. "Can I fix you something to eat?"

"What we really need is sleep," said John.

"We can put you up in two empty bedrooms," said Emmett, realigning his metal rimmed glasses that had tipped to one side of his small nose. "And one of you girls can have the extra twin bed in our daughter, Carolyn's room. I'll wake her. We didn't expect you to arrive this late at night."

"Thank you for giving us a place to stay," said John.

"It is our pleasure," Emmet's thin lips parted in a soft smile.

Nina volunteered to sleep in Carolyn's room. Ruth and I shared the second bedroom and John took the third.

Not wanting to impose on the Lyfords' hospitality, we scoured the limited job listings in the local paper the next morning after breakfast. Ruth and I offered to help clear the table and wash the dishes, but Doris and her soft-spoken daughter insisted that, as their guests, we were not to trouble ourselves. They had exchanged their bathrobes for plain house dresses and aprons.

I noticed that John struggled not to stare at Carolyn. Her endearing amused expression had a calming effect in contrast to her mother's concerned servitude. Even without makeup, her pale skin conveyed a simple beauty under a crown of light brown curls.

Wearing a double-breasted brown suit, as he departed, Emmet mentioned that the city Chamber of Commerce had an opening for a typist where he worked as an accountant. Ruth said that sounded right up my alley. "She's the fastest typist in Colver." Not what I wanted to be known for. An ad for switchboard telephone operators had caught her eye.

Carolyn invited Nina to accompany her to the Weise department store where she worked and to apply for a salesgirl position.

We ironed our wrinkled dresses, did up each other's hair, applied makeup, and went off for our interviews. We were somewhat embarrassed having to wear socks with our low heeled shoes, but socks were an acceptable fashion in those days. Nylons were a luxury we could not afford.

As soon as we pooled enough money to pay the rent for an apartment, Ruth, Nina, and I moved.

John found a job with a local dairy as a delivery milkman. Not to our surprise, he stayed with the Lyfords at their invitation and became active as a member of their Kingdom Hall. Eventually, he delivered sermons at their meetings. Emmett and Doris loved him and planned that, one day, he and their daughter, Carolyn would marry.

Nina and I shared a room in the sparsely furnished two bedroom apartment and Ruth took the second room, since she worked the swing shift on the city central PBX switchboard and came home late.

We were euphoric with our newfound freedom. Saving some of our earnings and sharing the cost of groceries, we were able to upgrade our meager wardrobes and occasionally go out to a ten cent movie. I was an avid fan of Lauren Bacall and Katharine Hepburn, who portrayed strong-minded women. Nina preferred the glamour queens, Veronica Lake and Lana Turner. Ruth liked the comedians Carol Lombard and Rosalind Russell.

None of us dated for the first few months, but we hadn't really met anyone we cared for that much. Nina told us the driver of the bus she rode to work had the "hots" for her, but she wasn't flirting with him. "I don't see myself dating a bus driver," she said.

"At least he has a job," said Ruth. "He's lucky."

"I know I can do better," Nina primped the luxurious blonde waves that graced her shoulders. "I have my sights set on someone rich."

"Nobody's rich these days," I said. "I work at the Chamber of Commerce. I know. Even men who own companies are barely getting by."

Ruth smirked. "There's this guy who calls the switchboard and asks for me just so he can hear my voice, he says."

"That's creepy," I commented.

"Not really, he sounds like a nice guy. Has a big strong voice and a Boston accent. He told me his name, Richard Ainsworth. He said he'd like to meet me and just have a cup of coffee."

"Are you going to do it?" asked Nina.

"I'm thinking about it."

"Anybody at your office?" asked Nina. "You must get looks."

"I'm not in any hurry," I said. "I want to have a career first."

"Women don't have careers unless they're movie stars," said Nina.

"I'm going to get my GED and then go to college," I said.

"That's a noble goal but how will you afford it?" asked Ruth.

"Maybe not soon, but some day."

"I won't go back to school," said Nina. "I like working. I like having my own money. School wasn't so great for me anyway."

"You got good grades," I said.

"That's because you helped me. My teachers weren't that good. They didn't make anything very interesting."

"You have a knack for figures. You handle cash okay at the store?"

"Handling cash is easy," said Nina. "Even without a register, I can do it in my head."

"You got something out of school then," said Ruth.

"Math was the only class I liked."

"I did okay, but I didn't like math much at all." Ruth sipped her coffee. "I like to use my voice. I like talking on the phone."

"You just like talking," Mary smiled.

"That's me all right, motor mouth." She laughed.

I came across a photo of a fashion model who caught my attention in one of Nina's magazines. She was wearing tan riding jodhpurs and boots, a blue blouse, and a yellow silk scarf. That she resembled me captured my imagination. The model posed next to a beautiful light chestnut colored horse. The casual elegance of the model juxtaposed with the bright-eyed horse represented wealth and an elite lifestyle to me. Of course, I didn't have that kind of money. But some people did. I decided to indulge in a little fantasy. I splurged and spent some of my money on a pair of tan jodhpurs and shiny brown jodhpur boots.

The next weekend, I took the bus across town to a stable that rented out horses for leisure rides. I noticed other passengers wearing drab clothes catching glimpses of me, as though I were a celebrity.

I stepped off the bus at the end of its route outside the city in a rural area. The sharp odor of urine and stench of manure from the paddocks next to the barn belied my romantic vision of myself as an equestrian.

I could afford only an hour and I lied to the tall skinny stable boy, who led an imposing chestnut colored horse out of the barn, that I was an experienced rider. I would have thought he could tell by how I was dressed. I had never ridden a horse before in my life. He detected my falsehood when he saw I did not know how to mount the horse. He assisted me up onto the English saddle and arranged my boots in the iron stirrups. When I didn't pick up the reins, he placed them in my hands and instructed me how to hold them. When the horse didn't move, the stable boy told me, "Touch his sides with your heels." I did and the horse lurched forward, nearly unseating me, then settled into a lethargic walk, which was fine with me. I didn't want to go any faster.

The horse was wider between my legs and higher off the ground than I had imagined. I watched his bobbing head and his ears crank back and forth. I heard his tail rhythmically swish and flick at flies on his rump. I focused on the sensation of his broad shoulders moving with each step. I tentatively pulled on the left rein and he turned to the left. Then the right rein and he turned to the right. And so we ambled along the dirt lane between hay fields. The hot sun caused me to perspire and my blue blouse grew damp under my arms. My nose dripped from the rising dust. I wiped at the mucous with the back of my hand. My fanny and inner thighs began to grow sore with the repetitious sliding back and forth in the saddle. I had the distinct feeling I wasn't as fashionable as the model in the magazine.

After about twenty minutes, the horse suddenly stopped. I made clicking noises at him like I had heard the stable boy do. I touched his sides with my heels with no response. He suddenly whirled and sprang into a full gallop back in the direction of the barn. I dropped the reins and took a handful of his mane and grabbed the front of the saddle to keep from falling. My legs desperately clutched his sides and made him go faster. I shouted "Whoa!" to no avail. As we passed several riders on their way out onto the trail, I heard a man say, "Look at that girl go! Can she ever ride!"

I wasn't fooling anybody, especially myself. I didn't feel any elation flying over the ground at this equine speed. My heartbeat fiercely. I was afraid. I just hoped to arrive without falling and breaking my neck. Thankfully, the horse had the good sense to slow to a spine-jolting trot that bounced me up and down on the saddle. Then he stopped at the barn door, as the stable boy stepped out and grabbed the reins at the bridle. His smirk told me all I needed to know about how foolish I was.

He helped me dismount, which was me sliding backwards into his arms. I retrieved my purse from the tack room office and walked down the lane to the bus stop.

One week later, changes at work began happening for me more quickly than I would have imagined and not in the way I anticipated. I finished typing a stack of correspondence for the home front director to be mailed to businesses throughout the city regarding the need to hire more women, even for men's jobs in plants and factories that were losing male employees to military service.

I had noticed that in riding the city bus home, soldiers in uniform outnumbered civilians on the streets. Ruth was preparing to leave the apartment to go to the switchboard center but took a few minutes to describe her meeting with Richard Ainsworth for coffee.

"I didn't know he was in the Navy. He didn't say anything on the phone. He was wearing his uniform. He looked very dashing. I'm a sucker for a handsome guy in a uniform."

"When did you see him?"

"This afternoon. We had lunch together. His treat. He's quite the tough guy gentleman, very smooth and sophisticated, even the way he holds a cigarette. He could be in the movies."

"He smokes? How can you stand it?"

"I don't mind. He blows it out of the corner of his mouth like Humphrey Bogart. He reminds me a little of Humphrey Bogart only he's better looking, black-haired, blue eyed Irish, more like Tyrone Power. He has a kind of dished nose and face and a flashy smile that melts my heart. And I love the dimple on his chin."

"Sounds romantic."

"Oh, he is. Who would've thought I'd meet the man I'm going to marry because he liked my voice on the phone."

"He asked you to marry him?"

"No, but he will. I just know it."

Soon after we had moved into our apartment, one of Ruth's strategies to meet men was to place an advertisement in the local newspaper classifieds that she would be holding a kissing contest between the hours of twelve and three on a Saturday. Whoever was the best kisser would get to have a date with her.

I would have nothing to do with her escapade, as I called it. I told Ruth men would think she was a prostitute advertising for business. She just laughed and said a kissing contest was just harmless fun. That was Ruth. I made myself scarce by going to a movie alone that afternoon.

Nina thought the kissing contest was a great idea. Even though I disapproved, Nina stayed to take part. She had recently turned seventeen and her age had gone to her head. She wasn't a bobbysoxer anymore. She was a dish. Fun-loving Ruth was her role model. I was definitely not.

The war was a turning point for all of us.

For the past three years, the war dominated newspaper headlines and stories and radio broadcasts of Nazis campaigns in Europe and of the Japanese in the Far East.

The shock and fear caused a heightened emotional frenzy throughout the country, as young men enlisted or were drafted into the armed services. The bombings and fighting and battles we read about in other parts of the world didn't seem real to us until we started experiencing the effects of food, metal, and gas rationing. Even shoes were limited to three pair a year. The military needed leather and rubber. We couldn't even buy stockings. Nylon was used to make parachutes.

John handcuffed like a common criminal and led away by Federal agents brought tears of rage to my eyes. Scorn was not new to him or to any of us. Our whole family had been scorned when he and my sisters and I were disparaged and discriminated against for our religious beliefs back in Colver.

John was a compassionate, decent young man. What might happen to him at the hands of prison guards and other inmates disturbed me. He would be living behind bars in a concrete prison cell for two years, because he refused for religious reasons not to enter the military or to even wear a uniform in a noncombatant role and work in an alternative service building roads and maintaining forest lands.

He was despised by the FBI and labeled a traitor for not being patriotic. Winning the war demanded that every able-bodied man and woman had a definite part to play. You showed patriotism through the defense of your country.

As a deacon missionary in the local Kingdom Hall, he cited the Bible and the sixth commandment, Thou shalt not kill, as his standard. He also believed that the Government did not possess the moral authority to command warlike behavior from its citizens.

His incarceration confirmed for me and for him that the Selective Service System was not interested in recognizing conscience, but in keeping conscientious objectors out of circulation.

I read the statistics. John was among six thousand men sent to prison. Of those six thousand, 75 percent were Jehovah's Witnesses.

One day, Ruth asked me if I would be willing to go out on a blind date. "The Faust Hotel is sponsoring a social dance and the brother of one of my co-workers is trying to arrange a date for his roommate at Northern Illinois University. They're home on spring break."

"He's in college?" I gasped. "I can't do that. I didn't even graduate from high school.

He'll think I'm a drip."

"Don't be silly. Once he sees you, he'll be smitten just to have a date with you."

"I don't have anything to talk about with someone who's in college. I don't even know what subjects they teach."

"You don't talk about college courses. He'll want to know about you. Tell him about yourself."

"Never! Absolutely not! You think he wants to hear about growing up in Colver? What do you talk about?"

"I get the guy talking. Guys love to talk about themselves."

"You mean just ask him?"

"That's right."

"He'll think I'm prying, that it's none of my business."

"He'll think you're interested in him. That's what he wants from you. Make him feel you're interested."

"You mean just sit there like a bump and listen to him?"

"No, listen to him in an active way. Put your hand on your chin like this." Ruth cocked her right elbow on the table and rested her dimpled chin on her fist. "Stare deep into his smoldering eyes."

"You're joking."

"I'm not joking."

"That seems so hokey. I can look and listen without doing this." I imitated my sister's gesture.

"Do it any way that you're comfortable."

"What if he's shy like me and he doesn't talk much."

"Then you can both sit there and lay an egg. You have to take the initiative."

"What if he's not handsome? What if I don't like him?"

"Then pretend that you do."

"That isn't me. I don't pretend."

"Yeah, I know. You're tell it like it is Mary. Just don't embarrass him. Remember, he's your date."

"I hope you didn't commit me to doing this."

"I did." Ruth's lips parted in a wicked grin. "You're committed."

"You should have asked me first."

"Not a chance. I struck while the iron was hot. This is an opportunity."

"Says who?"

"Says me."

"Just because you're my older sister doesn't give you the right to push me around."

"As far as I know, nobody could ever push you around. You're as stubborn as a mule. Mary the mule. Besides, I'm not pushing you around. I'm looking out for you."

"I'm perfectly capable of looking out for myself."

"Not perfectly. You're afraid to meet someone for a blind date, because you don't know what to talk about. I'm giving you pointers on what to say. Just follow them and you'll be perfectly fine."

"When is this dance?" I asked.

"Saturday night. Two days away."

"You're crowding me. That's too soon."

"Too soon for what?"

"I need to get this straight in my mind. I need to practice."

"You don't need to practice. Just be your normal self."

"My normal self says don't do this."

"Oh, come on," Ruth grinned. "You're the bees knees, kid."

"I mean it. I'm not the bee's knees. I'm serious."

"I know you're serious. You're too serious. It's not often we get to enjoy much in life. So either we go out and find it or we grab it when it comes along."

Chapter 8

Blind Date

I had to admit I was nervous and excited. I had the jitters. Ruth acted as liaison and told me my blind date and his college roommate with his date would pick me up at seven.

All I knew was his name, Bob Wenger, and that he was in college. I didn't know what college. I wondered if his friend's date was in college too. That would make me feel worse than I did already.

I soaked in a tub at mid-afternoon, way early. I was grateful for the spring weather. It was not hot and humid, so I would not be sweating by evening.

I had borrowed a few of Nina's fashion magazines, which lay open on her bed. Wearing a bathrobe, I towel-dried my hair while sitting on the edge of the bed and slowly turned pages of the magazines in search of a suitable way to fix my hair. I didn't have Nina's luxurious long peek-a-boo locks like Veronica Lake. The Marcel waves and curls swept back from her high forehead held more appeal for her and fit the oval shape of her face and accentuated her high cheek bones more like Greta Garbo. For the most part, the perfunctory styles of the day were worn by women working in factories to keep the hair out of their eyes and to prevent dangling locks from being caught in moving machine parts. I didn't have pin curlers, so I used strips of rag to fashion curls while my hair dried.

I was on the slender side, so the lavender A-line evening dress with padded shoulders Nina had selected for me with her employee discount from the department store gave me a fashionable hour-glass figure.

"Who am I trying to kid," I told myself. "Hoping to impress someone I haven't even met?

All I had to brag about, and I wouldn't brag anyway, was I was the top typist at the Chamber of Commerce, the fastest and the most accurate. My boss recognized that and praised me for setting such a high standard. I saw both respect and envy in the eyes of my coworkers. I couldn't toot my own horn to a college man about being the best typist. Like Ruth had coached me, I had to get him talking about himself. I needed to have some questions ready and rest my chin on my knuckles.

I was curious what college life was like. I supposed I could ask him about that. But then what? If he asked me about myself, I needed to make up something. I could never tell him where I came from. I could tell him I had graduated from high school at the top of my class with straight 'A's and was working to pay for college and that I would be applying in the fall. If he asked me where, I would tell him that I had many choices and I hadn't decided yet. I had to lie convincingly.

Seated at the powder table, I looked intently at my image in the mirror and made what I thought was an honest expression. I couldn't look honest if I didn't feel honest. I would be lying. He'd see right through me. I couldn't even believe myself. This whole blind date thing was not going to work. I never should have let Ruth talk me into it. I never should have agreed. I had been coerced. That's what had happened. I was being forced against my will to go out with a stranger.

Ruth was leaving me on my own from the get-go. Richard Ainsworth was taking her to dinner before going to the dance. I was grateful to Nina for staying home to help fix my hair and do my makeup. She had learned some techniques at the department store cosmetics department.

I nearly panicked as the hour approached. But I couldn't back out. It was too late for that. Whoever the guy was would think I was a loser. I had to show some respect for myself even though I didn't think of myself as much of a date.

Nina would answer the door. I had arranged for her to come up to the bedroom to get me when the blind date arrived. I would make a grand entrance. From the expression on Nina's face and the way she rolled her eyes, I thought the guy was going to be ugly or at least a disappointment.

"Listen," said Nina, "if you don't want him, I'll take him. He's a real looker."

After a final glance in the mirror at my naturally demur expression, I preceded her out into the hall and started down the wooden stairs that creaked at each step and, I was sure, ruined the impression of my descending grand entrance. I thrust my shoulders back, held my head high, and parted my lips in an alluring smile like a movie star gliding down a mansion staircase.

As soon as I saw him standing in the entry, my preconception of how he would look vanished. He was incredibly handsome. His wavy blonde hair, gentle warmth and direct appreciation beaming clear across the room from his brown eyes captivated me.

I managed to reach the bottom of the stairs without stumbling. With a disarming smile, he stepped forward to meet me and graciously took my hands.

"Hello, Mary, I'm Bob Wenger." His soothing voice and calm manner put me at ease. Miraculously, my nervousness faded.

He wore a brown and tan tweed three-piece suit and light blue tie snugged into a white collar shirt.

"You look wonderful," he said.

Tongue-tied, I managed to utter, "It's nice to meet you." Impressed by his young, rugged face, I stupidly said, "You look wonderful too," then blushed as he laughed and said, "Thank you. My roommate has a car."

"A car? That's nice. I thought we might have to take the bus. You know, the gas rationing and all that."

"Well, this is a special night." He offered his arm. "Shall we go?"

I transferred my small evening purse to my right hand and slipped my left arm into the crook of his elbow.

Nina crossed from the bottom of the stairs and waved to us from the door. "Have a good time."

I was thinking I should say, "I won't be late," but decided that would be insulting to Bob. His next words confirmed my decision as we approached the light green Pontiac Streamliner Coupe parked at the curb.

"We might be a little late getting back. The dance is over at eleven," said Bob.

"Oh, that's all right. I don't mind."

"I understand you share the apartment with your sisters."

"Yes, we all live there." I thought, that's another stupid thing to say. But at least I had said something.

An attractive brunette wearing a tight red jitterbug dress and too loud red lipstick stood at the open passenger door waiting for us. With a vivacious smile, she motioned for us to enter. "Hi, Mary, welcome to Ronnie's chariot. I'm Deanna Grigsby."

I stupidly wondered how she knew my name. "How very nice to meet you."

"Ready to have a blast?"

Not knowing how to respond, I smiled and nodded my head and stepped past the canted front seat back into the rear passenger compartment. As Bob followed me and I slid to the other side and arranged my skirt, he introduced me to the hunk wearing a maroon and black plaid sport coat and drumming his fingers on the wheel.

"Ron, this is Mary. Mary, my college roommate, Ron Delevan. We're on the golf team together at NI."

Ron's boisterous features popped between the two front seats like an entertaining clown. "Great to meet you, Mary."

"How very nice to meet you, Ron," I enunciated graciously. I had no idea what NI meant, but assumed it was where they went to college. Also, Ron's broad shoulders gave him more the look of a football player than a golfer. Bob had a slender build, which was appealing to me. I didn't care for brutish men with bulging muscles. They were disproportionate and could be threatening.

"My sister works with your sister, Ruth, at the phone exchange," said Ron.

"Yes, she told me about that."

"This is quite fortuitous," said Bob, "for all of us."

My God, he's using big words, I thought. I knew what fortuitous meant but didn't expect to hear it used in casual everyday conversation.

"Mary thought we might be riding the bus," said Bob.

Ron's booming laugh filled the vehicle as Deanna slipped onto the front seat and pulled the door shut with a solid thunk. "Nope, my old man loaned me his bucket for the night." He glanced at me in the rearview mirror. "Ready? Let's blow!" He put the car in gear and we shot down the street.

Riding as a passenger in the Streamliner Coupe was my first adult exposure to what I would call luxury. The second was the Faust Hotel.

The fifteen-story brownstone building with a penthouse tower rose above all others at the center of town. The driving brassy musical sound of the swing band caromed off the walls, as we entered the ball room alive with whirling, jumping, gliding partners. Ron passed a few dollars to the tuxedoed host, who led us to a round dining table draped with a white linen cloth. Bob ordered us plain Cokes from a busy waitress and Ron and Deanna ordered theirs spiked with rum.

Within minutes, they were sucked into the jitterbugging whirl of the dancers. Bob's apologetic grin conveyed his lack of dancing skills. "Let's wait for a slow one," he said. "I don't know how to dance like that."

"My sisters do, but I don't either," I said. "I never went to dances back home," and immediately regretted my words.

"Where's home?"

I blushed. "Well, home is here in Rockford."

"Well, when you say back home, you're from somewhere else."

"I grew up in Pittsburgh," I lied and hoped frantically he wouldn't ask me anything more about where I came from. I quickly needed to divert him. "Is Rockford your hometown?"

"Yes, I've lived here all my life."

I nodded and sipped my coke. We watched the dancers and listened to the rousing musical numbers, Chattanooga Choo Choo, Tuxedo Junction, In The Mood, Boogie Woogie Bugle Boy, Sing Sing, On The Sunny Side of The Street, Dancing Cheek To Cheek, until a nice slow waltz came along that we could manage.

Other than an occasional hug from my Dad, I had never been held so closely by a man. With my chin resting on his shoulder, I concentrated on the sweet smell of his after shave, the light pressure of his hand on the small of my back pulling my body against him and arousing an unexpected erotic feeling. The romantic waves of the music washing over us made me wonder if I were falling in love.

Except for the slow dances during which we barely moved from a single spot on the floor, we spoke hardly a word to each other during the entire evening, which didn't bother either of us. Only walking hand in hand through a city park on a subsequent date and sitting on a bench, did he tell me about himself, and, of course, I listened intently, with my knuckles supporting my chin like Ruth had shown me.

The images he shared of his childhood caused me to shed my embarrassment over my impoverished upbringing and united us in an understanding and acceptance of our origins.

As he explained how and where he grew up, I could see him as a ten year old boy reaching out his hand to shut off the dissonant jangling of his bedside alarm clock at five a.m. In his sleep, he had unconsciously rolled to his knees and hugged himself to himself to keep warm. His left arm had become pinned under his chest and the circulation had been slowly cut off. His arm was numb with needles. He thought he had pressed the button, but still the ringing continued. He forced his eyes open. The room was bitter dark and cold. He heaved himself onto his side and tried to lift his right arm, but it wouldn't move. His left hand clamped over the alarm clock and silenced it, then lifted and moved his right arm. The pain coursed through in singeing flashes, as the surging blood flow dissolved the stinging needles.

The cold morning air rendered him practically immobile. He told himself he had to move. He had his job to do. He reached out his shaking right hand and pressed the light switch on the table lamp. The bulb cast only a small circle of light touching the shadowed sleeping lumps of his two brothers across the room.

His eyes were drawn to the loudly ticking clock. Twitching with spasmodic shivers, he slid out of bed and picked up his blanket from where it had fallen on the floor. He wrapped it around his body and hobbled along the dark, creaking hallway to the bathroom, fumbled for the light switch, and closed the door.

Gripping the handle of the plunger, he broke the thin sheet of ice in the toilet bowl and urinated. Cursing silently to himself at the lack of heat, he flushed the toilet and felt his way back to the bedroom. He eased his limbs into frost-stiffened clothes.

Only the dim glow of a single bulb illuminated the kitchen. With numb deftness, his fingers lit the pilot of the open gas oven. The ensuing heat thawed him awake.

He savored a breakfast of black coffee and a slice of his mother's homemade bread with jam and butter. He left the oven on for his siblings to warm themselves when they would wake.

His rubber boots were a half size too small and his coat worn at the elbows. He pulled his stocking cap down snugly over his ears and, carrying his school textbooks in a mittened hand, stepped outside.

The thermometer hanging on the front porch wall read fifteen degrees below zero. He wrapped his woolen scarf around his face so that only his eyes were visible and went down the icy veranda steps into the knee-deep snow, fresh and unbroken under the dim glare of streetlamps and the drooping, ice-covered skeletons of tall dark elms.

He huddled his shoulders against the biting cold and felt the mucous from his nose soak into his scarf and freeze. Evenly spaced dark holes in the snow told of his passing down a side street into predawn shadows and were later erased by a snowplow.

He fumbled for a key and unlocked the wooden door of the news shack. Closing it after himself, he pulled the light cord and stuffed kindling into a pot-bellied stove. When the fire was blazing, he took inventory of the stacks of newspapers which had been delivered to the station the night before. Of the eight routes in his district, one was his responsibility. With tin-snips, he cut the wires of one stack. To protect them from wet snow, he wrapped the newspapers in butcher paper as he folded and stuffed them into a canvas sack. He would deposit them on porches out of the elements to keep them dry.

One by one, other boys arrived runny-nosed and bleary-eyed for their papers. Amid mumbled greetings, Bob trudged off, the pouches of his sack filled with papers riding fore and aft with the weight carried on his thin shoulders.

He left school early, as he was allowed to do every day. His stomach clenched with hunger. He had skipped lunch again to save money. Two meals a day had to be enough to sustain him.

He arrived at the shack and unlocked the door. Eight stacks of the evening edition waited inside.

Winter night enveloped the neighborhoods before Bob finished his deliveries. Soft snowflakes drifted down under the hanging streetlamps and gently salted him and peppered his shadow.

He was home by seven when the rest of the family had already finished their supper. They were in their bedrooms doing school homework. An older sister reheated the macaroni, which was their basic meal, and set it on the table for him.

"My mother was always tired and never talked much," Bob told me. "We were a large family, three boys and four girls. Oddly, I felt like I never had anyone to talk to. Because I was working all the time to help support the family, I didn't really have any friends. We all had to work. My father didn't make enough as a barber, and a lot of what he earned, he drank away.

"I worried about my mother. She had been deteriorating from exhaustion and the extreme cold weather and was bed-ridden with a fever. We couldn't afford to pay for a doctor and my father said we were Christian Scientists and didn't believe in doctors anyway, which was convenient. We were expected to mentally overcome our ailments and illnesses. She died of pneumonia.

"She loved me and my brothers and sisters but didn't have the stamina to show us. She was always tired and relied on my sisters to do the cooking and housekeeping. The one memory I have of her showing how much she cared for me is the night she came to my room and held my hand when I was suffering from a chronic ear infection."

I didn't want to appear boastful by describing the contrast of the love expressed in my family, the one experience that gave me an intangible status of a different kind. I timidly shared my unaffordable ambition of wanting to go to college someday and become a teacher. "I know I'd make a good teacher," I said. "I love books and being with other students in the classroom."

"I'm sure you would be a great teacher. I received my draft notice three weeks ago. You know, the war won't last for long. After I'm out of the service, I can help you get through college."

His statement shocked me. I didn't expect him to ask me to marry him, but before reporting for basic training, he proposed to me. I said yes without hesitation. Following his completion of basic training at Camp Grant on the southern outskirts of Rockford, we were married in a civil ceremony. I would be able to visit him at the Army base from time to time.

My corsage was a cluster of pink, lavender, and white roses pinned to the brown knit piping on the shoulders and across the front of my cream-colored dress. A simple string of pearls peered from a high V neckline and small gold crescent hoop earrings completed my adornments. Nina expertly coiffed my light, blonde-streaked brown hair with Marcel sculpted waves.

Bob's smooth complexion and short blonde wavy hair gave him the appearance of a teenager wearing an Army dress uniform. Formal portrait photographs were taken before the civil ceremony attended by my sisters, Nina and Ruth, and her fiancé, Richard Ainsworth in his Navy dress blues, and my brother, John, and his fiancée, Carolyn Lyford. My parents had not yet moved from Colver. So John gave me away.

Bob's college roommate, Ron Delevan, acted as best man; and Ruth was my bridesmaid. Nina stayed just long enough for the brief simple ceremony, then had to return to work.

Ruth and Richard and John and Carolyn hosted a reception dinner at the Faust Hotel, where Bob and I spent our wedding night. We had spaghetti for dinner and hot apple pie topped with melted cheddar cheese for breakfast.

The next day, Bob boarded a troop train to Miami, Florida to undergo officer candidate training. I would follow and join him. And so began the journey and ordeals of our married life.

Chapter 9

Troop Train

Visiting a military spouse fell under the category of permissible travel by train with no guarantee you would have a seat. Many of the trains were designed to transport large numbers of tanks and jeeps on flatcars. Soldiers traveled on troop trains for military personnel in reconfigured Pullman sleeper cars. Even box cars with three tiers of bunks were used.

Because of the proximity of the Camp Grant induction and training center, many soldiers also traveled on civilian trains and were given priority when it came to seats. After waiting for an hour in a long line of irritable passengers at the depot, I reached the ticket agent's window only to be told there was standing room only on the train to Miami, a two day trip with no possibility of a sleeper. I would still have to pay full price for a ticket.

"Maybe another passenger might be willing to share a seat, but there's no guarantee," he explained.

I looked at his stony uncompromising face and said, "I'll buy the ticket."

Shouts and cries from wives and mothers with small children assaulted me, as I joined the jostling soldiers waiting to board on the wooden station platform.

Arms and hands wildly waved goodbye when the faces of sons or a husbands appeared at a passenger car window. Wind-driven clouds of black smoke chuffing into the air from the coal-burning engine drifted back over the crowd.

Hefting my suitcase, I clambered up the steps of the nearest car platform and stepped through the door into a bedlam of soldiers wearing summer tan uniforms.

I was one of three women in the car. I noticed the other two sitting on laps of soldiers, laughing and carrying on like this was all a big party. A soldier seated next to the aisle grabbed my arm as I tried to avoid colliding with another. I stumbled along the center in search of an empty seat. Even though I'd been told by the ticket agent there were none, I naively hoped a gentlemanly soldier might offer me his seat, but instead heard, "Hey, sweetheart, I've got a seat for you right here." The rough-featured young man patted his lap. His thick lips and lascivious smile were not encouraging.

"Thank you, no," I said. "I'll stand if I have to."

He glanced at my wedding ring. "Goin' to see your hubby in Miami?"

"Yes, he's training to become an officer."

"That's exactly where I'm goin', honey. All of us on this train are. You're in good company. So whattaya say? You can raise my spirits and tell me about your old man."

"You'll raise something else!" Other soldiers guffawed with laughter.

"Thank you, no." I glanced over the remaining rows. All seats were taken.

"You gonna stand the whole trip? You sure have got some legs."

More laughter. They just saw going off to war as a big party, having a good time.

I saw the conductor enter through the door at the opposite end of the car. I intercepted him coming toward me along the aisle, as the train started to move with a piercing foghorn whistle and a jolt that caused me to stagger and clutch his shoulder to stabilize myself.

"Can I help you, ma'am?" he asked.

"I was wondering if there might be a vacant seat in another car. There aren't any here."

"There aren't any on the whole train. Every seat is taken. I'm sorry you have to stand. The ticket agent should have told you."

"He said there might be a possibility of sharing."

"I told her she could sit right here," the soldier who had grabbed my arm slapped his thigh.

"Well, you can either stand in here or between cars on the platform," said the conductor. "Up to you. I can't ask any of these men to give up his seat. Soldiers come first. That's the law."

I nodded and leaned aside so the stocky conductor could pass.

The grinning soldier patted his thighs with both hands. "Right here, sweetheart, ready and waiting. Best and finest lap on the train." His comment brought another explosion of laughter from soldiers seated nearby.

I ignored him and walked out onto the connecting platform between the two cars where there was a safety wall enclosing the platform. The noise of the iron wheels grinding and clicking along over the rails along with the creaks and groans of metal couplings below was deafening. The greasy odor of oil mixed with coal smoke made the air nearly unbreathable. I knew I could not stand out there for long. I decided to try the next car.

Noticing my hopeful gaze as I entered the car, a plain-featured soldier with a pleasant smile motioned to me. "It's a long ride, ma'am. My buddy and I can squeeze you in. He's skinny."

The gaunt second soldier grinned up at me and gave me a brief salute.

"I won't sit on your lap," I said.

"Not asking you to. It'll be tight, but we'll share the seat."

"Okay."

He jumped up, took my suitcase, and stowed it on the overhead luggage rack. "You can have the middle or the aisle. Take your pick."

"I'll take the aisle, if you don't mind. Thank you. You're very kind."

"You're welcome." He extended his hand. "Name's Dennis. My buddy's Lester. We're going to OCS in Miami, Army Air Corps."

"That's where my husband is. I'm Mary."

"Nice to meet you, Mary." Dennis slid onto the center of the two seat bench.

My slender body fit the outside edge.

"There, not so bad," said Dennis. "Better than standing. We can take breaks. Get up and walk around. You just married?"

"Two months ago. My husband went through basic training at Camp Grant."

"Same with us. Lester and I aren't married."

"Do you have girlfriends?"

"You bet." Dennis raised slightly out of his seat to get at his wallet. He flipped it open to show a pocket photo of a gorgeous redhead with wide spaced green eyes.

"She's very beautiful," I said.

"Show her yours," said Dennis.

"That's okay. Later. Too tight here. Nice to meet you, Mary." Lester reached his hand across his friend's lap.

"Thank you for your generosity."

"Glad to, ma'am."

I exchanged pleasantries with primarily Dennis, since we were squeezed tightly together. I revealed little about myself other than I had worked at the Chamber of Commerce and had shared an apartment with my two sisters. Mostly, I spoke of Bob's achievements on a golf scholarship at Northern Illinois University. His education became a benchmark for my own life. After a few hours, depleted of content, our conversation faded while a few other soldiers around us engaged in loud games of dice in the aisle.

As the car filled with cigarette and cigar smoke, I began to cough. Dennis gestured to Lester to open the window. Many of the soldiers smoked, but a few opened their windows as a courtesy to the nonsmokers.

I tried to envision what would happen during the days ahead. I knew Bob and I had only a short time together before he would be shipped somewhere overseas, most likely to the South Pacific. We wanted to make the most of it.

In one of his letters, Bob had described Miami as a tropical paradise. When I arrived, he would move out of the officers' barracks, actually a converted resort hotel, and we would rent a room in one of the many houses or apartments on the beach that provided residential support to the thousands of troops undergoing training before deployment to either the European or the Pacific theaters of the war. 'We'll be having a vacation,' he had written. 'The white sand beaches here are incredible and the clear blue ocean is so warm, it feels like bath water.'

The train switched track routes in Chicago and headed southeast through Indiana farms and the rolling green landscape of Kentucky and Tennessee. Through the train window, I noticed the transition to the piney woods of Georgia and down through the palmetto swamps of Florida to Miami Beach, the central base of military operations.

Bob was among the first wave of soldiers matriculating through the OCS training center. Florida was as much of a new adventure for him as it would be for me.

Miles of luxury hotels had been converted to living quarters for officers undergoing training.

Bob stayed in one of the hotel room barracks, ate in the dining room mess hall, took written exams in a movie theater testing center, learned life saving techniques in the hotel pool and ocean, practiced synchronized marching drills on golf course parade grounds, and received rifle training on an isolated beach not so far from hotel and residential areas that the distant popping of gunfire could be heard.

I stepped off the train at the Miami station into a disembarking mob of soldiers being called into formation to board military trucks that would transport them to training barracks at Camp Blanding.

In a letter, Bob had written he would not be able to meet me upon my arrival and that I should go to the nearby USO center for soldiers and their wives and wait for him to come for me. Through a connection, he had been able to find a room in the high rent, limited vacancy tourist economy where there were no available rooms for low paid military personnel. He said the housing crisis left wives and children wanting to see their husbands and fathers, for what could be the last time, out in the streets.

Rent control did not ease the demand for the eighty thousand apartments leased to the Federal Government. Miami was a hive swarming with khaki uniformed men and women.

Tired and gritty with the stink of travel at close quarters, I spotted the USO sign posted high on a flat gray stucco single story building that had once been used to store freight and baggage. My suitcase thumped against my leg as I maneuvered through the crowd toward the service center.

Walking through the doorway, I encountered wall to wall soldiers and wives and children occupying all the available couches, tables and chairs or waiting in long lines to speak with military clerks and civilian hostesses. The rumble of voices and crying of babies filled the air.

I saw exhausted angry mothers with babies in carriages, with babies in their arms and with toddlers. Unable to find housing, they had been turned away to roam the streets homeless, sleeping on park benches or in deserted automobiles and dependent on emergency breadlines set up by the Red Cross to distribute food.

I waited in a long line to use the women's restroom where I could at least wash my face. With no place to rest, I removed my shoes and leaned against a wall, then eventually sat on my suitcase.

An hour later, I saw Bob come through the door and look over the crowd in search of me. His loose-fitting summer tan uniform accentuated his weight loss from the physical demands of training, but the familiarity of his broad smile when he saw me was unmistakable.

Flushed with relief, I slipped on my shoes, grabbed my suitcase, and worked my way through the blockade of people as he was coming toward me. He momentarily held me in a strong embrace, took my suitcase, and escorted me arm in arm to the door and out into the sunlight.

He kissed me. "I'm so glad you're here. I'll bet the train ride was an ordeal."

"That's putting it mildly. I need a bath and I'm starving."

"I hope you were able to get food on the train."

"I ate what they served, army chow."

"There's a restaurant down the street. I have a lot to tell you." He grasped my hand as we maneuvered along the sidewalk congested with milling soldiers and civilians.

"It's so hot and humid here and so many people," I said.

"The Army and Navy have taken over all the hotels and apartments. We're lucky to have a room in an older house. It's a nice place. A friend I made the first week I was here told me about it. He and his wife have one of the other rooms. We share a kitchen. So we don't have to eat Army chow."

"What about the owners? Are they still there?"

"An elderly woman, Mrs. Chelton. She's a widow. She's lived here in Miami for over thirty years. Seen all the changes, but nothing like what's happening now. Here we are." He held the door open for me to enter the Palmetto Café. "I ate here once. The food is very good."

A cute freckle-faced waitress wearing a blue and white dress and a candy-striped apron seated us at a vacated table toward the back of the restaurant. As we sat down and read the menu, we had to raise our voices to be heard above the chatter.

"Everything on here is fish," I said.

"It's a seafood restaurant. Seafood is mostly what they serve in Miami. There's a whole ocean full of it out there. Meat is rationed unless you live in the hotel barracks. Civilians can buy only a pound and a half a week from the butcher."

"Do you know anything about these fish? I don't know what to order."

"I'm not familiar with all the different varieties, but when I ate here before, I had grouper. It's a grilled white fish that's delicious. I'm going to have it again. It comes with French fries and coleslaw."

"Okay, I'm a vegetarian, but I do eat a little meat once in a while. I'll try it."

"They had to stop serving sweet tea here because of the sugar ration. Sweet tea is southern. We can have regular iced tea. You won't see sugar bowls on the tables. Can't get it for coffee either." Bob signaled to the waitress.

After we left the restaurant, I expressed surprise at seeing a woman driving the city bus Bob and I boarded on Flagler Avenue, the main street through the city.

"Women are doing most of the jobs that men used to," Bob explained. "There are even some training to be pilots. A lot of women are mechanics and building ships and airplanes in factories. There's a big push on nation-wide to get food and equipment and supplies from farms and factories to where the fighting is happening on the front lines. Some women are on tree-cutting crews and even building houses. You won't see a milkman anymore. Women deliver the milk. Almost every able-bodied man is in the service. According to the *Herald News*, we're living in the era of the new woman."

"I guess that makes me a new woman," I laughed flippantly.

I liked the sound of the phrase but didn't know how it applied to me.

The bus let us off at a neighborhood of two story Spanish style urban houses with red tile roofs.

"We're only a block from the bus stop," said Bob. "So it's easy to go into town."

"What about groceries?"

"There's a market within easy walking distance. You can shop with Gwen Gebhardt. She's the wife of the friend I told you about. I'll introduce you."

"Do we need anything for the room?"

"It comes furnished. We have to do our own towels and laundry. Mrs. Chelton has a washing machine. We're on the second floor. We have to share the bathroom with the Gebhardts."

"They sound like nice people."

"They are. Eddie is a bit of a character. He's training to be a fighter pilot. He's quite an athlete. He ran track when he was in college. He's a champion two-miler. Here we are."

The size and architecture and tropical foliage impressed me. "Mrs. Chelton must be rich to have a house like this," I said.

"Her husband owned a citrus fruit company for many years before he died. She told me he left her with a large inheritance, but most of the money was lost during the crash. The war picked things up here like everything else. She sold the company. The Government pays her six dollars a month for each room the Gebhardts and we are renting.

"We don't have to pay rent do we?"

"As an officer, I get a living allowance."

"That's nice since I'm not earning any money."

"We'll be okay. We can live comfortably on my commission."

"What will I do? I'm not used to not working."

"Talk to Gwen. She volunteers a few days a week at The Red Cross."

As we entered the house, Gwen and Mrs. Chelton came through the back door into the kitchen and unloaded baskets of vegetables from Mrs. Chelton's victory garden. Bob put down my suitcase and ushered me into the kitchen to introduce me.

"Gwen, Mrs. Chelton, my wife has finally arrived," he announced with an unabashed grin.

Mrs. Chelton crossed the kitchen to greet me with a hug. "Welcome, Dear. Bob's told us about you. You are every bit as beautiful as he says. Hope you don't mind my dirty hands. Gwen and I have been digging in the garden."

Dressed in a simple print dress and wearing low-heeled laced black shoes, Mrs. Chelton reminded me a little of my own mother. They had similar weathered wrinkled European faces.

"I'm Gwen." Wiping her wet hands on a towel, Gwen walked over and extended her clean right hand. "We should celebrate your arrival. Tonight, our husbands can take us out on the town." Her deep contralto laugh matched the exuberant glint of her brown eyes and direct forward manner bearing down on me.

Gwen stood a half head taller, her height and forceful personality accentuated by a hood of thick shoulder-length brunette hair. A slightly flared nose and wide sensuous mouth gave her the attractive appearance of a stage actress. I felt slightly intimidated by her aggressive lusty nature. The top portions of her tanned cleavage loomed from her tropical orange and lemon yellow summer dress. I noticed her sun-bronzed bare feet exposed in wedge sandals. She liked to expose her flesh.

"Mary's pretty tired from the trip," said Bob. "I think the weekend will be better, and besides, Eddie and I have to report at the crack of dawn. Is he back from training yet?"

"Not yet. He's flying around in one of those buzz bombs out there," Gwen spoke with the clipped enunciation, raised Rs and elongated vowels of a New England accent.

"We ate dinner downtown. Mary wants to soak in a tub and get some sleep."

"I know what you mean," said Gwen. "I rode one of those trains. Bet you had lots of offers to sit on a lap."

I grinned. "I turned them all down."

"You stood up the whole trip?"

"Two polite soldiers made room. It was snug, but okay."

"Eddie's father had some pull with the railroad. He's a congressman. So I got a seat."

"Tell Eddie I'll see him in the morning," said Bob.

"I know. Special night."

My face flushed with embarrassment. I touched Bob's arm and we left the kitchen.

"Good night, kids," Mrs. Chelton called after us.

Chapter 10

Sand In Our Shoes

Bob's kiss brushing my forehead woke me at dawn. "I'm off," he said. "See you tonight. Have a wonderful day."

"I love you."

"I love you too. I'm so glad you're here. There's some cash on the dresser, if you need to go out and buy anything," he said.

"Thanks. I don't think I'll go anywhere today. I need to wash some clothes."

"Mrs. Chelton will help you with that. We can take a tour on the weekend. Lots to see. Florida is nothing like Illinois. It's a tropical paradise. See you later."

"See you later." I watched him silently close the bedroom door.

With a sense of happiness and well-being, I snuggled back onto my pillow and inhaled the sweet floral scent of jasmine and orange blossoms wafting through the open window and listened to the melodic trilling of a mockingbird.

Stretching leisurely, I threw the covers aside and slipped out of bed. I padded barefoot to the bathroom to relieve myself and wash my face. Peering at my mirror image, I thought I looked different than before I was married. An expression of content had displaced the hardness of my blue-green eyes. A pink rosiness colored my lips and raised a glow in my cheeks. My body pulsed with an erotic sensuality aroused by Bob's gentle love-making that had followed my relaxing soak in the large cast iron tub the night before.

I returned to the bedroom and changed from blue cotton pajamas to a plain beige blouse, dark slacks and low heels. I brushed out my hair and moved the money from the dresser top to my purse, then walked downstairs toward the smell of coffee and women's voices coming from the kitchen.

"Good morning, Dear," Mrs. Chelton's cheery greeting and motioning me to enter dispelled my uncertainty that I might be intruding. "Did you sleep well?"

"Yes, it's a comfortable bed."

" 'Morning, Mary," Gwen raised a glass pitcher. "Orange juice? Coffee? Both?"

"I'll have both, thank you." I noticed that Gwen was also wearing dark bell bottom slacks and a tan short sleeve shirt.

"I'll bet you're hungry," said Mrs. Chelton. "I was just making scrambled eggs and toast."

"I saw Eddie and Bob off," said Gwen. "I'm in the habit of waking up early and going for a walk. I like the cool morning air before it gets hot and muggy."

"How do you like your toast?" asked Mrs. Chelton. "Light or dark."

"Sort of in between."

"Medium, I should have guessed. You're not an extreme person."

Gwen asked, "Would you like to do something today?"

"I don't know. I hadn't thought about it. I have to wash some clothes. What did you have in mind?"

"I volunteer a few days at The Red Cross. They can always use help. We can work a few hours, then hit the beach."

"Hit the beach?"

"Go to the beach. It's lovely. White sand, warm blue water."

"I don't have a bathing suit."

"We'll go shopping and buy you one."

"I don't know how to swim."

"You can wade in the surf. Get a suntan."

"How about tomorrow?"

"There's no time like the present. We're not here for that long." Gwen noticed my sudden anxiety. "I didn't mean that like it sounds. We have kind of a respite here, a short vacation. Eddie and Bob will ship out overseas in a few months. We have a taste of Miami. We have sand in our shoes. Eddie says he wants to move here after the war. You know, you're right. You need a day to settle in. Let's make it tomorrow." Gwen finished her coffee and pushed back her chair. "Well, I'm off. You both have a swell day." Her smile washed over me and Mrs. Chelton.

Mrs. Chelton nodded and raised her hand. When Gwen was gone, she glanced across the table at me. "Your eggs okay?"

"They're delicious. I've never had them cooked like this before."

"It's my version of a seafood omelet. I sprinkle a little cheddar and green peppers on it. I keep some chickens out in back. They give me fresh eggs every morning."

"When I was a girl, my Dad tried raising chickens, but they all died."

"Did you live on a farm?"

"My Mum and Dad kept a garden. They grew our vegetables and we had fruit trees. We helped Mum with the canning."

"So you had good years growing up."

I nodded.

"Where were you born?"

"I beg pardon."

"Where were you born?"

"A small town. I consider Rockford, Illinois my home. It's a city."

"My husband and I moved down here from New York."

"Bob told me you had orchards and a fruit company," I said.

"We did and we did well. Raised nine children, three girls and six boys. All the boys went in the Navy. Girls married with children of their own. You remind me of my youngest girl, Midge. She was a shy one too."

I wasn't sure how to respond to the implication.

"It's okay to be shy. Cautious I call it. Don't just charge in. Figure things out. Look before you leap. You and Bob are going to have children, aren't you?"

"If he makes it back."

"Don't think like that. Plan for it. Have a child. Just believe he'll come back. You religious? You pray?"

"No, I'm not. I don't think praying helps."

"Then you're realistic."

"What do you mean?"

"You don't bury yourself in wishful thinking, hoping some miracle will happen."

"I do wish for things. My brother and sisters and I did wish for things growing up. We didn't have much."

"That small town."

"Yes, but we didn't stay."

"Now, you're out in the world."

"Somehow it doesn't seem real here."

"It is and it isn't. Bob told me how you met in Rockford." Mrs. Chelton smiled. "Very romantic."

"It was romantic. We don't have much, but we have each other."

"That's what matters."

"The war isn't romantic," I said. "It's frightful."

"War isn't romantic. It's deadly. There are German U-boats off our coast and Japan has attacked us. Our men have to fight, just like any other warriors."

"I don't think of Bob as a warrior. He's very kind and gentle. I can't imagine him killing anybody."

"Actually, Dear, I can't either. Come. I'll show you the washing machine. There's a clothesline in the back yard to hang your things."

The next morning, as the bus pulled to a stop near the Biltmore Hotel, Gwen and I glimpsed several hundred shirtless men performing synchronized calisthenics on the beach. Caressed by warm sea breezes, we paused to watch for a few minutes.

"Our guys are out there somewhere," said Gwen. "Shall we go?"

We continued along the sidewalk in the direction of The Red Cross headquarters adjacent to a wing of the hotel which had been converted to a hospital for returning wounded soldiers.

I looked up at the unaccustomed drone of P-51 Mustangs, Navy Hellcats, and PBM Avengers crossing the Florida skies from dawn to dusk. A hovering flotilla of massive air dirigibles used to spot German submarines in coastal waters patrolled the shorelines. Military police carrying bayoneted rifles patrolled the beaches crowded with civilian women and children and off-duty soldiers.

A few miles offshore, low-flying B18 "Bolo" bombers in squadron formation skimmed along fifty feet above the azure Atlantic surface in practice raids to avoid enemy radar detection.

The rattle of automatic gunfire and distant explosions of bombs offshore farther up the coast caused me to feel a sense of foreboding in the "tropical paradise." Out of sight, amphibious landing craft loaded with young infantry soldiers stormed isolated beaches. The military presence was everywhere I looked and listened, air, land, and sea.

Gwen told me the entire city went dark each night in compliance with a blackout regulation to prevent enemy U-boats from seeing Navy warships and commercial freighters against the Miami skyline.

"I didn't know they were that close," I said.

"They're out there all right," said Gwen. "Eddie told me some Germans were captured and imprisoned at Camp Blanding.

A flurry of women volunteers rolling bandages and packaging medical supplies to be shipped to the front lines occupied The Red Cross center.

"Don't be put off by the number," said Gwen. "They can always use another pair of hands."

After a brief introduction to the serious mannered middle-aged woman in charge, wearing a white arm band with a red cross, I joined Gwen on the bandage rolling assembly line. The filmy gauze raised images in my mind of the bloody wounds it would be used to wrap. My anxiety increased as the morning progressed. The women along the line silently concentrated on their task. Relief flooded me when I heard Gwen say, "Time for lunch. I usually only work mornings. The afternoon is ours. After lunch, we'll get you a bathing suit."

"I don't have the money to spend."

"I'll buy one. My gift to you as a new bride."

"I can't accept that," I said, trailing after her out the door into brilliant afternoon sunshine and the swish and sizzle of waves crashing on the beach.

"Oh, sure you can. Eddie and I are flush. He made a killing at Hialeah last weekend. It's for me, for us to enjoy."

"What's Hialeah?"

"Racetrack. Horse racing. Eddie's a risk taker. He likes to bet. And by the way, I'm buying lunch. I hope you like seafood. That's most of what we get these days."

"Seafood is fine. It's new for me. We didn't have it where I grew up."

"Where was that?"

I tried to avoid giving a specific answer as we maneuvered through a crowd of rowdy off-duty soldiers jamming the sidewalk in search of prostitutes. "Pennsylvania."

"That's pretty far inland."

I was relieved she didn't press for details. To direct attention away from myself, I asked, "Where are you from?"

"Eddie and I are from Boston. We're not new to seafood. Plenty of it there. Practically lived right on the ocean. We got married while he was going to Princeton. His dad wanted him to become a lawyer. Eddie had made up his mind about that, but he was drafted before he could graduate. He had one more year to go before starting law school."

"How did you meet each other?"

"At a party. I was in my junior year at Wellesley."

"You went to college. How lucky you are. That's what I want to do after the war, go to college. What was it like?"

"Wellsley is a snooty all woman's school. I didn't like the snooty part," said Gwen, "but I liked my classes. I was majoring in Journalism and English literature."

"Journalism?"

"I want to become a news writer," said Gwen. "After Eddie goes overseas, I'm applying for a job."

"In Boston?"

"Here in Miami, at the Herald."

"Do they hire women news writers?"

"They're going to hire me."

I admired how Gwen could have such confidence in herself.

We stopped and waited at a street corner for a twelve military truck convoy of Negroes to pass by.

"Negroes. I didn't know they could be soldiers," I said. "Where do they come from?"

"You're in the South," said Gwen. "They're everywhere."

Other than the convoy, Negroes were nowhere to be seen on the streets. "They don't come into the city," Mrs. Chelton had later explained. "They have their own places in Color Town. You won't see them on white beaches either. They're not allowed."

Eventually, I learned the Depression and the war effort had created a level playing field eliminating the perceived barrier of a social and economic class for white military personnel, but not for African Americans. All soldiers' lives were at equal risk going into battle, but, with the exception of officer candidates, Negroes underwent training separately at Camp Blanding to become engineering regiments building living quarters, landing fields, and roads through mountain jungles. They were banned from commingling socially with white soldiers and the white civilian population of Miami.

As for white soldiers and civilians, the high spirits and good times in the city provided an interlude impregnated with the logistics and realities of aerial, land, and sea combat training.

“Here we are,” said Gwen. “I haven’t tried this place yet.” She pushed open the door to *El Cubana* and we entered, joining the noisy lunch crowd.

Chapter 11

Taking Risks

I disliked seeing Bob influenced by Eddie Gebhardt to bet even a few dollars, but I didn't say anything to discourage his youthful enthusiasm. Hialeah was part of the Miami tour he promised me. I would just as soon have foregone a visit to the famous racetrack.

Wearing a sleeveless summer dress and straw sun hat, I withered in the broiling heat and humidity. The stale odor of sweating bodies, cigar smoke, beer, and crushing bodies of uniformed men nauseated me. I covered my ears at the deafening roar of the crowd, shouting and cheering encouragement to the horses and jockeys on which the men had placed money at the long line of betting windows.

A close second to the maneuvers of aerial combat, the contagious thrill of gambling pulled at Eddie like a magnet. He discussed the racing form with Bob as though it contained the secret how the races would be run and their outcome.

Gwen sipped a beer and ignored her husband's heated discussion about the quality and bloodlines of the thoroughbreds and their racing history. She jokingly told me, "I think Eddie identifies with the horses, because he was a championship runner in college."

I could not deny Eddie's dark good looks and swaggering charisma. His restless hazel eyes reflected an intense competitive spirit.

At breakfast that Sunday morning, his certitude about any topic had dominated the conversation. I followed Bob's example and just listened politely as Eddie expounded on his feats of flying a P-51 fighter. Gwen seemed to tolerate him, until his brash statement, "There's always a chance I'll go down in flames over the Pacific, but I'll take thirty Jap zeroes with me."

"I really wish you wouldn't say things like that, Eddie," said Gwen.

"Oh, it's okay," he teased her. "It doesn't mean anything. Nothing's gonna happen to me. I can outfly anything and anyone up there."

Later, eating dinner at an open-air waterfront restaurant, tossing back rum punches, Eddie suddenly grew agitated at my reluctance to order a cocktail. "All I've seen you drink all evening is Coca-Cola. I've noticed how you watch me. You don't approve of me, do you, Mary? You're uptight. Go on. Have a drink. Bob, you need to teach her how to loosen up. Enjoy herself."

"I'm fine. I don't drink," I said. "I don't like how it makes me feel."

"I get it. You don't want to lose your edge. I'm sober as a saint when I'm flying, but off-duty, it's my time. Is it a religious thing with you?"

"No, everything in my life is not a religious thing."

"She's fine, Eddie," said Bob in a friendly tone to defuse him. "I love her just the way she is."

"Well, Mary doesn't seem to be merry."

"Eddie, that's enough," warned Gwen. "I'm hungry. Let's order."

"I'm sorry, Mary. I apologize. I was out of line. Bob, you're too nice. You should have punched me in the nose."

Bob grinned and shook his head. "Mary can handle herself."

Later at Mrs. Chelton's house, lying in bed alone in our room, I commented, "Eddie can certainly be obnoxious."

"Oh, he's not so bad, Honey. Pilots have it rough. Aerial combat is one of the most dangerous, more than infantry. He just likes to unwind when he's off duty. I told you he's a character."

"I hope all of your Army buddies aren't like him."

"We need each other. We have to look out for each other."

"I hope you never have to carry a gun and shoot somebody."

"I'll be a supply officer, behind the front lines. Because I'm an officer, I'll have a handgun. But there are a lot of unknowns out there."

"Where are they going to send you next?"

"Supply officers go to Mather Field in Sacramento, California. I'll be there for a short time, then ship out to Australia."

"Can I go with you to Sacramento?"

"It will be another long train ride, clear across the country. As an officer, I think I can arrange for you to travel with me, actually have your own seat. We might have to share a sleeping berth. Sleep in two shifts."

I wrinkled my nose.

"I'm kidding. You can have the berth. I can sleep fine on the seat."

After completing the twelve weeks Officer Candidate School training commissioned as a second lieutenant, Bob showed me his orders to report for duty at transport. I would be allowed to make the five-day train ride with him.

Upon our arrival in Sacramento, after processing in, Bob returned with good news to the USO center. "They have a house for us like in Miami." He dropped his duffle bag on the floor. "There's a military bus into town. Goes back and forth to the base every hour. Sorry I took so long. There are a lot of us here, thousands."

We moved into one of the Craftsman bungalow style homes being leased near the base for married officers. While Bob learned about the supply chain logistics for supporting military operations in the South Pacific, I made weekly trips on the bus filled with officer's wives to a local market for groceries and made occasional forays into downtown Sacramento to occupy my time alone.

Walking about the city streets teeming with civilians, I wandered into an area of deserted Japanese mercantile and retail businesses and saw large, posted evacuation notices with instructions to all persons of Japanese ancestry who were being relocated to internment camps.

Bob had told me that when he was a teenager, he had come out to California for two summers to work for his uncle, Floyd Wenger, who owned acres of citrus and walnut orchards.

"Except that his trees needed water, he hated the rainy season. He didn't like to be idle. He was happiest during the summer, and he was glad to have me here. He was always on the go from dawn to dusk. He hired a few Mexicans to work for him during harvests, but otherwise, he ran the whole two-hundred acres by himself. He was a small man, hard and strong as nails.

Several years before I came out here to visit, he lost his right hand to a power saw. He wore a steel hook. He never married, but he employed a housekeeper, Helga. The main thing I remember about her is she filled the farmhouse with the cooking smells of garlic and onions. She also hid garlic cloves all around in the house. It drove my uncle mad trying to find them." Bob laughed at the memory. "He'd search out every nook and cranny while she trailed after him shouting, 'They clean the spleen. They clean the spleen.' My uncle told me because he didn't have any children, he was going to write me into his will."

When Bob was off duty, he and I would sometimes see a movie in the crowded Senate Theater packed with men and women who were there not only for the feature, but for the propagandized newsreels about the favorable progress of the war without showing the bloody ravages of battle.

Bob shared with me some of the scope of what he was learning about procurement, purchasing, inspection, supply management, packaging, storage, and warehousing of perishable goods, and about inventory control and what conditions he would encounter of loss, waste, and pilferage. He emphasized this was knowledge and experience he might be able to use in business after the war. I listened attentively for any indication that he might be in the middle of the fighting.

"Once I'm over there, my main responsibility will be the distribution of food and supplies and ammunition to troops on the ground and for the fueling, arming and maintenance of aircraft. And it all depends on what the generals want and their tactical plans for where resources are needed."

"And you're behind the front lines in all this?"

"There aren't really front lines in the South Pacific, only islands. You don't have to worry. I won't be in danger."

"You said Australia."

"That's the jumping off point. From there, I'll be going to Port Moresby on New Guinea. It's across the Coral Sea from Australia."

"I'll have to get an atlas so I know where you are."

"Wherever I am out there, my thoughts will be here with you."

I had sent my parents a photograph of Bob and myself at the time of the wedding. The snapshot image and my description of him as a college student and training at officer candidate school were the extent of what they knew about him.

With Bob gone overseas, I moved in with Mum and Dad, who had left Pennsylvania and had bought a small two story, three bedroom bungalow in Rockford on the lower income east side of town.

After some hesitation, Nina overcame her resentment against our mother, but managed to stay at the apartment with Ruth and a friend to share the rent with her.

I wrote Bob a letter every week to maintain a connection and to describe any family news. Even the small daily things we did were important to him and gave him hope that he was constantly in our thoughts and prayers for a safe return. I always signed them, Just Mary.

To my own surprise, I had taken up praying privately, if you could call it that, more like thinking about Bob in an emotional spiritual sense. Despite their ardent request, I refused to follow my parents' religion. I vowed I would never again impose their cultist restrictions and worshipful mythological fantasies of Armageddon and resurrection to a Utopian afterlife on my life and the lives of my husband and children.

I received Bob's first letter one month later, after he had traveled on a troop ship from San Francisco to Australia. I found the initiation to Neptune's Court to which he was subjected when he crossed the equator to be quite bizarre and wondered why men did such foolish things to each other.

He described the ceremony of having his head shaved by sailors, being blindfolded, having his hands tied, called a pollywog, and then pushed over the side of the ship to waiting sharks, or so he thought, until only a few feet later, he splashed into a canvas container of shallow water. They removed his blindfold and he became a shellback, like others before him. What an odd ceremony.

Sometimes, a whole month would pass before I received a letter from him. After he moved from Brisbane, Australia, to Port Moresby, New Guinea, letters arrived containing the money he won in poker games. Knowing my aversion to gambling, he explained that there was little else to do in the camp at night.

During the first year of his tour, I listened to three daily broadcasts over the Zenith radio on the progress of the war. I also bought a weekly newspaper to read about campaigns, but quickly decided the statistics and names of soldiers dying in battle was too depressing. I believed that looking for his name might cause it to appear and I lived in dread of receiving a telegram from the war department.

Bob's redacted letters gave me a sense of the difficulties he encountered just trying to do his job. Regulations prohibited him from describing many details, so what he told me was always positive and that, except for the loneliness of being so far from home, things were going well, with one exception.

He suffered from malaria; a mosquito borne disease that was decimating the troops by the thousands. He wrote that despite taking Atabrine and quinine tablets, he was having bouts of nausea, headaches, and abdominal pain. The Atabrine had turned his skin yellow.

As long as the letters kept coming, I knew he was alive and I wanted him to know about the life I had growing inside me. Two months after he had gone, I learned I was pregnant. At first I thought I had a flu bug, because I woke up feeling nauseous and, for a week, didn't feel like eating anything but saltine crackers or toast and pickles and drinking tea. Since she had experienced the symptoms five times, Mum knew the signs and she told me.

I was elated and dashed off a letter to Bob that wouldn't get read for at least two months. Although two other letters arrived in the meantime describing the harsh living conditions in the New Guinea jungles and his contraction of malaria, I received his response to the news of my pregnancy three months later. He said the thought of being a father raised his spirits and kept him going. He wanted me to send photos when the baby was born.

The malaria worried me. It was a disease that didn't just fade away.

For a while, I experienced what I thought were gas bubbles that eventually evolved into pokes by tiny feet and elbows, as the fetus rolled over and turned around inside me.

I had gynecological exams three times during my pregnancy. When the doctor asked me if I were eating meat, I told him no. He said a lack of protein would harm the development of my baby. When I said that I was a vegetarian, he told me to eat lots of peanut butter, nuts, and cheese and beans. That was how I ate for the next eight months, and lots of it.

I imagined how our lives would be after the war.

When Bob came home, he would finish his college education using the G.I. Bill and get himself a good-paying job as a manager in a well-respected successful company. After all, he had the skills and experience from being a supply officer. As a captain, he was already a manager.

We would have two more children. Three would be the limit, two boys and a girl. I would take the test for my GED and get my high school diploma. Then I would enroll in evening college courses part-time, or even during the day, as the children became old enough to be in school and wouldn't need me at home. I could also work as a secretary to supplement our income so we could afford some of the finer things.

Based on Bob's salary and having a G.I. mortgage, we would buy a nice house in a nice neighborhood suburb in a nice part of town. As our children grew, we would enjoy gracious living as a family. They would wear fine clothes and take piano lessons. We would be cordial with each other and have intelligent conversations and informed discussions regarding topics of the day and what the children were learning in school. We would eat well, steaks and fried chicken, beef roast or pork roast on Sundays with all the trimmings. Even though I was a vegetarian, I wanted my family to eat a balanced diet. I didn't mind cooking meat and, occasionally, I would take a small serving.

Our dining room would have a chandelier. Sometimes, we would have lighted candles at the table.

Bob and I would regularly attend PTA meetings at the school to underscore the importance of our children's education.

I would make my dreams and wishes come true.

Chapter 12

The Homecoming

For the duration of the war, I lived with my parents in their white two-story frame house. Stately elms shaded the quiet street that belied the violent chaos and turmoil of war in Europe and the South Pacific and its effect on people and cities and towns throughout the country. The warm security of being with Mum and Dad in their home among the tall trees casting leafy green umbrellas over the neighborhood rooftops gave me a sense of existing in a protective cocoon.

Mum's familiar cooking smells of fresh baked bread, savory chicken and beef soups and stews, fruit pies, garlic and herbs and paprika drifted from the kitchen creating a pervasive presence of old world aromas.

Dad worked as a machinist in a local factory. Ruth continued her employment as a PBX phone operator. Wanting to financially contribute to Mum and Dad, I took a secretarial job with the Rockford Life Insurance Company. I would stop working when my baby was born.

Ruth bought a folding camera and snapped the first of twenty black and white photos of our son, Robbie, I would send to Bob over the next few months.

Photographs were the only means I had to establish an impression for Bob of his son. I didn't want Robbie to associate Bob in a uniform with the idea of Daddy, so I showed him a large photo of Bob wearing the suit he wore when I first met him. Bob and I were standing close together. I pointed repeatedly from one of us to the other and said, "Mommy, Daddy." Of course, Robbie was too young to have developed any language comprehension, but I thought he might absorb some of what I was telling him.

While I had been pregnant, I started reading *The Commonsense Book of Baby and Childcare* by Dr. Benjamin Spock. One of the points he emphasized about childhood development was that babies liked to explore the world around them. Infants were constantly taking in everything they saw, heard, touched, tasted, and smelled and that their brains were already processing and storing those impressions and information.

Robbie's birth caused an emotional sensation. My sisters spent more of their off-work time at the house and Mum and Dad nurtured these family gatherings with celebratory feasts that, during later years, became a weekend tradition.

We did not see my brother, John, who remained in prison for two years and was not released until six months after the end of the war.

The tone of Bob's letters conveyed his depression that he couldn't be with us and love his son with more than words in letters. Like many other soldiers, he was among the thousands of goldbrick papas, as they were called, whose child had been born while their fathers were fighting overseas.

We never left Robbie alone. Either I or Mum or a visiting Ruth or Nina watched over him, even while he napped. When he became ill, coughing and gagging on mucous with tiny infant coughs, I never slept.

He recognized me and could differentiate me from the other adults. His stubby little fingers pulled and entangled my long blonde hair and he burbled and chortled at its texture.

I enjoyed watching him clutch the bottle and hold it tightly while his puffy lips sucked and squeaked the rubber nipple. I handled him gently when I changed his diapers and he talked to me with his incoherent cooing and belching sounds.

When I bundled him up and took him outdoors, as I pushed him in his baby carriage along the quiet street, he was alert to the sense of motion, the multitude of smells in the air, the colors of the sky and lawn and flowers and the high-pitched melodic bird calls mingled with the slow chug of passing cars. And I would sing little songs to him.

Just as the impressions outside stimulated him, the world inside the house held his attention, the pungent garlic, onion, meat and fresh dough and paprika food smells of his grandmother's European cooking and the occasional bang of pots and the crackling of grease and blistering pop of stews and tomato gravies. So life beckoned him. And so did death.

Again, as with my baby sister, Margaret, during my childhood in Colver, death visited me and threatened to take my son.

Our house had been placed under quarantine. As our soft-spoken, kind pediatrician, Dr. Woodward, left us, he told me and my parents that nothing more could be done for Robbie. Thousands of infants and children across the country were dying from polio. He said the spread of infection could be caused by handling feces. When Robbie had begun crawling, I discovered him playing with his poop he had tried to hide from me behind the living room couch. From the squishy greenish-brown substance smeared around his mouth, he had even been tasting and eating it.

The polio virus invaded the brain and spinal cord and could cause paralysis, because the muscles that helped him breathe could be affected.

All we could do was pray for him. Being a disbeliever, even I prayed fervently and wept and went without sleep. We took turns holding him all through the night and never lay him down for fear he would stop breathing. We sponged his small quivering body with a cool washcloth in an attempt to reduce the discomfort of his raging fever. His eyes did not open and he began to die.

I was beside myself with grief. I couldn't let my son die like I had let my baby sister die. I stubbornly refused to let anyone else hold him, as though I alone could protect him from death. Bob would never see his child, only photographic prints just as the infant had seen him only in a photograph. My emotion choked me so that I could no longer pray. The rapid words of prayer uttered in the Czech language by Mum and Dad hovered around me like a flock of birds.

The doctor had told us that if Robbie lived for twenty-four hours, he might survive, but with the crippling effects of polio. By late morning on the second day, Robbie began breathing more easily. I detected a soft sibilant snore and his skin was no longer hot to the touch. He continued to live.

When he started walking, under my watchful eye, he careened about the back and side yard. His chubby legs protruded from bulky swathed diapers and pumped him along with a rubbery flexibility until he toppled forward or sometimes just sat down with a soft bump.

I had read in Dr. Spock's newly published book that I should have confidence in my abilities as a mother and to trust my instincts. The first line in the book stated, "Trust yourself. You know more than you think." Those words imprinted in my mind became my belief in myself for the rest of my life. I stopped listening to advice from others, including Mum and Dad, not only about childcare, but about everything else.

Spock said to be flexible and show affection for my child. My affection was naturally and instinctually demonstrated. Using common sense and being flexible were other issues. I had my own way of thinking about and doing things.

Spock said to treat my child as an individual, which I most certainly would do with Robbie and, eventually, my other children as they grew into early childhood and beyond, but on my terms. I trusted my instincts over any and all other considerations.

I believed our lives would be different after the war. I knew Bob and I would be able to provide the advantages and opportunities that we never had.

I had shown Robbie one particular photograph of Bob so many times that the image was imprinted in his mind. Although the soldier who walked through the door was jaundiced, thin, and gaunt, Robbie recognized him with a helpful prompt from me, "He's your Daddy."

Barely holding back tears, Bob tossed his officer's cap aside and dropped to his knees to get at eye level with his two year old son. Within a few minutes and some encouragement from me, Robbie felt his father's arms encircle him and draw him close in a gentle embrace.

Bob did not want to talk or even think about the past two years of his life where his home had been a tent in a deadly snake and mosquito infested jungle encampment, but he suffered from bouts of emotion, shaking and trembling uncontrollably and breaking into tears. I told me it was okay to talk to me, to tell me what had happened and to get it out of him. He needed release and relief.

He told me he had nightmares of dead and wounded soldiers he had seen with missing limbs, bodies partially covered with blood-soaked bandages pressing to hold exposed viscera, the bloodied remains of a face, bodies being carried on stretchers to waiting C-47s for evacuation and fly-encrusted corpses waiting to be flown to Australia for burial.

He described the lines of tents infiltrating the dense encroaching jungle that threatened to creep out over the airstrip. He saw unshaven emaciated bearded men wearing tattered uniforms stained with mud, diarrhea and jungle rot, oozing festering open sores on arms and legs, their fingernails gone, consumed by mold and damp.

He closed his eyes remembering the drenching downpours and invisible wall of humidity that sucked the strength from their bodies. The sky was filled with the endless sound of P-38 fighter aircraft taking off and rising up into the airspace over the bay to come together in squadron formation on bombing runs to the east.

He just wanted to sit with our child and me in a real house and see and hear men and women who were not soldiers or natives of New Guinea. But a reminder of that life had come home with him.

The malarial attacks usually occurred at night in the form of sweats and palsied shaking from severe abdominal pain, a latent side effect. I would leap out of bed to bring him water to wash down his quinine tablets, then hold his hand and soothe his brow until the drug had taken effect and he was once again calm.

The recurring malaria left him tired and listless and unmotivated. The reality of his son kept him in motion. With his silky blonde curls and large brown eyes mixed with chunky Slavic features from my side of the family, Robbie physically resembled both of us.

We moved to a small lakeside cottage in Wisconsin, where Bob enrolled at the University. He took courses in English, Psychology, and Physics. He enjoyed the study and excelled in his classes. But among his most pleasurable moments was taking his son on walks to watch the beavers at work on their lodges and dam on a nearby stream that fed into the lake.

The furry creatures with their flat tails, sleek heads and probing black noses held Robbie's attention and interest like nothing else he had known in his young life. He followed Bob's cautioning advice to remain still and quiet so as not to alarm the skittish animals. After a while, the beavers grew accustomed to their presence.

Every day, they would go and watch the beavers until the day Robbie went alone. When he turned up missing and I couldn't find him anywhere in the house or the yard, I frantically ran from the house and discovered him standing on the bank of the pond. He was talking loudly with unintelligible words at the animals swimming about.

Worried at the danger to our child of living near so much water, Bob and I agreed that I should take Robbie back with my parents during the final month of the school year. Within a week, Bob followed us without completing his final exams and lost credit for the entire semester. He protested that since returning from the war, he could not live without his family. He could not exist apart from us.

The needs and the brevity of life pressed on Bob. Time was precious. He wanted to hoard it. He never attempted to return to college again. He discovered his former desire for academic learning had vanished. There was no time for school. He must work, get on with life, support his young family, make a living. We wanted two more children, a girl and a boy. He took a job as a real estate agent.

He had an intense need to be near us and with us. He came home every day for lunch and right on time at 5:30 each evening for supper.

Chapter 13

Wandering Boy

Our first apartment rental was located across from a commercial raw lumber yard that steamed with the fresh cut odor of wood stacked in ten foot high piles in a three acre storage yard. I couldn't shake the sensation of being out of my comfort zone. The location and noise of high-powered saws and trucks and locomotive train engines coming and going reminded me of living in a manufacturing section of town. Throughout the day, we could hear the sound of flatcars being loaded by forklifts and a crane. As far as we knew, all those boards were destined for housing construction.

We didn't have a yard where Robbie could go out and play, only a narrow sidewalk running along the ten two story units of the pale-yellow brick building. With the understanding our situation was only a start and we didn't have much money, we simply furnished ours with a cheap Formica kitchen table and chairs and a second-hand couch and an easy chair in the living room.

I hated the feeling that we were struggling financially. Bob was trying unsuccessfully to build his real estate business in the post war economy. Professionally dressed in an impeccable dark suit and tie, looking friendly and handsome with a combed blonde wave, I didn't see how he could fail to find listings and buyers.

Despite the symbolic image of all that lumber across the street, there just weren't enough houses to meet the demand. Thousands of soldiers who had returned from overseas were living in extra rooms and garages of their parents and relatives. We were lucky to have found a vacant apartment through Bob's real estate office. Although his sales commissions were low, we were able to buy a car, make a weekly trip to the grocery store, and pay the rent.

Our entertainment was watching our child play with his few toys and reading picture books with him seated between us on the couch. During the evenings after we tucked Robbie into bed, we quietly listened to Les Brown and Doris Day, Perry Como, Frank Sinatra, The Andrews Sisters, and Johnny Mercer tuned low on the radio while Bob did paperwork he brought home from the office.

I read and reread the monthly Redbook Magazine I purchased from the Walgreen's drugstore and I read books checked out from the local library. Reading made me feel impatient that I wasn't advancing. I didn't think I would ever get a college education at this rate. But according to Redbook, I should be content with being a good wife and mother and cooking and keeping house and appearing attractive for my husband, and not be concerned with an education beyond high school and working outside the home. I committed myself to those priorities up to a point.

One of my occasional activities was to participate in a mommy's exercise class at the YWCA for women wanting to restore their figures after a pregnancy. Although I hadn't gained any extra weight, my muscle tone was soft and I wanted to firm up my thighs and fanny.

Despite efforts of the smiling, heavyset, childcare lady, Sybil, to interest my tearful son in the abundance of toys with which he could play, I left him screeching. She held him by the arms, so I could go to the class in the gymnasium.

Ten minutes later, her hair askew, Sybil came chasing after him out of the recreation room and down the hall to the gym. She said it would be all right for Robbie to sit quietly in the bleachers and watch the class. From time to time as I did the calisthenics and muscle toning floor exercises, I glanced up at him. He never took his eyes off me. His separation anxiety caused me to wonder why he would just wander off when we next moved to a new neighborhood.

Other than reading Dr. Spock's book, I didn't really understand all that much about how my growing child perceived the world and what was going on in his mind. Robbie carefully observed and scrutinized everything happening around him to the extent that, sometimes, I couldn't get him to respond to me calling him. A line of ants or a passing dog could divert and hold his attention when I needed him to hold my hand and look where he was walking so he didn't wander into busy traffic. Despite my firm warnings, for a three-year-old, he seemed oblivious to passing cars. In that neighborhood, I didn't dare let him go out alone. I prevailed upon Bob to find us a place in or near my parents' safe, quiet neighborhood.

One day after breakfast, leaving the door open so I could keep an eye on him, I let Robbie stand outside on our low cement porch stoop. He wore his customary tan coverall corduroy pants, a long sleeve shirt, and small leather shoes with laces he had begun to learn how to tie.

Always curious about what was happening over in the lumber yard, he had lost his focus, I assumed, experiencing a sense of vertigo at an altitude of two feet. Without using his hands and arms to break his momentum, he fell to the sidewalk and landed squarely on his chin, resulting in blood, high-pitched cries, tears, and a throbbing swollen jaw.

I leaped out of my kitchen chair and charged outside with Bob close behind. Fortunately, he had been working at home that morning. He picked up Robbie and carried him inside to the kitchen sink where I tried to stem the bleeding with a dish towel. Despite my applying pressure, the blood kept leaking out.

"We have to take him to the doctor," I said. "Bring the car around." It was parked in a reserved space behind the apartment building.

After seeing numerous incidents of wounds and carnage during the war, Bob had forsworn being a Christian Scientist as not being in our best interest as parents. Half-carrying Robbie, I clambered onto the front passenger seat of our 1948 Plymouth and we rushed to the hospital. The doctor closed the wound with ten stitches.

I associated Robbie's injury from his fall and the proximity of the lumber yard as a negative sign. I always equated where we lived as a measurement of my goals and our progress of how well we were doing as a family.

As we drove home from the hospital, I told Bob, "We can't stay there anymore. We have to move."

"We've been in the apartment only six months."

"That doesn't matter. It's not safe for Robbie."

"His falling off the porch was an accident."

"He's too young. He doesn't pay attention to things. He needs to have a yard to play in. He can't go outdoors here without me being with him. I have to watch him constantly or he'll get into trouble. You've seen how fast cars go up and down the street. He could wander into traffic and be run over. You're in real estate. Find a place for us. You haven't used your G.I. bill yet for a loan. Find a house."

He didn't answer immediately, which I did not take as a good sign. "All right, but there are no guarantees. I'll do what I can. Also, if we wait a while longer until more houses come on the market, we can get a better price."

"If you would sell more, you'd make more."

"That's the general idea."

"I'm giving you thirty days. If we can't move out of the apartment by then, Robbie and I can go live with my folks for a while so he can have a yard to safely play in."

Bob glanced at me with a shocked expression, then back at the traffic ahead of us. "You don't really mean that."

"I mean every word." What I said was not intended to be a threat, only to motivate him.

"You realize the position I'm in."

"If you'd stayed in school and gotten your degree, you could have a professional job instead of being a salesman."

"You know why I didn't go back to finish college."

"You can't blame everything on the war. We have to move on to get ahead."

"Real estate requires marketing and salesmanship, just like any other product. There's nothing wrong with being a salesman."

"There is in my book. Selling is like begging. It's demeaning."

"It's not like begging. I don't see it that way," said Bob. "It's how I make a living. It pays the bills. I look for your support and understanding."

"I understand we have to do better. I support that."

"I'll do my best, Mary."

"I'm sure you will."

From Bob's sober expression and body tension, I could see he was controlling and suppressing his feelings. He said nothing more, a sign he agreed with me and would comply with what I asked.

Our next home was a small two story yellow brick house in a clean neighborhood of either brick or wooden bungalows with neatly trimmed front lawns. Newly planted maple trees lined both sides of a quiet street used by the residents. Families with elementary age children lived in most of the houses. Unfortunately, they were a few years too old for our son to play with. He didn't indicate whether he was lonely or not. He had picture books, toys and coloring books to occupy him and spent hours on the swing set and digging with a shovel and pail in the sandbox until the heat and humidity and hunger drove him indoors.

With the exception of an occasional vendor or service truck, I saw no commercial traffic and did not hear machinery noise. My only concern was that the fenced back yard was barely large enough for a swing set and a sandbox and didn't have much room to run a clothesline. Shortly after we moved in, I told Bob I wanted a dryer to go with the Bendix Washer we owned.

These particular houses had been under construction during the past year. Bob had been watching for them to become available on the market and had used his G.I. loan guaranty to make the purchase. At a cap of four percent, our five-thousand dollar house was covered for a maximum of two-thousand dollars, if we should default, which we would never intend to do. Given the post war demand for housing and the rapid increase in prices, Bob said we could sell at a profit and buy an even bigger and better house. We were in tune.

Whether by coincidence or not, it seemed that this house, like the last one, had something I didn't care for. At least here, the location was acceptable until the day our son wandered off and became lost.

My justified liking or disliking of the various houses in which we lived over the years was related to four conditions, the cost, the location, the exterior and interior, and the well-being of our children. To say the least, the anxiety caused by Bob's disruption of our lives when he changed jobs that uprooted and forced us to move placed a strain on our marriage. There were moments when I hated what he was doing to us, but I was determined to tough it out. He understood in no uncertain terms the importance of meeting my needs and demands.

Robbie often sat on the front porch stoop and watched the comings and goings of mothers pushing baby carriages and listening to the high voices of their children tagging after them on tricycles or bicycles with attached training wheels.

I had just carried a basket load of laundry into the back yard to hang on the clothesline to take advantage of the warm breeze blowing under a sunny sky. I wasn't there for more than fifteen minutes, but when I checked to see how Robbie was doing, he was gone. I rushed out to the sidewalk and looked frantically up and down the street. He was nowhere to be seen.

I panicked and ran in one direction calling his name, then turned and ran back to the opposite end of the block. I stopped and asked a mother if she had seen him. She said she was sorry, she had not. Screaming his name, I peered into the side yards between houses. A large black Labrador Retriever came bounding out wagging his tail and acted disappointed that I wouldn't stop and pet him.

I raced back to the house, slammed through the front door, and snatched up the phone. My heart pounding, I waited at the curb for the police car to arrive. The lone young officer didn't have his lights on and wasn't using his siren. He took his time telling the dispatcher he had arrived and was meeting me. Obviously not thinking I was an emergency, he calmly stepped out of the patrol car.

"Hello, ma'am, I'm Officer Brent. Are you Mary Wenger?"

"Yes."

You called about a missing boy."

"Yes, my son, Robbie. He was sitting on the front porch and the next time I looked, he was gone."

"Did you search the neighborhood?"

"Of course, I did! I'm desperate! He's not here anywhere. He's been gone now for thirty minutes. You've got to find him."

"Could he be at a friend's or a neighbor's house?"

"No, we just moved in. He doesn't have any friends."

"Where were you before you discovered he was missing?"

"I was hanging clothes in the back yard. He's a curious and friendly little boy. Someone could have offered him candy and taken him."

"We haven't had reports of any kidnappings. It rarely happens. I know you're worried, but kids often wander away and get lost. If they don't find their way home, we find them. I'll find your son. Where's your husband?"

"At work."

"You should give him a call. Let him know. I'm sure finding your boy won't take me long. How old is he?"

"Three."

"Can you describe him?"

"He has curly blonde hair and brown eyes."

"I'm on my way." He slipped behind the wheel, made a turn using a driveway at the middle of the street, and, talking on his radio, drove back in the direction from which he'd come.

I raced into the house and called Bob at his office. In an aggravatingly calm voice that drove me up the wall, he said not to worry and that he would be right home.

I started to run back outside to wait at the street, then remembered the police officer had instructed me to stay by the phone. Even though he wore a blue uniform, he reminded me of the many young soldiers I had seen during the war. His air of confidence and authority gave me faith he would find my son.

Ten minutes later, Bob pushed open the front door and entered the living room. "Did the police find Robbie?"

"Not yet. I'm waiting for a phone call."

"How did it happen?"

"He was outside on the front porch. I was hanging clothes. When I checked on him, he was gone. I scoured the neighborhood, then called the police. The officer said he would find him."

"It sounds like he just wanted to go exploring," said Bob.

"He can't do that! He can't just go off like that!"

"He's just a little boy. He doesn't know any better."

"That's the point, Bob! I can't leave him alone for a minute."

"He has a sandbox and swing set in the back yard."

"The back yard doesn't have a fence. He can wander out to the street any time. He needs to be closed in. You need to build a fence. I can't be with him every minute of every day. I have housework to do. I have things to do. Besides, now that I'm pregnant, it's hard for me to go chasing after him."

"I understand."

"No, you don't understand. I even take him for walks up and down the block. I think he thinks it's okay to go by himself."

"Well, certainly, he's curious and wants to explore."

"That doesn't help, Bob. Can't you see I'm out of my mind with worry? You're not helping me with your unconcerned attitude. He could be run over by a car or kidnapped."

"I am concerned. I'm very concerned."

"You don't sound like it. You couldn't prove it by me."

"I don't know what to say. Do you want me to fence in the back yard?"

"That is absolutely necessary. You will build a fence."

Bob nodded. "I'll build a fence. How long have the police been searching?"

"There was only one police officer. He's been gone now about twenty or thirty minutes."

"Robbie can't have gone far and if someone sees a child alone, they're likely to call the police anyway," said Bob.

At that moment, through our front window, I saw the police car pull up to the curb. "They're back. He's here." I rushed out through the door left standing open and raced to the black and white car. I could see Robbie sitting in the back seat behind the screen. He saw me and waved. Officer Brent came around and opened the passenger door and Robbie scrambled out. I lifted him into my arms and hugged him.

"I'm Bob Wenger, Robbie's father," Bob introduced himself.

"Officer Brent," they shook hands.

"Where did you find him?" asked Bob.

"He was down by the stores at the intersection, in the alley behind the gas station and a restaurant. He was looking at fish in a tank. He's not hurt or injured, just confused. He probably hasn't seen an officer in uniform or a police unit. He wasn't afraid of me though. I just told him his mommy was worried about him and had asked me to bring him home."

"I am so grateful," I said. "Thank you so much. This will never happen again, never, if I have anything to say about it."

"He's lucky. Lot of traffic at the intersection. He might not understand about his own safety. Have you taught him how to watch for cars and cross the street?"

"No," I said. "I didn't think he was old enough to understand."

The officer shook his head. "Not at his age but at least he'll get the idea. It's for his own survival. You take your eyes off kids for a minute and they can get into trouble. I'll be on my way. Nice to meet you both."

"Thank you, Officer Brent. Nice to meet you," said Bob.

"Glad to be of service. Have a good day."

Bob trailed me and Robbie up the porch steps into the house. "If you're going to be all right, I need to return to the office. I'm getting more buyer interest now that new houses are coming onto the market."

"That's good. That's good news, but right now, I don't need or care to hear about it."

Chapter 14

Sisters

Absorbed with my own concerns, I still maintained contact with my sisters, Ruth and Nina. Ruth, less so, since she and Richard Ainsworth had moved back East to Massachusetts where he had taken a job with an insurance company.

Richard had been raised by a dark-haired wild Irish mother who was an alcoholic harpy, a vicious jealous woman to the point of driving away her husband and verbally and sexually abusing her son. Richard hated her. She disapproved of and despised Ruth and refused to even meet her. He felt no remorse when he learned of his mother's suicide.

Because Ruth had resented the restrictions imposed on her by our parents while we were growing up back in Colver, I could not understand why Richard's dominating personality attracted her. I supposed that unconsciously, that was the kind of relationship she wanted. Even as a child and as a teenager, she had enjoyed the game of rebelling against authority in a teasing manner. But Richard was all seriousness when it came to the assertion of his will over a woman. He often displayed a mean streak and I resented his condescending manner with me, as though that was his privilege, because I was Ruth's sister.

During the war, Richard had developed a drinking habit to dull the long hours of boredom at a radar outpost in Alaska where he had been stationed.

Ruth told me his heavy drinking at times curbed his sexual functioning and he would blame her for his impotency. He accused her of being frigid and incapable of arousing his desire.

From the day she was married, Nina's life became a catastrophe.

Socially, she acted like an adolescent, but biologically, she was a mature woman. Except that she confided in me and made me promise to keep her relationship with Charles a secret.

At a United States Naval Base hospital, he had been diagnosed with osteomyelitis, an inflammation of the bone marrow and had been given a medical discharge. Upon his return to Rockford, he had secured a job as a bus driver and had met Nina, who rode his daily route.

She never allowed him to call on her where she was living at our parents' house. Then, one Sunday, when Nina was not there, he came by the house.

I was visiting Mum and Dad. Robbie and I were sitting out on the front porch. I hadn't met Charles yet and didn't know what he looked like. I saw the slim, wiry man walk past the house a few times checking the address. He finally came up to us and asked if this was where Nina Woijcek lived. I immediately disliked his cold, blue eyes, skewed red hair, and taut, snub nose features. I responded that she did, but wasn't home, and asked him what he wanted. He introduced himself and told us that he and Nina were dating.

"When she gets back, tell her I came by to see her," he said, and walked away.

When Nina returned, I told her about Charles coming to the house and my impression of him. "I think you should stay away from him. He has shifty eyes. I think he's dishonest and not a desirable person."

"You got all that from his eyes?" she said. "I'm in love with him and I'm not asking you for your advice. He's just as nice as Bob."

"How can you even begin to compare him with Bob?"

"You're not the only one of us who can have a nice husband," she snarled.

"You're not actually going to marry him."

"You're damn right we're getting married, smarty pants."

"When?"

"That's none of your business. He told me we're going to elope."

"You've got be kidding, Nina. Come to your senses. That's a sneaky thing to do. If he told you that, he's definitely not right for you."

"Don't trouble yourself, Mary. You won't be invited."

"And what about Mum and Dad? Don't you care what they will think?"

"I don't give a damn what they think. What I do is none of their damn business."

"Of course, it's their business. They want what's best for you."

"They don't know what's best for any of us. They never have. They only know what's best for them."

So Nina and Charles got married in a civil ceremony and moved to a shabby little house in a semi-rural area west of town. It did not take Nina long to realize she had made a mistake. Two months later, she called me on the phone and could barely talk, her voice was so tight with sobs.

"He just has this mean streak," she choked. "I don't know where it comes from or why. He wasn't like this in the beginning. He treats me nice most of the time, but then just flares up for no reason. And at night when we're in bed, it's worse."

"You don't have to tell me this," I said. "I don't need to hear this."

"Who else am I gonna talk to? You're my big sister, for God's sake. I've always told you everything. So don't hang up on me."

"I'm not going to hang up on you. I have been worried about you. Mum and Dad have too."

"No, they haven't. Don't try to lie to me. I took Charles to meet them at their house and they wouldn't let us in. Charles hates them. He says he'd just as soon kill them as look at them."

"I don't like the sound of him, Nina. He's dangerous. He's unhinged."

"I'm sure he wouldn't do anything to Mum and Dad. He has problems like all of us. He just makes threats when other people look down on him."

"You know when someone makes a threat, there's more behind it. Where there's smoke, there's fire. Does he threaten you?"

"He wants to have sex a lot. I liked it in the beginning. But he changed, like he's a different person. He gets me hot at night. I mean really hot, just before we're going to have intercourse. Then he stops and just leaves me lying there. And he laughs at me, Mary. He laughs at me."

"I'm sorry, Nina. I feel so sorry for you."

"Why couldn't I have met a man like your Bob. You're the only one of us who ended up with a good husband."

"I guess I need to count my lucky stars."

"Sometimes he comes home with lipstick on his collar and a woman's handkerchief in his lapel pocket just to watch me get mad. I hate him. We've been married only three months and I already hate him. Sometimes he leaves me home alone at night and then he calls me to terrorize me. Even though he can change his voice to sound like a different person, I know it's him."

"What does he say?"

"He pretends to be this other person and says Charles told him to call me and that I sleep with other men for money. He wants to come over and fuck me."

"Nina, that's such an ugly word."

"Sure it's ugly. Everything about Charles is ugly. I shout into the phone that I know it's him, and he just laughs. He has this scary laugh."

"Like death?"

"What do you mean?"

"Does he sound like a devil, a ghoul?"

"I guess so. It gives me the creeps."

"I'm so sorry, Nina. The next time I see him, I'm going to give him a piece of my mind."

"Are you kidding? Don't ever come over here. He hates you and Mum and Dad. He calls them Jesus freaks and he says you're a frigid cold-hearted bitch. If you interfere, he'll just get worse with me."

"Is that what he calls me?"

"Yes."

"Does he slap you? Does he hit you?"

"He punched me the other night. I have a bruise on my face."

"Oh, Nina, you really need to get away from him."

"How? I can't. I'm trapped. I'm pregnant."

"I don't know what to say. Do you want me to tell Mum and Dad?"

"Not yet. Charles said he's looking forward to being a father. He said he'll treat his children different than how he was treated."

"Did he ever tell you?"

"Not really. He calls his mother a whore. He said he doesn't know who his real father is. His parents were divorced and he said his mother slept with other men."

"I wish you would have listened to me in the first place."

"Oh, shut up! You think you're holier than thou! You're not perfect, even if you think you are! You're just trying to be, but you aren't!" She slammed the phone down. The dial tone sounded ominous.

They named their daughter Jennifer. I told Nina on the phone I wanted to come and see her and I'd drive her and the baby to Mum's and Dad's. She pleaded with me not to. "I'm worried Charles might do something to hurt you."

"Just let him try. I'll scratch his eyes out," I boasted. But I did honor her request.

Eventually Charles came around to letting us see Nina and the baby. He dropped them off at Mum's and Dad's house and drove away. They stayed with Mum and Dad for a week. Then Charles came back and took them home. I was surprised that Nina would even go out and get in the car with him.

She visited us on and off during the next three years while I was contending with my own children. I genuinely felt sorry for her that she had such an unhappy marriage.

At age three, Jennifer blossomed into a charming, ebullient little creature with springy red curls and smiling blue eyes with no trace of her father's shiftiness. Humming and singing a little tune slightly off key, she loved and was affectionate with Bob and me and her grandparents. She was sharp and intelligent, qualities I encouraged and admired. She was an extremely sensitive child, who visualized her existence as a happy dream world.

To my surprise, Charles stopped avoiding us. He seemed like a changed man. He just came into the house with Nina and Jennifer as though there was nothing wrong between him and me and Mum and Dad. He enjoyed exploiting Jennifer's ability to recite poetry and have her sing and tell us a cute little joke.

Jennifer basked in his attention. Then, suddenly, one day, Charles said something in our presence to hurt her and make her cry. I angrily scolded him and he retorted with a sneer that I wasn't his mother.

A year later when their second child, Tommy, was born, Charles accused Nina of being unfaithful and that he was not the father. No matter what she said, he refused to be convinced.

When Tommy grew old enough to sense Charles' antagonism, he incessantly clung to Nina's skirts whenever Charles was in the house.

I observed that Charles harbored a bitter hatred for his family and for all of us. In his eyes, Nina was a woman like his mother, whom he referred to as a whore, a tramp. He had a story printed in the local paper about his and Nina's divorce, which deeply hurt and embarrassed Mum and Dad. They wanted to avoid any such smear on a member of their family, because of the implication of sin and what members of the Jehovah's Witnesses Kingdom Hall would think and say behind their backs.

Then one day, Charles drove by their house with Nina, Jennifer, and Tommy and hustled them out of the car to the front porch where Mum and Dad and I had come out to see what was happening. He unpacked three suitcases from the trunk and threw them onto the lawn in a fury, shouting, "Whatever I've done, your daughter did it too! And you, you bitch!" he shouted at me. "You screwed things up between me and Nina. But I'll get you for it, you and your damn brats."

Infuriated, I recoiled with a rush of maternal protectiveness.

He roared off in his car leaving his family behind in tears.

When I asked what had happened, Nina said that Charles had gone insane, screaming that she was a whore and that was why he divorced her.

Nina retained custody of Tommy and Jennifer. Living with Mum and Dad, she and her children were subjected to their religious beliefs. A condition of having a home with them was to attend the weekly JW Kingdom Hall meetings and become indoctrinated by the dogma. They came under the guidance of my brother, John, who was a deacon. He and his wife, Caroline, were childless. Their loving influence was a balm that soothed the children.

I thought that would be the end of Charles in our lives, but it was not to be so. For a whole year after, Charles made intermittent calls to Mum's and Dad's number and, in a disguised voice, threatened Nina and her children. Nothing came of his threats to take Jennifer and Tommy away from her, but Charles' stalking kept her on an emotional edge, which was his intention.

Chapter 15

Accidents

I didn't want to believe in curses and fate, but since my baby sister Margaret had died, a dark gloom revisited me frequently with my own children over the next several years. Perhaps the accidents and illnesses they experienced were not so unusual or uncommon, but to me the physical and emotional trauma they incited was unacceptable. In most cases, I held myself to blame for not being a more diligent parent.

Then there were so many other incidents that obstructed my personal development and threw my life out of balance and hung over me like a pall.

One afternoon, Bob called from his office with news that coincided with my need for help with Robbie, since we were expecting our second child.

"That brown brick house a half block from your folks is listed for sale," he said. "It has three bedrooms, which is fine for us. I'm driving over to take a look. Want me to pick you and Robbie up?"

"Yes."

"It's an established neighborhood. Twenty-three years."

"It depends on the condition, but I'd love to be that close to Mum and Dad."

"Give me thirty minutes. I have to finish some paperwork here."

"What about this house? We haven't been here that long. We can't afford a down payment and you used your G.I. Bill."

"I'll set up a contingency sale. Our house is worth twice what we bought it for. The appreciated value alone can cover a down payment. "

My excitement at the prospect of another change confused me slightly, since I really wanted a stable family situation of security and stability. But my folks' neighborhood would be a change for the better, as long as the house was suitable. As it turned out, despite its age, the construction of the brown brick two story bungalow was sturdy and solid. Given its proximity to my parents, I could live without kitchen and bathroom upgrades and modern touches in the living room, at least for a while. I did mention the need for modernization to Bob, as we initially toured the house. Somehow, modernization, taste, image, and making an impression didn't seem to be as important to him as to me. Yet, he was in a business where those considerations were of paramount concern to potential buyers.

I decided to supplement our income in the interest of paying for improvements. Until our daughter was born, I would go back to work part-time as a secretary at the Rockford Life Insurance Company. Robbie would stay with his Gramma during the day, which suited him just fine.

Grampa would wake him at five o'clock in the morning and fry several eggs in butter for their breakfast. Together, they would sop it up with large hunks of Gramma's warm bread. Then Robbie would walk with him down to the bus stop and wait until he had boarded and gone on to work at the factory.

Even though he wasn't a tall man, to Robbie, his maternal grandfather was imposing, gentle, strong, powerful, and commanding of respect. He called him Grampa, like it was his name, rather than the more formal grandfather. And he called his grandmother Gramma. Robbie liked his Grampa's warm strength and how he hugged him rough and hard with a wrestler's grip.

Gramma smelled like cooking and dusty tomato plants on a hot summer day. She let Robbie help her pull weeds and pick plants in her vegetable garden. She often wore a *babushka* over her tight brown curls and sometimes Robbie would have her tie one on him so he would look like her. She was wiry and tough and reminded him of an energetic sparrow darting around the yard or in the house. She told him he was not supposed to pick and gorge himself on the plums and grapes and raspberries. But he would, regardless, whenever she left him outside in the yard alone and if she weren't watching him from the kitchen window. These fruits were too warm and juicy and sweet to ignore.

Mum told me that what most concerned her was Robbie climbing the tall pear tree and clinging up there eating green pears while he swayed high in the wind like a koala bear. He enjoyed the sensation of a squirrel's eye view. His observation of seeing a squirrel scamper up that very tree had set the example.

Mum would charge out of the house shaking a finger up at him and scolding and commanding him to come down. He never immediately obeyed her. He would polish off a pear or two before coming down. She was worried that he might fall. But what she didn't realize was that the fear of falling out of trees never occurred to her grandson. Despite his experience with pain, being four years old Robbie did not believe he was vulnerable to personal catastrophe. For the present, he considered himself too skilled a climber and was impervious to such accidents. He could climb anything and hang on, even in a strong wind, the stronger the better. He could climb like that squirrel. And he knew that his Gramma could not climb up there after him.

He did waste a great many pears whenever he shook the tree, which he did often. Mum told me he liked to hear the loosened pears crash through the leaves and thump on the ground. More fell than a person could eat. So she used them for canning and storage in her cellar larder. Robbie once told her that she couldn't blame him about the cherries, however, because the robins always got to them before he had a chance. And he wouldn't dare eat cherries full of beak holes, especially when you thought of all the worms that had dangled from that beak.

For the last few years, my Dad had moved slowly and was generally always calm and contemplative, but with an ever present smile lingering in his blue eyes. Whenever he looked at Robbie, his ruddy face glowed with pleasure. He parted his thinning brown hair on the left side and kept it trimmed short with a bimonthly visit to the local neighborhood barber two blocks away at the corner. Mum's hearty European meals added to his girth and kept his body solid. *Halushki* and *pierogi*, handmade stuffed pastas accompanied the rich broth and noodles of beef or chicken soup. Flavors drawn from scrap meat and bones that simmered for two days in large pots commingled with the aroma of garlic and paprika like culinary Bohemian perfume.

After seeing his Grampa off to work at the bus stop, Robbie would return to the house and spend the rest of the day helping his Gramma make dough for bread and rolls, cakes and pies and cookies. At Robbie's request, Mum would tie a babushka like her own around his head. Then they would wash clothes together in the old tub and wringer down in the cellar and hang them out on the clothesline to dry in the sun and wind. Afterward, there were weeds to pull in the garden and beans and tomatoes to pick.

She would take him with her to the Piggly Wiggly grocery market. Her feet would often swell and feel painful during the summer months. Barefoot, wearing a plain cotton dress and her babushka, she would roam the store aisles with Robbie trailing after her, wearing his babushka.

Noticing how quickly our son was growing and how mobile and active he was, Bob and I decided he might be ready for a tricycle. The heavy black model with large metal spoke wheels that Bob brought home was much larger and challenging for a little boy than I had envisioned.

At first, the size of the tricycle intimidated Robbie. Bob lifted him up onto the A-frame seat and showed him how to hold the handlebar grips and place his feet on the pedals. I watched from our raised front porch. As Bob slowly pushed him along the sidewalk, the revolving pedals created the pumping motion. Bob grabbed the handlebar when the front wheel turned out of alignment heading them off onto the lawn. After fifteen minutes of encouragement and repeated tries, with a look of grim determination, Robbie grasped the concept of tricycle locomotion and Bob let him go in unwieldy fits and starts for several feet without supporting him. Bob didn't feel confident we should let him ride alone unsupervised, but from that moment on, boy and trike were nearly inseparable.

As soon as he finished his cereal and orange juice the next morning, Robbie wanted me to carry the tricycle down the porch steps for him so he could practice riding along the front sidewalk.

I noticed he had some difficulty figuring out how to make the turn at the corner to go back in the opposite direction and over-extended the turning radius of the front wheel enough for the tricycle to topple over pinching his left leg in a vice-like grip between the wheel and the center frame. His screams of pain brought me running. I disentangled him and righted the tricycle. "Maybe you should wait," I said. Without a word, using the back foot step, he clambered up onto the seat and started pedaling. He didn't fall again.

At another time, from the kitchen window, I noticed a small group of children playing with cardboard boxes across the side street in a neighbor's back yard. One of the little girls was swinging. I asked Robbie if he would like to go play with them. He dashed over to join the boys tumbling about the yard while inside the boxes. From the way the laughing boys emerged unsteadily from the boxes, the sensation of not knowing where they were made them dizzy and disoriented.

Robbie staggered up out of his box and didn't see the swing swoosh at him. It cracked into the side of his head. Blood instantly poured out over his face and into his eyes and, screaming, he came running for home.

Bob charged out of the house, picked him up and put him in the car while I held him in my lap with towels to soak up the blood. Bob drove fast, speeding, honking his horn to warn other drivers out of the way until a police officer stopped us. After one look inside the car, he led us the remaining distance to the hospital with his siren wailing.

When we arrived at the hospital emergency entrance, Bob carried Robbie inside. A nurse took one look and positioned him on an examination table. Robbie had stopped crying and was looking up at us with a mix of trust and fear. A young intern quickly moved to stem the blood flow while the nurse arranged a tray of gleaming metal instruments. I held Robbie's hand and smiled down at him, as the doctor sterilized the wound, administered a local anesthetic, then applied six stitches that left a scar once they were later removed.

Afterwards, the police officer gave Robbie a dollar for not crying while the doctor had stitched his wound. To alleviate pain, Robbie swallowed a pill along with a cup of water the smiling nurse held out to him and enjoyed the lollipop she handed him. On the way home, he fell asleep and didn't hear my empty promise to never let him leave the house again.

II

Different Houses

Chapter 16

Snapshots

The day after Pam was born, I looked out my third floor hospital room window to see Bob and Robbie waving up at me from the yard below. Leaning from the bed, I smiled and waved back. The birth had gone smoothly with no complications. I looked forward to getting home and settling our daughter into her nursery. Bob had pasted up light blue wallpaper with sheep and white fleecy clouds that would be among her first impressions. I wanted her to experience a soothing pleasant environment.

Mum stayed at the house with Robbie the morning Bob brought me and our infant home. Despite the hot humid August weather, I kept her double-wrapped in a soft pink cotton blanket. She had slept in my arms during the ride but woke as I carried her through the front door into the living room.

Robbie bounded up from his coloring book on the floor, dashed over to me with a shout, "Mommy!" and threw his arms around my legs. "Is that my baby sista?"

"She's your baby sister. Her name is Pam."

"Pam?"

"Yes."

"Can I see her?"

I bent down slightly so Robbie could see her face. He wrinkled his nose. "She's all red and smelly."

"That's how babies are when they're small."

With a broad smile, Mum leaned in to peruse Pam's rosy cheeks and gently brushed a hand over her head. "Hair like yours when you born. Doctor say she good?"

"He said she's healthy. That's what's important."

"She looks a lot like you," said Bob. "She has your eyes."

"She certainly has the Woijcek chin," I said.

Our first month with Pam was not smooth sailing. To begin with, her cries from colic kept Bob and me up most of the night trying to comfort her in shifts. Her piercing screams sounded like she was dying. I could only imagine the pain she was in.

I couldn't ask Ruth and Nina for support, since they were now raising families of their own. Ruth and her husband and two small boys had moved to the East Coast.

Trying desperately to support a three-year-old son and a four year old daughter, Nina's marriage to an abusive husband was on the verge of coming apart. I had to thank my lucky stars that at least Bob loved and treated us well.

After our second son, Daniel, was born, we decided we should move up to one of the new suburbs. As convenient as it was to live near my parents, the neighborhood was old and there were better schools on the other side of town.

After some looking, we decided on a two story white colonial style house with green shingles. Although cars traveled too quickly on the street that ran by the front of the house, our gravel side street was used mostly as a driveway to access our back yard and the next house up the hill. We didn't have a garage.

Against my wishes, Bob took a job as a sales representative for a drapery hardware company. I looked upon his decision as a come down once again.

"How can you settle for selling curtain rods?" I accused him. I was infuriated.

"I won't be selling just curtain rods," he tried to explain, but I didn't want to listen. "It's called drapery hardware and it's not just for house windows. It's also for theaters and museums and government buildings. I'll have my own territory to develop and will be paid a base salary plus commission. With all the new construction, there's a market. I'm sure I can do well in this."

"God, I wish you'd finished your college degree. The way you have with people, you could have been somebody."

I could see him shrivel up inside at my words. But I didn't care. He wasn't giving enough consideration for what I wanted for us as a family. It appalled me that he was willing to be content, to settle for less. He wasn't motivated. I couldn't be ambitious for both of us. I determined to do what I had to do to get my high school diploma. Then at the first opportunity, I would start taking college classes and earn a degree myself. Since his income was inadequate, I would also become a breadwinner.

He had realized only moderate success in the real estate game. Bob argued that the market had become glutted with brokers and agents and the profit margins and commissions had narrowed. So he had made the change to drapery hardware.

We were just able to pay our mortgage and pay our bills. He had bought the newest model Pontiac, a four-door fastback.

For our new house, I had been able to purchase the blonde birchwood dining room furniture I had wanted ever since I saw the advertisements. I also bought appropriate lamps for two blonde end tables. The off-white fabric couch and two maroon armchairs blended well with the wall-to-wall thick pile dark green carpet and beige walls. Bob and I had a double bed. The boys shared a bunk bed and Pam had a single bed with a wooden frame and headboards.

I regularly shopped for new clothes for the children. For myself, I studied the latest fashions in Redbook and Glamour magazines and watched the sales ads in the newspaper. I gradually created a suitable wardrobe for wearing in the home, mostly house dresses, tapered slacks and Cuban heels and flats. For going out in public, tweed suits and no waistline shag coats. Solid dark brown was my favorite color or in a subdued pattern for clothes. Although Bob bought me a mink stole one Christmas, I had no need for evening clothes, since we did not go out. Our entertainment was spending time reading stories and playing games with our children and going over to visit my folks. I had to store the mink high up on a closet shelf. The kids wanted to play with it as though it were a stuffed toy.

Bob bought a folding camera and several rolls of black and white film so I could take snapshots of the kids. I took a multitude of photos over the years to preserve the image of how they once looked.

Among the most memorable was a picture of them sitting on the back porch concrete steps of our South Rockford Avenue house. Wearing cool weather clothing, they all had guileless expressions. My five-year-old mop head Robbie looked at the camera with compressed lips askew in his version of a complaisant smile, a goofy smirk.

An uncertain impish grin lit up Pam's pie face. Her green tam perched rakishly on her head and her saddle shoes toed in on the bottom step.

His cheeks pouched like rose-colored fruit, two-year-old Daniel was mesmerized by a wooden toy truck cradled in his lap. He still wore white leather lace-up baby shoes. A small dark blue soft cap crowned his blonde hair. At my request, the barber had clipped the hair across the forehead in bangs.

I loved their half-formed, beautiful, innocent faces and small bodies. I wished I could keep them just as I had captured their image in the photograph. I wanted to protect them from the nasty things in life.

Our move to this house marked a milestone of memorable and not so memorable incidents. For me, Bob bringing home a one-month-old German Shepherd puppy, without my approval, was disturbing. He had a way of doing things without asking me first.

Of course, the children loved the puppy at first sight and couldn't keep their hands off it. They named him Tippy and cuddled and played with it in the back yard for hours. Bob explained that taking care of him and keeping his food and water bowls filled would be their responsibility. “Having a dog will be a good learning experience for them.”

The next day, the puppy appeared to be sickly and listless. I called Bob at work and told him he had to take it to the pound. “He poses a risk of disease to the children,” I said. Amidst the kids’ tears of resistance and remorse, Bob came home and explained why he had to take Tippy away.

Even if they think they are in charge, children are accepting and resilient. I knew they would get over their disappointment in a few days and forget about having a puppy. I told Bob to never bring home another animal again. I would not allow pets of any kind, not even a turtle or a goldfish whose soiled water gave off a rising odor of decay.

Chapter 17

Housekeeping

What could have been a catastrophe for Robbie's first day in kindergarten turned out to be somewhat humorous. I had walked with him to Highland Elementary School a block from where we lived. The short trek required using the subterranean underpass to cross a busy street to the school grounds.

The young, attractive brunette (long hair hanging halfway down her back) with expressive wide brown eyes who greeted us at the classroom door introduced herself as Miss Hathaway and explained that she had recently earned her teaching credential and Robbie's class was her first job. How I envied her that she had a college education. She wasn't much older than I was and possessed a kind, soft-spoken gentle nature that disarmed the children and made them want to pay attention to her and do what she told them, with one exception, my son.

Frustrated at his lack of skill to cut out colored paper shapes and paste them to look like tulips, as Miss Hathaway described to me later that day, he burst into hot tears and couldn't be calmed. She told him to go across the hall to the restroom and rinse his face with cold water and she would help him when he returned.

He took his cap and jacket off his assigned hook just outside the door along the wall, disappeared into the tunnel, and ran all the way home. I wasn't aware of what he had done until Miss Hathaway knocked on my door fifteen minutes later to inquire if Robbie had come home. He had not. Together, calling his name, we went searching for him. Since Pam and Daniel were taking their naps, I could momentarily leave the house.

I mentioned that Robbie and the neighborhood children played in a deserted lot, a field covered with wild wheat grass, across the gravel side street. In addition to hummocks behind which they could play hide and seek, numerous trees provided them opportunities for climbing. We spotted Robbie in the largest of the trees, an enormous elm with multiple side branches large enough for a child to walk on. He was standing on one such branch fifty feet up in the air and. When he saw us, he climbed higher. My heart nearly stopped. A fall from that height would certainly kill him.

"Don't shout at him," Miss Hathaway cautioned. "Don't scold him. We have to coax him down."

"If I order him to come down, he'll come down," I said.

"If he thinks he's going to be punished, he might misstep or lose his balance. We want him to pay attention to what he's doing while he's climbing down."

"I told him to wait until I came to school to get him," I said.

"Well, here he is."

"This is so unnerving. How can you be so calm at a time like this?"

"Practice. When you're supervising twenty hyperactive emotionally charged five year old's all day long, you don't have a choice. You have to be firm, but patient."

I raised my right hand to wave to him. It suddenly occurred to me he might wave back and lose his grip. I immediately lowered my hand. "You're the teacher. How do we get him down?"

"With these," she pulled an orange and a green lollipop out of her deep coat pocket and held them up. "Robbie," she called to him. "It's okay that you came home from school. When you come down, I have some lollipops for you. I'm going to help you cut out the tulips."

"Are all little children like this?" I asked Miss Hathaway.

"Yes, they can be delusional at times as the mood strikes them."

"Robbie, it's going to be supper time soon. You can't stay up there all night. You're going to get hungry and you can't sleep up there in a tree. Miss Hathaway is a very nice lady and she's not mad at you. She cares about you. She came all the way to our house to tell me. She wants to help you."

I couldn't be sure because of his elevation, but I thought I detected an expression of skepticism as he looked down at us. "Maybe I should call the fire department," I said. "They can go up and get him with their long ladder. A ride on a fire truck might lure him down."

"Wait," she said. "It looks like he's climbing down."

My heart was in my mouth.

"He is agile for such a little guy," said Miss Hathaway.

We watched him quickly descend the tree like a monkey. I wondered how he had learned to climb like that, but some of his friends were a few years older. He just copied what they did.

I didn't want to dwell too much on his making it safely to the ground. I gave him a hug and a kiss and Miss Hathaway gave him her two lollipops.

"I climb up there all the time," he said, which was what I was afraid of.

Miss Hathaway took his free hand and gave me a smile of relief. "The school day is over. I'll bring him home."

"Thank you so much. I could come and get him."

"No, he's my responsibility. Give us an hour. I'll have him home in time for supper."

"I never imagined being a mother would be like this."

"At least he's only five. He's very bright to do what he did. He's telling us something about himself."

"I would prefer he use words," I said.

"That will come in good time. We're heading back."

"I'll see you in a little while, Robbie. Do what Miss Hathaway tells you."

He removed the green lollipop from his mouth. "Okay."

I watched them walk up the road to the sidewalk. She talked to him all the way. He returned home later that afternoon proud of his cut and paste accomplishment that Miss Hathaway hung on the wall to be admired along with the other children's. We did not have a repeat incident of him running away from school. He had to learn not to run away from difficult situations.

The Lonsway family lived three houses down from us on our side of the street. Although Robbie played with their four boys, I discouraged him from ever inviting them to our house, because they were uncouth ruffians. How I knew was that one day I had to go fetch Robbie from their house.

When the oldest boy, Dale, answered the front door, I caught a glimpse into the foul cigarette-smelling living room of his father snoring on the couch with an array of beer cans scattered on the coffee table.

"I'm Robbie's mother. It's time for him to come home."

"He's upstairs," said Dale, scratching his ragged stiff hair hanging down to his eyes and that probably hadn't been washed for a week. Not only that, but he also had dirty bare feet and spoke with a drawl. I suspected the family had recently moved up from somewhere in the South.

A loud woman with the same drawl shouted from the kitchen. "Who's at the door?"

"The kid's ma. She wants him to come home."

"Well, go git 'im. Where is he?"

"Upstairs," Dale shouted back. "I have to go git 'im," he said to me and sauntered away.

I noticed his mother peek around the door jamb and quickly pull her unkept head back when she saw me, which was just as well. I had no wish to speak to her. My impression of the whole family reminded me of the sordid mining town lowlifes I had gone to school with and had encountered growing up back in Colver. I definitely did not want Robbie coming to this house and playing with these ruffians.

One week later, the unthinkable happened. Never in my wildest dreams did I expect to find what was going on in my house when I returned from grocery shopping at the Piggly Wiggly with Pam and Daniel.

One of Bob's associates had driven him to the office that morning so I could use the car.

Robbie had insisted he would be fine if I left him home alone so he could play with his miniature plastic horses and cowboys and cattle and Indian toys. He verbalized stories about them as he maneuvered them around inside miniature fences and on the street of a small western town. He preferred to play outdoors in the dirt, but I told him he could stay home alone only if he remained inside with the doors locked. If anyone came to the door, he wasn't to answer.

I parked on the gravel square at the rear of the house and assisted Pam and Daniel out of the car. Before I even opened the back door, I could hear boys' voices shouting inside through an open upstairs bedroom window. I put down the grocery bag I was carrying, quickly unlocked the door, and ordered Pam and Daniel to wait in the kitchen. The whooping and shouting from upstairs was now louder. I rushed into the living room and found Robbie sitting on the bottom step. Tears streamed down his crimson face.

My glance took in a table lamp on its side on the floor, its shade crushed. Scattered cookie crumbs dotted the couch cushions and a cracked lavender blue flower vase shattered on the coffee table caught my eye.

"What is going on?" I shrieked at Robbie. He sobbed all the harder. I stepped around him and dashed up the stairs.

Wearing his dirty shoes, one of the Lonsway boys was jumping on the double bed with the blankets skewed everywhere. Another was pulling socks and my bras and panties out of the dresser and pawing through the drawers. A package of Bob's condoms glistened on the floor. I heard two other boys shouting in Robbie's neighboring bedroom.

"Get out!" I screamed. "Get out of my house!"

The smirks on their faces as they scrambled past me and raced along the hall and down the stairs like rats further enraged me. "Your mother and father are going to pay for this!" I shouted chasing after them. "I'm calling the police!" They ran out the front door and left it standing open in their haste to get away.

I whipped off my coat and turned to confront Robbie, who was trying desperately to pick up the broken lamp. "What happened? How did they get in here?"

"They wanted to play. They said I always come down to their house."

"I told you that you weren't allowed to play with them."

"They kept ringing the bell and knocking on the door until I let them in."

They must have known I wasn't home, I thought. They must have seen me drive away. I couldn't imagine them pulling such a stunt otherwise.

"And do they act like this at their house?" I asked accusingly.

"They jump on the beds and have pillow fights."

"And their mother doesn't stop them?"

Robbie shook his head as his body convulsed with another sob.

"I told you not to answer the door."

"I know who they are," he choked.

"I said not to let anybody in the house."

"I'll clean everything up," the veins on his neck stood out.

"You're damn right you'll clean up everything. How do you think you're going to replace the lampshade and that flower vase?"

"I'm sorry, Mommy. I couldn't stop them. They wouldn't listen to me. They said I always came to their house and did this."

"Did you jump on the bed and break things?"

"I jumped on the bed. They did and said it was okay. They told me to jump on the bed but I didn't break anything."

"This will never happen again. Do you understand me? Never."

He nodded and trudged up the stairs to his room.

"I can't believe this. I just can't believe this." I walked to the kitchen where Pam and Daniel cowered under the table and went out to the car for the rest of the groceries.

I spent the rest of the day restoring my house to its original level of cleanliness and orderliness with the exception of the ruined lampshade and broken vase. Robbie did his best in his limited way to make amends, even volunteering to run the vacuum cleaner, to which I said no. Only I could vacuum the carpets to my satisfaction. The Lonsway boys must have come in with dirt and mud on their shoes. There was dirt everywhere.

When Bob came home that evening, his smile froze when he saw the irritation in my eyes. "Something happen?"

"Yes, something happened that should not have happened. Against my orders, Robbie allowed the Lonsway boys into house while I was gone shopping with Pam and Daniel. They nearly destroyed everything. I was furious. I'm still furious. I sent the children up to their rooms."

"Robbie wouldn't deliberately disobey you. It sounds like he made a mistake."

"You don't realize how much time and effort I devote to keeping up this house."

"Yes, I do and I appreciate all that you do for us, for me and the kids."

"Sometimes I wonder. Go up and talk to them. See if you can calm them down. It's not good for their digestion to be so upset before eating dinner. By the way, speaking of dinner, we're going over to my folks Sunday afternoon for dinner."

"That was part of what I wanted to tell you. The company president invited me to join him and two other regional sales representatives for golf on Sunday. Can we go to your folks the following weekend?"

"No, we're going Sunday, with you or without you."

"I suppose I can explain to him. He has children and in-laws. But playing golf with the boss is important to future advancement and our working relationship. It's a social commitment."

I bristled. "I have a social commitment with my folks. They come first in my book. Sunday dinners are special and important to them. They're important to me. Your boss is not."

"I'll talk with him. He's an understanding man. You should meet him sometime."

"I have no desire to meet him. With you or without you."

Bob drove us to my folks on Sunday. The kids always enjoyed playing out in the yard where their "Grampa" could watch them. Mum prepared her usual multi-course spread of paprika and herb European dishes.

Chapter 18

Streator

The smell of vegetation rot and decay coming off the muddy scummy Vermillion river smote my senses as my first impression of Streator, Illinois. The odor and noxious clouds of dark smoke rising from the stacks of a glass and tile works that employed most of the townspeople reminded me of the coal mining town where I had been born and raised.

Many of the residents lived in tacky low-class houses, some in shacks along the riverbank and others in farm homes that dotted the surrounding countryside through which we had driven two hundred miles downstate to reach this abysmal destination.

That Bob expected us to live here was beyond me. Only one month ago, he had announced that Streator was a hub right in the middle of his territory covering Iowa, Southern Illinois, and Missouri. Living in Streator would eliminate the need for him to be gone from home for a week at a time. In addition, his company's headquarters and manufacturing plant were located in Peoria, just eighty miles north on the interstate. He said he felt sad and depressed that he wasn't involved more in family activities and raising the children. He wanted to be able to come home for dinner every night and sleep in his own bed instead of in cheap motels.

He had leased a big yellow, two-level Victorian house with a wide veranda across the front, gabled roof, and a second story balcony that circumvented the front and sides. A raised foundation elevated the house several feet higher than street level. A wooden slat skirt concealed the foundation and several steps led up from the sidewalk to the front entrance. A crushed gravel driveway wound around to the rear where what was once a horse and carriage barn served as a garage.

We arrived two hours ahead of the moving van that trucked our possessions from Rockford. Bob proudly showed us the house, emphasizing the classic Queen Anne architecture and large spacious rooms. He sounded to me like a real estate agent pointing out the features of the house. He could tell from my expression that I was not pleased. I didn't care for old things. I didn't want them in my life. I wanted to leave them behind.

The kids started complaining they were hungry.

"We can't wait around 'til the movers arrive," I said to Bob.

"We'll drive into town and get some lunch," he said. "Okay, everyone back into the car. Lunchtime."

"They don't have any restaurants here, only cafes," I said. "Not even a Howard Johnsons."

"A café will be fine. The kids can order hamburgers or hotdogs."

"Cafes in a town like this are greasy spoons," I said.

"They are probably just fine. We can at least try one. There are a lot of cars parked in front of that one over there. That's usually a sign that the food is good."

"Or because there are few choices, the food quality is low and people just accept it. I want palatable food, not farm food. There was an A&W Root Beer drive-in where we turned off the interstate highway. We had A&W Root Beer drive-ins and Dairy Queens back in Rockford. At least I can trust them."

"It's a good fifteen miles to the highway. Since we're going to be living here, we can at least try the café. The sign says home cooking. I've eaten in a lot of home cooking places when I'm traveling and they've been very good. I'm doing the best I can to try and please everybody." Anger flushed Bob's face and he choked on a lump of sadness I hadn't heard before. "Whatever I do is never enough. If we go to the drive-in, you won't be able to eat for at least another half hour."

"Can I have a hamburger and French fries at the café?" Robbie asked.

"You certainly can."

"Café."

"Wouldn't you like to have a root beer?" I cast back over my shoulder.

"I'm sure the café serves root beer," said Bob.

"Café," said Robbie. "I'm hungry. I don't want to wait. I'll have a hamburger and French fries and a root beer."

"I'm hungry," said Pam.

"Me too," said Daniel.

"Here we are. Café it is," said Bob, and pulled in to one of the diagonal parking spaces a half block from the café entrance.

Robbie ordered a hamburger with French fries, Pam and Daniel, hot dogs with French fries. All three had frosty root beers in glass mugs just like A&W. At least I wasn't the villain, making them wait an extra half-hour. Bob ordered a cheeseburger, fries, and a tall glass of milk. Having inspected the knives, forks, and spoons, I ordered pancakes and a cup of black coffee. Although I would not admit to Bob they were delicious, I consumed the stack of four bathed in butter and syrup. Along with the kids, I was hungry and I didn't eat hamburgers anyway. I would have ordered a cheese sandwich at A&W. I did like toasted cheese sandwiches and often made them at home. The kids liked them too. Actually, they liked everything I cooked.

The big yellow house wasn't at all historically quaint as Bob tried to convince me. It reminded me more of a gothic house of horror alongside several others of similar architecture built during the mid to late eighteen and early nineteen hundreds when Streator was a mining town near vast beds of coal just beneath the surface, in addition to rich clay and shale which supplied the glass and tile and pipe industries.

The town had grown rapidly from a single small grocery store to a population of six-thousand with businesses, churches, four schools, and so called beautified historical residences like ours.

I read about the local history one summer afternoon when I walked with the kids to the public library, an imposing two story red brick structure with Ionic columns bordering the front door.

Our first night in the house, as Bob and I lay in bed staring at the high-pitched gabled ceiling, I asked, "How long are you going to keep us here?"

"I'm establishing a new regional territory. At least for some time, perhaps two years. That's what it takes. I'm very good at it. The company will likely use me to open up new territories, but I don't want to lose commissions I've established by leaving customers I've developed."

"I hate being uprooted. I hate how it feels, like we've been cut adrift. I have a hollow sick feeling at the pit of my stomach."

"I'm sorry," he mumbled. "I don't mean for you to feel that way. I'm trying to make things best for both of us and the children."

"Moving us here does not accomplish that."

"I'm sorry." He reached over to put an arm around me.

I jerked away. "Just go to sleep." He slowly withdrew his arm and rolled over. We slept with our backs facing each other.

Bob had purchased three fans for the house, but they only circulated hot, sticky, humid air. The air-conditioned library provided a respite from the sweltering Midwest summer heat.

Fortunately, Pam and Robbie liked to read. Not quite five, Pam was already reading at the above average advanced level of a fifth grader. She was gifted with a keen inquisitive mind and especially liked stories about horses and Nancy Drew mysteries. I wanted to encourage her intellect as much as possible.

I discovered a number of children's illustrated storybooks for Daniel.

I had no interest in getting acquainted with neighbors. To do so would be to imply acceptance of the move, and I refused to capitulate. As matters stood, there wasn't anyone with whom I would care to associate.

Daniel had met another four year old boy, Gordy Renfro, who lived next door.

I hadn't seen Mr. Renfro and had only exchanged a brief hello with Gordy's mother. A week later, it dawned on me that she was sending him over, not only to play with Daniel, but she also assumed I would take care of him during the day while she was gone, which was unacceptable.

His shock of short blonde bristles sprouted from his head accentuating his permanent expression of a pugnacious rodent.

The scowl on Gordy's flushed face and threatening expression in his feral gray-green eyes alarmed me. Even observing him and Daniel playing with toys and sailing small stick boats with paper sails in sidewalk puddles after a summer rain, I felt a degree of apprehension. He insisted Daniel do everything the way he wanted and shouted and screamed in frustration if Daniel didn't specifically go along with his orders.

When I confronted Mrs. Renfro, she explained she had to take care of her ailing parents during the day. They lived on a farm several miles from town. Her husband was a manager at the glass and tile plant and came home late at night and worked on weekends. She felt since the boys were good friends, I didn't mind her son spending the day with Daniel.

I told her this could not be a permanent arrangement. Her sullen gray eyes fixed me with a blank stare. An unimpressive overweight woman, her harried face shared her son's rodent-like features and washed-out blonde hair.

To avoid me, she left early each morning and Gordy continued to come over and play with Daniel. I let Bob know of my displeasure.

In his irritatingly calm manner, he said, "I'll go over and talk to Mrs. Renfro. There must be some misunderstanding."

"There's no misunderstanding, believe me. Mrs. Renfro is a dolt and an idiot and her son is crazy. Moving us here was a big mistake."

"But the reason was so I wouldn't be away traveling so much of the time."

"Damn your travel. Where we live is much more important than where you travel."

"At least give it a try. Streator is a nice quiet little town."

"There's nothing nice about it. I hate Streator. I despise this ugly place. It's a hole. I hate small towns, Bob. You should know that by now. They remind me of where I grew up, where I never want to go back."

"I'm sorry I can't seem to please you."

"Empty apologies mean nothing," I retorted.

"I'm being sincere."

"So am I, Bob. So am I. You knew coming here was a mistake, yet you persisted without my agreement and approval."

"I sometimes wonder why you married me."

"I married you because you were a nice guy." Although I didn't want to hurt his feelings more than I already had, I refrained from telling him that among the reasons I married him was to change my last name. I hated my last name, Woijicek. I was ashamed of my family name. It branded me and my parental origins as an eastern European immigrant from Czechoslovakia. I did not want to be thought of as a Czech. "Times were different during the war," I said. "Times are different now. It's not just about the two of us anymore. We have children. We have to move on."

"School will start in a few weeks for Robbie."

"And do you really think the teachers and schools in this Podunk town can compare with those in Rockford?"

Bob's silence spoke volumes.

"We are not settling here, Bob. Get that through your head. I want our children to have a bright future, not the dismal conditions you and I had growing up."

Despite my discontent with the move to Streator, I could see a difference in Bob's demeanor. As during our early days when he had been a real estate agent, he now enjoyed coming home in the evenings. He laughed and smiled playing games with the children and reading stories to them at bedtime.

With me, he tried to be calm, wanting desperately to have an uncomplicated relationship to the extent he repressed any anger and antagonism he felt against me. He just tried his best to please me and meet my needs and expectations for an acceptable family life and so often failed miserably.

Daniel had just turned four years old. Pam was five and Robbie seven. If we were going to live in Streator, what kind of future lay ahead of them? Even the thought of existence in a small town depressed me.

One evening, Bob brought home a large volumetric brown porcelain container and the ingredients and equipment to make root beer. The kids sat on the bottom step in the basement and watched with great interest as he combined the measured proportions of water, sugar, maple syrup, extract, and yeast. He siphoned off the liquid into a dozen bottles and set them aside for the brew to ferment.

Late at night we were awakened by a loud explosion caused by the carbon dioxide pressure. We ran down to the basement and found glass shards on the floor. Six bottles had become bombs.

I warned the children not to walk on the broken glass while Bob refrigerated the remaining six bottles.

To me the failed root beer experience was just another sign we had no business being there.

In July of that year, relentless torrential rain pummeled the Midwest leading to a great rise of water in the Kansas River and other waterways throughout the central states, including the Vermillion River that crested at eighteen feet, spilling over its banks and spreading along the lower side streets into the elevated main part of town. The surging current crushed and swept evacuated houses downstream. We were on high ground but could see the edge of the floodwaters from our balcony.

To me, the flood was a Godsend. At my insistence, Bob agreed to take me and the kids back up north to Rockford to stay with my folks. I made it clear we would not be returning to Streator.

Chapter 19

A Near Death

By the time the flood subsided during the early autumn of 1952 before the school year began, Bob located and moved us into a rented two story three bedroom red brick house in a nice neighborhood of hilly tree-lined streets within a few blocks of the elementary school where Pam would begin kindergarten and Robbie would begin second grade.

This custom home was a vast improvement over our first cape cod tract house on South Rockford Avenue. The cupboards, kitchen and laundry room, and the layout and amenities of the living, dining rooms and thick-carpeted upstairs bedrooms, and two spacious well-appointed bathrooms gave me the sense and satisfaction that we had upgraded our living status. The house fit my image of myself and my family. Even though we were only renting until Bob found a new house we could buy, I undertook homemaking and child-rearing with fervor and enthusiasm. I even complimented Bob, telling him he had chosen well. His pride and gratitude at my comment mended our emotional gap of the past few months in Streator. Understanding my approval became a driving motivating factor for him, I did not fail to use it as a means to get my way.

Occasionally, after leaving Pam and Robbie at school, Daniel and I would walk through the tunnel to cross the street to pick up a few groceries at the Piggly Wiggly. Daniel had a habit of daydreaming and sometimes lolly-gagged as we strolled up and down the food aisles, especially the cereal shelves and their array of colorful graphic illustrations. One day, I wasn't aware of how far he had fallen behind until I heard him screaming racing up and down in search of me two aisles over. When I found him sobbing, he endearingly clutched my hand and wouldn't let go. He held on to one leg of my slacks at the checkout counter and held my hand during the walk back home while I juggled a bag of groceries with the other and a purse strap over my shoulder.

Still unnerved by his traumatic episode in the Piggly Wiggly and suffering from separation anxiety, since he was home with me and his brother and sister were in school, he would not go upstairs alone to his new bedroom and take a nap. After a lunch of peanut butter and jelly sandwiches, potato chips, and an apple, we sat on the living room couch, and I read him an illustrated story of *Winnie The Pooh*. He fell asleep slumped against me.

Dense heavy snowfall floating down in a steady white curtain from a dark December sky coated the roofs, clotted the tall neighborhood trees and blanketed the ground with three feet of wet snow and six-foot drifts. Long icicles hung from the eaves like daggers and jagged teeth, creating the illusion of a giant open maw. Looking out my kitchen window, the world had transformed from the fallen dry leaves of autumn that crackled underfoot to a winter white cocoon that wrapped around the house and gave me a cozy snug feeling of security.

For the past two weekends before the winter storm, Bob had driven me and the children out to do Christmas shopping and to buy presents for Daniel's fifth birthday, which fell in December. Multi-colored lights and decorated window fronts festooned the downtown shops and stores. Inside, Christmas carols and jingling bells filled the air and I found myself humming the lyrics sung by Bing Crosby and Rosemary Clooney of the white Christmas about which they were dreaming.

As the temperature plummeted to below freezing, cars spun out of control on the glistening skein of ice-coated streets.

Next to our family decorated fir tree, through the living room window, I watched the children build a snowman and construct walled forts behind which they flung snowballs at each other. Their faces glowed red from the cold. Wiping their runny noses with the backs of their mittens, they came in for freshly baked cookies and hot chocolate and chattered at the table.

The sweet oven aroma of a flat yellow cake permeated the kitchen as I decorated the white frosting with 'Happy Birthday' in blue and red letters and five candles.

I placed a chicken, broccoli, cheddar cheese casserole to warm in the oven. When he had departed that morning, Bob had said he would be home in time for dinner and to celebrate Daniel's fifth birthday.

I pulled on my boots, gloves, and gray winter down jacket and trudged through the snow along a side alley over to where the neighborhood children were sledding. The sting of the frigid night air invaded my nostrils. I saw the car headlights turn the corner at the top of the street, the driver oblivious to the children on their sleds.

I heard Daniel shout, "One more!" and glimpsed a neighbor girl push him waiting prone on his sled at the top of a snow encrusted steeply slanted front yard terrace. He shot down the slope over the embedded runner tracks from the many trips other children had made.

My voice caught in my throat. I heard Robbie screaming Daniel's name over and over again as he disappeared at the center of the car between the front and rear wheels and bounced repeatedly against the undercarriage. The brakes locked the car in a skid. Robbie charged down the hill ahead of me through the churning snow, as the driver stopped the engine and stepped out of the car. Unable to talk or breathe, I ran the remaining distance across the street to the passenger side of the car.

The right rear car tire had stopped within one inch of rolling over and crushing Daniel's beautiful head. His eyes were closed, his face and snowsuit black-streaked with oil. Bleating and mewling like a kitten, he still lay on his sled.

"I'm sorry," the middle-aged driver knelt down in the snow beside me. "I didn't know they were sledding. I couldn't see anything. He's alive. He's alive." The man reached under the car and gently pulled Daniel out on the sled.

"Daniel, Daniel." My heart pounded uncontrollably. I couldn't stop my tears. Due to my negligence, I had nearly lost my own child. I should have been there watching out for the children or at least somebody should have been monitoring the street and shouted a warning that a car was coming.

The distraught man's kind brown eyes searched mine. "Do you live nearby?"

I nodded.

"I'll carry him to your house."

"All right. Be careful. Be very careful."

In extreme shock, Daniel kept making small moans.

"I'm here, Daniel. I'm right with you. I love you. I love you. You're going to be all right. We're going to the house now."

Pam and Robbie walked beside me. Pam held my hand. Robbie dragged Daniel's sled. The man carried Daniel in his arms, maneuvered through the front door and lay him on the couch. The odor of urine and diarrhea leaked from Daniel's clothes.

Pam and Robbie hovered next to Daniel, their red flushed faces imploded with panic and fear.

"I'm so sorry," the man said. "I have three children. We live at the end of the street one block over." He removed his hat. He wore a long coat over his business suit. "I'm Jack Lewis. I'll do whatever I can to help."

I didn't know what to say. I couldn't say anything. Through no fault of his own, this ordinary looking man had nearly killed my son. He was nice. He was kind, but, nevertheless, I hated him for existing, for turning that corner to come down the hill.

We heard a knock at the door. Robbie went to answer it and looked up at a police officer.

"The other kids told me your brother was in an accident."

"Yes, you can come in," said Robbie. "He's on the couch."

The man introduced himself as the driver of the car. The police officer knelt next to me and briefly examined Daniel. "Lucky, very lucky."

My eyes tearing, I nodded. I was removing Daniel's soiled pants and underwear. Daniel mumbled and cried in a state of shock. I barely heard what was being said.

"Excuse me, ma'am. I'm Officer Turner. I was called to the scene of the accident and was told you and your son had come to the house.

"I carried him," said Jack.

"Are you the driver of the car?"

"Yes, sir. Fortunately, my brakes locked. The wheels went into a skid."

"Those kids shouldn't have been out there, at least not without adult supervision," said the officer.

"The kids who aren't sliding watch," said Robbie. "But the kid who pushed Daniel didn't know. She didn't look first."

"You should not have moved him," the officer said to Jack. "He could have internal damage. I'll have some questions to ask after we see to the boy. Ma'am, may I have your name?" He opened a pad and began to jot down information for his report.

"Mary Wenger."

"And your son?"

"Daniel."

"He appears to be in a state of shock," said the officer. "We need to get him to the hospital."

"My husband will be home from work shortly. We'll take him."

"I'm calling an ambulance. He needs a paramedic."

"I can take care of him," I flared. "I'm capable of taking care of him."

"I'm sure you are, Mrs. Wenger. But your son needs immediate medical attention."

"Riding in an ambulance will only terrify him."

"I'm sure the paramedic will let you ride with him." The officer turned to speak to Jack, checked his driver's license, and asked him to describe what happened. I listened again to what was being said. It would be repeated in my mind for the rest of my life.

He had no idea children were sliding down that hill. The only overhead streetlight was at the corner where he had made his turn. If his wheels had not locked in a skid, the rear tire would have rolled over Daniel, crushing his skull. Officer Turner then listened carefully to Robbie anxiously wanting to explain what he had seen.

"My husband should be home soon," I said.

"The street conditions are dangerous. Does your husband's car have chains?"

"I don't know."

An emergency room doctor and a nurse wheeled Daniel on a gurney right into an examination station and quickly diagnosed symptoms of a concussion and of several contusions on his left leg. They checked for internal bleeding and found none. The nurse cleaned his wounds, then the doctor applied a soft cast to the injured leg. He told me Daniel would need to use crutches for a few weeks until his leg heeled enough to bear his weight.

Officer Turner stayed with us the entire time and talked gently to Daniel. He said he had a son about Daniel's age.

An hour later, Bob came to the hospital with a birthday gift for Daniel, an authentic large plastic dump truck. He had brought Pam and Robbie, who had explained what happened as soon as he arrived home.

Stretched out on the living room floor with her feet cocked up behind her, Pam was rereading one of her favorite horse stories, Black Beauty. Robbie Slouched deep in an armchair across the room and cradled an illustrated history novella about wagon trains and pioneers. I sat on a padded footstool next to Daniel sleeping on the couch. His medication made him drowsy and the blows to his head still left him dazed a week after the accident.

Fearful that tragedy would strike again, I confined Robbie and Pam to the house despite their wanting to go outside and play in the snow. Sifting through early snapshots I had taken of them reinforced my awareness of how vulnerable they were and the impermanence of their lives. The threat of losing them caused me such anxiety that I tortured myself with plans of suicide should anything fatal ever happen to one of my children.

For the next five weeks, (a coincidence of one for each year of his life) I waited on Daniel hand and foot, feeding him, bathing him, and dressing him until he regained enough strength and balance to manage those simple tasks himself.

I stayed at his side when he used his child-size crutches to move from the living room, where he spent most of his time and I would be able to hear him when I was in the kitchen. I assisted him negotiating the stairs to his bedroom and to the bathroom he shared with the rest of the family. Fortunately, a small downstairs half-bathroom just off the laundry room provided easy access during the day.

Knowing I couldn't restrict Robbie and Pam from going outside and getting fresh air, I allowed them to play in the front yard where I could see them through the picture window. I had Bob take down the tree the day after Christmas so that I had an unobstructed view. I prohibited them from sledding and tobogganing for the rest of the winter, except when Bob would take them to a hilly local park on weekends.

After the doctor removed the soft cast, Daniel began putting more weight on his injured leg and eventually didn't rely on the crutches. Although he was able to walk, he seemed a bit dazed and day-dreamed a lot. I still did not let him go up and down the stairs without Bob or myself supporting him. Months later, his full mobility returned, and he eventually was able to run a few steps.

Daniel's accident prompted me to want to move out of the red brick house and away from the neighborhood with its lingering aura of tragedy. I sensed that death was physically following me, not only lurking in the recesses of my mind, but hovering nearby, threatening me that it would always be there waiting for the right moment to strike. I vowed to ward away death. I would keep it out of our lives. We would escape it by moving away.

Chapter 20

Nina

"He's married and he's Italian," Nina's voice rang like hitting a tin pan in my ear.

"That's two strikes against him," my voice raised speaking into the phone. "Have you forgotten Colver?"

"And he has four kids."

"Oh, Nina, you must be out of your mind. Wasn't Charles enough? Certainly there are nice single men you could meet. I'm surprised you haven't at the Kingdom Hall."

"Are you kidding me? Not a one."

"How did you meet the Italian? What's his name?"

"Frank Soriano. I was waiting at the bus stop after work. It's just outside an Italian restaurant. He saw me through the window and came out and introduced himself and invited me in to have a cup of coffee."

"He owns a restaurant?"

"He and two brothers, Nick and Rollo. They were all smitten by me."

"That's because you're blonde and beautiful."

"Has something to do with it, I'm sure."

"For heaven's sake, Nina, don't let it go to your head."

"He invited me and the kids to have dinner at the restaurant, Sorianos' *tratorria* he calls it. Pizza, spaghetti, anything we want all for free."

"You're taking him up on it."

"Yes, I'm taking him up on it."

"Don't be stupid, Nina. He's just trying to seduce you."

"He's not even all that handsome, but he's really nice, a gentleman. He makes me feel calm and relaxed."

"That's not like the Italians we knew back in Colver."

"This isn't Colver. It's Rockford."

"What does he look like?" I could just visualize him, a typical wop like so many others we had seen growing up back in Colver.

"He's dark."

"Of course, I could guess that," I said.

"He has kind of rough features like a laborer, a big body, a little like Dad."

"Dad is handsome. He doesn't look anything like an Italian," I barked.

"What I mean is he's gentle like Dad. He reminds me of Dad."

"I'll bet he's probably old enough to be your father," I got in my zinger.

"Hardly, he got married when he was eighteen. He told me. He's in his thirties now."

"Four kids?"

"Yeah, they're all older teenagers about to leave the coop. I haven't met them, but I saw his wife, Louisa. She came into the restaurant the evening while I was there with the kids. She thought I was just another customer, but she noticed Frank sitting down and talking to me. She came over to our table. Frank is kind of loud and he smiles a lot. But he got testy with her when she wanted to know why he wasn't back in the kitchen. She's short and heavy with dark eyes and dark hair and an olive complexion."

"Typical Italian," I said.

"He told her he was with me and the kids as customers, but I know she didn't believe him."

"You're getting in over your head, Nina."

"We were just on friendly terms. He comes out to see me at five when I'm waiting at the bus corner. He said he wanted to take me on a date. When I reminded him he was married with four kids, he told me things weren't going well between him and Louisa and they were getting a divorce."

"He must be a Catholic," I said. "He's Italian. Catholics can't get divorced."

"That's not true. He told me divorces are allowed by a special arrangement. He said Louisa doesn't satisfy him anymore. He said that after the divorce, he wants to marry me."

"Did you ask him what about his wife and kids? What happens to them?"

"He said his kids are old enough to get jobs to help out and Louisa can do sewing and take in laundry. He said he told Louisa this is how he feels about me. He won't be happy again until he marries me."

"What about her happiness?"

"I didn't ask and he didn't tell me. This is not about her happiness, Mary. It's about mine."

The next day, I drove over to Mum's and Dad's and asked them if Nina had told them what she was planning to do.

Their dining room table was covered with a white lace cloth. At the center stood a large glass fruit bowl filled with pocket sized pamphlets of JW religious literature, loose buttons, and safety pins and several spools of colored thread.

Dad sat with his elbows resting on the table and hands supporting his forehead, as he unintelligibly mumbled grace to himself in his heavy Czech accent. He was still a handsome man and had a strong European visage about him of the old country. He wore comfortable soft leather house slippers, baggy trousers, and a loose-fitting undershirt.

As he concluded the long utterance and sat upright, he grasped an over-sized spoon in his gnarled heavy fist like a child and began siphoning down a spacious deep bowl of chicken and vegetable and cabbage soup with slurping, lip-smacking swallows.

He paused and looked among the other dishes before him and called out to Mum. "Eva, salt and pepper."

Mum flicked a fork through a large skillet of frying liver and onions.

I had forgotten how small and bent over she was beginning to look with encroaching age. Like the interior of her house, her face expressed weariness with warmth and vitality. She wore a white cotton apron over a dark blue cotton dress.

Dad heavily salted and peppered his soup and took another taste. "Good!" He emitted a loud basso belch. Mum returned to her skillet. Dad noisily cleared his throat.

"My back hurt again today," he said.

"Were you lifting?" I asked.

"No, I tell boss I can't do lifting. He give me job pushing now. I lift one time though. Too heavy."

"You should go see chiropractor again," said Mum from the kitchen.

"I go Saturday." Dad rapidly finished the soup and Mum brought him a plateful of steaming liver and onions. "You want coffee now?"

He grunted to the affirmative and voraciously attacked the liver and onions. Mum poured his coffee into a large white porcelain mug.

"You eat already?" he asked me.

I nodded, "Yes."

"Any mail today?" He asked Mum.

"There is bill from doctor."

"We just have one."

"I see him again last Tersday," said Mum. "I have to watch. He say my blood pressure worse."

"You go to Kingdom Hall alone?"

"No, Nina and children go with me."

"She still see Dago?" he asked.

"Then she told you," I said.

"I don't know," said Mum. "I ask Tommy and Jennifer and they say no. She might make them tell lie though."

Dad stuffed a forkful of liver and onions into his mouth. "Why she not be like Mary? She always do wrong thing."

"We're very different kind of people," I said.

"We raise you same way," said Dad. "How you turn out so different?"

"That's just the way we are," I said. "We have different personalities."

"She tell us she want to be like you. But she doesn't do like you."

"We want some of the same things, but we want different things too. We have different abilities."

"You smart. You do good in school. Nina not so smart."

"I'm not done with my education, Dad. I plan to go to college someday and get a degree."

"Why you need college? You have house. You have good husband and children. Why you want more?"

"I have the potential to be more than just a wife and mother. I have a good brain too. I want to use it."

"Jehovah's Witnesses say not good to know too much. Word of God in Bible is what you should know so you can spread his word."

"You know how I feel about the JWs. They're not for me, Dad. They're not for me."

"I know Dago married," said Mum. "Kids tell me. They know. Adultery is sin."

"Nina's not sleeping with him," I said. "She told me."

"I gonna pray for her," said Mum.

We didn't attend Nina's wedding to Frank Soriano. We didn't think what she was doing was right, but at least he treated her and her children with love and respect, so she told us. That was a lot more than could be said for their father, Charles Gibson.

Charles didn't just go away and stay out of their lives. He would periodically show up at their apartment late at night and terrorize them with threats until Nina had a restraining order issued against him, which further incensed him.

I didn't know where he lived or what he did. I assumed he still drove a bus, since the time he barred Nina from boarding, shut the door in her face and left her standing on the street corner. She took the next one and was late for work at the department store.

When she reported his behavior to the bus company, the management placed him on a different route and she did not encounter him again. However, a few years later, I did.

Nina was more of a problem. She had a nearly uncontrollable temper and would fly into a rage at the slightest provocation, especially with her own children. I witnessed it firsthand when we took four of the kids to go shopping. Robbie stayed home to play over at a friend's. I managed to cram them all into the back seat and, for the drive downtown, they laughed and joked and teased and got along fine.

The department store held no interest for them as we wandered around the crowded main floor to the boys' department. They raced to claim empty chairs in the waiting area next to the dressing rooms.

Nina flipped through piles of shirts in an agitated manner. She suddenly looked up and spoke to Tommy in a sharp voice. "Tommy, get over here. We came in to pick out a shirt for you. And what do you do? You sit over there as though you could care less. Now, come over here this instant!"

He quietly and obediently quick-stepped to her side. She continued to speak in an abrupt manner. "Here! Look at these! Do you expect me to do everything for you? What are you, helpless? Here, what do you think of this one?"

Tommy responded with a lethargic roll of his head. "It's okay. I guess."

"You guess? I don't know what possessed me to bring you shopping. I should just give you some money and let you shop for yourself, you and Jennifer. All she wants to do is giggle with Pam. It's miserable down here today. All these people. I've got a splitting headache."

A well-coiffed fashionably attired brunette saleswoman approached us. I could tell immediately her patrician manner irritated Nina.

"May I help you?"

"Yes, I'm trying to pick out a shirt for my son here." Nina held up another one. "What about this, Tommy?"

"Yeah."

"Okay, we'll take these two."

"Cash or charge?"

"Charge. I don't carry cash around."

"Charge it is." She took Nina's credit card, rang up the purchase, and slipped the shirts into a flat paper shopping bag.

Sensing Nina's agitation, I hurried our brood through the store and quickly purchased a few clothing items for Pam and Daniel. For no apparent reason, her mood darkened as a heavy rain began to fall on the drive back to her house. Bursting with anticipation, the kids planned to go in and make hot chocolate. As Nina unlocked and opened the front door, Tommy rushed ahead in a race with Jennifer for the bathroom.

"I get it first," she shouted.

"No, me first, I have to go bad!" Tommy howled and roughly pushed her aside, sped through the bathroom door and locked it with a loud click.

Daniel, Pam, and I stood clustered in the living room witnessing the ensuing tirade. I was thinking maybe we should not stay but didn't want to forfeit the hot chocolate Nina was making in the kitchen for the kids.

After a minute, the bathroom door opened and Tommy came out and stumbled against Jennifer waiting for him. She hit him in the head with her fist and lunged into the bathroom while Tommy pounded her shoulder. She got in her last licks in a silent scuffle in the doorway, then suddenly slammed the door in Tommy's face. He wasn't quick enough to withdraw his hand and the edge of the door caught his fingers. He let out a wild yell of pain and screamed over and over again as Jennifer continued trying to push the door shut.

"Open the door! Open the door! My fingers! Open the door!"

Nina rushed over in alarm. "Jennifer, open the door," she shouted. "Tommy's fingers are caught!"

The door opened and he pulled his fingers free.

"All right, what's going on here now?" Nina exploded.

Tommy clutched his left hand and sank to his knees moaning and crying, "My fingers! OOOhhh! My fingers! I think they're broken!"

Jennifer peered out fearfully from just within the door frame.

"She shut the door on them," Tommy sobbed.

"And why was that, tell me," Nina's accusatory tone made him cry all the harder.

Jennifer trembled in defense. "It was an accident. He was all through in the bathroom and I wanted to get in, but he kept hitting me and wouldn't let me! It was just an accident!"

"No it wasn't!" Tommy shouted through his tears. "When I was comin' out of the bathroom, she hit me in the head! She started it!"

Needing a target for her anger and seeing that Tommy was suffering enough, Nina attacked Jennifer, who cried out in protest, "Mommy! Mommy! Don't! It was an accident!"

"I'll accident you!"

Yowling and growling at each other, they fought like cats until I grabbed Nina's arms and broke her away from her daughter.

"Nina, Nina, stop! You're hurting her! That's enough!"

"You stay out of this!" she screamed at me. "These are my kids! Not yours!"

"Calm down. Please, calm down. We have to take care of Tommy's fingers."

Jennifer slammed the bathroom door shut and locked herself in. Nina struggled to break my grip on her arms. "Damn you, Mary! Let go of me! Let go of me!"

"The kids would like hot chocolate. Let's just give them hot chocolate, then we'll be on our way."

"You want hot chocolate; you make it yourself! I'm done here! I'm done!"

I released her and she raced down the hall into her bedroom and closed the door.

I knelt down to examine Tommy's smashed fingers. "Let's get ice on your fingers. I don't think they're broken." I helped him to stand up.

"They feel like it," he said.

I sat him at the kitchen table, filled a dish towel with ice cubes and wrapped it around his injured hand.

"Can I come out now?" Jennifer's tearful voice reached me from the closed bathroom.

"Yes, you can come out. Your mother went to bed. I'm making hot chocolate."

Jennifer rushed over to me, threw her arms around me, and hugged me tightly. "Oh, Aunt Mary, I wish I was your daughter. I hate it when Mommy shouts at me and hits me."

"I know, dear. I know. Your Mommy has some problems, but she still loves you. She loves you and Tommy very much."

"Sometimes, I think she hates us."

"She doesn't hate you. Believe me. You mean the world to her."

"Can Tommy and I come over and stay at your house sometime?"

"Yes, we'll talk about it."

"Can we have marshmallows in our hot chocolate?"

"Yes, you can have marshmallows."

Nina didn't come out of her room, even by the time my kids and I left to drive home in the rain.

Chapter 21

Edgebrook
The Happy Years

Upward mobility was taking place all around us and we were a part of it.

The name in the real estate advertisement Bob showed me about the suburb caught my imagination. On a sunny Sunday afternoon, he drove us out of the city along a two lane country road through a semi-rural area where farmland was being excavated and converted to residential tracts. Edgebrook featured semi-custom ranch style homes on half-acre lots. Most of the surrounding grassy hills and fields had not yet been touched by the giant earth movers and construction equipment. A corner location directly across from the tan cement block elementary school appealed to us.

Bob spoke with the builder at the sales office near the entrance to the tract. According to magazine advertising propaganda during the 1950s, wives were discouraged from making important decisions such as buying a house or a car. Since Bob was knowledgeable about real estate financial transactions, I did not get in my two cents other than the demand that in buying our house, there would be no turning back.

We were to be among the first wave of residents. Plans were being laid for a small shopping center a half-mile away along the main tar and gravel road. The distant buzz and whine of power saws and tapping of hammers carried on the warm spring winds like suburban background music giving promise of the growing, new community.

Our house was a simple single story ranch style model made of stained redwood siding and a shingled roof. Within two years, Bob added an enclosed breezeway for a family room and converted the carport into a two car garage. A red brick chimney rose from a fireplace at the front of the living room next to two picture windows facing onto the narrow street where no sidewalks or curbs existed. Intense green lawns tapered raggedly into the composite of tar and gravel. The development was still raw enough that there were no smooth edges.

We had finally arrived at a time and place that fit my vision of what our lives should be like, where we could realize intrinsic family values. Bob and I had left the poverty of our Depression Era childhood and the war years behind and now rushed to embrace the promise and prosperity of the '50s where family values displaced the previous necessity for our sacrifices in support of the war effort.

Our house was a symbol of that prosperity. Our house was also a home, an environment within which to create a suitable family culture. My vision of that culture included certain aspects of what I considered gracious living, mealtimes with well-prepared food and interesting and educated conversation. Most importantly, I would lavish a love and caring the like of which I had experienced from my Mum and Dad and brother and sisters despite our poverty.

I wanted to hold back nothing for our children, but money was always an issue. I decided to supplement Bob's income and increase our buying power by continuing to take part-time secretarial jobs. Although I just wanted to attend college and use my brain and experience the academic environment of which I had been deprived following high school, deciding on the goal to become a classroom teacher did not happen until many years later. In retrospect, I was undergoing a lifelong journey of personal discovery.

I would furnish our house fashionably, but affordably, according to Bob's base salary and sales commissions. I had started my collection in our first house on South Rockford Avenue with blonde wood and pastel accents as my preferred style with one exception. I now added a George Steck counsel piano made from mahogany and cherry wood. Buying the piano was my turning point for upward mobility and gracious living. Our children would have advantages that were never available to Bob and me. They would learn to play the piano.

The back yards of seven houses on our block faced each other and merged to form a few acres of a shared inner complex undivided by fences. This playing field rang with the jubilant shouts and cries of the neighborhood children. Our house in Edgebrook on Spring Creek Road was a safe haven for our young ones, a fitting place for a family.

Robbie shared a bedroom with Daniel. The room housed two twin beds and was paneled with clear-stained knotty pine. The boys envisioned animal shapes in the grain and whorls of the lightly stained wood. Robbie's bed was next to the windows facing out onto the front lawn. Daniel's was snugged against the inside wall. Pam's knotty pine room was on the opposite side of the wall. Robbie soon discovered with what ease he could slip outside late at night through the detachable bottom window at ground level.

Being the oldest child by two and three years, Robbie was protective of and responsible for the safety and well-being of his brother and sister. At the ripe old age of nine, he became a worried parent long before his time. Responsibility was expected of him and was positively reinforced by Bob and me and every other adult he encountered in his young life. Adults held him in high regard for his positive behavior and I could tell he liked the way that made him feel. He didn't goof off and make mistakes and he was always respectful.

His peers held him in high esteem for the thoughtful way he related to them. He always deferred to what his younger brother and sister and friends wanted to do, what card games and board games they wanted to play, who would be "good guys and bad guys," and where they would fish "down at the creek" that flowed from the outlying farmlands through the watershed basin at the low end of the tract hills. Because he cared about them, he made them feel good.

Along with responsibility came his self-imposed need to be perfect. He insisted that any embarrassing flaws he thought he possessed must not be revealed in public. The recognition by others of his deficiencies caused him intense incapacitating embarrassment.

Pam and Daniel took advantage of his easy-going nature and teased him mercilessly. They had a knack, however innocent, for pushing his primary deficiency button, which was that he had long toes, inherited from Bob. He dreaded when I took them to the shoe store. Invariably, Pam and Daniel would deliberately and loudly chorus (enough for everyone in the store to hear) that "Robbie has long toes! That's why we call him Robbie Long Toes!" The blood would surge up into his face leaving him apoplectic and wanting to depart immediately from the store. But Pam and Danny would wait until his shoes had been removed and the salesman was about to fit him with a new pair. To make matters worse, they would giggle and tee-hee during the fitting and, in sheer amusement, I did not shush them.

He loved Daniel's fine flawless features, brown wide-eyed enthusiasm, and golden-haired perfection. He loved the cherubic flatter face of his sister, her curly brown hair and serious eyes tucked in above wide full cheeks, similar to her grandmother. The corners of her nostrils turned white and quivered whenever she cried and caused a rush of sympathy in Robbie, who would protectively encircle her with his arms. He did not like to see his brother or sister unhappy or in pain.

The day Daniel was hit on the head with a rock wielded by an antagonistic neighbor boy, Bobby Klugman Robbie wanted to immediately go to his house and exact revenge. He ranted and raved, but I would not allow him to leave the house. He sat on the back door stoop and mentally projected his anger across the lawns to the Klugman house high on a knoll in the next block.

From the dull expression in Daniel's eyes and the open gash on his blood-stained blonde head, he had suffered a mild concussion. My anxiety level shot up and off we went to the doctor.

In retaliation, Robbie spread the word among his friends of Bobby Klugman's aggression, and Bobby Klugman was no longer welcome to play among them. Robbie believed that balance must be restored, that justice must be done, the bad guy must lose in the end. He did not yet realize that life was uncertain and unfair, that he and his friends were not invincible like cowboy movie and fiction heroes, that they were transparent and vulnerable and subject to pain.

When Daniel started school, I noticed he was quite immature, and younger than the other first graders. He was only five but I enrolled him anyway, since the school did not offer kindergarten. He liked his tall, imposing teacher, Miss Johnson, but he occasionally got in trouble due to daydreaming and staring out the window.

Edgebrook was populated with young families. Fathers were employed professionally or in median income jobs. One in the area, Russ Olafson, managed his own construction company. Another, Brian Crump, had his own hardware store. Without exception, wives and mothers did not work outside the home. They cleaned and cooked and maintained the household and ensured the education and well-being of their children. I was violating conventional values by even doing part-time secretarial work. A few were Cub Scout den mothers or Girl Scout group leaders. The community shared the values of wholesome family life and post war economic security.

On the surface, all of the immediate neighbors' families appeared to be healthy, happy, and stable. There were a few problems here and there as might be expected that I heard about while playing bridge with the neighborhood bridge club. I had been invited to join by Betty Johnson, the mother of Johnnie Johnson, one of Daniel's new friends. Eight months prior, the Johnsons had bought a gray ranch style house across the street one lot up from us.

During the morning while the children's school was in session, four neighborhood wives and mothers met either at Betty's or at Mrs. Crump's home, one block down the street in the other direction. I had never played bridge before but caught on quickly. I found the rules of play intellectually stimulating and challenging. Betty was an expert player and, together, we excelled in doubles. Our gatherings were also an excuse to have free time to ourselves and to share recipes, information about our children's school activities, and to gossip.

Valuing my privacy and respecting the privacy of others, casual gossip was not something with which I was comfortable, especially when the topic turned to husbands and their sexual prowess or, in Betty's case, her husband, Larry's, lack of interest in bed. Despite my wanting to remain outside of these discussions, and I offered nothing about my relationship with Bob other than, "We're happily married," sitting at the bridge table made me an involuntary recipient of others' information regarding their personal lives that should have remained private. I listened politely to what they had to say and they either respected my noninvolvement or envied my marriage.

Melanie Lane's complaint of being frigid shocked me. She said she never had an orgasm, not even on her wedding night. She said her husband tried his best to bring her to climax to the point of exhaustion, but the promised sensation and experience never happened.

She and her husband, Grant, had been unable to have children. Wanting to believe she was sterile; he had ordered her not to see a doctor in case he would be blamed for having the condition. To compensate, she over-indulged in eating chocolates, pastries, ice cream, cake, and desserts and put on the pounds that widened her girth and gave the impression her mouth spoke from within the folds of a double chin. A wedding photograph taken of her showed she had once been a buxom fair young woman. On the heavy side, with a receding hairline and plain looking himself, Grant told her he found her overweight condition unsightly and that she no longer aroused him, which complicated matters.

The wife of a general surgeon, tall, attractive former Nordic model, Estelle Gunderson, with uncontrollable curly red hair, was an alcoholic who, other than bearing him five children, felt inadequate in the shadow of her husband. He himself went on an annual bender for one week out of the year, his form of vacation, as he described it.

A tall kindly man with a gregarious aggressive demeanor, Ray had rakish dark hair and eyes that twinkled good-naturedly under bushy brows. I always felt that he spoke to me in a congenial bedside manner. He had a natural social ability to make people feel included. For me, feeling socially accepted by others required energy and effort that left me anxious and exhausted.

Understandably, Estelle's attention would sometimes lapse during a game and she would lose track of what was at play. The rest of us felt sorry for her but did not discourage her from coming. Since she checked in at a detox clinic once a year for three weeks and suffered from embarrassment, she herself arrived at the decision to discontinue. A few years later, Bob and I learned from her husband that she was being hospitalized for leukemia.

The emotionally demonstrative Betty Johnson was unhappy because her husband rarely showed her affection. I could not understand why he was so physically stand-offish with her. She maintained her shining brunette hair in the most current Hollywood style. A ready smile and cheery voice leapt from her uplifting coquettish face like a singing bird.

Her husband, Larry, owned a custom carpet store downtown that did a thriving business with builders and new homeowners in the booming housing market. His near-sighted blue eyes peering through the thick lenses of his black frame glasses reminded me of an owl. Otherwise, he was a tall, slender, good-looking man with close-cropped brown hair.

Gloria Mason was known to throw wild parties, to which none of us were invited or even wanted to be invited and was generally thought by parents and teachers to be promiscuous because of the tight knit dresses she wore and the cleavage she flagrantly exposed in public trying to emulate sex goddesses featured on the covers of movie magazines.

Her husband, Max, owned and operated a mortuary, which I thought might account for her flighty behavior. Although bald and heavyset, he seemed cordial enough, but people tended to avoid him, including myself, because of his profession and association with death and dying. I met him once briefly coming out of the new shopping center grocery store. Even though I said hello, he didn't seem to recognize me, which was just as well. I imagined that anyone he met he would be mentally sizing up for a casket.

Although only the wives seemed to have problems, we all knew that husbands had a hand in them.

I never mentioned that Bob and I had arguments about our finances. And as for my part-time secretarial work, I explained that, although raising children and doing housework were fulfilling in themselves, I wanted to expand my horizons. They could see me eye to eye with that, because they all agreed, which was why we sought outside activities like playing bridge, being den mothers and brownie leaders, and participating on school PTA committees and events.

During one of our conversations, the name Gwen Gebhardt came up. I knew she had worked as a journalist, but I didn't know she had become a feminist author and had a book published. No one in our group had read the book, only a review in the local paper. The book had just come out and wasn't even in bookstores yet, but the general consensus of opinion among the neighbor ladies was that she had gone too far with her diatribes. I didn't let on that I knew her and that we had been good friends in Miami during the war when our husbands were undergoing officer training.

I thought I would buy her book when it became available and read what Gwen actually had to say instead of relying on catty opinions. I didn't have long to wait. In about one month, she would be coming to Rockford as a stop on her promotional tour for a book signing.

Chapter 22

Piano and Wood Ticks

A few months after we moved in, Bob bought me a used car, a 1951 Fleet line Chevrolet coupe, so I could work as a part-time secretary and go shopping and run errands while the kids were in school and without his having to be home to drive me. With the high price of gasoline at 20 cents a gallon, I had to be conservative and limit the number of local trips I made during the week. At a cost of $1,492 dollars, the purchase of the car added substantially to our debt, but Bob's commissions had increased considerably with business expansion in the region he covered. He now exceeded his base salary of $3,600 dollars a year by $1,000 dollars in commissions. Theaters, businesses, and public buildings were now among his largest customers. I could no longer say he just sold Newell curtain rods, although many were sold in hardware stores. The heavy duty drapery hardware had to be custom designed and manufactured, as he explained to me one evening, despite my lack of interest, after we had put the kids to bed.

Still, his annual income was not nearly enough to cover the increased cost of living and further expenses to come. My paltry part-time clerical salary of $20 dollars per week working at an insurance company mainly paid for groceries. Clothing for the kids, who were rapidly outgrowing everything they wore, and for Bob and myself came out of his earnings.

And the kids' bikes and toys were not cheap. Bob had to buy a gas-powered mower to control the growth of our lawn. Thankfully, the fee for Robbie's weekly half hour piano lessons was a nominal one dollar.

Although I found details about Bob's sales activities boring and uninteresting, I did pretend to listen. He was very good at what he did and his bosses praised him highly and often invited him to weekend golf outings at their country club. Not wanting to leave the kids at home alone or with a sitter, I didn't attend any of the company award dinners. I did congratulate him when he showed me the performance recognition plaques he brought home, but I would not allow him to hang them on any of the walls. They were too unsightly. He ended up storing them in a box in the bedroom closet.

My search for a piano teacher brought Claudia Brent to my attention. I learned of her from Lorraine Hartman, whose perky bespectacled daughter, Phyllis, was in sixth grade, two years ahead of Robbie. I heard her play a short classical piece by Bach at a PTA meeting and, afterwards, asked Mrs. Hartman from whom her daughter took lessons. Claudia Brent specialized in teaching children and teenagers. I began Saturday morning lessons for Robbie, who discovered he had a natural flair for the music and quickly memorized his assigned easy pieces in the John Thompson Teaching Little Fingers To Play and the John Thompson for Beginners book. He quickly improved to an intermediate level. Within a few months, I started lessons for Pam and Daniel.

Sitting in her living room adjoining the piano parlor, I watched and listened to the lessons. Claudia was perfect to be working with children. Her calm manner and patience in showing and communicating with the kids the relationship of the keyboard to the written notes amazed me.

She reminded me of an old fashion bespectacled schoolmarm with her dark brown hair pinned up and kind, soft-spoken expression that won over every child who sat on the piano bench beside her. She never pushed or reprimanded or cajoled her students but gave them the information they needed and allowed them to discover and achieve step by step successes playing progressively more challenging pieces. Robbie, Pam, and Daniel proudly displayed the little red, green, and gold gummed stars she affixed to pages of their sheet music.

The kids collected the miniature white sculpted busts of the heads of classical composers, Bach, Mozart, Liszt, Chopin, and Beethoven that Claudia gave them upon learning beginner and intermediate versions of their compositions.

Listening to their repetition of scales and keyboard exercises and playing songs in the living room while I was preparing supper was another reality of my family dream coming true.

Robbie's frustration at not being able to immediately execute a difficult passage surprised me. He would burst into a fusillade of pounding keys that I feared would destroy the piano. Once when he threatened to get a hammer and smash all the keys, I ordered him to get away from the piano and calm down. He had to promise to control himself. I had no idea as to the emotional source of his anger.

At the end of the year, Robbie and Pam played in Claudia's first Christmas recital she held for all of her students at the Mendelssohn Club. The auditorium seats were filled with parents and their nervous excited children. Seeing Robbie and Pam perform at the ebony grand piano were among Bob's and my most joyous and satisfying moments as parents. The accomplishments of our children meant everything to us. Just seeing them running in and out of the house to school and to play and having them sitting at the kitchen table doing homework and chattering about their activities gave me a warm glow.

Wearing a dark suit and tie, Robbie played *Theme From Lebensraum* by Franz Liszt. Wearing a stylish young girl's dress, Pam played a country dance by Edward Grieg. As they took their bows, they appeared awkward, embarrassed, and pleased at the audience's enthusiastic applause. Bob, Daniel, and I clapped the loudest.

A series of images and memories recur to me as I look back on that period as being the happiest. The interconnecting neighbors' back yards became an open theater for much of the children's playtime activities.

On hot humid summer evenings, they captured fireflies that swarmed out of the night and created glowing lamps in empty jars.

Camping in a neighbor's large cabin tent, they told each other ghost stories and spooked themselves into screams of terror that brought me running from the house to ensure they were all right. As I poked my head through the door zippered tight to keep out mosquitoes, they looked at me aghast that I was encroaching on their imaginations.

Being the oldest, Robbie roamed farther afield than Pam and Daniel. From my kitchen window, I would watch his comings and goings, striding across the back yards to join his friends.

His first and best friend was Tim Olafson who lived three houses away. He and Robbie had quick and easy access to each other through their connected back yards. Robbie was impressed with Tim's realistic western six gun and holster rig and persuaded me that he needed to have one just like it. He could load blank cartridges containing little round caps into the revolving chamber. Their guns were just like the one Randolph Scott used in the movies. The boys galloped about the back yards and fields surrounding the school grounds on their imaginary horses and provided the sound effects of whinnies and snorts to add an element of realism to their make-believe.

Unlike my own childhood dominated by the religious beliefs of the Jehovah's Witnesses, I did not hold back on such make-believe toys and birthdays and the observation of Christmas and Halloween and the Easter Bunny which the JW's branded pagan rituals.

Although Robbie stood a head taller than Tim, short and blue-eyed like his father, who had intimidating bushy white eyebrows, Tim was experienced and knowledgeable in subjects and activities in which Robbie was not. So Tim became the leader in their relationship. He was small-boned and athletic like his mother, whose brunette hair and Elizabeth Taylor movie star looks he favored. The owner of a construction company, Tim's father's passion was freshwater sports fishing. He had taught his son the skills of handling rods and reels and bait and tackle. Tim passed along the fishing basics to Robbie and taught him how to cast. Robbie persuaded Bob and me of his necessity for a rod and reel, tackle box and artificial lures, along with extra Eagle Claw hooks, various sinkers, corks, and plastic bobbers.

During their first summer together, Tim showed Robbie his favorite fishing holes along Spring Creek which originated many miles out in remote farm country and passed through the hills and knolls being transformed into a suburban landscape. The creek was a draw for their adventurous impulses, although it yielded little more than chub, tiny blue gill, an occasional bass, frogs, turtles, and crawfish. The wildlife had not yet been displaced by residential development. They saw pheasants, quail, rabbits, chipmunks, skunks, possum, muskrat, and a variety of harmless snakes. They discovered a foxes den containing small broken bones and pieces of gray fur. They crawled on their hands and knees following small animal trails through tangled briar patches and stumbled into tall itch weed that caused them to break out in a spreading rash that worsened with scratching.

At the end of each day before going to bed, Bob inspected Robbie's hair and body for wood ticks. Distinguishing the tiny brown parasites was often difficult because of their resemblance to skin moles and pepper spots. Tim's father used the lighted end of a cigarette to cause the ticks to back out. Bob used rubbing alcohol. There was always concern that a tick's head would break off and become absorbed into the skin and that the germs they carried would cause Rocky Mountain Spotted Fever. My cautions, however, did not keep the boys out of the woods and fields.

Chapter 23

Stress

I watched Robbie depart from his friend as they entered Tim's back yard and trudge across the expanse of two more yards to our own which rose in a mild slope to the back door. He stomped his tennis shoes against the door stoop and wiped the loosened dried mud on the black rubber mat before entering the laundry room adjacent to the kitchen where I was preparing dinner. The smell of beef and vegetables and biscuits browning in the oven permeated the house.

"Are we having French fries?" he called through the door, as he placed his rod and reel and tackle box in the broom closet.

"Yes, supper will be ready in about thirty minutes. That gives you just enough time to practice the piano."

"I'm too hungry to practice right now. I'll do it after supper. Can I have some milk and cookies?"

"They'll spoil your dinner. Have a carrot instead."

Robbie always wondered why I thought cookies would spoil his dinner. He never had trouble eating even when he did sneak cookies when I wasn't looking. He settled for one of three peeled carrots on the kitchen counter and was about to walk back to his bedroom.

"Wash your hands first."

"They're clean."

"You've been handling worms," I said.

"We used lunch meat and cheese. We only caught crawfish."

"Wash anyway."

Robbie held the carrot between his teeth so that it protruded from his face like Pinocchio's long nose and washed his hands at the kitchen sink, then used my white dishcloth to dry them. His fingers left dirt smudges on the dishcloth. He bit off a piece of carrot with a loud chocking noise.

"If you're not going to practice, run over to the Gunderson's and tell Daniel it's time to come home."

"Where's Pam?"

"With the Brownies at Mrs. Macklin's. She should be home any minute."

Robbie crossed the dining room into the breezeway and went out the connecting door through the garage. As he crossed the narrow street, he watched the Olson's tan-skin boxer come over into his yard, raise a hind leg, and pee on one of the low-lying junipers.

Robbie had helped his dad plant the shrubs. He was responsible for mowing our big yard. We didn't own a power mower, so pushing required concentrated labor, during which Robbie made frequent stops to drink from the garden hose. He usually ignored the intense heat and humidity of summer as long as he was at play with his friends. When he mowed the lawn, the steaming air aggravated him and made the job unpleasant.

"Hee-yah!" He waved his arm at the dog. "Go pee on your own bushes."

The dog ignored him, finished his pee and trotted further into the side yard to investigate new smells. Robbie continued across the road into the Gunderson's driveway littered with evidence of five children -- tricycles, a wagon, two hula hoops, and various plastic push toys. He could hear his brother's loud voice and the softer one of Daniel's friends through the screen door. Daniel raised his voice on a regular basis to overcome being interrupted by Robbie and Pam whenever he tried to say something. His desire to be heard caused him to be vocally dominant when playing with his friends.

Peering through the screen's mesh, Robbie saw the shape of Estelle Gunderson in somnambulant motion in the kitchen. He always felt embarrassed for her in her alcoholic stupor and avoided engaging her in conversation. He had difficulty understanding her slurred speech and never knew quite what to say to her. He considered going back to his own house and calling on the phone. Past experience told him that the phone rarely got answered. He knocked gently on the aluminum door frame. "Hello."

"Who's there?"

"It's me, Robbie."

"You can come in."

"Can you tell my brother it's time to come home for supper?"

"Sure, I'll tell 'im."

"Thanks." Robbie waited a moment to be sure she followed through with what she said. When he heard her speak to the boys in the living room, he quickly left the back door and crossed the road again to his own house where Bob's gray Chevrolet coupe was pulling into the driveway.

Now that he had changed jobs and worked for a company in Rockford that manufactured aerospace fasteners (no more drapery hardware), he was often home in time for dinner, an event that eased Robbie's anxiety. Bob being late upset my expectation of family togetherness and I would angrily scold him as he walked through the door. I recognized that Robbie disliked emotional tension and confrontation of any kind. Bob handled it well. He handled everything well when it came to dealing with people. He even understood why I was angry and accepted it calmly, just as he accepted all things that came at him and to him. The children never saw him become angry or outspoken to anyone. They saw only me.

Robbie did not know what emotional stress was. He had experienced stress himself in school (particularly when Miss Wersen was teaching sixth grade arithmetic) and sometimes at play as high excitement. He had observed Bob laugh and smile, but he had never seen him become excited or agitated. What

Robbie didn't know, but I did, was that Bob internalized his stress and his anger instead of letting it out and getting rid of it.

The first time Robbie heard the word stress mentioned was late one night. I raced into his and Daniel's bedroom and shouted at them, "Wake up! Wake up! Go get Doctor Gunderson! Your dad's having a heart attack!"

As he and Daniel leaped from their beds and ran into the hall, they paused a moment to glance into our bedroom and saw their father clutching his abdomen and writhing and gasping for breath while I tried to get him to remain calm. The boys dashed out of the house and across the street to the Gundersons.

Ray Gunderson was a general surgeon. Accustomed to being called out of bed to respond to emergencies during the middle of the night, he answered the ringing doorbell and (barefoot, wearing only his pajamas) did not hesitate one moment to follow the two boys jabbering up at him about their dad having a heart attack.

Robbie especially liked Doctor Gunderson, because of a medical problem he had experienced during the sixth grade basketball season. (Their local school covered first grade through eighth.) Robbie was convinced that the reddish-brown spreading rash throughout his groin area that itched to distraction was cancer. I made an appointment for him to see Doctor Gunderson at his office downtown. At the doctor's request, Robbie had scrunched down his blue jeans and Fruit-of –the-Loom underpants in an embarrassed obligatory manner and exposed his scabrous inner thighs.

"How long has it been since you washed your jock strap," Doctor Gunderson asked.

"I don't know. A couple of months, I think."

"Do you keep it in your locker at school?"

Robbie nodded.

"How many do you have?"

"Just one."

"You should have at least two and wash and rotate them. Have your mom buy you another one. What you have is called jock itch."

"Jock itch?"

"Yes, I'm going to write you a prescription for an ointment you can apply and it should go away in a few days."

Robbie grinned with relief. "I thought I had cancer."

Doctor Gunderson swallowed his sudden impulse to laugh. "Nope, just old-fashioned jockstrap itch." He finished scribbling his signature on a prescription form and handed it to Robbie, who quickly pulled up his pants. "Have your mom pick this up for you."

"Thanks." Robbie took the little piece of paper while fumbling awkwardly with his belt and zipper. He felt incredibly embarrassed. He told me it concerned him that now, every time Doctor Gunderson saw him in their neighborhood, he would associate Robbie with jock itch. So thereafter, Robbie did his best to avoid seeing or talking to Ray. At the moment, however, as they raced back across the street to save his father, the thought of jock itch didn't even occur to Robbie.

When they arrived, Ray sat on the bed next to Bob. "Hello, Bob, it's Ray. Now I want you to concentrate on my voice and relax your body. Stay focused on my voice." His voice was soothing and calm. He took one of Bob's hands and slowly unclenched the tight fist. Keeping the fingers spread, he massaged them while also gently rubbing Bob's abdomen, which was tight and knotted with cramps. His breath came in little gasps, grunts, and wheezes.

A few minutes later, the kids and I saw Bob's body visibly relax and his shallow breathing expanded into a normal pattern of inhaling and expulsion of air. "What happened?" he asked. "Did I have a heart attack?"

"No," Ray observed with a kindly smile. "You must be under a lot of stress. You had an anxiety attack. The symptoms are similar to a heart attack. But you're fine. You might want to consider taking a couple of days off work and play some golf."

Bob nodded. The president and CEO of the former company had given territory and customers that Bob had established to a newly hired employee who would take over Bob's commissions. Bob had been directed to go out and develop another sales region which meant extensive travel and longer periods of time away from home. Every moment lost away from his family could never be recaptured – each meal, each bedtime, each hug and a kiss and utterance of, "I love you and I like you goodnight." To be gone saddened him and caused him great emotional suffering.

To the chagrin of the CEO, who had tried to convince Bob to stay, Bob had resigned and taken his recent new job with an aerospace fastener company as a business development manager.

He took great pride in describing how he worked with aerospace engineers helping them design special screws and bolts and rivets made from processed steel that could withstand aircraft structural stresses of flight and temperature and weather conditions of high altitudes. Technical descriptions of heads and shanks and torque and alloys populated his written purchase and sales orders I saw spread on the dining room table. I noticed that when he spoke of associating and interacting with, "engineers of such high caliber," it raised his self-esteem.

Robbie studied his father's elongated features in profile. Bob's previously frightened expression was once again calm.

Robbie told me he felt a sudden rush of shame at the remembrance of a moment at the dinner table when he had told his dad he didn't like the way he chewed his food. Although probably deeply hurt at the criticism, Bob had said that Robbie's observation was okay and that it was a normal part of growing up for children to be critical of their parents. The memory of what he had said to his father was the equivalent of Robbie's jock itch associated whenever he met Ray Gunderson. The only difference was that Robbie did not try to avoid his father, who was very attentive of his three children. He never failed to sit nearby and listen to them practice the piano and he was patient and helpful when they had problems with their homework. He was very good at arithmetic and algebra. Going back to being a supply officer during the war, math was one of his strengths.

As a result of the anxiety attack episode, I decided I was limiting myself and was excessively preoccupied with domestic concerns. I enrolled as a part-time student at Rockford College to begin realizing my personal dream of a higher education. Being late for dinner was never mentioned again. Happy greetings became the order of the day.

***

On another day, waiting at the open front door, I watched Robbie approach the car from the driver's side, as Bob stepped out. He had removed his gray suit coat, but still wore a tie loosened at the knot.

"Hi, Dad."

"Hi, Robbie. Will you help me with these?" He handed Robbie an expanding file containing engineering blueprints sales records.

"Sure."

Daniel dashed across the street from the Gundersons'. "Hi, Dad."

"Hi, Son." He gave his wide smiling golden haired boy a hug. Together they traipsed into the house.

"Tonight's rec night," Robbie reminded me. I have to get there early to set up the movie projector."

"You'll be ready in plenty of time."

"I have to get there early." Robbie had been asked by the science teacher, Mr. Rowley, if he would run the movie projector at the Friday Recreation Nights. The school provided the facility for the children of local families to come and dance, do crafts, play games, and watch a full-length movie. Mr. Rowley respected Robbie and considered him among the most responsible students in the school. The principal, Mr. Nicholson, also did and had appointed Robbie as the playground monitor, a position that came with the wearing of a white web bandolier style safety patrol belt. As playground monitor, Robbie kept an eye out for potentially unsafe situations among the screaming oblivious children on the swings and jungle gyms and racing madly after each other about the school yard. The kids his own age didn't present any problems. They either clustered in groups trying to "be cool" or played baseball or basketball on the blacktop.

During dinner, Pam told about her meeting at Mrs. Macklin's with the Girl Scout troop. They had made chocolate chip cookies. She had brought home ten that they could eat for dessert, two for each.

After supper, Robbie took a quick shower, put on his sun tans, saddle shoes, and red-checked cotton shirt. He rolled up the short sleeves and elevated the collar in the rear to emulate the photograph of Pat Boone on one of his record albums. He carefully combed his hair, making sure every strand was in its proper place, especially the slight wave drooping rakishly just above his left eye. I didn't understand how he allowed himself to be so influenced by those popular singing stars. I prohibited having any Elvis Presley albums in the house. He sounded and moved in a much too suggestive and provocative manner. As for Jerry Lee Lewis, his, "Whole Lotta Shakin' Goin' On," was outrageous and totally unacceptable. He should have been banned from the radio. I didn't want my children coming under their influence.

Robbie vigorously brushed his teeth and swallowed a glob of Pepsodent toothpaste so that his teeth sparkled, and his breath was fresh.

"I'm going now, Mom," he shouted as he passed through the laundry room and headed out the back door.

"Have a good time. Be careful crossing the road," I called out from washing the dishes at the kitchen sink.

The school loomed across the street from our home as an extension of where we lived. It was a safe, moral omnipresent influence in the life of the community. The elongated tan brick building contained pockets of experience and information that the children came to gather each day, invisible concepts that registered in their growing minds as learning.

The school was a natural cocoon for young people. Our children's teachers and the rows of desks in classrooms with walls and bulletin boards lined with the children's work and that of their peers formed the chrysalis of their development. There would be many such rooms before they finally emerged as adults.

Robbie liked the security of being with the others, gaining his identity from them, from his teachers, from Bob and myself and his sister and brother, and from his friends. He talked about how he liked the smell of paste and watercolors, of old wooden desks gouged with initials. He enjoyed drawing birds in art class. Unlike their parents, our children were unconcerned about the future. They enjoyed the present. They lived in the moment.

Robbie liked the gymnasium bounded on one side by a stage on which was presented school plays, holiday pageants, and assemblies, when the principal would make "announcements." The gym was also where the local Boy Scout troop met every Tuesday night and where the initial impulse to embrace a strong sense of morality was reinforced and nurtured in Robbie.

I felt I had finally achieved a major goal to which I had aspired. Our family life was wonderful. Everything was within grasp of what I wanted it to be. Nothing could go wrong until the day I saw Charles Gibson in an old car with a crushed bumper and a broken headlight parked in front of our house. I was busy vacuuming the living room and happened to glance out through the picture window. He was looking straight at me.

I turned off the vacuum cleaner and walked to the front door and stopped. If I went out to confront him, what would I possibly say to him. I wondered if I would be better off ignoring him. Maybe he would just go away. Bob was out of town for the next two days. Whatever happened here I had to handle alone. A sudden fear seized me that Charles might harm my children like he had threatened to do five years ago when he had deserted his family and dropped them off at Mum's and Dad's.

I wondered if I should call the police, but all he was doing was sitting out there watching the house and obviously waiting for me to appear and do something. I was at a loss for what that might be. His being there was an implied threat to my family. I needed to let him know I would protect them at all costs. I opened the door and stepped outside. I stood looking across the front lawn at him as though we were in a duel. Then I walked firmly to the car. He had lowered the front passenger window, but I didn't stand too close.

"Hello, Mary," he said. I was wondering if you'd come out. How are your beautiful children these days?"

"My children are none of your business. What do you think you're doing here?"

"Just thought I'd stop by and say hello for old time's sake."

"How did you find out where we live?"

"Oh, I have my ways." His foul smile exposed his nicotine-stained teeth and infuriated me. "I saw Nina where she works at Weises. She told me."

"She would never give you that information."

"I know she remarried that dago. I read about it in the paper. She told me she wasn't happy that you didn't come to her wedding."

"You're just a lying sneak. She never talked to you. She never told you that."

"She didn't have to. I know the both of you too well. I was married to her for three years. Remember. She told me all about you and your Mum and Dad. Gave me an earful about how all of you treated her."

"We're close. We care about each other."

"Couldn't prove it by me."

"We don't have to prove anything by you. You are out of the picture."

"And yet here I am parked in front of your house talking to you like an old friend of the family."

"You have nothing to do with our family, not with any of us."

"I'm Tommy's and Jennifer's father. That makes me part of the family."

"Not in my book you aren't."

"You can't ignore the facts, Mary."

"The facts are if I ever see you in this neighborhood again, I'm calling the police. I'm letting the school know who you are and what you look like and I'm telling all the neighbors to warn their kids about you."

"Warn them? I haven't done anything. I'm not going to do anything."

"I don't trust you and I never have."

"Same old suspicious Mary. Scared of your own shadow. Scared something might happen to your kids."

His reference to my children put me on guard. "I'm not afraid of anything, especially you."

"That's encouraging. Maybe now we can shuck the old baggage. Get to know each other. I'm not the same man as when I was married to Nina. Why don't you invite me in and we can talk about this over a cup of coffee."

"Never. Just because you can change your voice on the phone doesn't mean you're a changed man. I think you're sick. I'm surprised you're not in prison or a mental hospital."

His face suddenly flushed scarlet and his lips twisted in rage, reminding me of a writhing snake. "You fucking bitch. You think you and your family are safe and have it made in this shitty suburb. Think again, you frigid cunt."

"Don't you dare use that word and threaten me."

"Or what?"

"I know Nina has a restraining order against you. I can do the same."

"That's a lie. I can see her and my kids any time I want."

"And if you try, you'll be arrested. We're done here, Charles. Move on and don't ever show your face in this neighborhood again. Don't ever come back."

He started the engine and put the car in gear. "You haven't seen the last of me."

"Oh yes I have."

"Bitch! Fucking whore bitch!" His vile words floated out the window as he drove away.

I called Nina and told her about Charles coming to the house and what we had said to each other. I didn't even hold back on repeating his foul language. She said he had come into the department store one day while she was working. Because he was violating a restraining order, she had summoned store security and an armed guard had ushered him out.

I then went across the street to the school and told the principal about Charles. I described what he looked like. Then I went door to door around the neighborhood and described Charles to the mothers and warned them he was a child molester, an evil man.

When school let out in the afternoon, I walked my children home and warned them to never get into a car with a stranger.

Chapter 24

The Signing

I hadn't considered going to Gwen Gebhardt's book signing. Although I was curious, I almost dreaded to meet my old wartime friend. After all the years, I didn't think seeing each other again would be of much use. I was loathe to admit I was envious she had really made something of herself, and I had not. Not only was she an educated literary person, an achievement I longed for, she was famous for what she had written between the covers of a published book. People paid money for the book and to hear her speak. What would be her impression of me, a drab suburban housewife and mother and still no college degree?

I watched in the paper for an announcement about the book signing. It was to take place in the lobby of the Faust Hotel on a Tuesday from 1:00 to 3:00 in the afternoon. The kids would be in school. I would have to be back by 3:00 when they came home.

Wanting to make an appropriate impression, I debated with myself what to wear, then decided I should at least look like a businesswoman. No sense in embarrassing myself. I had the dark low-heel shoes and wool suit I wore when I did part-time secretarial work. A plum blouse topped with a single strand of fake pearls rounded out my image. A subtle touch of rouge, lipstick and eyeliner restored my youthful glow. I couldn't compete with Gwen and her upper-class style, but I could at least be presentable.

I brushed my hair to a high gloss so the waves bounced when I shook my head. I wasn't a babe like Nina, but I did look attractive.

The traffic going into town wasn't heavy at that time of day and I arrived at exactly 1:00 pm. I parked on the street to avoid the cost of the valet service, even though it meant having to walk three blocks. I wasn't alone. Many women were rushing along the sidewalk in the direction of the Faust Hotel like it was some kind of mecca.

I could barely edge into the packed lobby that had been set up with velvet ropes and stanchions for crowd control. I joined the long line moving at a snail's pace up one row and down another, edging us closer by increments to a white linen-covered table stacked high with copies of the book. A seated cashier and her smiling assistant were busy at one end taking money and handing out books.

Through the shoulder-to-shoulder line of women ahead of me I caught momentary glimpses of Gwen signing copies and chatting briefly with each customer. She looked every inch the successful businesswoman whose professional black and white photograph dominated the back cover of the book. She did appear a little tired and older than I remembered her, but her luxurious shoulder-length hair and flawless skin hadn't changed. She had added a few pounds that did not detract from her voluptuous figure. She looked like a movie star.

I crab-stepped and edged along until I was finally in front of her. Her sparkling brown eyes widened as she recognized me.

"Mary! I was hoping you would be here. How many years has it been?"

"Hi, Gwen, congratulations on your book." I handed my copy across the table to her. "I wouldn't miss seeing you. You look gorgeous as always, even more now that you're famous."

"Oh, stop it. Give me a minute to sign this." She chattered on while I watched the brief note and slash of her signature appear on an inside cover page.

"I figured you and Bob would settle in Rockford after the war. I'm sorry we lost contact with each other. Life has a way of doing that to us. How is Bob?"

"He's fine."

"He made it through the war okay."

"Some recurring malaria."

"Eddie shot down the thirty Jap zeroes he was always talking about."

"I remember," I said.

"Now he's following his father's footsteps in Washington. He's a congressman."

"That sounds right for him."

"What about Bob? What's he doing?"

I hesitated. I hadn't expected the question, but I was prepared with an answer. "He's an aerospace sales executive. Large territory to manage. He's hardly ever home."

"That happened to Eddie and me. Divorce. Not seeing each other. Only, I was the one hardly ever home. But the real reason is that I was writing news stories critical of the military industrial complex and he's a war hero in congress. I was an embarrassment to him. We have a son though, Edward, Eddie Jr. He goes to an elite boarding school. We only see him on Holidays. I'm sure you and Bob have children. How many?"

"Three, two boys and a girl."

"Listen. I'm here for only one night and I have to keep this line moving. Could you and Bob join me for dinner here at the hotel this evening around seven?"

"Unfortunately, Bob's out of town on business and I wouldn't be able to find a sitter for the kids on short notice." Nudged by the next woman in line next to me, I started to move on. "I look forward to reading your book. Congratulations on your success."

"It's wonderful to see you again, Mary. Here," she pushed a notepad across the table to me. "Write down your address and phone number. Maybe we can get together next time." Her eyes focused on the woman now standing in front of her.

I quickly jotted my address and phone number, raised my hand in a final farewell, then maneuvered to the exit.

I had lied about Bob being out of town. He was home for dinner that night. I showed him the book titled, *Paper Dolls*, and told him about meeting Gwen. “She’s doing a book tour,” I said. “Goes from one city to another for a couple of months.”

“Sounds like sales.”

“I never thought of that, but you’re right. It is sales.”

“So she and Eddie are divorced.”

“Yes, she’s too independent for him. She lives the life she describes in her book. I have to admire her for that, but I think she’s a horrid woman for isolating her only son in a private school and hardly ever seeing him. How must that make him feel, Eddie Junior? She might be an independent career woman, but she’s selfish. That’s just selfish. I would never do such a thing to my children, even if I had the money.”

“People like Gwen and Eddie live differently than people like us.”

“Yes, people like us,” I said with a tinge of bitterness.

“We have a loving family. We’re happy. It doesn’t sound like she is.”

“Oh, she’s happy all right. She has what she wants. She can buy what she wants.”

“You can’t buy happiness, Mary. We both know that.”

“It helps to be able to buy what you want.”

“We’re doing fine now. We’re doing just fine.”

“For the time being. The kids are still young. If only we could keep everything like it is. But our family life will change. I’m not where I want to be, not yet.”

It took me three evenings to read *Paper Dolls*. Gwen had obviously put in a great deal of journalistic time and effort researching and writing the book. She had conducted hundreds of interviews with women of our generation. The book covered a range of topics that included how men in the post war society undermined the identity of women, stereotyping the ideal woman as a sex object and second-class citizen whose primary domestic role was to serve her husband and be a wife and a mother.

She talked about the economics of the manufacturing world and its strategy to make women consumers of home products to fulfill their lives and to confine women to shopping with male oversight and protection and not making decisions in the workplace.

Since we, as a country, were in an unstable cold war with Russia, a family was supposed to be a fortress against fear and foreign aggression. An independent woman was considered a threat to the country's social order. Men wanted us to keep our place.

As I read, I realized she was describing me.

Chapter 25

Summertime

During the summer, among my favorite outings with the kids was the one hour road trip to Lake Geneva, just north of the Illinois-Wisconsin border. The expansive natural lake afforded us a respite in its chilly green waters from the intense ninety to one-hundred degree temperatures and humidity that kept us in a constant state of perspiration. Even during the night, there was no cooling off. We didn't have air conditioning. Our bed sheets were soaked and there was no point in changing them until wash day.

Robbie was the swimmer, but he didn't go out beyond the line of floating red and yellow buoys that identified a drop-off. The lifeguard whistle sounded from his stand whenever a swimmer ventured beyond the line or the teenagers became too rowdy diving off the springboard at the end of the wooden dock that projected thirty yards from the beach.

I coated the kids' bodies and my exposed arms and legs with Johnson's baby oil to protect them from the sun. The use of baby oil was long before we knew of such things as UV rays, although I did occasionally see billboards and magazine ads that said "Tan, don't burn. Use Coppertone." A cute blonde toddler's exposed white bottom from a partially dropped diaper illustrated the contrast with the rest of her tan.

We usually arrived an hour before lunch and spread our towels on the grass or on the sand, so the kids had time to swim and play in the shallow water. Having never learned how to swim, I waded in up to my knees with Pam and Daniel.

At noon on the dot, I heard their hunger signals and handed them lunch meat and cheese sandwiches made with Wonder bread. I munched on a cheese sandwich and poured potato chips from a family sized bag onto their paper plates. They requested numerous refills from the blue lemonade jug I had brought along with our red picnic cooler. Topping their meal with two chocolate chip cookies, they were anxious to return to the water, but I made them wait for a squirming half hour to let their food digest "to avoid cramps." A breeze off the lake carried the smell of roasting hot dogs along the beach and seemed to aggravate them. I told them to go build a sandcastle, which took their minds off the imposed health restriction which I had read about in a summer edition of Redbook Magazine.

After three hours, I noticed the kids' sunburns. They were lobster red and complained loudly when I rubbed on more baby oil and said it was time to go. We gathered up the towels, empty lemonade jug, and picnic cooler, and meandered back through the crowd of beach goers toward the car.

They held their noses at the odor of a decaying bass bobbing in the slight ebb and flow of shoreline water sloshing near the boat docks next to the parking lot. I had them wipe off the grains of sand that clung to their legs and swimming suits. They hopped and cried out as the hot asphalt seared their tender feet. I quickly opened the doors so they could jump into the oven-like car. We rolled down all the windows and began the long drive home.

Not more than fifteen minutes down the highway, led by Robbie's strident voice from the back seat, the expected root beer chant began, as the orange and black A&W sign loomed ahead. "I want a root beer. I want a root beer." I was just as hot and tired as they were, but I didn't really want to stop. Seeing that I wasn't slowing down to turn at the drive-in parking lot, the three various pitched cries assaulted me like agitated birds.

"Okay! Okay! Just stop shouting," I shouted back and abruptly braked to make the turn. The momentum threw Pam forward off the front passenger seat against the dash. As her tearful cries filled the car, a rush of fear electrified me that she was injured. I was angry at myself that I had not thrown out my arm as a barrier. Cars didn't come with seatbelts.

I pulled into one of the dozen spaces shaded by a long white aluminum roof and turned off the engine. I quickly looked Pam over and found only a red mark at the center of her forehead. "I'm so sorry, honey. I am so sorry." I held her against me and kissed her on her head. Her tears abated and she looked up at the cute gum-chewing, roller skating carhop approaching the driver's side.

"We'd like four frosty root beers," I said, as she braced the serving tray against my open window.

"Any hamburgers, hot dogs, and fries with that?" she jotted on her order pad.

"No, just the root beers."

"Got it." She popped a pink bubble and zipped away to the order window.

When the root beers arrived, I paid and tipped the girl and carefully handed each child their cherished frost-glazed glass mugs filled to the brim. "Handle them carefully so they don't spill," I said, knowing they would not risk spilling any of the dark savory brew. But I was all too familiar with the fact that accidents happened.

I drank mine quickly and listened to their slow slurping, prolonging the enjoyment, a reminder that they lived in the moment. Although they forced me to from time to time, when they had an injury or emergency or threw a temper tantrum, or I witnessed their achievements, for myself, I consistently would not and could not live in the moment.

With expressions of reluctance and remorse, they gave up their empty mugs and I placed them on the tray for the carhop to remove. Then we were on our way again with the kids belching and burping from the root beer carbonization that bloated their stomachs.

While we were at the root beer stand, I noticed dark gray storm clouds gathered on the horizon roiling toward us over the farmlands. Gold lightning flashes laced the bruised purple mass at its core, making me fear a tornado was in the making. I told the kids to roll up the windows. Minutes later, a deluge struck the car with such pounding force I had to pull off the road. The wipers could not move fast enough to clear the windshield and I would have been driving blind. Lightning bolts danced across an adjacent cornfield and deafening explosions of thunder made the kids cower on the floor of the car. Ten minutes later, the storm moved on and so did we. We rolled down the windows and cooled the interior with the fresh verdant smell of rain.

Not five minutes from home, something under the hood started making chugging clanking noises and the car periodically hesitated and jerked along. As we pulled into the driveway, the engine died and would not respond when I turned the key in the ignition and tried to restart it.

That evening after supper, Bob looked under the hood and listened to the clicking of the starter. "It needs a new alternator," he said. "The car will have to be towed to a mechanic tomorrow and repaired."

"We're lucky we got home in one piece," I said.

"Well, it is a secondhand car and parts do wear out."

"You'd better have the mechanic check for other problems. I can't go somewhere with the kids and have the car die on me."

"It will be ready before you make another trip to the lake, which reminds me. I'm taking a vacation in two weeks. I made reservations to rent a family cabin at Lake Louise."

"A cabin? What kind of cabin?"

"It's a nice place. It's in the woods along the shore and has its own boat dock with a rowboat."

"For how long?"

"Four days, then we'll be back home and I can do some things with the kids. Take in a movie, go to the county fair. We can all go to the fair."

"You can take the kids. I don't like fairs. The animals smell."

"You don't have to walk through the barn. The kids will want to go on rides most of the time anyway."

"That may be. Does the cabin have a name?"

"Hernando's Hideaway."

"It's named after the song?"

"I guess so. It's hidden from the road."

"How did you learn about this?"

"It belongs to Ben Carlson, one of the men I work with. I thought renting it for a few days would be a nice inexpensive vacation."

"Staying in a cabin is not my idea of a vacation. That sounds like it's more suited to my sister, Ruth. She was always the outdoor girl. She and Richard have a summer cabin at a lake in Maine. They have a sailboat and mosquitoes."

"It's only a few days."

"I'll let you know how I feel about it when I see it," I said.

"I'm sure it will be fine."

"I'm sure there will be mosquitoes."

Chapter 26

Highs and Lows

The yellow headlights pierced the gloom of the night and pulled the car forward with jerks and bumps over the dirt ruts of the service road deep into the inky blackness of massive pines and firs.

"Are you sure you made the right turn?" I asked, steadying myself with one hand on the dashboard. "This looks very primitive."

"That's because of the tall trees." He referred to the encroaching presence of the massive firs and pines that marked the shoreline of the lake. "It feels like they're closing us in. Watch for the sign," said Bob. "I'm following the directions Ben gave me. It should be coming up shortly."

"This does not bode well," I said.

The rustic wooden sign appeared in the glare of the headlights as though it suddenly sprouted up out of the bushes.

"We're here," said Bob.

I stared at the black hand-painted letters, Hernando's Hideaway. Bob turned in at what I would loosely call a short driveway overgrown with weeds and there was the genuine log cabin looming out of the black forest wall.

"It looks spooky," said Robbie.

"Real spooky," Pam echoed him.

"Are there ghosts?" asked Daniel.

"No ghosts. It's just a cozy cabin," said Bob.

I discerned a narrow footpath through the trees down to the water's edge. Moonlight glistened off the lake illuminating the boat dock. The eerie cry of a loon floated from somewhere across the expanse.

"Is that a ghost?" asked Daniel.

"No," said Robbie. "It's a loon. I read about them in my Scout manual."

Robbie had recently joined the local Boy Scout troop that met at the elementary school on Tuesday evenings.

Bob kept the car's headlights shining at the front door so he could see to unlock it and enter. He turned on a light switch as the kids crowded in and explored the rooms adjoining the kitchen, eating area, and living room, which featured a large stone fireplace.

"It's a fully stocked kitchen," he said. "We have everything we need here to cook meals except the food."

"Mom, Mom, come and look," Robbie shouted from one of three bedrooms. We've got bunk beds. They're made out of wood."

I stared disapprovingly at the plaid wool blankets spread on the mattresses. "The blankets probably have fleas and I know there are mice. There are always mice and rats in remote cabins. That means droppings and disease."

"Ben told me he has traps set out."

"We are not sleeping here," I remonstrated. "I'm not allowing the kids to sleep here, definitely not with rats and mice running around in the middle of the night. Rats and mice carry rabies. You know that."

"Mom, it's okay for us to stay here," Robbie interrupted. "It's okay. It's just like camping, only better."

"We want to stay here," Pam's mild voice barely filtered through my anger and resistance. "We like it."

"We want to stay, Mom," said Daniel. "We like it."

"Well, I for one will not stay here," I said. "I will not lower myself. I refuse to lower myself."

"You're not lowering yourself," Bob fought a losing battle trying to console me.

"There's nothing compelling about this cabin. And I'm not going to cook in that outdated kitchen with someone else's old pots and pans. There's dust in everything here. I can smell it. It's musty."

"All it needs is a little fresh air, once we open the windows."

"Staying in a place like this is lowering my standards. I refuse to sleep here with these dirty old blankets. You'll have to take me back out to the motel we saw on the highway before we turned off."

"It's not a Howard Johnson."

"It's still better than this."

"All right, I'm not going to argue. Okay, kids, back into the car. We'll take Mom to the motel and then come back here to spend the night."

"Can't we stay here 'til you get back?" asked Robbie. "I picked out the bed I want."

"No, I won't leave you here," said Bob, which was the first indication he was showing some good sense since we arrived.

The motel was not any I would choose to stay in while traveling. Despite its spare tacky furniture and uncomfortable mattress, at least the room was clean. A Denny's restaurant was a short walk across the parking lot. "We can have breakfast there tomorrow morning," I said. The kids gave me hugs and kisses and we exchanged our customary goodnights, then Bob drove them back to the cabin.

I wasn't pleased with the arrangement of being separated from them, but under the circumstances, there was no alternative.

The next morning, the kids were very solicitous, asking me if I had slept well and how glad they were to see me. I wondered if Bob had coached them, but they seemed to be genuinely concerned and a little down. I guess I had that effect on them.

I did go into the cabin to use the bathroom three times during the next day and refrained from making any more critical comments and observations. Although I put on my swimming suit, the lake was not as clean and clear as Lake Geneva. Moss and algae were visible floating in the water. Bob and the kids went in jumping and diving from the dock and seemed to enjoy themselves. They shouted how warm the placid water was.

Snapping turtles lurked in lakes and ponds like that. I sat on a lounge in the shade on the shore and kept an eagle eye on them splashing about, since they were in unknown water. Bob was a much better swimmer than I was and carefully monitored them, since I didn't swim at all. I was thinking I should take lessons someday.

Later, after lunch, they went out fishing in the rowboat. I insisted the kids wear life jackets, but there were none to be found in the cabin. I was apprehensive the entire time they were on the lake. Bob assured me he would stay near the shore.

That evening, he and the kids tried to convince me to change my mind and join them at the cabin. I refused and we settled for a cheap dinner together at Denny's, despite Bob offering to cook a meal in the cabin kitchen.

The next day, we all went for a walk along a lakeside path. Birds sang in the treetops and squirrels chattered at us. I asked Bob if there were any bears in the forest. He said no, but I had my doubts.

Before we left the cabin on the third day, the kids joyously took a final swim. I asked Robbie why he was suddenly so happy, whooping it up. He looked at me in surprise, unsure of how to answer. "Because the water feels good," he said. But I suspected his good spirits were because I would no longer be spoiling their experience. Once we were home, I could return to my normal self.

***

Sibling rivalry wasn't unknown to me. My sisters and I had bickered when we were growing up. But hiding behind cereal boxes at the breakfast table was a new twist. "Robbie's hiding from me. He's hiding," Pam complained sitting across the table from him.

"No I'm not," said Robbie. "I'm just reading the box."

"No, he's not. He's ducking his head. He's hiding."

"I'm not hiding. We can't see Dad because he's holding up the paper to read it and he's not hiding."

"I'll lower the paper so you can all see me," said Bob with a grin.

"Then it's okay if I read the cereal boxes," said Robbie.

"Yes, but you don't have to scrunch down in your chair. That looks like you're hiding."

"All right, I'll sit up."

"Respect your sister," I said.

After Bob went off to work and the kids went off to school, I would sit at the kitchen table and have a cup of coffee and a pastry and think about my day. Fresh bread products were my favorite food. Back in Colver, Mum had nearly raised me on bread and cheese, since I wouldn't eat meat. Oddly enough, I liked the flavor of crisp bacon, even though, when I was a little girl, I had seen a butchered hog hanging in Dad's smoke house and had run away screaming.

I liked to sing popular songs from the radio while vacuuming and dusting. Among my favorites were Que Sera Sera, sung by Doris Day. "Whatever will be will be. The future's not ours to see, Que sera sera." Although I could not see the future, I envisioned the way I wanted it to happen.

As for the present, the kids enjoyed our family centered activities like playing board games and, fannies up, reading the funnies on the living room floor. Bob took us for Sunday drives through the countryside after breakfast.

We didn't own one of the newly invented television sets. The kids would watch certain programs at friends' homes that had sets. They wanted us to buy one so they could watch *Leave It To Beaver, I Love Lucy,* and cartoons. Bob and I refused. We were a reading family.

***

Not long after she turned ten, Pam surprised me by saying she wished she had never been born a girl. She felt she was different than other girls her age in school. All they wanted to do was have boyfriends and neck and play spin-the-bottle at parties. Pam would always run into the house before her date could have a chance to steal a quick kiss at the door.

Many of the mothers in surrounding neighborhoods hosted the parties because they wanted their daughters to be popular even at their young age. Pam became fearful about attending them and finally stopped going altogether. After that, her "friends" dropped away with the exception of Sandy Macklin. Her mother wouldn't let her go to the parties in the first place either. She considered them immoral.

I noticed that Pam cried a lot and buried herself in the reading of books and gorging on sweets. I admonished her about growing fat. In an attempt to turn Pam around, I enrolled her in "charm school" to learn social skills and emulate the young models dressed up in magazines. I took her shopping for nice clothes and praised her improved appearance. During the evening while she read or did her homework, I brushed her glossy brown hair. I was living a different childhood through her, a much kinder, more abundant, gentler one than my own.

After three weeks of charm school, learning how to walk and pose like a model, and how to politely converse, Pam protested that she hated it and refused to go back.

Not giving up on her and to be supportive and do my part, I took her shopping for a uniform when she told me she wanted to join her friend, Sandy Macklin, in the local Girl Scout troop, organized and led by Regina Macklin, Sandy's mother.

Mrs. Macklin had been the Brownies leader and, when her daughter was in Girl Scouts, became the troop leader. Because Pam and Sandy were friends, she asked me to be the assistant troop leader and conduct the second meeting. Pam's affiliation with the Girl Scouts provided Robbie and his friend, Tim, an opportunity to get into mischief.

The meeting took place after school in one of the empty classrooms. The boys sneaked around to an open window and spied on the girls. Tim let a garter snake loose in the room and all the girls screamed and ran out into the hall. Mrs. Macklin was not there, only me. Being fearful of snakes, I promptly located the custodian and had him remove the reptile.

I noticed Pam fidgeting expectantly at one of the desks, as I put up the movie screen at the front of the room. The other twelve girls murmured to each other in excited whispers, conjecturing what the surprise was going to be. I had promised them something very special for that meeting.

I felt that my idea was the most educational and worthwhile activity to be attempted since the organization of the neighborhood Girl Scouts troop. Up to that point, I had found my position as assistant leader to be a bothersome chore under Regina Macklins' dictatorial personality. A strait-laced religious person who wore dull colored dresses that failed to hide her ample figure, she constantly negated my creative, original suggestions for improving the nature and quality of our weekly gatherings.

This time, I had vowed to come prepared and to prove to Mrs. Macklin (she had even asked me not to call her by her first name), the value of my progressive approach from the standpoint of the girls' reactions. I felt this was a wonderful means and opportunity for the girls that would alleviate the stigmas and ambiguities which so often formed the basis for education in the realm of human reproduction. Our family doctor had been helpful in obtaining the short film and pamphlets. He had advised me to wait until after the showing of the film to hand out the pamphlets. The contents would then be more meaningful and the girls would have a better understanding.

After threading the film leader through the projector, I returned to the front of the room. "All right, girls," I said. "We're ready to begin. Mrs. Macklin won't be here today. She isn't feeling well. I'm glad you were able to make it anyway, Sandy. What I have for you today is something I wouldn't want any of you to miss out on. When the movie is over, I have some wonderful material to pass out for you to read and take home and discuss with your mothers. Okay, Sandy, will you see to the lights. Thank you."

As I walked back to the projector, I smiled at Pam. Her questioning blue eyes glowed under her brown bangs and green tam. She was sitting next to Sandy, who looked like a sister, but with an identical blonde ponytail and freshly starched and ironed Girl Scout dress.

The girls sat in the darkness enthralled from the beginning to the end of the ten minute film. When I handed them the pamphlets, their enthusiasm had been limitless.

As I rewound the film and returned it to its can, I felt a glowing warmth that I had set these girls on the right path with a wholesome informed attitude toward the most beautiful and important force in their lives. Their reactions had been just as I expected and they had all parted more attuned to each other than when they had entered the classroom.

That evening while I prepared supper, Pam sat at the kitchen table and exclaimed at the wonder of it all. She told me she was proud that I had been the one to present such interesting information. The next day after school was a different story.

She said she wanted to talk to her friend, but Sandy's first words were, "Oh, wasn't that just awful! How could your mother ever show us such filthy immoral things? My mother said your mother isn't going to be assistant leader anymore because of that."

Later that night, I received an unexpected call from Mrs. Macklin informing me that I could no longer be the assistant troop leader.

Following the Girl Scout episode, Sandy told Pam she couldn't be her friend any longer. Pam started hating everybody.

She came in after school and dropped her books on the table. She didn't look at me or say anything. I was ironing clothes and asked, "How was your day in school?"

"Not very good." She went to the refrigerator.

"We'll be eating soon. I don't want you to start nibbling now," I said.

"Robbie's nibbling," she glanced at her brother eating a cookie.

"He's not the one getting fat."

Pam swiped her finger in a bowl of chocolate cake frosting I was going to spread later.

"I said don't eat anything now."

"I feel like it. I'm hungry."

"Well, just stop feeling like it. You're putting on too much weight."

"So who gives a damn anyway!" Pam picked up her books and started to leave the kitchen, then suddenly turned back, her face in tears. "Why did you lie to me?"

"Lie to you? What's the matter?"

"I'm not pretty. Why did you ever tell me such a stupid thing?"

"What's gotten into you?"

"Oh, hell, it's like I'm not even there in school. Nobody even says hi to me!" She ran to her bedroom and slammed the door.

I stopped ironing and just sat stunned for several minutes, then started again. I wondered what was happening to her, then decided it was growing pains. We all had our highs and lows.

I made every effort to support and to be an involved cheerleader in the kids' activities. Bob and I attended the boys' basketball and baseball games, the holiday skits and operettas, Boy Scout ceremonies, and children's local horseshows. In search of a pursuit that satisfied her emotional needs, Pam had begun taking riding lessons. Equitation began her lifelong love of horses.

Occasionally, Bob and I would dress up and attend neighborhood parties. I wasn't always socially comfortable, but I managed. Bob said I looked just as gorgeous and beautiful as when he met me for the first time, which made me feel pretty good, since I placed great importance on how I looked. He said I resembled Doris Day, because of my hair style. Mainly, I went along to the infrequent parties because Bob enjoyed socializing and was very good at drawing people out and getting them to talk about themselves. They recognized he was genuinely interested in what they had to say. He listened. I listened, but I wasn't always that interested, except for the fear of a nuclear attack from The Soviet Union.

There was much discussion about building bomb shelters, but none of the neighbors actually did. Despite what we read in the news and heard on the radio, other than keep emergency supplies, we didn't feel threatened enough, although schools had regular bomb drills. Whenever my children had something to say, I did listen, and I was interested.

They talked about the atomic bomb movie they were shown at a school assembly and how they practiced crouching under their desks and shielding their heads with their arms.

Like nearly everyone, of course, Bob and I had voted for President Eisenhower during the 1952 election. He did marvelous things for the country that contributed to the prosperity we were experiencing.

Bob barely escaped being called up from the Army reserves for the Korean War. Fortunately, thanks to Eisenhower, that one came to an end. He did intervene wherever there was a communist threat and still avoided using the bomb.

I earmarked my educational progress. Attending college classes made me feel as though I were soaring. I was so proud when I received my first 'A' on an English composition paper about a green worm in a bowl of green peas.

My first philosophy class opened new worlds of thought, not that any of them personally applied to me. How the great philosophers expressed their elevated views and reasoning about life and the world excited me beyond anything I had encountered. Most importantly, I was in a college class. I was in seventh heaven.

Chapter 27

My Shadow

I thought I had seen the last of Charles Gibson, but he persisted invading my life and adding to my fears. I started getting phone calls from someone who remained silent at the other end of the line. His heavy breathing was more terrifying to me than if he said something, anything. I knew the person had to be Charles. No one else with whom I had come into contact or with whom I associated would do such a thing. Our suburb was a safe, close knit community of families who shared the same values and concerns and we pretty much knew each other's business. No one among our circle of friends and acquaintances was so unhinged.

When I expressed my anxiety to Bob, he told me whenever I got a call like that to just hang up. But disconnecting Charles on the phone did not erase him from my thoughts. He personified the presence of death that the satisfaction and joys of our family life had banished from my mind. His image became a recurring nightmare that I could not dispel.

At the fifth time he called late one night when I was home alone with the children and getting ready for bed, I told him, "Charles, I know it's you. You need to stop doing this." His response was steady heavy breathing. I hung up, only to hear the phone ring again a moment later. I didn't know how I could stop him. I didn't know what to do.

I told Bob I wanted to change our phone number to see if that would stop the frightening calls. Only two days after the number was changed, Charles reached me again late at night. Only this time, he spoke – a few terrifying words that forever embedded him in my mind as the source of the fear that possessed me.

"You can never escape me, Mary. You should realize that by now."

Not wanting to give him the satisfaction of knowing how much he upset me, I quietly hung up the phone, then raced to the children's bedrooms to confirm that they were safely sound asleep.

I wondered how Charles knew to call me only when Bob was away on business. He never called when Bob was home. Charles timing led me to wondering if he were somehow spying on us. So the next time Bob was gone, I stayed up late with the lights turned out and sat waiting in the darkness of the living room.

Normally there wouldn't be any traffic in the neighborhood close to midnight. A single set of car headlights approaching along the side street that intersected with ours caught my attention. Then they suddenly went out, but the barely illuminated dark shape of the car continued moving slowly forward, which struck me as odd and made my heart clutch at my throat. I had deliberately left the living room drapes open so I could detect any movement out in front of the house.

I dropped to the floor and hid behind an armchair where I could remain concealed and still see out through the picture window. The car turned the corner and crawled to a stop at the curb.

I knew Charles was checking to see if Bob's company car was parked in the driveway. We never put both cars in the garage. So Charles had to have observed our habits and that was how he knew when Bob was out-of-town.

To my horror, the car pulled into the driveway and stopped. After several minutes, Charles got out and walked slowly over to the window. I ducked completely out of sight behind the chair and I was sure he hadn't seen me. But he must have somehow sensed I was there in the living room. He tapped on the window. I stayed frozen. I didn't dare move.

I carefully raised my head enough to see that his shadow was gone, but his car was still parked in the driveway.

On my hands and knees, I crawled around the couch to the hallway and leaped to my feet when I knew the wall would conceal me from the front window. I knew he must be walking along the edge of the house toward the children's bedrooms at the end of the hall.

I waited and listened at the open doorway to the boys' room. Their curtains were closed, so he couldn't see them. I heard him tapping on their window, not loudly enough to wake them. I was convinced he knew I was standing there listening.

The tapping stopped. I waited. My heart fluttered. I was drenched with sweat. A few minutes later, I heard his car engine start. I walked to the beginning of the hall and peered around the corner to see the car back out of the driveway and move down the street without headlights.

Charles stalking us raised a chill at the back of my neck. I went to bed. About one hour later, the phone rang. Only this time, I did not pick it up and hold it to my ear. I immediately replaced it on the cradle. It rang again. I repeated my action and, at the next first ring, I hung up. At the third ring, I pulled the phone cord out of its wall connection and wondered why I hadn't thought of doing that long before. I had been too distracted to think clearly.

What alarmed me was that Charles had not heeded my warning. He clearly surmised that under the cloak of darkness, he could do what he wanted and get away with it. Since I had spoken with him, I had not seen his car anywhere in the neighborhood during daylight hours.

When Bob came home the next evening, I told him what had happened. This time, his brow furrowed with concern. "The police won't arrest him unless he's caught in the act."

"We can report what he's doing. We can tell about the late night phone calls and who knows how often he comes skulking around here at night. I'm afraid he'll do something to our kids, Bob. I'm afraid for our kids."

"I'm not sure we can even get a restraining order. We don't have any evidence. It's not the same as with Nina and her children."

"It's what he's doing to me, Bob. When you're not here and I'm home alone with the kids, he's taunting me like a cat and mouse. It's what he's doing to me. You have no idea how he terrifies me. Starting tomorrow, I'm not even going to let the kids walk to and from school without me, even though it's just across the street."

"He wouldn't dare try to snatch one of them, not in broad daylight."

"How do you know what he will or will not do. He's insane, Bob. He's a maniac. I don't feel safe letting the kids go out and play with their friends."

"You need to just ignore him."

"Ignore him? What are you talking about? He's there. He's a voice in my head. He's a shadow outside our window at night."

"Just be vigilant. That's all you can do."

"What does that mean, be vigilant? I'm thinking we should buy a gun."

"No, Mary, no gun. We would endanger our children to have a gun in the house."

"Be vigilant? I am vigilant. I'm vigilant all the time. All the time. I'm frantic, Bob, frantic! You don't know what it means to be frantic all the time."

"You said you pulled out the phone cord. Just disconnect the phone when you go to bed at night and I'm not here."

"And if he comes snooping around the house again like he did?"

"Plug in the phone cord and call the police."

"He'll be gone before they ever get here."

"He won't try to break in. That's not what he's doing. He just wants to antagonize you and leave."

"So what do you suggest we do?"

"We can't let him get under our skin."

"It's too late, Bob. He's already under my skin."

"Well, I guess we could at least let the police know he's harassing you. They might give him a warning."

"And are you going to call and ask the police to do that or shall I?"

"I'll do it. This should be handled in a calm manner."

"Don't you realize by now, Bob, that everything in life is not calm?"

"Of course, but there are effective ways to address our problems."

"If I had a gun and he came around here like he did last night, I'd open the door and shoot him. I want to get him out of my life! I want to kill him!"

"You shouldn't say things like that. You're overly upset. I'll handle it. He'll stop what he's doing and go away."

"You know, Nina's married to an Italian. Maybe her husband can get the Mafia to whack him."

"Whack him?"

"Murder him. Take him out."

"Now you're being ridiculous."

"Am I? I think not."

"I'm sure we've seen the last of him."

"How can you be sure? You have no idea what he's capable of."

"If you just don't respond to him, he'll go away."

"Just pull the phone cord out every night?"

"If he can't get a connection, the phone won't ring and he can't talk to you."

"I think we should at least keep a baseball bat handy. Robbie and Daniel have one. I'll keep it next to the bed at night."

"If it makes you feel safer, by all means."

"Yes, by all means."

Chapter 28

Uprooted

The house stood off by itself on a low rise, a cheap, tacky, pale box of a tract home with miserable pretensions to being a ranch type. Thinking of the beautiful redwood ranch style home we left behind in Edgebrook for this made me sick to my stomach.

I remained sitting in the car and stared beyond the roofed-over, wall board symbol that locked me in despair. Our three children stood beside Bob's company station wagon, a 1958 Yeoman Chevrolet, parked a few feet ahead. The station wagon was one of the "perks" he received for moving us to Wayzata, Minnesota. He was commissioned to develop new aerospace fastener business in the region. Again, as before, he had to follow the money and our children, and I had to follow him.

What distressed me most was that our life in Edgebrook had come to an end. Robbie and Pam and Daniel were no longer young children enjoying the advantages of our innocent sheltered existence. They were in their teens. The sense of change and unraveling of their childhood years was unsettling to me. That I wanted to sustain what we lost was not meant to be, but I could not accept what was happening, not for this.

Bob walked to my car and held the door open for me to get out. I remained transfixed. "How could you do this to us?"

"Isn't it like Edgebrook here? There's even more space."

"There's no need to look inside," I said.

He gazed down at my frozen face. The drive from Rockford through Wisconsin and much of Minnesota had been long and wearisome. He realized the moment was too emotionally charged to say anything further. He returned to his station wagon.

"All right, kids. Back in the car. We won't look inside now."

Pam walked back to my car. Robbie and Daniel climbed into the station wagon passenger section.

We followed them along the rolling, open country freeway. Bob eventually signaled with his blinker lights to take an off ramp which brought us to a frontage road restaurant. He parked and he and the boys got out. I backed my car in a few spaces away from his and turned off the motor. Pam opened the door and joined her brothers. I opened mine only halfway, then suddenly slammed it shut and gunned the motor to life with a roar. They heard my anguished cry as I drove blindly and recklessly out of the parking lot.

"TAKE CARE OF THE CHILDREN!" I shouted through the open window.

"MARY! MARY!" I heard Bob call after me and the children's voices clamoring, "Dad, we've gotta stop her! Did you hear what she said?"

I sped unseeing, hot tears burning my face, no place to go, nowhere to turn, back and forth swerving through the multiple clover leaf complex until finally, I stopped, lost.

Bob and the children found me a half hour later. Knowing how upset I was, he asked me to ride with him and Pam and Daniel in the station wagon. I said I was okay to drive. Bob told Robbie to ride with me, probably to keep me from going off the deep end again. I couldn't think straight. I felt fragmented. We followed Bob out of the freeway maze and into downtown Minneapolis.

Outside, snow flurries shrieked around the impersonal buildings of the gray, windy streets. Inside, Robbie shouted at Bob and me in a great emotional rant peppered with sobs of anger. He grasped the hotel towel hanging around his neck and strangled it like a surrogate snake, heaving it into the bathroom. Bob and I just sat there, numb to our son's violent tongue-lashing, our blank, introverted stares crossing somewhere between us and being absorbed into the gray carpet.

Pam and Daniel huddled away to one side of his burning, wet blast, their fearful eyes casting back and forth from Robbie to us, hoping for a positive reaction.

"SHHH…IT! You both sound real great! Yeah, just great! Like a couple of God-damn spoiled brats who aren't having everything their way! Hell, you go around telling us about intrinsic values and then you act like this! It's nothing but a hypocritical pile of shit!"

Despite the castigating truth of what he was saying, we remained immobile in our chairs. The room throbbed with silence. Finally, Pam couldn't take any more. She came over to Bob and me and made us get up out of our chairs by pulling on our arms. Daniel joined her efforts, then Robbie; and my pride became melted putty, as arms and five bodies intertwined.

Shortly after supper, we left the hotel in downtown Minneapolis and walked the cold streets to a movie theater where we saw *The Dark At The Top of The Stairs*, a family drama starring Robert Preston. Our faith in compassion and the human spirit having been reaffirmed for the second time that day, we returned to the hotel.

The moving van arrived at the house early the next morning. While Bob and I supervised the furniture placement and checked for chargeable scratches, the children went for a walk nearby.

The neighborhood was in a sparsely settled area of Wayzata, a suburban community near Minneapolis. We were in farm country and the ragged tops of dead field grass perforated the thin layer of wet snow. The houses were near a small pond and spongy bog, a haven for breeding mosquitoes during the spring and summer months.

Completing their meager exploration, a half hour later, the children slowly trudged back along the gravel road to the house and waited patiently while the movers maneuvered the piano through the front doorway into the living room. The sound of scuffing feet reverberated through the cramped hollow void. Pam came into the kitchen to help me unpack the dishes and silverware. Robbie and Daniel found their father in one of the two small bedrooms lining up bed parts for assemblage.

That night, Robbie's near maniacal laughter howled through our small confines and infected the rest of us bellowing and cackling awake; and the whole house rocked with the purgative sound until we drifted off to sleep again with sore abdominal muscles.

The next morning, Bob drove the children to their combined junior and senior high school, due to the sparse population in the area. Robbie was now a junior, Pam, a freshman, and Daniel an eighth grader. Pam and Daniel were first to be whisked away to their home rooms.

As for me, I sat at the kitchen table and bemoaned how a move could so affect our lives. We had everything our family could wish for back in Rockford; and now, here we were stuck in a dumpy tract home out in the middle of nowhere. How Bob could even suggest this hole was like our home in Edgebrook was beyond my imagination. It paled by comparison.

I felt immobilized. Getting the children's breakfast had taken a Herculean effort. I was too sad and depressed to even wish them a good first day at their new school. I recognized their worry and sympathy for me, when I knew they were filled with anxiety about this abrupt change in their lives, not Robbie so much, but Pam and Daniel especially.

Robbie took a dramatic approach to nearly everything. He had a flair for it, as though he envisioned himself and the rest of us and everyone he encountered as characters in a story. I suppose his view provided him with a sense of actual or fictional understanding that was his coping mechanism. (A term I later learned from a child psychology course.)

As he told me later that day after returning home on the rural school bus, he had been worried because no third year Latin course was offered in the curriculum.

He described how he had sat fidgeting in the principal's office until he was met by the junior class president, Dwayne Eaton, who was three inches shorter. Robbie was six feet and one inch tall. Dwayne wore his hair in a crew-cut. His bird-like face matched his outgoing personality. Robbie reacted to him in a cordial manner, but maintained an attitude of aloofness, as he began to feel his way into this new social environment.

I recalled Robbie had actually welcomed the move from Rockford with a positive attitude. He told Bob and me he was glad for the chance to leave behind the rut of old mistakes and fading relationships and to start in fresh. He said the students here knew nothing about him, his past, what he had done, and what he planned to do. He determined to maintain this mystique of a newcomer, stand out from his peers in chosen endeavors where he had failed in the past at a larger high school, notably on the basketball court in the face of greater competition than his grade school and junior high days.

He had incessantly warmed the bench and had lost his confidence. The few minutes he had been on the court during games, he described how his legs had turned to rubber and the rest of his body felt numb and paralyzed. "I couldn't even handle the damn ball," he shouted.

Now that he was in a hick school, by comparison, nobody would know about those embarrassing moments and he could establish himself as a leader on the court, or so he thought to himself.

He had described his first day when he came home after school.

The bell rang signifying the end of the ten-minute morning home room period. His first class was chemistry. As he followed Dwayne from the office down the hall through the shuttling students, his self-conscious awareness grew more acute. By the time he entered the chemistry lab, his anxiety level rose to a fever pitch.

The teacher, Mr. Driscoll, appeared plump and jovial in his stained white lab apron. He immediately and deliberately embarrassed Robbie by reading from his class entry card the courses he was taking. The language requirement wasn't listed. When questioned, Robbie haltingly explained that he planned to take third year Latin in a tutor program.

"What do you need Latin for?" When Robbie told me what Driscoll said, I was furious. "So what did you tell him?" I asked.

"That I was going to med-school someday."

"German 'ud do you more good," Driscoll said. "That stuff about Latin is a fallacy."

"Oh, well, maybe." He was a teacher, so Robbie had to be respectful. I had to somewhat agree.

"There is no maybe about it," I said. My ambition for him was to become a doctor, a pediatrician. I told him he had the perfect personality for it. I could envision him wearing a white lab coat and a stethoscope hanging around his neck while he advised an anxious parent. "So what happened next?" I asked.

"He handed me back the card and told me to take a place in the second row next to the side aisle."

"That sweet little cutie next to you is Jill," he said.

"Jill was just as embarrassed as I was," said Robbie. He slid onto the high metal lab stool and concentrated on positioning his books in front of him on the counter. Then Mr. Driscoll started writing formulas on the blackboard and everyone opened their lab workbooks.

"I hate moments like that," Robbie told me, "when the teacher just turns his back on the class and writes symbols without a word of explanation. I have to rack my brains to understand what I don't know and what I don't want to have to trouble myself about, especially since I was new and didn't have a lab workbook. Jill smiled at me, leaned over and shared hers. My mind blocked out the squeaking chalk and focused on the perfume fragrance she was wearing. She was brunette, slim, pretty, with a ski-jump nose and a slight acne rash on her cheeks. She wore a dark blue sweater and short pastel pink culotte skirt.

"You noticed a lot about her," I said.

Driscoll turned to face the class. "Okay, you know where the supplies are. So, get started."

"I wanted to shout at him," said Robbie. "I wanted to say what supplies? I don't even know what you're talking about. But I kept quiet."

I watched some of the students make hesitant movements toward the open supply shelves at the back of the room. Jill pointed to a column in the workbook. "You get these things and I'll start the Bunsen burner going."

"But what are they?" I thought to myself. "I don't even know what they look like." "Okay," I said, feeling really stupid.

Robbie continued his narrative. "Throughout the entire day, fellow students looked after me, as though they had been assigned as my personal escorts. Sure, I valued their attention, but disliked the intrusion on my privacy. They weren't allowing me time and personal space to brood and observe from outside the social group, and, to maintain my status as a mysterious stranger. I wanted and needed that time and space."

"Mysterious stranger? Are you imagining something to write about?"

"I always think of what is happening. And, yes, I'll probably write about it someday. I realized that most of my classmates had been together since grade school. They held no secrets from each other and acted in a predictable, acceptable middle-class manner according to the expectations of teachers, parents, and of each other. I was determined not to fit the mold."

I smiled inwardly. Robbie sounded like me, something I would say.

He described the first efforts to pin him down at a lunch table in the cafeteria. Two guys asked him if he would like a ride to the football game that evening and then to the post game party. He accepted out of courtesy, even though football didn't interest him.

Chapter 29

Maple Square

I attentively watched the names on the street signs. As Bob and I approached the corner, my gloved hand expectantly clutched the want-ad section of the Lakeshore Weekly News folded on my lap.

"This is the street," I said. "Turn right."

Bob slowed at the corner. "How far down?"

"The end of the block."

We turned in at a steep downhill driveway by a small rustic sign that read: Maple Square. Secluded behind a thick wall of trees and shrubs and sunken below the street level, four apartment duplexes, painted yellow with brown trim, formed three sides of the square. The fourth side opened on a sparse winter woods and swampy bog.

"Does it look okay to you from the outside?" Bob asked.

I reached for the car door handle. I didn't want to comment yet. "Let's see what it's like inside."

I considered the apartment small for a family of five, but adequate in respect to its unlived in cleanliness and modern kitchen electric facilities. The den could function as a third bedroom. The rent was two-hundred twenty-five dollars a month. Bob signed the contract with the polite, business-like resident property manager before we departed. Earlier that day, he had terminated the month-to-month lease governing the house in the weeds.

I found it amusing that Robbie had been writing about our family and that he allowed me to read some of the descriptions, especially about his social adjustment.

The roaring bleacher crowd surrounded me under the lights and cold night air. At times, I chanted long and loudly with the jack-in-the-box, blue-sweatered cheer leaders, jumping, jiggling, ass-wiggling and dancing in choreographed unison along the sideline.

Dwayne and the other guy, Ron, who had brought me would then at least think I had school spirit. I wouldn't give myself a sore throat for any other reason. I was superior to school spirit. I didn't really yell to cheer on the tumbling players on the wet chalk—smeared field, but only for myself, for the acknowledgment of being accepted.

I didn't like to play social games. Shouting helped me draw warmth from the crowd. Being silent left me cold and shivering.

The post-game party was held in a rich kid's pine paneled basement. I sat alone stuffed deep in an armchair confronted by the staring others, wondering how they should approach me, wondering what they should say to the silent stranger.

A ping pong ball spat back and forth across a green tabletop and several couples danced to rock and roll music, Elvis Presley songs and Bill Haley and The Comets. Light flickered from the warm shadows of an earth tone design set in the hearth carpet before the fire and from low key florescent overheads. In my imagination, the mood was ripe for murder, but I didn't know who would be the victim or when or why. I didn't know who the killer in the group might be either.

I didn't care for the way Jill's boyfriend was giving me the once-over. He was tall, skinny, and ugly. No, give the poor guy some credit --- slim and tolerably handsome. So scratch Jilly-Billy. There was something about her that didn't set right with me anyway. I thought it was the tiny acne pimples on the right side of her face under the pancake makeup. Also, her rear end slanted to a point. I hated girls with pointy rear ends. Somehow, they didn't meet my expectations for the ideal girlish figure.

And then too, during chemistry lab that morning, she had deliberately and vainly drawn attention to her figure by telling me she was fat when obviously she ranged from being skinny to just right, depending on what angle you looked at her. She had just been begging for a compliment and like a fool, I'd paid her one. I had told her she was just right. There wasn't really anything athletic about her anyway and it was important that any girlfriend of mine had to be athletic. She was just too feminine in a way I liked, but I didn't much care for either.

I noticed how the girls casually clustered for me to notice them. I realized how handsome I was. I was clean cut and had a good build, but my vision was going bad. Still, I couldn't risk putting on my glasses at such a crucial moment so that I could actually clearly see their faces. I had to maintain my image, the big strong silent type sitting in an armchair by the fire in brooding contemplation. I puffed out my chest slightly and arranged my left arm in a more casual manner, then stared deeply into the fire.

A girl arrived as a latecomer. From her uniform, I recognized her as one of the cheerleaders. She had long blonde hair, blue eyes, an athletic figure and she was the prettiest of all the girls for my taste in females except that the shape of her nose bothered me slightly. It was straight and I preferred ski-jump noses. This preference was the result of a cultural peer influence when I had been a sixth grader back in Rockford.

Linda Harrison, one of my classmates who came from a rich family and was a style setter, constantly pushed up the end of her straight nose in an attempt to give it an upturned shape. An upturned nose rendered you the appearance of being smart, precocious, and superior to others, even if you were dumb and inferior. Linda's lead in this nose-pushing behavior was emulated by other boys and girls in the sixth grade who were not already blessed with a turned-up nose. Of course, over time, pushing at your nostrils created a visible line of demarcation where the soft flesh met the cartilage. And, of course, my mother noticed this line on my nose and asked me what I thought I was doing.

I had explained about Linda Harrison and my need to have a fashionable nose. My mother ordered me to cut it out before I did some serious damage and that my nose was perfectly fine.

The nose-pushing fad passed for everybody but Linda Harrison, who ended up with a misshapen tip, a permanent line of demarcation between flesh and cartilage, and flaring nostrils that exposed her nasal hairs and any accumulated dried mucous (boogers) she might have missed in blowing. This was not a good image for a rich girl to project, because it tended to be unattractive to boys. As an adult, I'm sure she had her nose straightened to its original shape by a plastic surgeon.

Despite my brief encounter with the sixth-grade fashion leader, I still preferred girls who had natural ski-jump noses. Later in life, as an adult, I planned to marry a girl who was blessed with a perfect ski-jump nose. At the moment, sitting before the fireplace and projecting the image of myself that nobody else actually recognized (they just thought I was either shy or anti-social), I was in search of the perfect girl with the perfect ski-jump nose and who was also athletic. She had to be out there somewhere --- waiting for me to find her.

As the cheerleader stood aloof from the meaningless chatter of the crowd (Standing aloof was a good sign.), she did seem different to me. Her gray knee sox and the petite quality of her blue sneakers caught my fancy and I thought that maybe I could like her. So, I leaned over and asked some guy sitting next to me, "Who's that?"

"Chrissy Olafson. Do you like her? I'll introduce you."

"No, no that's okay. I might ask her to dance in a little while." Chrissy Olafson. With a name like that, she had to be Swedish, which was another point in her favor. I was attracted to Swedish girls since I had read in a Playboy Magazine that Swedish girls were the sexiest in the world. And Minnesota had as many or more Swedes than Illinois, which was a good sign.

I wondered why all the other kids wanted so desperately to introduce me and bring me into the group. They were so anxious to get me linked to some girl. I could sense their collective psychic force bearing in on me as though they could not stand to not have me classified and labeled for quick social identification and easy reference so they would know immediately how to relate to me and where I fit in.

I remained sitting in the armchair for exactly five more minutes, by the wall clock, then decided the moment had arrived for me to circulate. I needed to get close enough to some of the girls to see (without my glasses) what they looked like and partly so their interest in me would not falter. As I rose and moved about through the crowd, I could feel all eyes upon me.

I danced with two not-so-hot looking girls first so they would be flattered I had acknowledged them and not consider me a snob. In addition, I didn't want to hurt their feelings. I was a good guy, a former Boy Scout, after all, --- better yet, an Eagle Scout, but my achievement was not something I went around announcing and bragging about, especially at a post-game party of teenagers. To say you were an Eagle Scout would be really out-of-place and totally uncool. The knowledge would have to remain part of my mysterious self.

The silent stranger, however, is always a good guy, even to ugly girls. However, this move turned out to be a serious mistake. The unfortunate uglies took severe advantage of me after that. Believing they had a chance for my affections, they lined up standing right there in front of me every song every time I turned around, practically forcing me to ask them to dance. One large bony girl seemed incapable of keeping her breasts from roughly and firmly and deliberately bumping into my hands. Each time it happened, I stupidly apologized as if it were my fault. The girl smiled pleased and nodded at me and kept moving in for the touch. I finally decided that she was horny.

Even though I didn't think of myself as a great fast dancer, my style was still more dynamic than the others. Mainly I overdid the gestures to cover up my lack of true ability. By the time I got around to dancing with Chrissy, I was the sweating center of attraction, which worried me because I had forgotten to saturate my pits with deodorant after taking a shower that evening. I was still going strong when the final record on the stack of 45's ended.

It was not so difficult after that exhibition to eat popcorn, drink apple cider (even though it gave me gas) and to talk socially, but not excessively. A silent stranger had to be silent at least eighty percent of the time or his image would be ruined. Of course, I was among the last to leave the party.

As she told me of her experience with our move, Pam's description startled me into realizing I was not the only one adversely affected by our rootless wandering.

I pictured her as she closed her locker and scuffed down the hall in a three o'clock shroud of loneliness. A popular boy who was in her homeroom class came walking toward her with a friendly smile. Her spirits lifted. "Hi," he said.

"Uuhh."

But he followed his gaze right on past her to the attractive girl mincing along a few steps behind her. Pam's cheeks heated with embarrassment. A hard lump choked her as she pushed through the big glass double doors at the front of the school. Recently familiar, yet unknown faces, children waiting for rides home stood framed against the red brick porch columns. Other young groups milled about in the yard scuffing the shallow powder snow oblivious to her passing.

Where there were no sidewalks, she paralleled the waist high earth embankment lined with barren winter trees and moved on to follow the black-tarred street cracked with frost. She glanced up at a sudden swirl of snowflakes materializing before her eyes against a backdrop of slate gray clouds.

During school, some girls had talked about a party they were going to that night. She had more edifying preoccupations to fill her time than parties, a special book to read when her homework was finished. So, no reason to hurry.

Back in Rockford, she would have been rushing home to get ready for a party too. Then, it was understood that she would be going with Jeff Mulloch. She winced at remembering her discomfort with him when, after each party, she had jumped out of the car and run to the door ahead of him to avoid the inevitable goodnight kiss. A non-kissing relationship was a standard that she had established and that he had tried to overcome. At parties, she had refused to have anything to do with spin-the-bottle or sitting alone with him necking in some corner of a recreation room.

Certain mothers in their former neighborhood would become very worried if their sixth and seventh grade daughters weren't going steady and having at least some preliminary sexual experience necking and petting. Pam never understood why she ended up going to those parties. Both she and her mother had imagined they would be nice social occasions. Now, less than a year later, a cancerous fear and disgust gnawed at her young mind. She wished violently that she hadn't been born a girl. Her peers had thrust sex down her throat until it made her psychologically gag. She kept snatching at her frayed jumbled emotions, trying to reconnect them, but discovered no outlet for her frustration, only tears of depression and self-pity.

Daniel openly and unabashedly told me of his impressions about our move. He didn't have as much of a problem with it as his brother and sister. The lake afforded him a new experience.

On a Saturday morning, right after breakfast, he left the apartment and walked down to the shore. He stepped out onto the frozen sand and watched the wavelets lap against the beach. The lake was long and wide and dotted with small islands from which tall spruce speared raggedly at the winter gray sky. A cold gust shimmered the surface and swept over him wind-milling his wheat blonde hair. He bent down to pull up the elastic of his ever-falling socks. They were mustard and clashed with his dark shoes and trousers. His family teased him good naturedly about his taste and combinations of colors in the clothes he wore. So he wore them deliberately. He picked up a flat stone and threw it far out into the lake, then walked back along the beach access road to the main street on the waterfront. His face glowed from the crisp air, but his brown eyes were sad.

With his family's move to Minnesota, he had been yanked mid-term out of his eighth-grade class in Rockford. He felt adrift on some foreboding sea filled with unseen dangers. While he missed his friends and even his teachers, Daniel found one solace from his fears and loneliness -- fishing. Daniel became obsessed! His new Wayzata home was just a few blocks from Lake Minnetonka, which contained plentiful populations of every warm freshwater fish he had heard of.

Daniel had one other extra-curricular interest -- basketball.

The eighth-grade basketball coach was holding try-outs that night. Daniel planned to go, but the discrepancy between what he was and who he would like to be churned inside with a burning sensation. He had a late birthday, December, and he was not nearly as tall or physically developed as most boys his age. He often wished he were a year back in school. The competition wouldn't be so stiff then and he felt he would be able to excel in both sports and academic studies.

Crossing the street, he slipped on the ice under a thin layer of powder snow. The ice had been like that on the night of his fifth birthday, only the snow had been falling heavily creating a slick wet crust. His mother had had a terrible dream the previous night and had warned him to be extra careful. She had specifically ordered Robbie to keep an eye on him. Still, the accident had happened just as she had dreamed it.

Taking a side street away from the waterfront, Daniel watched the local firemen turn on their hoses over the park playground to flood the area for ice skating. He decided he would have to buy a good hockey stick. Other boys even carried them to school. He had also overheard some of the boys talk about ice fishing on Lake Minnetonka. The ice froze from three to six feet thick, they said. Some people even drove their cars out onto it and set up fishing cabins. He had never fished through a hole in the ice before. He looked forward to the experience with great anticipation.

I finished washing the supper dishes and gave the counter a final swipe with a damp sponge. Bob was away in Madison for the week on business. The three children were silent at their studies. I leaned back against the refrigerator and listened to the long, low howl of the wind and the rattle of ice coated branches. An entire day of house cleaning and grocery shopping had exhausted me. I glanced over at Robbie sitting at the kitchen table swearing under his breath at a difficult chemistry problem. With a weary shrug, I wandered over and sat opposite him. I looked about the living room where Pam and Daniel were draped over chairs and diligently reading. I returned my attention to Robbie. "How was basketball practice?"

"Damn it, Mom!" he shouted. "Will you be quiet! I've got to get these problems done."

The hard lump that never seemed to quite leave my throat during the past two months expanded, choking me as I rose from my chair and hurried away to my bedroom. My muffled sobs drifted out to them. Pam immediately dropped her books and came in to comfort me.

Robbie stalked to his own bedroom where he lay fighting back hot tears of shame. After several minutes of cursing and chastising himself, he came in to apologize to me. "I'm sorry, Mom. I don't have any right to yell at you like that. You can talk as much as you want."

My reddened, tear-stained face remained half-buried in my pillow. "No, No, it's partly my fault too. You children have to study. It's just that it gets so lonely around here all day with none of you to talk to and then, when you come home in the evening, it's still the same. You have your homework and things to do. I'll just have to find something to keep me busy, that's all."

Robbie knelt beside the bed and stroked my hair. "I'm sorry. I love you."

"I know you do. I know all of you do. I'll be all right. I'm all right now."

The following week, I enrolled at the University of Minnesota, taking classes in child psychology, children's literature, sociology, and physical geography. Being an intelligent woman and a diligent worker, I discovered that the intellectual stimulation excited and motivated me to further goals for personal achievement, particularly that someday, I would earn a bachelor's degree in education and a teaching credential.

To add to my distress, I observed Pam continuing to gain weight. I compelled her to go on a rigid diet that she would violate behind my back at every opportunity. If truth be told, I really didn't want to see her maturing into a young woman. I wanted to keep her a thin girl. Her soft flesh of puberty disturbed me.

To escape studying chemistry, Robbie attempted to write one act plays for his personal glorification. His favorite placed him in a situation for which he imagined himself widely acclaimed for his intense portrayal of a man trapped in a cave during the dead of winter. He actually let me read the play. To emphasize the symbolism of the ordeal, he titled his dramatic work *The Cave,* although he toyed with the more intriguing title, *The Dead of Winter*. He liked the double meaning of the word Dead.

Daniel went off fishing alone on a regular basis at the end of each school day and sometimes almost entirely disappeared on weekends except to come home for dinner. He took his lunch with him.

Chapter 30

Daniel's Ear

When Daniel told me one day after school that his woodshop teacher, Mr. Stapleton, had jerked him out of his seat by pulling on his left ear and that his ear was hurting, I went on the warpath. The next morning, I strode into the school principal's office with Daniel at my side and said to the secretary, "I'm Mrs. Wenger. I'm here to report the abuse of my son in the classroom by Mr. Stapleton. I'm bringing a charge of child abuse against him."

The secretary, a middle-aged matron, looked at me aghast, struggled up from her chair and waddled into the principal's office. I heard her mumble something I couldn't discern, then return to the counter. "Mr. Rafelson will see you right away. Please come in."

Daniel and I walked around the end of the counter. Mr. Rafelson rose from his desk to greet us with a concerned expression as we entered. I immediately didn't care for his mud-colored mustache and black-rim glasses. His dark eyes stared at me through thick lenses as though I were some kind of insect. I figured he would take the teacher's side. I didn't trust him. "Mrs. Wenger, I'm Mr. Rafelson." He offered to shake my hand, a gesture I ignored. "I understand you have a complaint against one of our teachers, Mr. Stapleton."

"He brutally pulled Daniel out of his chair by the ear and may have caused internal damage. I will be taking him to see the doctor this morning. I want my complaint to go on record and be forewarned, if there is evidence of injury, I will hire a lawyer and file charges against Mr. Stapleton for student abuse. I'm studying to get a degree in teaching. There is a law against teachers physically punishing students, especially like that."

"I am very sorry, Mrs. Wenger, and I sincerely apologize. Punishment of students in that manner is not allowed in my school, regardless of the behavior. Daniel, may I ask what you were doing?"

"I was just talking to somebody."

"That's certainly not anything unusual. I will speak with Mr. Stapleton."

"I understand a teacher can be fired for doing something like that to a student," I said.

"I can assure you I will investigate the situation," said Mr. Rafelson, "and I will deal with Mr. Stapleton. Please inform me of anything your doctor might tell you."

"Oh, I will. Believe me. I will. I entrust my children to the teachers in your school."

"I understand, Mrs. Wenger. I'm sure all parents share your feelings about their children."

"I'm going to his class and give him a piece of my mind."

"Please, don't do that, Mrs. Wenger. It would likely be embarrassing for your son. Let me talk with Mr. Stapleton before I arrange a meeting between the two of you. I would like to hear what your doctor has to say first."

"It doesn't matter what he has to say. Mr. Stapleton deserves to at least be reprimanded by you."

"Believe me, Mrs. Wenger, he and I will have a serious discussion."

"Daniel will not be returning to school today."

"I'll have my secretary notify his classroom teachers."

"In the event I don't confront Mr. Stapleton, I expect a report from you as to what he had to say and what you are going to do about him."

"Oh, you'll be able to talk to him all right, but here in my office, not in the classroom. He owes Daniel and you an apology. I will definitely arrange that."

Two days later, I still had not heard from Mr. Rafelson. Fortunately, the doctor had confirmed there was no damage to Daniel's ear. I still wanted to know from the school principal that he had disciplined the shop teacher. Daniel told me his full name was Harry Stapleton. Daniel also told me the principal must have said something to the shop teacher, because Stapleton completely ignored him, wouldn't even look at him.

I would not settle for a lack of explanation and for being ignored by Mr. Rafelson. When I called to speak with him, his secretary always told me he was busy. So I just showed up in his office again unannounced. His door was closed, and the secretary told me he was having a conference. I told her I would wait. Ten minutes later, a tall, lean, sharp-featured man came out of the office. He had straight red hair that reminded me of my nemesis back in Rockford, Nina's ex-husband, Charles Gibson. His blue eyes stared at me through brown rim glasses with instant recognition. From how Daniel had described him, I was certain he was the shop teacher. Without a word, he hurried around the end of the counter and rushed out the door.

"Who was that?" I asked the secretary.

"Mr. Stapleton."

"The shop teacher?"

"Yes."

"So, Mr. Rafelson is free to see me now."

She glanced at her switchboard. "I'm sorry. He's on the phone."

"Would you inform him that I am waiting."

"After he gets off the phone."

I took a seat on the waiting bench. Fifteen minutes later, the office door opened, and Mr. Rafelson came out, clearly surprised to see me.

"Mrs. Wenger, I didn't know you were here. I've been trying to reach you at home on the phone. Mr. Stapleton has received a reprimand and has been advised that he needs to find appropriate ways to keep his eighth-grade shop class under control. He told me what he did was unthinking and that one time, in anger, when the boys were talking out of turn, he singled out Daniel and pulled him by the ear. He is extremely sorry."

"Lucky for him there wasn't any damage," I snarled.

"I'm very glad that Daniel is okay."

"He shouldn't even be in the shop class," I said. "He's not a general student. Daniel has enjoyed a solid 'B' average ever since the fifth grade."

"Actually, Daniel told me he elected the shop class in hope he could learn some skills working with his hands, something he apparently has not been exposed to in his other school. All his other classes this spring term are prep-track. When he arrived mid-term in the fall, we had to enroll him in a few general classes due to a lack of openings in some of the prep classes."

"Believe me, he's brighter than those others in the shop class."

"I'm sure he is, Mrs. Wenger. He gives every indication that he is. He'll be enrolled for prep in the coming fall."

"If we're even here."

"Oh, you're planning to move?"

"Not just planning. We will be moving," I said.

"Be sure to let the enrollment counselor know."

"I will."

"Where are you moving to, if I might ask?"

"California."

"I'm sure you won't miss the Minnesota winters. We'll miss your son, Robbie. He's quite a basketball player."

"Thank you."

"Is there anything else?" Mrs. Wenger.

"No, I'll be going. Thank you."

I turned and left. I didn't have occasion to speak with him again.

Even though Daniel and I were done with Harry Stapleton, Harry's red-headed nephew, Roger, was not. Daniel told me that Roger had been held back one year. He was a big tough, blue-collar kid, not in prep, who lived in Oakwood, a lower economic area next to Wayzata.

On the last day of school, he and his Oakwood buddy told Daniel they would get back at him for "embarrassing" his uncle. They nearly succeeded in catching him but, in desperation, Daniel ran all the way home when the bell rang and beat them to our house by a couple of minutes.

There they were facing the park and the school with their backs toward him when he emerged onto our second-floor balcony carrying his BB gun. He fired a shot in the air and called to them to get their attention, prompting them to turn around and face him. They shouted at him to come down and "meet" them. He told them no thanks and walked back inside.

After only one year, Bob had discovered that the northern regional market for his employer's company offered little opportunity for expansion to warrant his attempts to develop it. There were more competing aerospace companies in the Midwest and in California than in Minnesota. The sharp decline in his sales commissions depressed him and his anxiety grew.

I suffered from the cold and dampness of the winter months because of my rheumatism. So the entire family was pleased to hear Bob announce one evening that we would be moving to sunny California in June, at the end of the school year. We all believed the opportunities and fulfillment of our dreams would be discovered in The Golden West.

III

The Golden West

Chapter 31

Smog

Numb with despair, we stared out the windows as the car raced along through the frightening confusion of traffic. Upon entering the regional basin, we had been in stark sunlight. Now we were inextricably bound in the churning mass of cheap housing, fast food franchises, rushing people, an incessant rumbling viscera of freeway systems, and exhaust pipes spewing carbon monoxide fumes. Looking upwards we saw only an occasional shabby palm tree bowing to intertwining wires and roof-top antennae and acres of industry belching smoke into a dirty yellow-brown poisonous cloud hovering low over the endless confused urban sprawl that comprised the metropolis called Los Angeles.

We spent the remainder of the day recuperating by a motel swimming pool. The following morning, we began to search for a new place to live, a tiresome, thankless ritual. After many hours of driving and inquiries, we discovered we had to settle, as usual, for conditions far below my hopes and expectations.

The apartment was located on the ground level of a fifty-four unit two story complex. It provided two small bedrooms, one bathroom, a tiny living room, and a small kitchen-dinette combination. Thin gray carpeting matched the barren mood of the beige walls constructed of thin plasterboard that allowed the noises and flushing toilets from the immediate neighbors on either side and overhead to be easily heard. With the addition of furniture and drapes, the atmosphere of the close living quarters grew increasingly claustrophobic. Daniel and Robbie shared one bedroom and Pam took the other, while Bob and I slept on an uncomfortable rollaway couch in the dinette.

The local high school was two blocks away in one direction. Set against the dry purple San Gabriel Mountain range, the Santa Anita Racetrack was two blocks in the other direction. Throughout the day, we could hear the announcer's voice calling the races over the sound system.

Bob responded as though he heard a siren call. I hated to acknowledge that he liked gambling, probably influenced by his success at poker in the jungles of New Guinea during World War II. To me, gambling was a lowlife addiction. Playing card games for toothpicks with the kids when they were young children was one thing. Gambling at the track was entirely unacceptable. Our proximity to Santa Anita went from annoyance to agitation to fury.

He had been studying racing forms on Sunday afternoon and jotting copious notes. Robbie was practicing the piano in preparation for the high school talent show tryouts. Pam was doing homework in her bedroom, and Daniel had gone over to the school basketball courts to shoot baskets. I had just finished a load of laundry and was getting ready to iron clothes in our tiny living room when Bob spoke up from the rollout couch that doubled as our bed.

"I figured out their system. It's a code they've devised using the horses' names. All the races are rigged. The jockeys are in on it. I can pick who's going to win and who's going to place."

Robbie came to the end of the song he was playing and listened.

"Look here," Bob continued and stood up from the couch to show me.

"I am not interested and neither should you be." I turned away from him and began vigorously ironing one of his shirts.

"I was thinking of going over to the track this afternoon."

"No, do not get started with that. We can't afford for you to lose money we need to live on. We have groceries to buy and bills to pay."

"But I'm not going to lose. I'm going to win. I've broken their code. I read the clues. I can win every bet I make."

"If you think you have money you can squander away, why are we living in this atrocious apartment?"

"This is only temporary. You know very well prices out here are not like in the Midwest. The cost of living is much higher. Anything else we really like is too expensive. We can't afford them. We're in a holding position. As soon as I establish myself with aerospace customers here, we can find a house to rent."

"Not here in Arcadia. The smog is horrible. Some days, we can't even see the mountains. And the kids and I constantly have sore throats and Pam has trouble breathing. I have trouble breathing. We all have trouble breathing. We're breathing in poison every day."

"There are days when the wind blows it out over the ocean."

"How often does that happen? Not often enough. It is not healthy for us to live here in Los Angeles. We need to move at the first opportunity."

"You need to give me a little time," Bob started for the door. "We can look. We'll take a drive. The man I'm replacing here in Southern California is retiring. He's handing over his customers to me. It's a transition. He lives in Palos Verdes. It's on the coast."

"I'll bet it's a place for millionaires."

"He has done well. He owns a sailing yacht and a house worth a half-million dollars."

"Can we expect as much from you?"

"I can do just as well or better. We'll take a drive up the coast. See what's north of L.A."

"Do you have a limit how much you will gamble?" I asked.

"I always do. I know when to walk away. That's why I did so well in New Guinea. If I started losing, I folded and left the game. I know I'm going to win at the track. Here, look at this," he coaxed Robbie off the piano bench and motioned to sit next to him on the couch.

Fully aware of my disapproval, Robbie shot me a quick glance of apology.

"These are the names of the horses for the first race today," said Bob. "I've completed an analysis for every race. But look at this. Once I figured it out, it became so obvious how the races are fixed. Here, look at this sequence I've deciphered from the original list. Northern Lights is Daddy's Dawn. Delilah's Desire is the Dream Catcher. Flight Leader is a Flaming Ace. Magic Moment is Taylor's Choice. Ruby's Son is Rise to Glory, who brings us to Jackpot. Jackpot will win. He'll be first place. Rise To Glory will come in second and Taylor's choice will be third. So I will bet accordingly. Don't you see it? You do understand the logic and relative positions of the names."

"I doubt that they fix the races, Dad," said Robbie. "There are laws against it."

"The machine behind racing makes up its own rules. The commission laws are just a façade. I know I'm right and I'll prove it today and I'll keep winning and no one will be the wiser. This is how I can supplement our income. I can make as much and more money betting than I do working."

"You're the one who needs to wise up, Bob," I said. "You're being delusional."

His hurt accusatory stare during the past several years had become a habitual expression in response to my criticisms of his choices and behavior. He couldn't argue with me, because I was right. I could not be swayed. His silent blunt denial like a petulant child was his way of shutting me out, which was what he was doing to me now.

After he spent the entire afternoon at the track, I imagined him gambling away everything we had; but he walked through the door with a triumphant grin and dropped a stack of bills on the dining room table.

"I won eight hundred dollars," he announced. "My system works."

"Did you lose any?" I asked.

"No, I was very conservative in placing bets. I was testing my system. Now that I know it works, I can place larger bets."

"Don't you dare," I warned him.

"Mary, it's all right. I know what I'm doing."

"You're risking our livelihood is what you're doing."

"This is my relaxation, my recreation."

"I thought you played golf for relaxation and recreation."

"In good time. There's no point in discussing this further. You're not in the right frame of mind."

"I will never condone your gambling. You're risking our future. You know that."

Shaking his head, he sat down on the couch and opened up the newspaper to block me out, a technique he had learned when Robbie was small and claimed to be reading cereal boxes at the breakfast table and Pam accused him of hiding from her.

The next weekend, Bob lost one-hundred dollars. "But I had the good sense to walk away," he explained. "I slightly misinterpreted the clues. Afterwards, I could see where I went wrong. That's how we learn, from our mistakes."

"But you don't learn from your mistakes, Bob. Where you went wrong is engaging in such absurd behavior in the first place."

"I have no doubt I can win it back and a great deal more."

"I have no doubt that you had better not try."

"It's just a game, Mary, a puzzle. It's no different than doing a crossword puzzle."

"It doesn't cost money to do a crossword puzzle."

"Believe me they can't outsmart me on this."

"They already have, Bob. They've conned you into going there in the first place. Gambling is a disease. You've got to stay away. You're hooked just like any other drug."

"I'm not hooked. I'm completely rational and in charge and responsible for what I'm doing. I'm using logic to beat them."

"You haven't beaten them. They've beaten you. You were just lucky the first time. The second time, you lost one hundred dollars. That could buy a weeks' worth of groceries."

Another incident that pushed me to the edge was an alcoholic neighbor upstairs. He and his wife and young teenage son had just moved in only a week ago. We could hear him come home drunk every night and shout at them. We knew he beat her, because sometimes, we heard her crying and screaming at him to stop.

One afternoon, I saw her and her son carrying bags of groceries up the balcony steps to their apartment. She appeared to have bruises on her attractive face and ducked her head to avoid looking at me. I couldn't place her ethnicity, but she had burnt reddish brunette hair and her body was a little chunky in a plain dress. Her son had close-cropped dark hair and an anxious suffering expression. I instantly felt sorry for them. They obviously didn't want to talk to me, although I'm sure they knew I lived in the apartment below them.

Bob complained to the apartment manager and asked him to speak to the resident. The manager said he didn't interfere in renters' personal lives.

Shouting and raging at Robbie to shut up, the father beat a chair against the ceiling when Robbie practiced the piano at night, especially the loud dynamic *Malaguena*. Bob cautioned Robbie to play quietly, but the drunkard came running down and pounded at our door. When Bob answered, I rushed across the room and positioned myself between the two men.

The man from upstairs was taller and heavier than Bob. He reminded me of the Italian mine workers from my childhood back in Pennsylvania. He could easily punch out Bob, who wouldn't know how to defend himself against such a raging lunatic. I, on the other hand, was spitting fire. I firmly told the man, "You lay a hand on me, I'll scratch your eyes out. Bob, go call the police. This man is threatening us with bodily harm."

Always soft when it came to a conflict, Bob said, "I think we can discuss this and resolve the situation peaceably."

"You tell that fuckin' kid of yours not to play the fuckin' piano at night when I'm home. If he don't stop, I'll trash your fuckin' piano and break his fuckin' fingers."

"Bob, I said call the police. Now he's threatening Robbie."

"Sir," Bob spoke from behind me over my shoulder. I sensed him trembling with defensive anger, as well. "Mister, get control of yourself. Go back to your apartment. We can hear you beat your wife. If the police come, you're going to be arrested and go to jail. You need to calm down."

Shaking his head, the man backed away and I immediately slammed and locked the door. I turned to Bob. "I refuse to live in a ghetto. Do you understand? I refuse to live in a ghetto."

"This is a stressful moment for all of us. Let's just calm down. He's just an irrational person. Arcadia isn't a ghetto. It's a community of professionals."

"Then what are we doing here, Bob? You and I aren't professionals of anything."

"Listen. He's gone. I'll talk to the manager again tomorrow. He will have to address this situation."

To my relief, the lunatic and his poor wife and son moved out the next day.

By the time the following spring arrived, we all agreed we did not want to live in Los Angeles. The ideal location and atmosphere was not to be found there for the money Bob was earning and what we were willing and able to pay. For another reason, I wanted us to move away from the vicinity of the racetrack. Its location was just too convenient and encouraged Bob's addictive small stakes gambling. A two hour drive up the coast to Santa Barbara rekindled my hopes.

As we came over the last hill along the coastal highway approaching Santa Barbara, we fell instantly in love with the seaside tropical garden town. The Mediterranean Riviera rose in steps up the grassy foothills overshadowed by deep chaparral green and purple hues of the Santa Ynez mountains. Startling yellow and orange and blue wildflowers blanketed sun swept slopes and the vast chameleon blues and greens of the sea shimmered to the Channel Islands and the far horizon. It was the California of our vision, of our dreams.

We wanted passionately to make our home there. Bob did say he would not be happy about the distance between Santa Barbara and Los Angeles but decided he could deal with the commute for the sake of living in such a beautiful setting.

Two months later, following Robbie's graduation as a high school senior, we moved out of the hole in Arcadia where we had lived for the past year. Late at night, Bob brought us to the house he rented, a single-story California ranch made with an eye to outdoor living with patios in both the front and back. Every room was large. The living room boasted a beamed cathedral ceiling and a tall picture window overlooking the Pacific Ocean moonlight from where the house stood high on a mesa. Robbie was the first to praise his father's choice, as the family stood together staring out over the nocturnal tropical island paradise.

"Man, Dad, you really hit on it this time."

Chapter 32

Dreams

I loved Santa Barbara. Robbie began his freshman year at the university as a Zoology major to go into premed. I occasionally saw him on campus since I enrolled full time and worked toward getting my degree in education. Pam and Daniel attended a local high school, San Marcos; and Bob drove the commute to Los Angeles twice a week, coming home on Wednesday nights and for the weekend.

We loved the house on Cliff Drive overlooking the harbor filled with private boats. We walked on the rarely crowded mile long beach in the salty air and swam in the ocean. At least Bob and the kids swam. I didn't feel comfortable doing anything more than wade in the surf and the water was too cold for me. I enjoyed watching sailboats skimming back and forth out in the bay, the keening seagulls and squadrons of brown pelicans coasting by overhead. I enjoyed walking the downtown streets lined with shops built of white adobe and orange tile roofs and mingling with tourists and college students.

With the exception of morning fog that burnt off by ten, we were drenched with sunshine and blessed with blue skies. There was no smog. We lived in a virtual paradise. Wherever we looked, tall palms, eucalyptus trees, and climbing bursts of red and purple bougainvillea on walls and in gardens and the sweet scent of jasmine and orange blossoms surrounded us. But just before the lease was about to run out, Bob's company reassigned him to San Francisco and we were forced, once again, to move, this time to an apartment in Menlo Park near San Francisco in Northern California.

***

Disgust and frustration gnawed at Bob's innards like some abrasive flux as he studied the income tax form. Putting down his pencil, he stared across the room and was silent for a long time before speaking. "As of right now, I owe the government twelve hundred dollars in taxes."

Daniel looked up from his homework at the opposite end of the table. "I thought they took that out of your pay."

"They do but I still owe them money. I'm supposed to set it aside and budget for it, but how can I when we're living beyond our means as it is. We just have to start being practical."

"You'd better see about getting a loan, then." I set aside my iron to fold a shirt.

"That isn't necessary. There's no need to increase our debt when we have the money to account for this."

"That money in the bank is for one thing only," I insisted.

"Now, Mary, before we start on that, let's get ourselves in the proper frame of mind to discuss it. This has to be viewed in a practical sense."

"There's nothing to discuss, Bob. Just take out a loan and that solves the problem."

"No, it only increases it. We're in debt enough as it is."

"Well, you'd better find some other way then. Anyhow, don't bring me into it. It's your problem, not mine."

"It's your problem as well as mine. It's ours together."

"That money is not to be touched. Let's stop talking now so the children can study."

"We have a problem to contend with here and we're going to have to decide how to face it."

"I already told you, take out a loan."

"No, that's out of the question."

"So is the other."

"Now, Mary."

"Don't now Mary me. Just don't start on that."

"We have to face reality."

"That money is for something far more important than paying our income tax." Anger tinged my voice. "Don't touch it. I warn you. Don't touch it."

"Warn?"

"Yes, warn – If you use that money for other than what it's intended, I'll sue you for divorce."

He looked at me askance. "You're talking nonsense again."

"I'm not talking nonsense. I'm telling you. This is no idle threat."

"Don't you realize the position you're putting me in? If we continue at this rate, we're not going to make any progress. We'll just keep sliding backwards. Within the next two years, we're going to have to finance the college educations of three children, not just one. Where do you think that's going to leave us?"

"I'll not lower myself," I said. "I absolutely refuse to lower myself."

Lower yourself? Where do you get the idea that you'll be lowering yourself? We have three fine intelligent children. You have a good sound education. We all live moral and decent lives. We have good tastes and ideals and our health and happiness as a family. We're far better off than most people."

"I refuse to discuss the matter any further."

"Mary, will you please just for once get behind me in making a decision and help me out. You're always fighting me. Be reasonable for a change."

"Get behind you? Be reasonable? Good Lord, Bob, just how much do you think a woman can stand? You've moved us all over the country. You put us in that little shack in Minnesota and then nothing but rents and apartments ever since. And look at the children. They don't have any friends. They don't live in a home where they can bring friends and feel some sense of pride. They don't have roots, just because you couldn't stand the bosses you had to work with. Oh sure, you're too nice and they were in a position to step on you. And that's what I can't understand. You letting them do it. You're meant for something better."

"I did it for us . . . for all of us. It wasn't just my bosses. I've been trying to get ahead ever since the war. And I'm not in something better and maybe never will be. You have to realize that. The war took a chunk out of my life that can't be replaced. I'm not in my twenties anymore. We have to go on from where we are – now."

"Well, I still say this is your problem."

"If matters like this don't involve us both, then why did you marry me?"

"Why? I married you because you were nice, a handsome guy, that's all. You weren't like most other men. We really shouldn't have been married. We're too different from each other. I'm too pushy. Robbie wouldn't be in the failing position he's in at school now if it weren't for me. And you wouldn't be, either. I'm not good for you – any of you. Pam hates me for harping at her all the time about food and Daniel for not acting more like an adult. All he cares about is hiking in the hills. I'm just not good for you."

"Did you really mean that, what you said? You married me because you thought I was *nice*? That's all?"

"Yes, I meant it."

Bob rose and quietly left the kitchen for the bedroom and closed the door. I suddenly had to move and find another space, another location. I walked firmly, but with inward unsteadiness, into the living room, plunged into an armchair and stared stonily into the room's space. Pam came over from where she had been studying on the couch and kneeled at my feet. Taking my hand, she tenderly smoothed it.

"Mom?"

"Yes, dear?"

Pam spoke gently, uncertain where she could go with her words, yet wanting to probe and provoke thought where she had no access to who her mother was. “Daddy was awfully hurt.”

“I know,” she sighed. “I didn’t want to do that to him. It just came out.”

“Don’t you think – well, couldn’t you maybe just try to make it all right again?”

“How?”

“Well –” The turnaround threw Pam, to be asked for an answer a daughter might well ask her mother instead one day. “Oh, Mom, I want you to be happy. That’s all that’s necessary. I wish that war hadn’t come. This never would’ve happened if Dad could have stayed on in college instead of going away and coming back too tired. Nobody can be blamed entirely that everything’s not the way we want it.”

“You would all be better off without me around. I make everyone unhappy. Your father and I never should have gotten married.”

“Mom, don’t say that. We need you. We love you. And you and Dad love each other. I know.” Pam stood and put her arms around my neck and kissed me on the forehead. “My little mommy, you’re so pretty. Please don’t think like that ever again. And, Mom, what you were talking about before – sure, we’d like to live in a bigger house and be settled down and have roots. Sure we’d like a real place of our own to call home like back in Edgebrook. Times are different now. It’s not gonna kill us to live here. We’re only unhappy when you’re unhappy. Home is supposed to be where the family is. Anyplace can be home. You don’t have to have a real nice place to hold up your head. You want it really more than we do. I mean just so you won’t be ashamed to have people visit you and all that. Besides, this is a nice place as far as most people care.”

“Pam, what do you want to do after you’re married someday? Live in apartments and rented homes? Is that what you want your children to have? You think this moving around hasn't hurt you, but would you want your children to go through it someday?"

"Well – no."

"What do you want?"

"I want a few acres of land and horses for them to ride, and one's going to play the violin and one the piano, and one is going to like art and singing and dancing. Maybe they all will. I want them to be able to come home to a – to a homey warm home that makes them want to cry for gladness when they come back from vacations. And I want my children to learn good manners and to love one another. We'll all sit together in the dining room for dinner and talk and be happy with one another. And my husband – that sounds odd – he'll come home every night and we'll sit around the fireplace with the children and eat popcorn and apples sometimes and read books to the children like *Robinson Crusoe* and *Treasure Island* and we'll play music on a hi-fi. And I want to live close to you, Mom, so my children will know their gramma and grandpa. I want you to have a lot of influence on them. Oh, Mom, I know what you mean. I love you so much." She kissed my hand.

"How do you suppose you're going to get all that? It seems so simple and natural to talk about having, but even ideals cost money. I don't think I'm materialistic, at least not in the hard sense."

"No, Mom, you're not. You're the greatest idealist that ever lived. You're even romantic. Keep fighting. Don't let anyone beat you down, or anything, or us. You're strong and you're right."

Bob came out of the bedroom to the front hall closet, grabbed his coat and left with a slam of the front door. Pam leaped up, snatched her coat and followed him. I started after her, then stopped. I could see them through the front window. He was walking rapidly, just crossing the street under the light down the block. She called out. "Dad! Dad! Wait! Wait for me!"

He didn't stop. Pam sprinted and caught up to him.

Later that night, she told me what they had said.

"I can understand a lot of things about her," he said, "but I would never have believed that she could say a thing like that."

I told him he was wrong. You didn't mean it and he knew you didn't. It's just that you both have to deal with things, and you don't feel you're getting ahead fast enough. But you really didn't mean it. It was just a stupid thing that just came out because you aren't happy about things right now."

"He said it always ends this way. We just can't ever discuss these matters without letting emotions enter into it. He said you're so idealistic and you don't seem to realize what you already have accomplished. He knows what you want but he doesn't have the money or the likelihood of getting it. He said he just comes up against this wall.

"I asked him if it would make any difference if he had to repay a loan or replenish the savings account."

"He said if he takes out a loan, he has to pay interest. He doesn't see why you should discriminate with the method."

"It's a matter of principle with me. That money is our only hope of having a real honest to goodness home again like in Edgebrook. I'm afraid I'll never see that money again.

Chapter 33

Psychosomatic Syndrome

I stared with anxiety at the ominous lump protruding under the skin of my right arm. For two weeks, a severe pain in my throat had made it difficult to swallow, and now the lump. A racing fever drained my energy so that I felt unable to function, yet I continued to get up each day, prepare breakfast for the family, then go off and teach school for eight hours, return home to prepare supper, correct papers and do my lesson plans for the following day, iron clothes and finally return to bed where I should have stayed in the beginning. I averaged only four to six hours of sleep each night, other than on the weekends.

Then there was Dad's accident. My sister, Nina, had sent me a letter about his heart attack that occurred while he was painting his house. He had fallen from a ladder. Mum said that he was recovering, but, in addition, had to have an operation to straighten a displaced septum in his nose.

Growing increasingly aware of my ailments and discomfort, my family encouraged me to see a doctor but I tacitly refused by never getting around to making an appointment. Then one morning I wasn't able to get out of bed. The alarm clock rang, and I reached out a hand to silence it as usual. When I threw back the covers and slid my legs around to a sitting position, the room whirled before my eyes causing me to ease back down to the pillow again. A slight moan escaped me and Bob, who had been emerging from sleep for the past ten minutes, glanced over at me.

"Is something wrong?"

"No – no, I'll be all right in a minute."

He sat up abruptly. "You look awfully pale." He touched my forehead. "I think we'd better take your temperature." He slipped out of bed, went quickly into the bathroom and returned with the thermometer. "Here, hold this under your tongue."

I lay there half-conscious for three minutes while he stroked my hand. Then he removed the thermometer from my mouth. "One hundred and five. I'm calling the doctor to make an appointment for you to see him today." He hurried to the kitchen phone.

My dreams had been filled with witnessing my father in his final convulsive death throes. At Thanksgiving, I had received another letter from Nina with the message Dad was dying of cancer. My thoughts dwelled on him constantly and I could have no peace of mind until Bob and the kids and I returned to Illinois for a visit during the Christmas break.

Dad's face was badly scarred from the radiation treatments and his once twinkling blue eyes were rapidly going blind. His suffering did not prevent him from happily gathering us all into his strong arms. Robbie commented to me he never forgot his Grampa's warm strength and how he hugged him rough and hard like a wrestler. It was the last time the kids saw him alive.

By spring, the cancer had metastasized and taken over his body. He had been moved to the hospital. I went back to Rockford alone to be with him during his last days. My brother, John, met me at O'Hare Field in Chicago. We said very little on our silent pensive drive to Rockford.

After a three-week vigil, my nerves were frayed to the breaking point at my helplessness to do anything for Dad. A doctor entered the room and stood looking at me sympathetically. "Why don't you go home? There's nothing you can do," he said.

I glared at him. "You do something for him! He tries to talk to me! At least operate on his throat so he can talk!"

"He wouldn't be able to talk anyway," Mrs. Wenger. "Why do you want to prolong his suffering? Let him go as soon as he can."

"Go to hell! What do you think I am?"

"At the moment, I think you're acting like a bitch. Have you seen yourself in the mirror lately?"

I rose numbly and went into the bathroom. My hair was stringy and dirty. My face hung haggard with exhaustion. With bowed head, I slowly returned to the doctor. "I'm going but I'll be back."

"Go home and get some sleep. Clean yourself up."

At Dad's bedside, I placed my hand in his and gently pressed in communication. His wrinkled aged hand slowly closed around mine. I watched in agony, as his mouth and throat moved in a futile attempt to speak to me. There was no sound, only the stench of decaying flesh. His unseeing eyes had closed long ago. His abdomen formed a distended bubble of gas under the sterile, white sheets. His thin white hair had grown long and shaggy and then shed itself in mangy patches.

Two nurses entered to change his bedding. They let his head fall against the steel frame of the bed, sending a shudder through his pain-racked body. I stepped to the other side of the bed and cushioned him from their rough handling. Then the nurses were gone, leaving us alone again. I sat down, took his hand and gazed at his face where oozing pus and mucous had dried and caked around his eyes and in his ears, nose, and throat.

I wept. Why did his life have to end like this? He lived a good life. He didn't deserve this. "My God," I silently prayed. "Help him. See who he is. See what he has done – made us our lives. See where he came from. Don't let this happen."

Another week passed. I held Dad's tongue down with a depressor stick so he wouldn't choke as the convulsions started, but I couldn't remain doing so.

"Take the stick. Take the stick," I gasped to Nina standing nearby. I just made it to the bathroom and had violent diarrhea as I heard his death rattle. Feeling faint, I left the hospital room in a cold sweat and took an elevator to the first floor to find a phone booth. Leaning against the glass door, I picked up the receiver, put in a quarter from my purse, and dialed the operator.

"I would like to place a long-distance call collect to San Mateo, California." When Bob came on the line, my voice trembled. "Dad just passed away. Will you come and get me now. I need you."

Following the funeral, Bob bought a small car and we started the long drive back to California. My children found me greatly subdued upon my arrival. Bob had temporarily rented a house in San Mateo, on the San Francisco Peninsula. I didn't care for the house. It was just another ticky-tacky box in a development, but I was moderate, not vehement, in expressing my disapproval.

He asked, "How do you like it?"

"Do you want me to lie?" I responded.

A month later, we found a spacious home in Menlo Park and moved there.

The summer dragged slowly and dully for us all except Robbie. He found a job working in a curtain rod assembly line company (of all things). In September, he left to return to Santa Barbara. I achieved my goal of securing a teaching position in an elementary school in San Carlos. Pam and Daniel returned to their senior and junior years in high school, respectively.

In my dream, as I watched my Dad die, the pain in my own throat increased to an intolerable degree. I tried to speak, to communicate with him as he had tried to do with me, but there was no sound, only the futile effort. Then he was gone, being lowered into the dark earth. I tried to follow him, but the grave was suddenly covered over, preventing me, until the pain in my throat started and the lump formed in my arm. Then I could see him again. Always he was trying to talk to me and I to him, but there was never any sound.

I screamed to myself, "I should have been there. I never would have let him see that doctor in the first place. He didn't know what he was doing. He left that report on his desk for a month." I had unleashed my wrath on my sisters for letting that happen. They were the ones who lived nearby. It could have been prevented if they had monitored and kept after the doctor. It was all that doctor's fault. It was all his fault. We never should have moved. I never should have agreed. It was all my fault. It was all my fault.

"Mary – Mary –"

"Mmmuhh –" My eyes opened slowly.

"You were dreaming. I'm taking you to see the doctor this morning. Do you want me to help you to the bathroom?"

"No, I can make it myself."

He helped me to a sitting position. "Feel pretty dizzy?"

I nodded, then slowly stood with Bob supporting me.

"There, just take it real easy."

As I entered the doctor's office, he motioned for me to take a chair. For the past week I had been subjected to numerous tests and had been carefully examined by several specialists. He cleared his throat.

"Mrs. Wenger, we are unable to determine any physiological cause or causes to account for your symptoms. At first, we suspected cancer, but tests don't bear that out, fortunately. There was nothing out of the ordinary in your blood tests except a slight anemia and a higher-than-normal white cell count in conjunction with your fever, but we can correct that. My conclusion at this point is that there might be some psychosomatic connection with your father's recent death. I want you to stop in and see me once every day for the next three weeks and I'll give you one of these pills. They're cortisone and will help kill the pain. In addition, before you leave today, I'll give you an injection for thyroid deficiency. Are there any questions you'd like to ask?"

"No."

"Very well, will you wait here a moment." He rose and left the office.

I pressed the lump and winced at the flash of pain that electrified my arm.

The doctor started me on three cortisone tablets each day, then gradually decreased the dosage during the following three weeks until I was taking only a half tablet. I continued to teach school during that period until the day I was taken off cortisone altogether.

I woke feeling restless and went about fixing breakfast and readying myself according to my regular routine. As I drove from the house and joined the morning traffic, my nervousness increased so that I found it difficult to concentrate on driving.

Thirty minutes later, I sat in hot silence watching the children file into my classroom as the bell rang for what seemed to me an endless duration. And the children were so incredibly slow in taking their seats. Finally, the bell stopped and the class quieted. I felt the muscles in my legs shudder as I rose. "Will you please pass your homework forward."

The rattle of the incoming papers caused my skin to prickle. I placed my hands on the edge of the desk to steady myself. When the papers were all in, I said, "Today – today, we're going to – learn about the base ten. So open –" I hesitated. "Open –" My entire body shook with spasms breaking into a cold sweat. I slowly moved away from the desk and walked unsteadily to the door amid worried buzzing from the class.

The school nurse helped me to lie down on the cot and the principal was notified. "You'd better go home for the rest of the day. You have a very high fever," he said. "Shall I call your husband, or do you think you can drive all right?"

"I can make it all right. I just have to lie here a minute."

"I'll call a substitute immediately."

As I drove home, the oncoming cars kept swerving over into my lane honking at me. Nobody was home. Tearing off my clothes, I barely made it to the bathroom and retched. I lay naked and moaning on the floor, clutching my cramped abdomen. By the end of the day, the withdrawal symptoms had diminished, and I slept a restless sleep.

***

"I want to go to Colorado," I told the family. "I just want to get away for a while. I want to go to Colorado for a vacation . . . alone. I want to be alone."

Bob and the kids stared at me in silent empathy.

"When do you think you'd like to go?" Bob finally spoke.

"As soon as possible. I just want to get away from here."

"You don't have to be on the defensive. None of us are trying to stop you."

"I'd go even if you did."

"I'll call and make a plane reservation for you," he said. "How about Wednesday?"

"Nobody's saying anything. I can see how anxious you all are for me to leave."

"Now, that's not true and you know it."

"Isn't it? I don't blame you. At least you'll be getting a vacation from me for a while. Things should be more pleasant around here without someone bitching at you all the time."

"I'm not so sure you really want to go."

"Of course I want to. Get on that phone and make that reservation. And make it for tomorrow, not Wednesday. Why waste time. The sooner I leave here the better. For me, for you, for all of us, right?"

Amid the rancid sting of tears, Pam rushed to her bedroom. Bob picked up the phone and called the airline office while I stared distracted at the floor. Daniel could no longer concentrate on his page of homework. Robbie was at the UCSB campus and knew nothing about my plans.

The following morning, we arrived at the San Francisco airport one hour before my flight departure. I waited with Pam and Daniel while Bob carried my two suitcases to check them in at the baggage counter. Then with a sudden rush, I lunged forward before the agent could send my luggage away on the conveyor belt. "Bob, wait. Wait. Cancel my reservation. I'm not going."

"Are you sure?" He studied my face. "Why not?"

"Never mind now."

"You do need the rest," he said.

"I'll tell you later. Just cancel the reservation."

"All right."

When we all returned to the car, I confessed, "I can't do it. I never really wanted to go in the first place. I – I was just trying to punish myself by leaving all of you and – this is where I want to be. I don't want to be away from everybody. I'm afraid – I'm afraid I'd kill myself. You're all I have. I'm so sorry about the way I've been acting. You're all I have."

Their arms encircled me despite the awkwardness of car seats.

"You're all I have," I sobbed. "You're all I have."

Chapter 34

A Year Apart

Bob lingered over the evening meal longer than usual. He was still finishing dessert twenty minutes after the rest of the family had left the table and lay sprawled about the living room reading books, except for me, who had begun the kitchen clean-up.

Robbie had been home from college for the first two months of the summer working as a playground supervisor for the local Palo Alto School District. In retrospect, I knew what was going through Bob's mind. He feared the confrontation because he could predict our reactions, the way we would relegate him to a position outside our circle, a manner of treatment he had been subjected to many times during his youth and for nineteen years as a husband and a father. It was not something he could order us to do. He could only present the problem and explain his perspective of the situation and hopefully appeal to our love for him, if it were in fact there.

As he carried his empty dessert dish into the kitchen, he intercepted Pam about to leave the house. "Where are you going?"

"Out for a walk."

"Can you stick around a bit? I've got something to discuss that concerns all of you."

"Oh, all right, what is it?"

"Come into the living room. Mary, this includes you as well."

We sat about watching him and waiting, apprehensive that he had essentially called a serious meeting.

"My company is transferring me back to the Midwest, which means we're going to have to make another move."

Robbie dropped to the couch. "Not me – this is where I plan to make my life. Anyway, I'm nineteen now. That's old enough to be out here on my own. I've got too many things going for me here to move back to Rockford."

Pam shook her head. "I'm not going to any college or university except Santa Barbara or Berkeley. I like it here."

"I'm sure not going back there." Being the youngest with no alternative but to do his parents' bidding, Daniel nevertheless voiced his refusal. "There's no mountains. It's nothing but flat and ugly."

"I stay wherever the children are," I said. "Anyway, my rheumatism can't take those Midwest winters."

"All of you don't seem to understand. There isn't any choice. It's not a matter of what you or I want to do, unless I quit my job and try to start over at the same level, which is not going to happen at my age. Now, Robbie and Pam can remain out here, but, Mary, you and Daniel can move back with me. You can easily get a teaching position at Edgebrook, and Daniel can enroll at Rockford College."

Daniel sprang from his chair. "Hell, I'm not going anywhere."

"You're acting very selfish," Bob retorted.

"I don't care. I'm not going to live where there aren't any mountains."

"It doesn't bother you that I'd be living back there alone for a year then?"

Mary cut into the silence that followed. "Why did your company have to do this to you? We've already committed ourselves to a life out here. Can't they understand that?"

"Yes, I believe they understand our situation as I've explained it to them but this is a matter of business. They're a corporation. I'm just an employee. If I want to remain employed, I have to do what they tell me."

"That's the extent of their understanding."

"All I can say is I'm sorry this has to happen."

"Couldn't you go back alone for a while and see if you can sort out something to get transferred to the Los Angeles area?"

"If I went back alone, a while, as you put it, would turn out to be at least one year. And what if I couldn't work out something? Daniel would be in the middle of his high school senior year and it wouldn't be fair to pull him out. And what about you? You couldn't leave a teaching job right in the middle of the school year. Your contract wouldn't allow it."

"I guess you're right, but as I said before, where the children go I go."

"Well, that makes me feel real good."

"Don't you turn this back on us," I retorted. "It's your company's fault, not ours."

"It shouldn't matter that much," he was visibly hurt. "You should want to let me be with you."

"We've moved around far too much as it is, I'll tell you that. You go back for a year – alone – and get things settled but try to get transferred back out here to the coast first."

"I'm afraid that's an impossibility. We already have another representative down in the Los Angeles area."

"All right, I'll agree to move back after a year. All three children will be in college. But I'm going to live near them when they all graduate, even if it means moving back to California."

"What you're asking me to do . . . A year is a long time."

"I know, but it's for the children."

"No, it's really for yourself."

"A family is for the purpose of children and it's wrong to split up."

"You mean it's only wrong for you to split up, not for me. What kind of position do you think you're forcing me into?" Bob's shoulders slumped. "They each have to go their own way eventually."

"Don't you think I realize that? So there's no sense in rushing that time is there?"

"No, but circumstances just aren't right. There are times when we can't pick and choose, and this is one of them."

"One year." I raised my voice. "That's the most I'll compromise. I've made more than enough sacrifices already and now I think I deserve a respite."

"And I haven't made any sacrifices? I don't deserve a respite?"

"I never said that. One year. That's my last word."

***

Bob carefully hung his best suit in the rear of the station wagon, then slowly turned to face us, his family. The time had come for him to return to the Midwest – alone. He could not hold back the tears as he said goodbye and embraced us one by one. To get into the car was the most difficult feat of his life and even more so to back out of the driveway. He straightened the front wheels and as he slowly moved away down the street, gazed back over his shoulder at where we all stood on the sidewalk waving goodbye. He half hoped we would call him back and tell him we had changed our collective mind and would come with him, or at least follow. Then the corner loomed at the right. He had been away on the road for most of his working life when the children were growing. So they could accept his absence without difficulty and did not possess sufficiently deep empathic understanding as to how this happening tore him apart. His hand lay on the horn for a long loud duration. The car seemed to slide around the corner of its own volition, and we passed from his vision.

The mainstream of traffic was the only force that kept him moving in the opposite direction from the drawing magnetic attraction he was compelled to leave behind. He drove late into the night, then stopped at a motel after passing through the northwest corner of Nevada into Utah.

Early morning discovered him on the road again, breakfast, then continue, munch a sandwich and a cluster of grapes from the lunch I had packed for him, stop for gas, to relieve himself, to splash his face with cold water, then drive for several more hours stop at a cheap restaurant for supper drive on into the night until the motel signs blurred before his eyes, stop, sleep and so each of five endless days consumed him as he consumed oncoming highway into his eyes, into his mind, into his system, numbing his brain until finally, early the last evening, he arrived in Rockford and drove through town to Gramma's house on the west side. He parked the car at the front curb and walked to the porch, his eyes bloodshot, a suitcase in each hand. As he mounted the wooden steps, she opened the door to greet him. "Hello, Bob."

"Hi, Gramma." They met with an emotional hug as he entered.

"How was trip?"

"Oh, fine, just fine – tiring."

"I have supper ready for you. I expect you little earlier."

"I'll leave my suitcases here for the moment."

"Sure, just put there. Go wash hands and come eat now. I put food on the table."

He climbed the rickety carpeted stairs that, years before, his then-small children had scampered up and down pretending fright at the creaking noises or attempting absolute stealth while spying on others or playing hide and seek with their cousins. These were the stairs his wife had climbed and descended daily for two years during the Second World War when he was stationed overseas on an isolated jungle outpost in New Guinea. His son Robbie had been born then and Bob had not met him until his return to the United States. The irony of this separation from his family nineteen years later halted him halfway up the stairs and he had to support himself for several moments against the wall.

Gramma had returned to the kitchen, and he knew she would be waiting to serve him. The warm sweet smell of her embrace mingled with the aroma of frying steak and onions from the back of the house still clung to him. Yet he did not want her to see that he had been crying.

The atmosphere of every room bespoke warmth, age, hominess and informal comfort that was alien to modern homes with jet-age tastes and design. The old walls had been replastered, repainted, and repapered many times in the past thirty years.

Gramma salted and peppered, then flicked a fork through the steak and onions spluttering in the black skillet. Her short quick movements and rapid walk had not changed, still much like a mother sparrow looking after her offspring.

Ten minutes later, Bob returned and entered the dining room with an appreciative smile and sat in what had been Grampa's chair.

"Aaaah, Gramma, it certainly smells good."

She smiled, pleased, and wiped her gnarled arthritic hands on her apron. "How you like steak?"

"Medium rare."

She served him with the same energy and loving attention as she had her husband in the past. She asked to hear about me and the children and he savored telling her about our activities and, in turn, inquired about herself, listening with interest and sympathy. Then, exhausted, he went to bed early, silently saying his prayers, because he knew that Gramma would be kneeling in the next room saying hers and the house drew a prayer from him.

The next morning, he reported to the main office to review his territorial assignments. The director of marketing expressed his sympathy that Bob was going to be living a half-continent apart from his family and told him not to worry about flight expenses as far as the major holidays were concerned. Bob thanked him for his generosity.

He returned to Gramma's for supper. Afterwards, while they were sitting in front of the television set watching Lassie, Gramma's favorite program, to Bob's amusement, she suddenly leaped up and turned off the set at a moment Lassie was about to encounter danger. In her child-like naiveté of dramatic conventions, she believed that what she was seeing on the screen was actually happening in real life, her emotional involvement was so intense. So by switching off the television at critical moments, she thought she was saving Lassie from an evil fate.

The same thing happened at ten o'clock when the opening prologue of *Gunsmoke* came on. Her religious beliefs wouldn't allow her to accept or tolerate guns and violence. So there was nothing left for Bob to do but retire to bed. He respected her values and wishes. There were times, however, when she would attempt to explain to him and sell him her religion in hopes that he would become a convert to the Jehovah's Witnesses. He would listen patiently for a while, then politely avoid further discussion by telling her he had to get an early start in the morning and had better go to bed. They had little in common to discuss and he never wanted to hurt her feelings in any way, so he exercised extreme tact. Every Thursday and Saturday night when she would attend "meeting," except when he was out-of-town, he would always be there to bring her home at the end of the service.

Bob spent half of his time calling on buyers in Chicago where he would stay overnight. He had the ability to make an immediate favorable impression and to communicate and sell the values and benefits of the products and the company that he represented. His intuitive knowledge of human nature and behavior was highly developed from years of contact in the world of selling. There were some buyers of executive rank to whom he never made a sale, but with whom he became good friends. And then there were others suffering from insecurity and lacking knowledge of their buying position who were arrogant and inflexible, refusing to listen to anybody, sheltering the egocentric belief that their opinion and only theirs had to be the right one.

For individuals of this nature, Bob learned he had to bring them around to the realization that his way was the better one, but in so doing he had to let those individuals believe it was their own creative revelation and that he had not actually persuaded them to accept an opposing opinion at all. At times, he failed, but he left a greater percentage of buyers feeling important and pleased with themselves and their decisions than not. He approached selling as a counselor who helped his prospects solve their problems instead of trying to force them to buy.

He often thought of using his spare time to study and improve himself intellectually, but soon realized that he was not motivated enough and did not have a goal to achieve in relation to the effort. Instead, he spent the majority of his evenings staring at a television set in lonely motel rooms. As soon as he turned off the program, his thoughts would immediately dwell on his family as he lay back in bed choking on a lump in his throat.

On weekends, he spent entire days on the golf course he had frequented as a boy. Occasionally he saw a familiar face and would stop and chat or play a round or two.

***

Bob was to leave for California by jet on Friday evening to be with his family during the Christmas holidays. His anticipation was keen as he drove through the busy Chicago loop on Monday thinking about the trip. He figured that the calls he had to make on Friday could be made on Thursday instead, and so he would be able to depart on Thursday night, giving himself an extra day. But then thinking further, he never made any calls in the afternoon, so why not fly back then. On another impulse he recalled that Thursday morning business could be easily shuffled back and handled on Wednesday and Wednesday's calls were made in the morning, so why not leave Wednesday afternoon. He stopped at a phone booth and changed his plane reservation from Friday night to Wednesday afternoon.

Chapter 35

The Letters

With the end of another school year, Robbie found a job as a desk clerk at a guest ranch resort in the Santa Barbara foothills.

Daniel graduated from high school with a solid 'B' GPA and had just been accepted at UCSB. He spent the summer months in restless anticipation of attending college in the fall. He would be on the same campus with his older brother and sister.

Bob flew out to San Francisco from the Midwest at the end of the summer to handle my moving arrangements from Menlo Park to be with him in Rockford. I went weighed down by the greatest reluctance. Plans for maintaining contact, and rejoining my children became my primary preoccupation.

Daniel started his freshman year and two weeks in, he called me on the phone to report he had gone to a party and gotten drunk for the first time. I responded with anger and disgust and told him he was on the path to end up like his paternal grandfather, Lloyd Wenger, who, as Bob recalled, had become a pathetic, habitual alcoholic. I'm pleased to note that Daniel, through the rest of his college career, never reported "getting drunk" to me again.

Pam began her sophomore year as a resident assistant in a supervised apartment complex for women students. I dreaded the elusiveness of time passing and the distance between us, a sense that my three children were growing away from me, and I did not want to lose connection with them. They were the center of my life.

Surprisingly, Pam kept up a regular correspondence with Bob and me in letters that revealed a disturbing inner-conflict of self-discovery and change on which I did not comment. I was just grateful we had a form of communication.

At first, the letters were just chatty descriptions of her experiences as a resident assistant, her meetings with the house mother and supervisor in preparing for the arrival of the girls and their parents, and, oddly, complaining about Daniel thinking he had special privileges because she was an RA. He was aggressively pursuing six girls for dates and wouldn't listen to her regarding not barging into the lounge and living areas. She wrote that both Robbie and Daniel would bring their laundry there to save money, instead of going to a local laundromat. She was afraid her brothers might get her into trouble, and she was supposed to set an example for the girls.

She discouraged an "overly passionate" date by psychoanalyzing him. She wrote, "The trouble with guys is that they're too egocentric. So ends chapter one of my social life."

She elaborated how much she enjoyed her philosophy course, and that philosophy suited her temperament, especially the concept of supernaturalism. She said she felt free and complete as an entity in her own right. That was something I had never experienced in my life.

I didn't know whether to take some of her comments as red flag warnings, especially the influence of her professor of the History of Western Civilization, Dr. Eckert, or to be glad for her personal discoveries and revelations.

From Pam's Letters

I talked with Dr. Eckert about a book by Mercea Eliade called *The Sacred and The Profane* or *The Myth of The Eternal Return*. We got into a most exciting conversation, and he complimented my intelligence and hoped I would come back. He said I had infinite potential for success.

In contrast, the house mother told me to spend less time studying and to visit my girls socially, instead of always on business. I guess I care too much about myself to be a resident assistant. I would rather not partake of tete-a-tetes much less instigate them. I'll just have to remain in the middle of house rules and studies. I know what extreme I'd rather pursue. Just think if I had freedom . . . . . .Infinity. . . . . .On the other hand, this RA job is giving me a different kind of freedom, freedom from myself. My relationship to other people is more pleasurable, though I have torturous regressions because of my ingenious frankness at times. The house mother is after me for that too. "Speak your opinions or your ignorance in private," she says. I may upset the potato wagon yet.

In your last letter to me, you mentioned you weren't sure I was being wise switching over from English to history as my field of study. In so doing, it doesn't mean I am going away from literature. On the contrary, it is giving me a much more mature view and understanding of philosophy and literature than would otherwise be possible. Also, I'm being exposed to more literature as primary source material than I ever came in contact within my English courses.

For the first time in my life, I don't want to be an eighth grader anymore. I feel like someone has died in me and someone else has been born. It is an exaggerated feeling, but acute. I don't know whether to laugh or cry. Today, it rains. Tomorrow, there will be sun. I guess that is enough to answer by. I am a scholar now. It's what I was born for.

I just got your letter. Don't be so melancholy. You make yourselves despair over what should give you joy. I don't want to live in the paradise of naiveté. I have opened the door and to close it would be a kind of spiritual death. We take our past so much for granted that we have no awareness of it at all. The

Twentieth Century is the great age of the search for self. Who thinks it can be found entirely in the present is mistaken. The pattern of our world is a direct line from the past despite the apparent chaos of history. I desire to use the tools of my intelligence and of the past and present to create a life for myself that is my own as far as is possible for me to create in a world of plurality and interdependence.

I quit my RA job so I can spend more time working on my History of Civilization term paper. I told Mrs. Levin I have found what I want, that I am alive. She hates me for it. She thinks I am so wrong. I have never been more certain of myself, but I hate to have people disapprove of me.

Dr. Eckert has set higher standards for me than anyone else in the class. I told him it was too much, but he says I can do it. Anxiety kills. I must work on my books for cure.

You should see the neat boots I bought. I wear them constantly because of the rain lately, also, because they're neat.

We children are your creation. My creation will be the work of my life itself. I will not spend my life in introverted seclusion. I am creating future. History is not past. There is oneness between us. You cannot lose us.

Anyway, I probably sounded unenthusiastic on the phone about coming home, which is not true. I want so much to come home, but how I wish I could be free of the black cloud of intellectual obligations hanging over my head.

I realize how truly far away I am from the crowd. I no longer care for secret sisters and Christmas decorations, for contests and hootenannies. I have been introduced to the world of books and people who like books about thinking and deep feeling. This is the world I have chosen, with freedom to be a slave to my own curiosity.

Right now, I feel intensely the need to escape from apartment dwellings and pretty blue swimming pools. If I must be alone, I would rather be alone among mountains and glaciers and trees and meadows and deer than among people and cars. I am dissatisfied with the present. Someday, I must have a ranch, not even a big one. It must be in rugged land near or in the mountains. And I will have horses.

You say I will get married and end up in an apartment or a nice suburb where my children will go to a good school and meet nice friends. Oh, for a magic spell or a dream world.

Chapter 36

Fragmentation

Bob and I waited expectantly among the crowd at Chicago O'Hare as we watched the American Airlines jet taxi over to the terminal.

Passengers grabbed belongings from overhead racks and maneuvered for positions in the aisle, Daniel, Pam, and Robbie among them. Daniel stood six feet tall now with long blond hair badly in need of a trim. His trousers were too short and revealed that he was wearing mustard-colored socks that clashed with his dark suit. He set down the portable typewriter and suitcase he was carrying and struggled to put on a ski jacket over his suit coat.

Pam's long unkempt hair swept down like a thick poncho over the length and width of her back. Her overweight excess of thirty pounds externalized the gravity of pulsing expanding intellect and a preoccupation with self-search and identity. Robbie's bushy hair was also in need of a cut but he had allowed it to grow long for a part in a university theater arts production and there hadn't been time to stop in at a barber shop before the flight. He discovered he enjoyed wearing his hair longer than usual.

Unfortunately, to my regret and despair, he had discovered and changed majors from pre-med to theater arts. He had a D in chemistry and Bs and Cs in other science courses. His raging emotional outburst over his failure to live up to my expectations that he become a doctor had ended my hopes and ambition for him. I finally had to submit to his choice and decision. He had to at least graduate. His threat to quit school would have landed him in the Army. Working toward a college degree was the only thing preventing him from being drafted and sent to Vietnam.

The three of them resembled country bumpkins edging away from their seats into the aisle and slowly moving toward the door at the front of the aircraft. Ten minutes later, parents and children met in a flurry of kisses and greeting embraces. Then as a group, we hurried away from the waiting area and terminal lobby.

I couldn't help laughing at Daniel. "What are you doing wearing a jacket over your suit coat? And your pants – what happened to your good pair I sent you?"

"I have to carry my jacket this way and my other pants are wool. I can't stand to wear wool, especially for five hours on a plane."

We stepped onto a passenger conveyor and rode silently to the baggage claim area. Daniel retained his almost ever-present smile, while Pam pointedly averted her glance to other people and activities around us. Her rebellious impulses steamed from her. I observed her expression and condition with disappointment. Pam caught my glance and shifted so that her back faced me. Bob placed an arm around Robbie's shoulders.

"Well, how's Santa Barbara?"

"Okay."

We came to the end of the conveyor. Pam and I stood aside to wait while Bob and the boys claimed the baggage. As we all headed for the main exit, Bob asked Pam, "Why are you wearing your hair so long? It looks much nicer on you when it's shorter."

She wrinkled her nose. "Oh, I think it looks better on me this way."

"You boys both need haircuts too."

"Yeah." "Yeah."

Fifteen minutes later, we were driving along the Chicago Tollway.

"The scholarship goes into effect the same time I leave for Germany," Pam was bringing us up to date on her future academic plans.

"Is your departure date still the same?" I asked.

"No, it's been changed to July tenth."

"That gives you even less time than before."

"Oh, yeah, but I'll be glad to get started. It will give me more time to spend in New York and France."

Bob methodically cleared his throat. "How many other students will there be besides yourself?"

"Twelve . . . only three of us are from Santa Barbara. I met a guy at school who's from Gottingen. His name's Gerd Winke and he told me that the people in southern Germany are friendlier and most of the ones in northern Germany are cold and business-like and not to expect loud back-slapping Germans."

My gaze hardened unseeing at some distant point on the horizon. "We'll have to get you slimmed down before you leave. You certainly don't want to go looking like you do."

"Mary, let's not now," Bob attempted to unobtrusively warn me.

An expression of hurt flooding her eyes, Pam shifted her gaze to stare at the passing countryside.

Bob smiled at them via his rearview mirror. "What are your plans, Daniel?"

"I don't know. I guess I'll try to find a job out there for the summer."

I asked, "How well did you do on your finals?"

"Well, I really studied like mad. I mean I didn't even go out on a date or even go to a movie with my roommates since two weeks before finals started. I did real good in geology. Got a 'B'. The other profs sent me grade cards too. Anyways, it looks like I've got about a 2.3 grade point average."

I tensed inwardly. "That could give you some trouble with the draft board, couldn't it?"

"Oh, hell, I'm not going to worry about that now."

"Yes, but your two-S classification expired at the beginning of this month, didn't it?"

"Yes, but don't worry about it."

"They could reclassify you 1-A with only a 2.3 grade point average. You can certainly do better work than that. I should have stuck to my guns and had you live at home for your first year. From the way you sounded in your letters, I don't think your roommates are a very good influence on you."

"Oh, Mom, come on now. I'm all right."

"I'm going to fly back with you next fall," I said. "Your father can work things out here and then come out later."

"Now, Mary, you know I'm in no position to ask anything like that of the company. I thought it was agreed that we were going to make our home here in Rockford."

"Not with the children two thousand miles away. And besides that I swore that I'm not going to suffer through another Midwest winter. My rheumatism can't take it."

"Well, we'll discuss this some other time."

"Now, when we finally have a home for them to come home to instead of moving around the country, they're all grown up and going off on their own. We never even had time to establish roots."

We opened doors and pulled out luggage, which we promptly deposited in the entryway. Pam silently walked out into the spacious cathedral-beamed living room. Daniel followed her and moved around with arms extended wide, matching his expansive grin. "Hey, man, this is really neat."

"Isn't this nice, though," Bob appreciated Daniel's observation. "We've never had so much room in one house before."

"Yeah," said Daniel, "I'll bet this is the nicest house you've ever had."

"Your mother likes it," said Bob.

Pam nodded with sarcasm. "That means it's nice then. Seems kind of cold to me though. I like something smaller and more homey."

A brief shock of hurt and antagonism fluttered within me, leaving me puzzled at Pam's statement. It took Daniel to break the sudden gloomy mood again. "What's for supper? I'm starving."

As I removed the hot casserole dish from the oven, Bob entered the kitchen and went over to her. "Well, now they're home, safe and sound. Glad?"

"Yes, but Pam certainly doesn't seem to be happy to be here."

"Oh, just give her a few days to adjust herself. She'll be all right. I think it would be better if we didn't say anything more about her weight for the time being."

Robbie aimlessly wandered into the living room and sat hunched at the piano staring abstractly at the keyboard at which he had spent hundreds of hours practicing as a child. He talked about Margo Maier, the girl he had written us about who he had been dating back in California. She would be home now too with her family in Los Angeles. He intended to call her long distance the following evening and wish her a Merry Christmas. He knew that would not be sufficient contact, considering the thousand miles that separated them, and he would probably call her at least two or three more times during the vacation break. He said he wondered if being apart affected her as much as it did him. It irked him to think that perhaps she took it in stride as a matter of fact and it didn't bother her emotionally.

He had met Margo in the speech and drama department through another girl with whom he was infatuated, Susie, but who skillfully dangled him along with some one hundred other college Joes who had to see and arrange dates with her by appointment a month in advance. He and his latest roommate had cast Susie, a pixie-faced brunette, as the heroine in a promotional film they were making for the university to screen for incoming freshmen during their orientation.

In addition to not particularly wanting to encourage him, Margo was having difficulties in ending a relationship with a former boyfriend whom she had known since high school. Given time, she had warmed toward Rob, as he now preferred to be called, because of his genuine concern, attention, and love for her, although she had not yet arrived at a point in their relationship where she could honestly feel and express that she loved him. Rob had accepted that and assumed that she would finally come around to it because of his persistence and dedication to their relationship. A good two years would pass before that was to happen.

A few hours before driving to meet them at the airport, I had my hair frosted a sandy blonde and was slightly miffed that the drizzle had ruined its fullness. I was an intelligent, accomplished, aggressive, poised, energetic woman from whom they had all taken an example to become high achievers and move toward personal independence. Yet, just as my own mother had difficulty coping with my personal growth and direction, as a mother, I now experienced the same difficulty in relinquishing control and no longer being able to make the destinies of my children part of my own.

Robbie admired us both and felt deeply our mutual love for all of them and between themselves in spite of a flux in time and exposure and awareness of new values and new opportunities to become who they would as adults. He had once told us we made a very handsome couple.

I focused on listening to him playing the piano in the living room.

"All that nonsense about Pam becoming a Catholic," I said. "I've brought up my children to be individuals – strong. It makes me ill to think she'd even consider such a thing. Believe in God, fine, but to have to depend on a bunch of fat priests to brainwash your guilt when they're just as corrupt as their congregations, it's beyond me."

"I'm sure she sees more in it than that."

"If you don't stop talking like that, I'm going to leave this house. I swear I'll just walk right out of here."

"All right, but you know this will come up again with her."

"I refuse to discuss it with her."

"You're being highly unreasonable."

"It's too bad it has to be this way, but I'll talk to her sometime when we're home alone," said Bob.

"You do that. It's a good thing she'll be home for a while at least, so I can get her back on the right track. She needs me more than ever. If nothing else, I'm glad she is going to Germany just so she can get away from the influence of that professor."

Daniel's sudden entrance ticked off my other major concern. "And another thing, I'm terribly worried about Daniel and the draft board. That 2.3 grade point may be the start of trouble. I firmly believe he would be doing better if he enrolled here locally and lived at home. I know he has the intelligence and that he is probably being negatively influenced by his roommates to spend more time socializing than studying."

"Now damn it," Daniel ruffled in the doorway towering over us both. "Don't bother me about that. I just got home. This is my vacation and I want to relax."

"We're ready to eat anyway. You haven't lost your touch," I complimented Robbie's piano playing as he entered the dining room. "It sounded very nice."

"I've been away from it too long. I haven't sat down at a piano all semester."

Robbie considered it about time to direct some interest toward his father. "How have you been doing, Dad?"

"Business has been good." He was genuinely pleased that Robbie should ask. "I've been working with aerospace engineers for the past few months on designing a new type of specialized belt they need for rocket parts. So far I've established three accounts worth seventy thousand dollars each."

"That's good. That sounds real good."

"Something is developing, though, that may or may not be better. The company is offering me a more substantial position as a result of my work here in the Midwest. It's in the area of top executive management. But now is not the time to discuss it."

"Who wants dessert?" I asked from the kitchen doorway.

"No."

"I do."

"I'll have some."

"Except you, Pam. Chocolate cake is the last thing you need."

A sense of déjà vu consumed Pam and she restrained herself from leaping up and screaming her rage.

"I'll have mine later," said Bob. "I'm the only one around here who knows how to enjoy a meal."

Instead of screaming, Pam came back at me with a cold, "I overheard what you said before about Doctor Eckert. The vents in this house carry loud voices quite well. You're wrong. He's the one person I can talk things over with intelligently and he gave me a sense of direction."

Ignoring Pam's challenging statement, I withdrew into the kitchen and served the cake.

Chapter 37

Confrontation

Three-quarters of the entire back wall of the living room consisted of a window overlooking a flagstone patio and expansive back yard shaded by several tall elms.

I silently gazed at Pam lining up a lounge chair with the angle of the sun. She was wearing a two piece bathing suit and sunglasses and carrying a paperback novel in one hand. I was disturbed by her visibly overweight condition. I crossed the living room to the kitchen back door and walked out onto the patio where she was just settling herself comfortably on the lounge chair.

"Doesn't it seem odd to be sitting out in the sun here instead of in California?"

Pam glanced up from the page she was reading. "That's for sure. It's too bad the owners didn't build a swimming pool. This place could use it."

"They probably didn't think it was worth it. They can only use one about four months out of the year out here," I said. "California and Florida are the only places worth having a pool."

"Oh, maybe, but most people don't have time to swim except during the summer anyway, even in California."

"Pam, I want to talk to you seriously about your weight."

"That's what I thought."

"Don't you realize what you're doing to yourself?"

"You really don't love me then, do you?"

"What do you mean by that?"

"Oh, if you really did love me, it wouldn't matter to you how I look. You act like you don't even care about my intellectual accomplishments."

"Now, there's no need to cry about it. I just want us to arrive at an understanding."

Pam wiped her runny nose and tried to restrain herself but was unable to. "Oh, yeah, you should talk about understanding. Yeah!"

"I realize I'm not a very rational person."

"That doesn't matter. That doesn't matter. You don't understand. You just don't understand anything but what you want."

"What don't I understand? That's just it. Somewhere, I've really gone wrong with you to make you do this to yourself. I don't want you to be unhappy. You know I don't."

"Oh, I know. I know."

"I don't know why, but I think you're trying to get back at me for some reason, for something I've done. But you're really not hurting anybody but yourself."

"I always thought. . .you and Dad once said you'd be behind us and support anything we decided we wanted to do."

"Yes, but that didn't include making yourself unhappy. You know as well as I do that you don't want to go around being fat."

"That's just it! If you really loved me, it wouldn't matter to you how I looked or what I believed either."

"Pam, do you think I don't love you when I care enough to want to help you? Some mothers just completely forget about their daughters."

"I don't want you to help me! Why can't you just accept me like I am?"

"What I don't understand is how you can accept yourself. I do love you, Pam, and I do admire your intelligence very much. But there's more to it than that. How with a mind like yours you can even think to let your body go is beyond me. I don't at all respect you for it. That's not to say I don't love you though. And another thing, how do you expect to attract any boys looking like you do?"

"Who wants to? All they're after is sex and none of 'em even cares about having an intelligent conversation. All they want to do is make out and fuck."

"Watch your language."

"Hell, I don't want to be kissing anybody just to be kissing them. I want it to mean something, not just because I'm a body. It's sickening."

"If it's carried to an extreme, yes; but you'll never attract the kind of boy you want if you let yourself go like this. You're just driving everyone away from you."

"Can't you see? Oh, God, forget it! I want to be loved for who I am, not for what you or anybody else wants me to be. You can't separate my mind from my body."

"That's exactly right and nobody is going to respect you if you don't care about your appearance. Your mind doesn't matter a damn to anyone then. It's you that people see; and as far as they're concerned, you may not be much of a person at all. How you look represents your mind whether you want it to or not."

"I don't care what other people think."

"Oh, come on now. You don't really expect me to believe that."

"Well, it shouldn't matter, especially for you. At least you know me."

"I'm not sure I do. Apparently, I've gone wrong somewhere."

"You want to know where you've gone wrong? I'll tell you. You're always talking about making sacrifices and not being selfish and all. Just for us. Boy, I sure know one thing. If I ever get married, I'm not going to push my husband and children around."

"And you really think all I've done all these years is push you and the others around. My family is all I have in this world, Pam. I'm just trying to do what I feel is right and best for you – for all of us. I want to be proud of you, Pam, proud of all my children. Not just your intellectual capabilities, but in every way. That means being strong on your part."

Pam rose from the lounge chair. "Yeah, Dad told me what you said about that before. I've gotta think." She entered the house and went to her bedroom.

I remained alone, thoughtfully on the patio in troubled contemplation, then also entered the house. I rinsed the lunch dishes and put them in the washer. I went out front to get the mail. There was a letter from the selective service board for Daniel with our house as the address of residence.

By mid-evening, I nervously paced the living room with anxiety. Bob sat thoughtfully in an armchair. Daniel was on the edge of another chair with his elbows resting on his knees, head down, depressed. I stopped for a moment and stared at the invading letter on the dining room table.

"I tell you," I said to Bob, "when I saw that letter, I became sick, actually sick. It gave me such chills I had to take a hot shower and put on my robe. What's the matter with you anyway? Do you care that little about your son that you won't even write the letter for him?"

"Don't be ridiculous. It's just that unfortunately it's too late now. He has no choice."

"What do you mean he has no choice? OOOOOHHH! How can you even think to say such a thing? I knew I shouldn't have asked you in the first place. I'll have to do it myself like everything else."

"Now you know that isn't true."

"Oh, isn't it? Who's gone back to school so she can teach and put her children through college? Who's made all the sacrifices of moving around this damn country and the children never having a place they could put down roots and call home? Do you think for one instant that we would have come along as far as we have if it wasn't for me? Somebody has to have the drive in this family."

Bob stared at the floor and passively absorbed my comments. "All right," he said, "I'll tell you what to write; but this is something that Daniel has to go through himself. He has an obligation the same as every other young man."

"I can't believe what I'm hearing. I can't believe you're saying this. He is not the same as every other young man. He is our son and that makes him special."

"Yes, but only to us."

"That's all the more reason we have to do something about it. How cold you are, Bob. I never realized you could be so cold. It's a pity you had to come from a family where nobody cared about each other."

"That will do, Mary. Daniel, get a pencil and paper."

Daniel rose from his chair, entered the kitchen, and returned with a ballpoint pen and a notebook pad.

"You write down what I'm going to dictate," said Bob.

Daniel resumed his seat and I took a position looking over his shoulder from behind the chair.

Bob extensively cleared his throat. "Dear sirs, I am writing in acknowledgement of receipt of a 1-A classification and notice to report for my induction physical examination. I would like to request an appeal to have my deferment extended. I am currently pre-enrolled for the fall quarter as a full-time student and my occupational intention is to become a teacher. I readily acknowledge my military obligation and will gladly serve my country upon completion of my education."

Daniel slumped forward. "Oh, what the hell. Why don't I just forget it and go in. The world's nothing but a damn mess anyway."

***

Before she left for Germany, Pam at least lost a few pounds. She continued to wear her hair long, but in a much neater manner than previously.

"I'll write you from New York and France," she said when we arrived at the terminal. "If I've forgotten anything, you can mail it to me later."

An airline official opened the door of the entrance tunnel and unsnapped the rope that blocked off the waiting passengers. Pam warmly embraced each of us, bringing tears to her eyes.

"Goodbye, Mom, I love you."

"You look real nice, Pam; and I love you too."

"Dad."

"Take care of yourself and keep us informed on how you're doing. This will be a great experience for you."

"You take care of yourselves too."

"Bye, Pam." Daniel kissed her on the cheek. "You have a good time over there."

Robbie gave her a hug and a kiss. "You look out for yourself."

Pam wiped her eyes, took her two handbags from Bob and started backing toward the gate. "Goodbye, everybody, I love you." Then she turned and walked away into the tunnel.

Chapter 38

The Wedding

At the end of the school year, I resigned my sixth grade teaching position at Edgebrook Elementary in Rockford. Bob's company honored his request to transfer him back to Southern California to develop new aerospace-related fastener business, his specialty. We rented a condominium on the north side of Santa Barbara and I was hired as a sixth grade teacher at Jefferson Elementary School located in the foothills overlooking the city.

The year was a turning point in our lives for a number of reasons.

After underachieving somewhat in his collegiate freshman year, Daniel had recovered nicely and was performing well in his upper division classes. [He was to graduate his B.A. with an overall 2.9 grade point.]

Pam returned from her year in Germany and was finishing her senior year and preparing to apply to graduate school in the field of psychology, which had become another of her academic peripatetic interests. Whatever subject she studied never seemed enough to satisfy her. She was on a constant search for understanding that eventually became exploration and experimentation with a range of spiritual cultist and New Age religious experiences.

I abhorred the direction she was being led into by some personal inner emptiness, some inner need. I didn't know from where it came, but it reminded me of what I had escaped by leaving my growing years in a Pennsylvania mining town behind. I thought I had shed all that, but I now saw that it was reappearing and coming around to haunt me through my daughter's insatiable intellectual curiosity and pursuits. But initially, Pam wasn't the carrier of this spiritual virus and delusional escape from reality that had been cumulatively building in her life. Her experiences came later. As things turned out, Bob was pathologically consumed by it.

Most significantly, Rob and his fiancée, Margo Maier, were married.

Although I was happy for Rob and my delightful blonde, well-educated daughter-in-law, the wedding left me personally feeling depressed that a stage of my life as a mother had come to an end.

Rob's and Margo's honeymoon followed late on the heels of a reception that extended far too long into the night for Rob. He came to a realization and anxiety crept up on him of his lifetime commitment to have and to hold. What followed was the astounding fact (astounding to himself and to Bob and me) that he had crossed a major threshold of his life.

As the two families stood in a congratulatory cluster out in the church foyer, I detected a distinct reserve from Margo's parents. Not in words, but in body language I interpreted as questioning his worth to be their daughter's husband. Their mutual expression was so intense that Rob felt compelled to walk over to them and thank them, to which Margo's father replied, "Just take care of her. You hear me? Take good care of her."

Finally, Margo changed into her traveling or honeymoon dress, a soft cream-colored chemise with a large brown collar that extended down frontally to create a bodice, a simple but dramatic design. Rob dutifully kissed Bob and me and Pam and Daniel and received hugs and kisses from Margo's cousins and relations, then waited impatiently at the door to depart.

They arrived at the Porto Fino Inn at one o'clock in the morning. Rob wrote both of their names so the clerk would not question their right to share the same room, even though his father had reserved the honeymoon suite for them. Upon cracking open the magnum of Mumm's champagne they pirated in their suitcase, shedding their clothes and gazing out their window at the moonlit marina while erotically enfolded in each other's arms, somehow all the nervous shit disappeared. They were alone together, Rob and Margo, as they had been alone many times before. The ceremony had been only a temporary interruption of their previous relationship, only now the relationship smacked of a new reality. There was no longer a need to play at it.

Santa Ana winds swept out of the desert and rattled dry grasses and chaparral in the foothills of Southern California with an ominous caress. Warm nights drew the people out and they roamed the streets. We left our windows open and inhaled the heady sweet scent of orange blossoms and jasmine.

For weeks, the Santa Barbara Channel lipped whitely with steady chopping froth. The chameleon sea surged in fluctuating swells from slate gray to emerald greens to cerulean blue struck by curtain cascades of roving sunlight.

On a gusty Sunday afternoon, Rob and Margo drove into town from their apartment in Isla Vista near the campus to visit us.

Rob squinted against the stark sun glare off the white adobe style condominiums, rested his eyes on the plum colored Santa Ynez peaks, a startling soothing backdrop. Wary of rattlesnakes that occasionally visited the shiny green mottled ivy, his steady glance shot to the sidewalk ahead, scanning for a ropey shape or ground level movement.

They entered the condo at the back door to a vaporous draught of prime rib beef emanating from the kitchen oven and were greeted by my open arms and sparkling energetic pleasure at their arrival. We all greeted each other with animated hugs and enthusiastic kisses.

I always tried to look my best whenever they came to visit. As a middle-aged mother, I took pride in my slender prepossessing womanliness, my attractive high cheekbones, startling youngish blue eyes, and expertly coiffed sandy blonde hair. I wasn't competing with my new daughter-in-law for my son's admiration and affection, I just wanted to be presentable.

The robust noises of greeting and laughing chatter attracted Bob, broad smiling from the living room. He leaned in with brown-eyed exuberance through the doorway. "You're here. Just in time." He encircled both Rob and Margo in his arms, planted his tan rugged features against one, then the other. His hands squeezed and patted love expressions of enduring strength.

Rob had recently told Bob and me that he perceived and loved us as if we were his own children, rather than the reverse. He described how moments on the beach flickered across his visual memory of our awkward moves at play in the sunlight. With child-like smiles and eagerness, we dashed about amid the roar and swish of surf, the hushed scrape of hot sifting sand and cool wet packed sand and caused hordes of black flies to erupt in clouds from where they nested in the bladders of beached kelp. Robbie (I still thought of him as Robbie) had watched his father's wiry athletic body, enviable even to younger men and to his peers and to old men. He had watched me in my white cotton pants rolled halfway up my shins, my open-toed leather sandals rendering me flat-footed on the shifting inconstant sand as I launched a bright orange Frisbee into spinning flight that elevated in the wind.

"Where's Pam?" Rob led the group into the living room.

"Oh, she was here for a while this morning but she had to go back to her place and study for her orals," I explained. "She said she might be over again later."

"How's she doing?"

"She doesn't think she'll pass them."

"Aahh, she'll pass," said Rob. "Don't know why she even worries about it with a brain like hers."

"One of her professors said something that put her down and he's on her committee. So she's afraid of him."

"Bullshit." Rob's use of profanity disturbed me a little. "She'll do all right. She should have more confidence in herself." He turned to his brother. "Any job prospects yet?"

"I sent out applications for the state and national parks," said Daniel. "There's nothing though. Not at this time of the year. The jobs are seasonal. I sent mine in too late. When the fires start this fall though, I'll pick up some money in the National Guard." He had enlisted in the Guard to avoid being drafted.

"Did they call you out for that riot the other day?"

"No, I had Mom tell 'em I was off camping in the mountains."

"I watched it all from the second floor of the library," said Rob.

"I know. You hear what they said on the news? They blamed the students. If those assholes wouldn't have brought the Guard in, there never would have been any riot."

"Mmh -- I did see a bunch of students cut loose with rotten eggs and tomatoes first. But hell, they aren't firebombs."

"Well, maybe, but you don't know how scared you are running around out there in that uniform," said Daniel. "Hell, I'm not the enemy. I'd rather be throwing tomatoes."

"To hell with this talk." Rob slouched off to a chair. "I'm so god damn sick of politics and all the daily crap they feed us on the news. It's enough to drive you insane. They saturate your mind with it so you can't even relax anymore. All they do is keep you anxious. No wonder people go out and protest."

I looked in from the kitchen. "We're just about ready. The salads are on the table so why don't all of you sit down and start if you'd like."

They trooped into the dining room. At the head of the table, Bob opened and served a bottle of zinfandel. Rob selected herb and spices dressing and crunched into crisp lettuce, cucumbers, cherry garden tomatoes, and fresh avocado.

I carried in the roast, then followed with hot vegetables and sat down.

"Mmm, looks good and smells even better." Rob watched his dad carve the thick pink prime rib. "Looks perfect."

Bob offered me a well-done end piece, which I immediately returned to the serving platter. "No, I don't want any. I'll just eat the vegetables and a potato."

"It's good lean meat."

"No."

"Okay."

"Margo, help yourself here." He held the platter for her.

"Did you wear a hat when you were golfing?" Daniel asked.

"No, I should have. Got a little too much sun."

Pam returned an hour after we had finished dinner. Tension and an inner struggle with her shaken self-confidence and identity peeled away from her in raw layers. Withdrawn, now quite thin and underweight under a lion's mane of brownish-blonde hair, she silently snuggled into a corner of the couch. Her observant small features pinched with anxiety. "I can't stay long. I have to get back and study." Notes of disillusionment, arrogance, and naiveté bubbled in her voice. She was volatile, a sensitive soft bird.

I reheated the remaining roast and vegetables for her and Pam ate ravenously with a sense of sadness that left the others quiet and sympathetic after their ineffective efforts to boost her morale.

I viewed her with head and shoulders bowed, crossing the room with long boyish strides, staying only a short time, leaving quickly as if she shunned us, an image enclosing a wraith of seething unhappiness in a long magenta dress with thin strung beads around her neck. I remembered when she was happy in books and walking in the mountains, playing in fields and flowers and riding horses when she was a child. The playing was gone, snuffed out of her life, passionately desired, clutched at, never to be possessed again. It had flashed by slowly at the time. Then life had become an imbalance, a disoriented experience, a movement of constant change.

Daniel abhorred the world outside, except for the purity of mountains, clean rivers and sometimes the sea. He could not find what he sought, did not know what he wanted to find, so he sat in the home of his parents, slept late and played his guitar for long hours in order to accomplish something personal as well as to escape, to create a meaning and structure of living for himself. The sick sordid bombardment of television riddled him with despair and harangued him with futility. He felt totally ineffective and believed that it was senseless to even go out and try in the world -- for what? Disillusion and fear overwhelmed him, crushed his innocence and ambition. Bob and I understood and afforded him a retreat of love and childhood security, and for the moment he was content.

Chapter 39

The Episode

Rob described to me what happened.

Adrenalin jagged through his morning sleep at the distant ringing phone. He woke and sat for a moment trembling and quaking at the edge of the bed and stared at the clock. It was 5:30 A.M.

"You want me to get it?" Margo mumbled, curled in a warm ball under the blankets.

"I'll get it." Rob slowly stood, coping with pulsing sensations of an erection accompanied by bowel spasms. Bracing himself through the door frame, he sliced the phone in mid-ring and ticklishly touched the cold receiver to his still-warm ear. Chills crept over his nude body like a sharp breeze rippling the placid surface of a pond. His thick tongue nudged to expel the cotton dryness in his mouth. "Hello."

"Don't ask any questions. Just do as I tell you," his father's emotionally charged voice hammered into Rob's drifting mind and burst the bubble of soporific stupor. "We haven't got much time. There's going to be a catastrophic earthquake and a giant tidal wave will cover the city. Hurry! Hurry!"

The frenetic tension in his tone unstrung Rob, the credibility of what he had just heard. It came to him as an intense domineering command, and overcompensation to convince him of the necessity for immediate action. It caught him up abruptly. He paused, questioning, wondering why, brushing the tenuous outer edge of fear and sanity. His mind whirled back, skeptic. "How do you know?"

"Don't ask questions. Just hurry and get over here. There isn't much time remaining."

"Listen, Dad. Did you hear something on the radio or what?"

By this time Margo's anxious face bobbed at Rob's shoulder. "What is it? What's happened?"

His father continued to insist. "Please don't ask any questions. I'll explain it all later." His urgency grew anger pitched. "Just hurry. Our lives depend on it. We have to go up on the mountain. We don't have much time."

A pause, then Rob said, "All right, we'll be over as soon as we can."

"You've got to be here in the next half hour. It's going to happen at ten o'clock and we have to be well ahead of it."

"Where's Mom?"

"She's taking a shower, then going on to school."

"Have you talked with her?"

"She's all right. The school's located high enough on the Riviera. We'll go by and pick her up. Don't say anymore now. Just hurry." His father hung up.

"What is it?" Margo still waited for an answer.

Rob quickly dropped the receiver and turned, conjecturing. His imagination suddenly consumed his rational mind with the reality of what he'd just been told. His bowels jellied with fear. "There's going to be a massive earthquake and a tidal wave. It's supposed to cover the whole city. My dad must have heard it on the radio or something."

"I don't believe it. Earthquakes can't be predicted." She flicked on the clock radio searching for the morning news. There was no sense of emergency in the announcer's voice as he commented on the exceptionally fine clear weather, they were experiencing throughout Southern California.

Rob began to dress frantically. "He said it's supposed to be a catastrophic earthquake. We have to get over there fast and find out what's going on."

Margo tried several other stations. "How come they're not making announcements and giving warnings all over the radio and television?"

"I don't know. He said he'd explain everything. There's something wrong. He sounded a little strange, not like his usual self. Get dressed. We'd better get over there. I hope I have a chance to talk to my mom before she leaves for work."

"Do I have time to eat?"

"No. Take something in the car, yogurt."

"Well, I'd better call the school and tell them I won't be in this morning."

"Okay, but hurry."

She shook as she picked up the phone. Rob had communicated his nervousness to her.

"Nobody else is on the street," Margo observed. "If it was really going to happen, there'd be a mass exodus out of here."

"A tidal wave would bury this place in nothing flat. It's right at sea level."

"I really think we should stop and ask someone else if they heard anything on the radio or TV."

"No, let's just get over there. It might not be true and I'd just feel stupid. People might think we've freaked out on drugs or something."

"I think the whole thing is stupid, if you want my honest opinion."

"Maybe it is. Maybe it is. But I think we should at least find out what set my dad off like that. He looked like he had too much sun the other day when we were over there."

They rode the remaining distance in silence. When they arrived, they burst through the door without warning. Pam was there, woodenly snuggled into her couch corner while Daniel rushed out of the condo and stuffed sleeping bags and camping gear into the trunk of Bob's car. The two of them seemed convinced.

Harassed by violent psychic interruptions, Bob erratically paced the house, unable to come to rest for even a moment. "You're here, finally, thank God."

"Dad, are you sure you feel all right?"

"I'm fine. We have to get out of here. We have to get to higher ground. If we stay, the water will reach us here."

"How do you know there's going to be an earthquake and a tidal wave? We listened to the radio and they didn't say anything. Nobody else seems to know anything about it. I think we should call the geology department at the university and see if there have been any tremors or if they expect the widening of a fault or something."

"No, they don't know. Don't fight me on this. Don't fight me." Bob gestured in wild desperation. "Please, trust me. All of you. Trust me. I'll explain everything to you. There's no time now. There's going to be an earthquake and a tidal wave."

"How do you know?"

"They -- they came to me -- so clear I could reach out and touch them -- hear their voices."

"Who?"

"Jehovah's Prophets. They've been telling us all along this would happen in the world. Armageddon. It's a sign that God has come to cleanse the world."

"It sounds like you just had a bad dream."

"It was real. It was real. It came to me in a vision. It was so real I could reach out and touch them and hear their voices. We have to go up on the mountain to be safe."

Rob trembled, sweat-chilled at what he was witnessing, and now he understood Pam's withdrawal and horrific riveting stare. She knew.

"Dad . . ." Rob could not find the words nor the direction to act. He half-believed and feared to offend his father by airing his suspicion or by any expression of incredulity. Humor him, he thought. Humor him. When none of this happens, he'll see for himself it was just a dream. Everything will be all right. It has to be all right.

"We have to go now. We're running out of time." Bob's voice croaked with intensity.

"Do you have the snake bite kit?" Rob inanely asked Daniel. "Where we're going, there may be snakes."

"Yes, in my pocket."

Bob's glance suddenly riveted on the front page of the morning newspaper spread across the coffee table. He picked it up, waving it in the air and held it out to him. "Here, there's a sign. A man is having a heart transplant. No one will say who he is and there's an armed guard at the door. Why? Strange things are happening in the world. Here it tells of two Russian mig fighter jets that passed over an American ship, and for no reason they mysteriously crashed into the sea."

Ten minutes later, Rob and Margo wordlessly followed Bob's car along the tropically lush road winding across the face of the Santa Barbara Riviera. They pulled off and stopped at a broad promontory high above the city.

A faded adobe gray elementary school dropped away below the street level on the steep terraced hillside. Bob sent Pam in to fetch me from my classroom. With a hurried muttered excuse to the principal about a family emergency, I left the building and trudged after Pam up the long flight of concrete steps to the street. It was a warm clear day. They had opened the car doors and sat waiting at the curb. As I came into view, Rob got out and walked over to me and accompanied me to the other car. He pitched his voice low. "Mom, there's something seriously wrong with him."

"No, there isn't." I smoothed my gray suit and rearranged the green and yellow silk scarf about my neck. "I'll talk with him. The same thing happened when he thought he had a bleeding ulcer that night down in Los Angeles. It's just an anxiety attack."

A flow of images related to that traumatic incident pumped through Rob's mind. Nursing the last of a quart bottle of beer that night, he had been splayed across the couch when I had called him about his father. Rob was in no condition to suddenly leap up and drive off into the night. Margo fixed him a quick mug of coffee while he shocked his face with cold water. He had called the motel where Bob was staying to get instructions from him as to its location. He questioned Bob on his refusal to go immediately to a hospital if it was so serious.

I had explained to Rob how Bob had phoned in a panic at a raging burning sensation throughout his stomach and abdomen and had asked for Rob and Daniel to drive down to him in Los Angeles immediately with a quart of milk to soothe his stomach lining. I said Bob wouldn't go to a doctor because of his Christian Science upbringing, an impulse which he consistently denied but for which he offered no alternative explanation. So in the dead of night, the two brothers had shot down the coast from Santa Barbara to a small motel in Pasadena squeezed in among a congested neon-lit business district. They found their father flushed and feverish in his room. He expressed relief and pleasure at their arrival and slowly drank the entire quart of milk. They stayed with him for the remainder of the night. He felt recovered the following morning.

I slipped onto the passenger seat next to Bob, while Rob and Margo and Daniel and Pam stood listening, leaning in close over the open door.

"How are you feeling, Bob?"

"I'm fine." His pensive brown eyes momentarily focused on an accusing distracted manner, a high penetrating energy emanating from his flushed features. He didn't understand why he couldn't convince me that his vision and personal transformation were real.

"This probably all seems very strange to you, but the vision and these symbols are so vivid. Maybe I'm the only one gifted to see them . . ." He gazed out over the city and the encroaching sea. "We have to go now, before the earthquake happens."

"Dad --" The kids shot futile groping glances at each other, not knowing how to cope with the situation. I diverted to a new tack. "Listen, Bob, this is the first time I've ever really seen you let yourself go. Are you sure this isn't just your way of lashing back at me?"

"Just trust me. We're in the hands of God."

"You're talking nonsense."

"It happened in the Bible. Why do you doubt me? Why can't it happen now? I read how the prophets received their revelations from God. Now, it's happened to me. Why can't you accept this? Why can't you believe me?"

Rob squatted on the sidewalk and talked across his mother's lap to his father. "Dad, you've interpreted everything too literally. The Bible is only a story. It's mythology. Sure it's based on history, but most of it is myth."

"Do you believe in God?"

"Not necessarily a Biblical God," said Rob.

"Do you realize what you're saying?"

"Yes, and I don't think you realize what has happened to you, Dad."

Bob withdrew with a defensive pout of impatience unfolding from his previous expression of hyper-agitation. "Are all of you going to deny me the chance to save you? I've been endowed with the power to give you everlasting life."

"Bob," I projected a matter-of-fact attitude, "If we go with you and nothing happens, will you promise to stop behaving like this?" My manner was mother to child.

"I'll be relieved if it doesn't happen. It's time for us to go now. We can't afford to wait any longer."

Rob stared out over the panoramic slope below curving along the dark blue bay dotted with tiny white sails like distant floating gulls and then the darker ominous blue beyond where the channel deepened and merged with the purple island haze. He visualized the tranquility of this foliated garden city, a mosaic of white stucco with orange tile rooftops, suddenly crumbling into ruins, and the sea surge and swell into a three hundred-foot mountainous wall, and with prophetic doom descend over the city. He turned back to his father. "Listen, Dad. Let's just go up to the botanical gardens. That's high enough. If there really is an earthquake, we don't want to be up in the mountains with all those rocks and boulders."

"All right, we'll go to the botanical gardens. That will be our new Garden of Eden."

At that, I climbed out of the car. "I'm not going."

"But you have to."

"You go. I have a class full of children waiting."

"It's not safe here and I want us all together."

"There's not going to be any earthquake, Bob. I can't take any more time standing out here arguing with you. Miss Getlin will be coming up those steps any minute looking for me. Now please, Bob, try to get a hold of yourself. You shouldn't let a dream disturb you like that. I have to go now. You kids take care of him. I'll see you after school tonight." She quickly descended the steps.

Confused and frustrated, Bob stared after me, then started the engine. "It's time for us to go now." They closed the car doors and continued along the narrow winding road.

Later in the day, Rob told me what happened at the botanical gardens.

Only a few visitors wandered through the gardens during weekdays. The natural landscaped foliage lodged in a cut high in the foothills, a sumptuous spread of native golden plants, a meadow of wildflowers, a deep dank valley carpeted with ferns out of which suddenly towered clawing live oak and tall ancient redwoods. In another environment grew a mound of desert shrubs and spiny succulents.

They left the parking area and straggled as a group along the earthen walkways and footpaths to a shaded bench at the center of the park. Pam crawled up onto the bald dome of a sun-splashed boulder. The others sat on a bench constructed of weathered split logs and waited.

Bob leaned forward, elbows resting on his knees, and studied the purposeful movement of an ant at his feet. Sunlight filtering through the overshadowing oak struck one side of his face. The warmth soothed, then suddenly discomfited him. He shifted slightly to escape the rays and stared at his hands.

Passive, weary with their own collective impotence, the others sadly watched him. They nursed a fearful expectancy that decomposed the natural calm beauty of the surrounding gardens. Their sensations flitted with portents of lurking supernatural forces mingling with earth and plant smells and silent sunlight blinking among the leaves, breeding a flux of dappled shadows on the hard ground. Tiny lizards rattled about through the dry brush.

A small black sheltie snuffled by with twitching nose, lured into a stream of enticing scents exciting his imagination. He paused to cast a reticent glance in their direction, then continued on his course with a deft wave of his white-tipped rhythmic tail.

Moments later, a tall man followed by a woman and a small child appeared along the quiet path. They walked in silent single file, exuding a sense of ritual and formality in passing. The woman was tall and beautiful, slightly dark complexioned. The fair, curly-headed child laughed and talked to himself with delight, oblivious of their staring eyes. Sitting next to his father, Rob felt embarrassed that they would hear what his Dad was saying, but the group moved on.

"That was the Baby Jesus," said Bob. The man and the woman are Joseph and Mary. God put them here to walk by for us to see. It's a message from him."

"You're just reading into everything, Dad," said Rob.

"It's in the Bible. It's all there."

Pam slid down off the rock and stood slightly above and behind her father in utter disbelief. She eyed him with a strange compassion, a blend of quiet pity and absolute horror. "Oh, God, Dad, you've flipped out. What's happened to you? You've really flipped out."

"Dad," Rob gently touched his arm. "It's about twelve o'clock. There wasn't any earthquake. You said it would happen at ten o'clock . . . remember, you said it would happen and if it didn't happen, you'd laugh right along with the rest of us. Do you remember?"

"It won't happen. There's not going to be one."

"I think we should go home now. We have things to do."

Bob opened his eyes and looked around as if refreshed from a nap, yet still weary from his long ordeal. "Yes, we'll go home now." He stood and walked slowly, haltingly back through the garden to the parking area.

Manipulative, they were still wary, watchful, coaching, gently urging him along, dreading to antagonize him and set him off chasing some new metaphysical impulse like a berserk hound on a rabbit scent. They managed to herd him to the car and lock him safely inside.

Rob started the engine and drove away from the lot. Pam and Daniel followed with Margo driving the third car.

When they arrived at the condominium, Rob decided not to stay, but would return later to check in on the situation. Instructing his brother and sister to call should any problem with their father arise, any further unusual behavior, he and Margo departed with some trepidation.

When Rob returned alone later that evening, Bob was gone. I was preparing supper. My movements were slow and uneasy. Daniel and Pam had secluded themselves in other sections of the house in attempts to personally cope with their trauma. As it grew late, I began to worry.

"He took the car," I said.

"He really shouldn't be driving," said Rob. "Did he leave a note or anything?"

"No, at least I didn't see one."

"Where do you think he might have gone?"

"I have no idea."

The door suddenly slammed open, and Bob stumbled in staring glassy-eyed.

"You're just in time," I said. "Where were you?"

"Are you feeling better, Dad?" asked Rob.

"I'm not hungry." He moved on into the kitchen. "I'll just have some ice water."

I noticed his flushed feverish appearance. "Your face sure looks red."

Bob sipped his water with focused enjoyment. "I'm terribly thirsty. I feel like I can't get enough liquid."

"Where did you go?"

"To the ballgame." He walked slowly to the couch. There wasn't any team or baseball game in Santa Barbara.

"You don't look too well," I said. "Do you feel all right?"

"I'm fine."

"You must have been sitting out in the open."

"Yes, I was. That's a lie. I wasn't at the ballgame. I -- I was at the track down at Santa Anita. I lost three hundred dollars. I don't know why I felt like I had to lie. Why should a man ever lie? There should be no need for him to lie."

I sat on a chair opposite him. "Are you sure you're all right, Bob?"

"Yes, I just need a lot of water is all. I feel a little dehydrated."

"Do you want me to fix you some orange juice?"

"No, water's fine. You don't mind that I lost the money?"

"Of course I mind. I guess I shouldn't make you feel guilty and want to lie about it."

"That's strange . . . that's very strange. Everything's so obscure now all of a sudden. When I left the track, a cloud of fog came over the road. I followed a set of taillights on the car ahead of me. They led me all the way down through the city to Fisherman's Wharf.

"I went to the Harbor Restaurant where we ate that one time. You remember? I went in and sat at the same table. There were flowers at the center of the table . . . a beautiful bouquet of fresh flowers. The waitress brought me one glass of water. But I told her I was meeting another person, so she brought me another. I waited for about twenty minutes, Mary. And you never came. I left, then, and drove up into the mountains. I found a little dirt road and followed it back into the woods. There was an old, deserted cabin there. I got out and looked around. No one lived there anymore. The door was swinging open and shut in the wind. The name 'Lucy' was painted in white letters on the door." He looked at me with a vacant smile. "You know, Mary. I never realized until that moment, but you're my Lucy. . . you're my Lucy."

Chapter 40

Work

Bob refused to eat and retired to bed as soon as the others had finished supper. When we thought he was asleep, we gathered in a family huddle to discuss his bizarre behavior and what we should do.

"He acts like he's on a trip," said Daniel.

"It could have been the sun," Rob said. Mom said he kept getting up and drinking water all last night. Maybe he's so dehydrated, he had a sunstroke."

"But it seems like he's almost in a schizophrenic state," Pam muttered hesitantly from her corner.

"Maybe we should call a doctor."

"No," I said. "I don't think that's necessary. This is just some experience he's going through. It doesn't warrant all this preoccupation with his mind. He'll snap out of it."

"But what if it's really serious?"

"Let him go through this. It may do him good to release himself. Half the time he's so coherent and rational. I've always said he should let himself go once in a while. I just wish he'd picked something besides religion. When he talks that way, it makes me ill."

"Not me," said Rob. "He's got me scared shitless."

Daniel slowly shook his head. "I never would have thought this could happen to him -- especially him. He's always so steady and predictable, but now, hell, I don't know how to act with him. I don't want him to know I think he's crazy."

"He's not crazy. Don't even say that word," I bristled.

"Well, he's sure not acting normal."

"None of us are normal, especially me. I'm crazier than anybody -- any of us."

Rob went home and returned early the next morning before breakfast. I was vacuuming the carpet. He wondered why I had not gone to school. I glanced up from my intense concentration on imagined lint and dirt. "Did you have breakfast yet?"

"No."

"Would you like some eggs?"

"No, cereal's fine. How come you're not at school?"

"I decided to stay home today."

"Dad all right?"

I nodded, then shook my head.

"Anything happen last night?"

"No -- only he tried to get me to touch his robe. He said it was a holy garment."

"He's gettin' all that shit from readin' the damn Bible," said Rob. "What did you do?"

"I told him to cut it out. I said he could immerse himself in religion if he wants, but not to try to include me. I won't have it. The excessive gush is repulsive."

"Where is he now?"

"Out taking a walk."

"How does he seem?"

He seems to be completely recovered. He said he wanted to take a short walk. Then he's going to work."

"He said he was going to work?"

"Yes."

"That's good to hear." Rob poured a bowl of cereal and sat at the table. "How are you feeling?"

"Cynical." I began a vigorous round of dusting the living room furniture.

Rob finished and was rinsing his bowl at the kitchen sink when Pam and Daniel came downstairs barefoot and sleepy-eyed. "How is he today?" Pam yawned.

"He went out for a walk." I flashed them a harried glance. "He said he'll be going to work later."

"That's a relief," said Pam. "I couldn't take much more of what happened last night. I never would have believed this could happen to us. The mind is so powerful. You never really know what's going on in there. We all should have learned something from what happened."

"If you're referring to what I said last night, my feelings haven't changed," I said. "You let us worry about our relationship. Just be concerned with yourself."

"My self happens to care."

"Your dad and I have always had a good relationship."

The front door opened. Bob entered beaming an expression of content. We all noticed he was clean-shaven, dressed in slacks and a sport shirt. He acknowledged our barrage of greetings with a broad smile.

"How are you feeling?" Rob had to reassure himself.

"Wonderful, just wonderful, never better."

I moved toward the kitchen. "Would you like some breakfast now?"

"No, I'm not hungry. I'll just have a little orange juice." He poured himself a tall glass from the pitcher on the counter.

Daniel savagely chewed and swallowed a mouthful of mushy cereal. "Mom says you're goin' back to work."

"Yes, I am. I had to find my work first."

We all fidgeted with a tremor of renewed anxiety. "What are you talking about?" I asked.

"I just had the most wonderful walk this morning and -- I found my work. I discovered what I really want to do."

"What's that?"

"Let me tell you how it happened. I walked up to that church on the hill. There is a larger-than-life size painting of Jesus Christ next to the door. You've all walked by there before, I'm sure. I stood and stared at him for a long time -- and his eyes moved, and he looked at me."

Rob gripped the seat of his chair. "Yes, but that's a common psychological phenomenon. You look at any painting long enough with figures on it and you can imagine that it moved."

"This wasn't like that. This was a miracle."

Daniel's fist smashed down on the table. "Come off it, Dad. You know his eyes didn't really move. I've had the same effect when I looked at it."

"You have? Then you know. This is a sign to me that our whole family has been singled out."

"Bullshit!" Rob rose abruptly from the table and refused to waver under Bob's disapproving glance.

"Listen," said Bob. "Listen to what I have to say. I felt overcome with a warm glow while looking into his eyes. I was unable to move from where I was standing. I felt paralyzed. Finally, he directed me to walk into a small field of flowers. Thousands of bees were swarming there. I carefully sat down among them. They landed all over me. I felt no fear, only this all-pervasive warm glow. Not one bee stung me. Can you imagine, out of all those, not one bee. After about twenty minutes, I stood up and gently brushed them off, then walked away. It is a divine revelation like in the Bible. He has shown me my work. I will study the Bible and go out and teach His Word."

"You mean you're just going to forget about working?" I said. "You're not going back?"

"You don't seem to understand. Teaching His Word is my work."

"How do you propose to continue supporting a family ?" It took a considerable effort for me to remain standing in a state of rigid calm firing these questions at him.

"We'll live in the mountains where the air is fresh and clear. Daniel has shown us the way to life in the mountains."

"Dad, you need money to exist and get along in society, even in the mountains."

"Don't worry, son, there will be no society. We will be provided for."

"How?"

"God will watch over us and take care of us. We will be provided for. Please now, no more questions. I'm going to study for a while." Misinterpreting the tears streaming down my face for tears of happiness, he left the room with a smile of serenity.

"Mom, we've got to get him to the hospital."

"I know. I know. Call somebody."

Rob lunged for the wall phone and ravaged the yellow pages under psychiatrists, as I stiffened with sorrow and anxiety.

Rob waited for the duration of three rings. "I'd like to speak with Dr. Ellison. It's very important. This is an emergency. . . Hello, Dr. Ellison, my name is Rob Wenger. I'm calling concerning my father. He came home from the racetrack yesterday afternoon and it looked as if he had had too much sun. He's suddenly changed completely. He won't eat anything. He just drinks water and orange juice and refuses to go back to work." Rob went on to explain the events relating to his father's disturbed behavior. He listened intently to the doctor's instructions, thanked him, then hung up the phone.

"He wants us to bring Dad into the hospital as soon as we can. But he told me not to force him. Dad has to want to go in of his own free will or it'll be harder for the psychiatrist to work with him. He said he didn't want him brought in kicking and struggling if at all possible. It's going to be hard, the doctor said, and to just keep our heads and play it cool. Don't force Dad in any way. And he said that -- that Dad could potentially be very dangerous to us and not even realize what he's doing."

"How could he be dangerous? Look how he's acting. Anyone so full of love couldn't possibly hurt anything or anybody." I wept brokenly.

"That's just it. The doctor said he could be acting extreme to repress the inclination to do bodily harm."

"I don't believe it. I won't believe it. We've been married twenty-five years and I know him better than that."

I sat on the couch. "My god, what did I ever do to deserve this?"

A large wasp had come into the house when Bob entered earlier. Looking in on his father, Rob discovered it respirating where it clung to the bedroom drapes. Blanketed in bed reading his Bible, Bob warned Rob not to disturb the wasp, that he was communicating with it. Rob expressed anger at the freak incident which only further encouraged Bob. A while later, Bob opened the balcony door, and the wasp flew free.

Later that morning, Rob and Daniel went grocery shopping with me, leaving Pam to watch her father. Seeing that he was sedate enough, engrossed in his Bible, she went out for a swim in the pool. A half-hour later, she woke sharply from a doze in the warm sun.

One of the neighbors, a compassionate elderly man, was guiding Bob across the courtyard to the apartment steps. She sprang up from the lounge and raced over to them, thanking the man, who offered a quick explanation: he had discovered Bob in a field up on a hill near the church, crying out and braying and bellowing animal noises at the sky.

Pam helped her Dad inside. She noticed that he still carried his Bible, but his eyes were closed and a constant unwavering smile stretched frozen across his face. His breath smelled like a foul gas rising from a decomposing carcass. He slowly raised his arms in supplication. Horrified, she backed away with a soul-piercing scream that flooded into a ranting raving tirade. "STOP IT. STOP IT. I CAN'T STAND IT ANYMORE. DAD! OH, GOD, OH MY GOD!"

The smile dissolved into an expression of injury and withdrawal. He slowly, mechanically sat down and again thumbed through the pages of the Bible to where he had left off his reading.

Pam watched and waited with apprehension that he would attempt to go out again and she would not be able to prevent him. When the rest of us finally returned, she confronted me with hysterics.

"Mom, we have to do something. We can't just let him go on like this. I sat and talked with him for a while like you said. Then when he started reading again, I went out and fell asleep by the pool. When I woke up, Mister Landingham was leading him back home. He said Dad had been wandering around up on the hill making animal noises. Mom, we've got to get him to the hospital."

"I know. I know. But the doctor said not to force him."

"Damn it, Mom, we have to try to get him out of here," Rob moved in. "We can't just let it go on. It's going to get worse."

"Robbie . . .Robbie." Bob stared forward glassy eyed as if he were blind.

"Yes, Dad."

His voice rattled, hoarse and failing. "Sit down here beside me. I want to read something beautiful to you." When Rob was sitting shoulder to shoulder with him, Bob spoke slowly and with great weariness. "I'll never have to drive down to Los Angeles again. I've always hated to go down there. Now I've found my work. You will be my first disciple. The world will be cleansed. You will not have to go into the military service and fight Satan's war. Our family will always be together now. Listen."

"Dad," Rob spoke calmly, "We're going to take you to go see the doctor now."

"Do you believe I could receive a great revelation from God?"

"I -- Dad --"

Bob grew petulant and persistent. "Do you believe I could receive a direct revelation from God?"

Perplexed, Rob could only stare at his father's profile.

"Tell me, yes or no."

"I don't think it's very probable, but I believe in the possibility."

"Yes or no."

Rob looked desperately at the rest of us for help but we only returned numb stares of emotional impotence and the inability to act out of a lack of knowledge. Rob looked directly back at his father. "Yes."

"Listen." Bob read slowly in halting phrases from a page in the Bible. "And anything that my eyes asked for, I did not keep away from them. I did not hold back my heart from any sort of rejoicing, for my heart was joyful because of all my hard work, and this came to be my portion from all my hard work. And I . . . turned toward all the works of mine that my hands had done and toward the hard work that I had worked hard to accomplish, and look! Everything was vanity and a striving after the wind, and there was nothing of advantage under the sun."

Tears filled his eyes as he continued. "And I hated life, because the work that had been done under the sun was calamitous from my standpoint, for everything was vanity and a striving after the wind. And I myself have seen all the hard work and all the proficiency in work, that it seems the rivalry of one toward another. This also is vanity and a striving after the wind. Do you understand?"

"Yes."

Bob gripped Rob's arm and hand so that their fingers desperately interlocked. "Dad, you have to go see the doctor. It's for your own good. You're not well, Dad. You're not well."

He closed his eyes and released Rob's hand. The vacuous smile returned to his face. Rob carefully rose from the couch and went determinedly to the phone. He dialed 911.

"My name is Rob Wenger. We need an ambulance. My father has suffered a mental breakdown and we have to get him to the hospital . Yes, Doctor Ellison . No, he hasn't been violent at all, exactly the opposite . I see . Blue Cross . All right. I'd like to request that you please don't use the siren . No, it won't be necessary. It will only frighten him . 6092 Ridge Road. It's a condominium, number five. My brother will be outside watching for you. Thank you."

As Rob returned to the living room, he saw Bob suddenly rise from the couch and with eyes remaining closed and the vacuous smile stitched into his features, shuffle to the center of the room, stop and stare upward. He threw the Bible to the floor, then brought his hands together in an attitude of prayer with his fingers pointed upward exaggeratedly under his chin such as in artists' renderings of saints. He began to rock slowly back and forth. Rob moved near to prevent him from falling. "Daniel, you'd better go outside and wait. The ambulance will be here any minute."

Bob stopped rocking, then shuffled on to the front door Daniel had left open. With Rob sheltering close beside him, he stepped outside onto the green lawn. He raised his head at the electronic hum of a tiny hovering hummingbird. It vanished. The sun rained down on them with a startling, heightened intensity. They stood drenched in sweat, absorbing the verdant smells of the orchard below.

Bob's breathing increased from shallow to long, slow, deep rhythmical breaths. The momentum increased gradually until he was hyperventilating at a rapid rate, each expulsion of breath accompanied by a small plaintive hoarse groan and salivation at the corners of his mouth. Again he rocked back and forth. The frenzy subsided. He slowly placed his hands palms down, before him a few inches from his thighs and knelt, with Rob balancing him, until he was in an extreme squatting position, a fetal position, with hands resting on the ground to support himself. He remained so for a short period, moved further down on one elbow, as his mind slipped further from reality, and he toppled over. Rob supported his head to prevent injury as the muscles locked in a state of catatonia, the smile still frozen on his father's face. He checked to make sure his father had not swallowed his tongue. And then the paramedics rounded the corner pushing a gurney.

Chapter 41

Guilt

Unable to do anything more for Bob, we returned home from the hospital haggard and emotionally exhausted.

"He'll be all right," I kept murmuring. "I know he'll be all right." I caught Rob's accusing glance. "Why are you looking at me that way?" Low anger kindled my voice. I rose from the couch. "You blame me, don't you?" I turned, my hurt stare including Pam and Daniel. "You all blame me."

"Oh, Mom, come off it," said Daniel.

"You do, though. I can see it in your eyes. Well, let me tell you something." I stalked each of them. "If you think you can sit there and accuse me, you've got another think coming."

"We're not accusing you of anything."

"Oh, but you are. You may not come right out and say it, but you are."

"All right, so you see it for yourself," said Rob.

Shot with pain, I winced away from them with a shudder. My voice grew quiet, distant with love and memory. "When you were small, I used to stand at the window at our house in Edgebrook and watch all of you cross the street to school and my heart would be in my mouth that something would happen to you in all that morning traffic. Now I know what you really think of me." I was crying brokenly. "I came from a poor family and we never had anything but we knew what love was. We had that. We loved each other. You hate me. You all hate me." I rushed to my bedroom and slammed the door.

Pam immediately turned on her older brother. "See what you did."

"What the fuck are you talking about?"

"You didn't have to tell her that."

"I didn't tell her anything. She's got it in her own mind."

"You put it there."

"Bull shit. We all put it there. We're all to blame. Hell, the doctor said Dad would be able to come home and go back to work in a couple of weeks. This is just something we all have to live through."

"Okay, but what about Mom?" said Pam. "You hurt her feelings pretty bad."

"I hurt -- oh, for shit's sake. Whattya want me to do? All right. This thing's gotten to all of us. After seeing what he went through, I'm sure going to be strong enough to never let it happen to me. I'm hungry." He and Daniel went into the kitchen and made lunchmeat and cheese sandwiches. "You hungry, Pam?"

She shook her head, began to cry and went to her bedroom. Rob and Daniel followed me. They clearly wanted me to hear what they had to say.

"You know," said Rob, "When I was seven years old, I was helping Dad wash the car once and I shut the door on his fingers. He told me to open it fast and I just stood there and laughed. I don't know why and I didn't know why then, probably just a nervous reaction. I couldn't help it. It just came out of me. He finally had to open it himself. He was mad and told me to get away from him. I could never figure out why I laughed though. A lot of things I see that are funny nobody else laughs at. In the movies sometimes, I'll be the only one laughing. I saw a war movie once. There was this young German soldier trapped in a trench with bombs and dirt falling in all around him. Actually, he was only a boy, about sixteen. Anyway, he was screaming with fear because he was going to die. I mean really screaming and the camera just held on his face. And the look on his face suddenly made me laugh. Then somebody behind me was shouting at me to shut up and I suddenly saw that everybody else in the theater was quiet. It kind of bothers me but it was just a reaction I guess."

"Do you remember when I was dating Nancy?" Daniel asked.

"I remember," I said.

"We got to be good friends, but you know how you and Dad felt about her. Well, Dad told me he wasn't just a parent, but that we were friends too and that he wanted us to always be honest with each other and there would never be any hard feelings about something. So he asked me if I'd been having sex with her and I told him yes. Boy, did he get pissed off. I'd never tell him anything personal again after that."

"That's how parents lose their credibility," said Rob. "They're not friends. Parents are parents and children are children. And even though you're growing up and finding out about yourself and the world, never tell them something you don't want them to know about. You're entitled to your privacy. Just don't tell them everything. They look at us ideally, you know, which we aren't, and they don't want to see what they don't want to see or hear in us. It happens anyway, though. It can't help but happen. They have to learn too. I suppose it's harder for them than it is for us, because they're losing something and we're gaining something. That's why I can't see that it hurts to hold back what is private and personal to you. It's a hell of a paradox. They want to push you on and hold you at the same time and finally it reaches a point where everything explodes. And it's going to happen no matter what, because that's the way life is. The love is still there, but it's different. It's not dependent love anymore. It's independent. There's more respect involved -- at least for me -- and gratitude. In a sense the love is even stronger. But they have to accept us for what we are then."

"Yeah -- shit."

"I know."

I felt confused by what they had told me.

Later, Pam looked in on me.

"How's Mom?" Rob asked.

"I gave her a couple of aspirins. She's taking a nap."

"Did she say anything?"

"No, she just wanted to be left alone. Do you have the keys?"

"Yes."

"I'll take them."

"Why?"

She shrugged. "I've got to get away for a while."

"Where?"

"I don't know. Anywhere."

"Maybe you'd better stick around."

"What for?"

"Well, when she wakes up."

"It won't matter if I'm here or not," said Pam.

"I think we should all be here."

"Why are you so concerned about it all of a sudden?"

"She needs us. That's why."

"I won't be gone that long."

"How long?"

"What's the matter with you?" Pam challenged hard.

"Just stay here, huh?"

Daniel interrupted. "You sure don't sound like what you were just talking about."

"What do you mean?" Rob glanced at him in irritation.

"Breaking away."

"That has nothing to do with it, especially in a family crisis. You have to be together because you don't have anything else."

Pam snorted. "You really do think we're the cause of it, don't you?"

"I'd say we had a lot to do with it."

"What about Dad though," said Daniel. "A lot of men go through worse and they don't crack up."

"Yeah, but look at Dad, all the shit he had to put up with when he was a kid and always being stepped on right up 'til now, and he never lets it out. He keeps everything inside. He never gets mad."

"Well?"

"I mean really mad. He's never even tried to shout any of us down, including Mom. Hell, we've done nothing but take advantage of him all our lives."

"Bull shit," Pam shot back. "He got married and had a family because he wanted to. He's like he is because that's how he wants to be. Just because things don't work out the way you want, you've got to be strong enough to adjust and change."

"You're one to talk."

"Oh, no, you're the one who's scared. You've got just as big a security hang-up as Mom does."

"I admit it, not as bad though. Scared, yes, but let's not kid ourselves. We're all scared. We're all --" Rob suddenly reached into his pocket for the keys and tossed them to her.

"What happens if Dad doesn't get better?" asked Daniel.

Pam traced the jagged tooth pattern of the keys with her forefinger. "He will. You heard what the doctor said."

Rob brushed several loose crumbs from the counter into the sink. "The doctor said if he does, he should snap out of it fast. He didn't guarantee it was positive. Even if he does, I kind of worry about it happening again."

"From now on it's going to be him and Mom anyway," said Pam. "This will probably bring them closer together."

"We're still hanging on."

"Once we find where to break off, we'll break." Pam went to the front door.

Daniel chugged his glass of milk. "I'm coming too."

"No, I want to be alone."

"You can drop me off someplace then and pick me up later."

"Where?"

"Cold Springs Canyon. I want to go on a hike."

"That's too far out of the way."

"I don't care, dammit, just drop me off."

"Oh, all right."

When they had gone, Rob rinsed the glasses and was putting away the bread and cheese when I came downstairs red-eyed and puffy-faced.

"I thought you were taking a nap."

"I can't sleep. Is there any coffee in that pot?"

"Yeah, want some?"

I nodded and sat at the table half-angled toward him. "Where are Pam and Daniel?"

"They went for a drive."

"Oh."

"I told them."

"What?"

"I told them they probably shouldn't leave right now."

"That's okay."

"I'm sorry about what I said before."

"Don't be. It's true."

"No -- it's all of us and Dad too."

"Not your dad." Her eyes flooded with anger. "What do you know about it? Don't ever underestimate your father. He's got a lot more strength than I have. He has to put up with the likes of us. I'm the weak one. I depend on him."

"He depends on you too."

"Don't you think I know that? Sometimes I think you're very critical of your dad and me. Just remember he loves you very much."

"I know."

"He couldn't help being away all the time when you were younger. He wanted to be home and be able to spend time with you, but he couldn't because of his job. We know that."

"I'm not blaming him or you."

"And when he was home, you always took off to be with your friends. That hurt him but at least he was understanding about it."

"I never knew that."

"We never do until it's too late."

"I wish this never happened."

"It doesn't do any good to wish."

"Yeah." Rob poured the coffee. While placing the cup and saucer on the table, he awkwardly touched my arm. We suddenly embraced in mutual comfort and sympathy. "I'm sorry, Mom. I'm the one who's not strong. It's got me scared. To see it happen to him. I know he's strong. I've always known it. Both of you are. I -- I'm worried about it happening to me some day."

"You'll never have to worry about that. You've got a better start in life than Dad or I ever had. Maybe now you can see how important it is to get into a lucrative profession. This never would have happened if he were in the position, he's capable of holding and making the money he should."

"He was offered that position once, but you said you wouldn't go with him."

"There you go jumping at me again."

"Mom, I'm not jumping at you but you've got to stick with Dad. You've got to. By the way, are you going to call his boss?"

"I suppose I should, tomorrow."

"He won't lose his job because of this, will he? My god, I never thought of that."

"No, no, they'll understand."

"I sure hope so. Oh, shit this is such a fucked-up world."

"What's bothering you now?"

"Not knowing. The not knowing. I'm just trying to hash out some things in my own mind. What did the doctor say about visiting Dad?"

"I'm supposed to call him Wednesday. He did say we can't all see him at the same time. Just one or two for short periods. The doctor said the most important thing is to show Dad how much we love him and need him. He thinks we all hate him."

"Damn, damn, what a mess. Hate him? How are we going to face him? I don't know what the hell to say." Rob looked away.

"You'll know what to say."

"It's going to be awkward though. Will he know he's in a psychiatric ward?"

"Yes, I didn't want that because I know he's not that far gone. But the psychiatrist said he would feel safe in there."

"I know what you mean. The way those medical aides kept staring. They looked like they were inmates themselves. And that damn Dr. Ellison and his cock-of-the-walk attitude. All he could keep saying was Dad's crazy. I felt like hauling off and clobbering him. But it is serious. Dad I mean. You can't ignore that."

"Where did Pam and Daniel go?"

"They didn't say." Rob gazed out the window. "Why is it that Dad would never express to us what he really felt? I mean if he was angry, why didn't he just come right out and blast us?"

"That's not his way. He never had any love and affection when he was a child. You remember him telling us about that. He was selling newspapers to help feed and support six brothers and sisters when he was thirteen."

"Is he afraid to? Maybe he's always been afraid to -- afraid of driving us away from him." Rob noticed my fresh tears. "What's the matter? Are you all right?"

"Can't you quit harping on it? Can't you leave it alone?" I quickly left the room. Rob turned away with frustration at himself. "God damn son of a bitch."

***

When I visited Bob, he watched a man pacing up and down the hall. The entire ward offered a fishbowl effect so the white-coated attendants could always see at a glance what the patients were doing. The pacing man was bald except for the furrows of brown hair clinging to either side of his shiny scalp like two enlarged caterpillars. He clutched a large bowl pipe in his teeth and, smoking like a steam ship, walked along bent slightly forward, his hands clasped behind him. Bob watched him sail steadily back and forth hour after hour like a mechanical target shoot in an amusement park arcade.

A tall kindly Black attendant came in several times a day to give Bob a relaxant drug washed down with fruit juice. The attendant always waited to be sure Bob swallowed the pill. He also encouraged him to drink several glasses of water during the day, since the dehydration had contributed to Bob's chemical imbalance.

When the psychiatrist consulted with him, Bob was always aware of his control in questioning and assessing answers, getting him to open up and talk, motivating him to think inwardly upon himself, evaluate and attempt to understand what had happened to him and the current state of his mind. Bob told me he found the psychiatrist to be pleasant, slow-speaking and unthreatening, a man younger than himself by fifteen years, although he showed signs of balding which gave him a sage aspect.

Bob would sometimes talk with a young red-headed man, a patient who wandered into his room on occasion and sat on the adjoining bed and stared at the floor. He was congenial, conversational, but incapable of maintaining direct eye contact.

From a sitting position propped up in his bed, Bob had a clear view of the Santa Ynez Mountains framed by flaxen plumes of pampas grass just outside his window. His eyes were glazed from the effect of soporific drugs and his movements were slow and torpid from the constant state of being tranquilized.

He was seized with a sensation of being trapped in the ward, but the feeling was shared with a simultaneous sense of security. When members of his family came to visit, a strong desire to leave with them consumed him. The attendant always accompanied us to the door at our departure to insure he didn't attempt to follow when we said our goodbyes.

The period of rest and observation allowed him time to relax and reflect and remember. After two weeks, the psychiatrist released him from the hospital, and he returned home just before Rob was inducted into the Air Force.

Chapter 42

Dream House

During his spare time, Bob spent hours sketching and drawing the design for what was to become our custom final dream house, a place for our children and grandchildren to visit and stay with us and for holiday gatherings, birthdays, and summertime fun.

For only ten thousand dollars, we had purchased a one acre lot in an exclusive residential area in the foothills of Santa Barbara a few miles up the road from Montecito Village.

I had achieved my educational career goal and was migrating from teaching sixth and seventh graders to teenagers at Santa Barbara High School. I especially enjoyed English literature, stimulating class discussions about novels by such literary authors as Conrad, Hemingway, Faulkner, and F. Scott Fitzgerald.

Oddly enough, many of my students gathered around my desk at the end of class during the lunch hour to talk with me about how much they were learning and about their personal problems. Unlike with my own family, I guess I was a nonjudgmental, sympathetic listener.

Armed with architectural blueprints, Bob hired the lowest priced general contractor he could find to make our dream home a reality. He went over the excavation plans with Glenn Burgess in explicit detail to support the tri-level structure and incorporate a double staircase that we loved but would one day become an unforeseen problematic feature for me.

Despite congenial Glenn showing up on the construction site every day with a wine bottle in a brown paper bag, the framing and skeletal walls seemed to grow out of the ground. He was never drunk, just weathered, unshaven, and cantankerous directing his two sons to do the heavy work. Glenn's expertise was as a mason. He constructed a massive stone fireplace that nearly filled the entire wall at the far end of the living room and became a stunning visual focal point next to the large picture window looking out onto the black asphalt driveway and a forest of redwood and pine trees Bob and Daniel had planted together shortly after we moved in.

Anywhere we looked from any room, upstairs and downstairs, trees, flowering plants, and foliage graced our view. The beautiful redwood siding was Bob's pride and joy. Our house looked like a mountain chateau in a woodland setting. Built for only forty-five thousand dollars, it appreciated significantly in value during the years we lived there.

Bob hated the commute up and down the coast on the 101 freeway to Los Angeles twice a week. Having established customers who thoroughly trusted him, he discovered he could work from home. They called him on the phone to place orders that he relayed back to the manufacturing and distribution plant in Rockford, Illinois. The fastener parts would be shipped directly to the aerospace companies in Los Angeles.

No longer having to commute to Los Angeles, he was finally able to just relax into retirement and enjoy our house and the visits of our children and grandchildren.

I showered our grandchildren with gifts on holidays and throughout the year as the impulse struck me, unconsciously seeking their love and affection in return, not realizing how very much they loved me without the gifts.

Rob's and Margo's ten-year-old daughter, our granddaughter, gave us a wonderful gift that captured the essence of our home, a charcoal drawing of the house accompanied by a description of what it symbolized to her. I framed the drawing and caption, so dear to my heart, and hung it in prominent view on the kitchen wall.

Bob told me that the last ten years were the best years of his life, because I was happy. We actually had a congenial relationship free of tension.

He designed and built a wooden observation deck extending the back porch from the kitchen sliding door overlooking the pool. Then later, he constructed a larger wooden deck with steps leading down to the water at the far end of the pool.

Such home projects gave him great personal satisfaction. He loved the details of precision measurement, buying wood, sawing and trim, screws and nails, framing and support, and finally, diligently applying the wood stain.

He went for walks along the quiet neighborhood streets lined with tall eucalyptus trees and abundant varieties of desert cacti and sprouting spreading succulents. His route usually took him through the natural environmental park that backed our property and was frequented by deer during the early morning. Occasionally, we heard the high-pitched wails of coyotes loping through the park in search of rabbits and up and down the hilly streets hoping to find a small pet loose in someone's yard.

The only issue I had about how he used his time was that he watched far too much television. I would have preferred that he read good literary books. He did learn to play the piano, however, simple tunes self-taught on a spinet we bought to replace the piano we had owned since our Edgebrook days and was now in Rob's and Margo's home in Orange County.

Pam lived with us while teaching part time at Santa Barbara Community College until she was edged out by academic politics. She decorated her bedroom in the lower level of the house with Native American medicine artifacts and paraphernalia and filled her shelves with books about tribal medicine culture and New Age spiritualism. As part of her experimentation and religious search for something more meaningful than the here and now through mythological cosmic spiritual influences, she submerged herself in

New Age cultist worship. When she tried to describe it to me, I told her it was nothing more than Satanism.

At a loss for gainful employment, she invested and lost five thousand dollars from her savings in a Ponzi scheme that she said had to be kept under the radar. Being gullible and trusting in the goodness of humanity, she vehemently denied she had been conned when the promised doubling return on her investment never materialized.

What burned me was the hours she spent on the phone trying to get other people, even relatives, to invest. She finally stopped when she learned she was an accomplice in criminal fraud and could be arrested. She said she would manifest wealth, which meant she would wish for it to magically happen for her. I didn't understand what was happening to her.

Bob basically let her know he wasn't interested in what she had to say about her New Age philosophy. Her obsession limited our communication with her, except when the two horses she kept in the paddock Bob had built behind the house were the topic of discussion. Wearing a straw hat, Bob enjoyed going out and feeding the horses and shoveling up manure which he added to a growing pile, available to anyone wanting fertilizer.

Because of the association, our four grandchildren dubbed him Farmer Bob, better known to them as Poppa. Farmer Bob suited him well. He was a down-to-earth, no-nonsense plodder, most content when he was out working in the corral, cleaning up horse manure or planting something. He was tied to the seasons, to the clock, to stability. But his best characteristic was a penchant to often be droll. If he was Poppa Bob, the farmer, what did that make me? An excitable, compulsive, exercise prone, squeamish vegetarian whose mind buzzed faster than I could keep up with it, but who frequently stopped to apprise her wrinkles and spidery legs.

Being who I am, never satisfied, I wanted to push out the dining room glass wall to better accommodate the long dining room table. Always wanting to please me, Bob set about the task. To avoid a property tax increase, he managed to convince a contractor to do the job without a city code inspection. He regretted his decision when the roof leaked during the first heavy rainfall.

Raised in poverty as a child of The Great Depression, he had always been overly conservative, miserly, when it came to spending money. I, on the other hand, also raised in poverty, did not share his sentiment. I had long ago turned my back on The Depression and had no problem spending money. The faulty roof reinforced for me the adage that when it comes to quality, you get what you pay for. Bob had a difficult time getting the contractor to return and rebuild that section of the roof.

Chapter 43

Bob's Goodbye

I quit my teaching position several years before I was ready to retire in order to take care of Bob when he was diagnosed with colon cancer. We made many trips for him to be seen by an oncologist who had discovered evidence of cysts throughout Bob's liver, and scanned images, and biopsies of cysts taken from his lower intestine. The size of his lymph nodes had increased and the cancer was traveling to other internal organs. Every day for several weeks, I drove him to the hospital to undergo chemotherapy.

As he continued to lose weight, his very existence deteriorated. He refused to look at his image in the bathroom mirror. He turned off the light and washed his face and brushed his teeth in the dark.

For several years, in her search for personal relevancy and meaning, Pam had been reading about Native American medicine and Qi gong, as practiced by Asian mystics and self-proclaimed healers. She believed she possessed the mental power to heal others, which was ridiculous in my book.

I was so desperate and fearful at the inevitable loss of Bob, I agreed to let Pam bring a pseudo shaman into the house who claimed he could cure Bob's cancer. What a travesty that turned out to be. He wasn't a Native American. He was a young barefoot, bead-wearing hippy Caucasian man Pam had met at one of the various alternative medicine groups in which she participated. He had not been compensated for contract information technology work he had completed for a company and had turned his back on being conventionally employed. His claims to have healing powers fit right in with what Pam wanted to believe.

He spent two days alone with Bob in his room. From time to time, Pam and I heard him beating a drum and singing Native American chants. On the second day, we heard Bob coughing and gagging. The pseudo shaman came running down the stairs shouting, "He's throwing up the cancer! He's cured! He's cured!"

That did it for me. I screamed at him to get out of my house. I shouted at Pam, "Don't you ever bring someone like that here again! Do you hear me? Never again!"

Bob's pain and suffering and transformation from a healthy man to a skeleton of his former self horrified me. That I could do nothing to prevent him from withering away and dying in such pain devastated me. I sat by his bedside for hours while he spent his final days in our home under hospice care. I watched him self-administer morphine through an IV by using a small pump.

Whenever I came into the room, his eyes flooded with an expression of love as he gazed at me. He expressed his gratitude to the hospice caretaker, a gentle, soft-spoken middle-aged woman, who tended to his functional needs.

With deep sadness, our children and grandchildren came to see him and say goodbye. He told them not to be sad, but to remember the wonderful times they had had together, to remember him as their Poppa.

Just before he died, he asked Robbie to mount a round clock where he could see it high on the wall from his bed and know the time. The only clock available had gold numbers against a black background, but no hands.

"Where are the hands?" he asked, panic in his voice. "It doesn't have hands."

The morphine caused him to hallucinate. In his delirium, he said he was a wizard creating his own life.

I went berserk the moment he died. Screaming and crying at the horror of his death, I ran wildly throughout the house. My anguish echoed in every room. I was insane with grief.

Bob had always taken great pride in his lovely wavy hair that had turned gray with age, but remained lovely and wavy, except for the effects of the chemo, which caused some hair loss, but not all.

When Robbie and his wife took me to see his corpse at the mortuary, Bob's embalmed body was lying prone in his casket. He was a skeleton with a thin layer of skin. Grief engulfed me at his closed eyes and lifeless desiccated face. He was dressed in the favorite tan tweed sportscoat that he had worn to meet with business customers during the years he commuted to Los Angeles. His favorite ordinary brown tie appeared to strangle what remained of the thin strands of his neck.

I fussed at the mortician and wanted him to restore Bob's lovely hair, an impossibility. As a gesture to accommodate my request, the mortician took out a hand comb and made a futile effort of combing Bob's gray tuft of stiff dead hair.

As we left, Robbie held my hand and said, "That isn't Dad in there. It looks like a shrunken version of him, but his body is more like the exoskeleton shed by an insect. He's moved on."

Our daughter, Pam, had been with him during his final moments and had steadily increased the morphine dosage against the pain at his last words, "More. More." Although, as she told me later, she wondered if what he really meant was "No more."

Since Bob died one day shy of his seventy-fifth birthday, the kids handled the funeral like a birthday celebration, including a frosted cake, recorded piano music, and helium filled balloons floating up to the ceiling at the conclusion of the eulogies.

A few of his business associates who had driven up to Santa Barbara from Los Angeles expressed their condolences to me.

Several close relatives and family friends were in attendance. Seated in the front row of the small cemetery chapel, I watched and listened to my children and grandchildren share their remembrances of their Dad and dear Poppa.

We did not have any clergy preside over the ceremony. I did not want the taint of religion in his passing.

Following the funeral, I was in mourning and could not overcome the deep sadness, depression, and regret I felt at his loss. I visited his gravesite every day to honor his memory. I brought fresh colorful flowers. After arranging them in the sunken metal holder at his headstone, I would recall our life's journey together and tell him that before long, I would be joining him in the plot next to him.

We would rest side by side in this beautiful cemetery on a bluff overlooking the blue Pacific on one side and the purple chaparral covered Santa Ynez mountain range on the other. We had a great panoramic view of a tropical Mediterranean landscape paradise.

I would outlive him by sixteen years.

Chapter 44

Falling

I had always done everything in a hurry, running around the house, rushing up and down the two sets of carpeted stairs, my feet flashing from one step to the next as though they were in a race with one another, until the day they slipped on the bottom step. The jolt traveled from my tailbone up my spine like an electric shock and compressed the vertebrae in my neck.

Not long after, I underwent surgery for spinal stenosis, relying on one or the other of my children to take me to the hospital. I already suffered from rheumatoid arthritis, scoliosis, and osteoporosis, old lady diseases.

To my disbelief, my body was failing me. I was a geriatric mess. I had a litany of medical problems and was operated on for breast cancer. I, who had never smoked in my entire life, also showed a spot of lung cancer. I was losing control of my body. I wore a personal lifeline button to call the paramedics when I fainted and fell and couldn't get up, which happened seven times while I was living alone, once headfirst into the sunken bathtub.

I had grown deaf during the past few years and was isolated from the world of sound, including words spoken to me. Even when my children shouted at me, I could only pretend to hear them. I guessed at what they were saying. Robbie bought me a white board and black marking pen so he and others could write questions or information to me and I could answer. The technique barely suited me and reinforced how handicapped I was becoming. Having to use a walker and a cane was more than I could tolerate. But without them, I had no mobility, not even to take myself to the bathroom.

I absolutely refused to be tested for and wear a hearing aid. Despite my daughter-in-law describing how technologically advanced they had become (she was a speech and hearing pathologist), I would have nothing to do with them. First of all, they were too expensive. During the last years of his life, Bob had worn two, one in each ear. They were unsightly and acted only as sound amplifiers and were intolerable. He rarely used them. But he had bought a cheap non-prescription set from Sears. That was all the experience I wanted to have with hearing aids.

Depressed and distraught that I was no longer able to care for myself without assistance, I wanted my life to be over. Ninety-one years was long enough.

How long were my mind and body going to last?

I had outlived my older sister, Ruth. Her husband, Richard, had died of a stroke and a few years later, a stroke had taken her.

Nina's husband had died of heart failure, and she had numerous medical problems and was on dialysis.

Having worked as a JW missionary financially supported by members of his congregation all his life, John had died of congestive heart failure.

Over the years, we had all shared letters and family photographs of our grown children and grandchildren that I considered our legacy.

Pam was my short-term care giver. I denied access and refused to let anyone in the house that she hired to take care of me. We had a few enjoyable moments together until I grew increasingly impatient and cranky and restricted her and ordered her to do things as though she were my personal servant. I also wouldn't let her voice her opinion. I made caustic slighting comments that would shut her down. I could dominate her and she would not stand up to me.

Unable to cope with me and my demands, she started leaving me alone and went to help out at a ranch in the Santa Ynez Valley near where she boarded her horses.

In my condition, I wasn't able to prepare meals. I couldn't even operate the microwave to thaw frozen food. So I stuffed myself with bread and rolls and pastries and ate lots of nuts and cheese, which raised my cholesterol. I wished for a fatal heart attack or a stroke that would end my life.

Getting up and down the stairs became an ordeal. I viewed the stairs as a challenge. A fall might have killed me or only incapacitated me even more, which would have been intolerable. I used the wrought iron handrail and my cane to walk slowly step by careful step up and down the stairs. Each successful journey was an ordeal that left me breathless, but jubilant, and I would say, "Okay. Okay."

I finally set Pam free. In the diary I started in an attempt to understand myself, I wrote, *Did I dim your glow? I love you, Pam. My fervent hope is that one day, you'll glow happily again. In your senior year at high school, you said, "You're not just my mother. You're my friend." When did that begin to change? Why is more important.*

What are friends anyway? Who are friends? I can easily answer the second question. No one attributed to my preference over the years to shun closeness and sharing with anyone other than immediate family.

Friendship, as I perceive it, is synonymous with kinship. I equate kinship with caring and selflessness. That must be it. I don't care now (nor have I in the past) to be caring and selfless with anyone but family. The demands of friendship loom too great. So much so, I will not stretch any acquaintance into what might be experienced as a relationship more binding. So I sometimes ponder why I chose to be a non-friend.

Yearning is so chest heavy. Why so weighty since that which is yearned for has no substance. It is nucleus, just a feeling, sometimes blazing with intensity, other times hard to rest as trivia of the day demands attention – shopping, food, cleaning. How I despise my concentration on them. The good little girl doing what she ought – and ought not.

I'm not that person. I don't want to be!

I loved you Mum and Dad, but why did you place such emphasis on rewards for being good and for Godliness?

There is that side, dark and threatening, that I fear, yet want to admit – yes, admit.

Fuck you, teaching. I wanted to throw the food against the wall. Rattle the pans in my fury, tear off the astronomical price tags, kick, scream, throw a tantrum. And then, what will I have accomplished? But why do I have to accomplish anything?

Oh, image builder, how you have strait-jacketed yourself. The thing I have imprisoned is me, the me that no one shares.

I yearned for what I sat seeking on the east side of the house of my youth. I escaped the nothingness, the void of mindlessness and no development, imagining a pulsating vibrant in-command me, assessing the economic stresses of loved ones, and I failed.

The naturalness is what I yearn for. It has escaped me, but when or why I do not know. My three children know me not. I'm just Mom to them attempting to thread my way through family relationships, wondering if love is a form of bondage when parents grow old.

I was a child bringing up three rewards in my life, attending well to the physical nurturing, yet inhibiting them with my own social and spiritual inadequacies. The child in me weeps. There are no second chances in the total nurturing of a child.

During one of Robbie's stopovers on the way to see consulting clients in Buellton and Santa Maria north of Santa Barbara, I was feeling so guilty about my treatment of Pam over the years that I had to unburden myself. I projected my guilt onto him. I knew he disapproved of his sister in some way and I thought that he blamed me. I challenged him with the accusation, "You don't like Pam, do you?"

"What?" he responded. "What are you talking about?"

"You don't like her. You don't like who she has become."

"I love Pam, Mom," he insisted. "I love her very much. I just have a problem with her freaky religion."

"What she does with her life is okay. I want to be proud of all my children."

He looked at me wondering why I had raised the subject. "Of course you do. You should be proud of all of us."

Little Mary from Colver knew so little yet felt so much. Now in my twilight years, I know more, but too late.

Wrinkles mock me, fiends of inner hell. Angelical fiend is mostly what I've been. In speaking, know thyself, prune face.

Chapter 45

Bye, House

I based my life on raising a family. I hoped one day to follow Bob and pass away in my home just as he had, but mitigating circumstances interfered with my plans. I stayed alive too long.

When Robbie moved me out of my house, I realized that my time, my turn had come. I could tell he was anxious I might resist in some erratic senile way. But I didn't. I said, "Bye, house," and got into the car without looking back. As inadequate and troubled as they were, I had my memories to sustain me and Robbie had made assisted living arrangements for me where my children and grandchildren could come and visit.

My children split the good pieces of furniture between them. What remained was sold in an estate sale and a property management company leased the house.

The first assisted living residence I called The Rabbit Hutch. The gray wood framed Cape Cod style architecture reminded me of a rabbit hutch.

The ignominy of being subjected to a bodily physical inspection for bleeding or bruises by three Amazonian Philippine attendants made me feel like a prisoner, an inmate, not a resident. I was told by the resident nurse such inspections were their policy. I made it known that I did not want to stay, that their policy was a violation of my personal civil rights. Robbie's daughter, who was a college professor, even expressed my opposition in writing for me in a letter to the management. I never stopped being a fighter.

One day, when Robbie came to visit me, I asked if any changes had been made of my house for the new tenants. He had just described how I was making more money leasing the house to strangers and combined with my retirement pension than when I had been a teacher, about one-hundred thousand dollars a year. Much of that went to pay for my care.

Upon learning that the entry stairs wallpaper had been painted over with white paint, I shouted, "Those shits! Those shits!"

The wallpaper was an old style turn-of-the-century pattern of burnished gold that I had carefully selected.

"Why?" I asked. "Why did they paint over it?"

"It was part of the upgrade to be able to rent it. The property manager said it wasn't modern enough."

"He's a shit! That's what he is, a shit!"

"You won't see it, Mom. Just keep the memory of the wallpaper."

"Someday, I'll move back."

"Of course, I never did or could move back. Robbie did relocate me to a nicer, upscale assisted living residence near his home with an adjacent skilled nursing facility. I had a private room with a balcony overlooking the landscaped grounds. The interior décor reminded me of a resort hotel featuring burnished wall sconces and a wide floral pattern pink and green carpeted hallway providing access for wheelchairs and service carts.

My room was quite large. Most of my clothes brought from home hung in the closet. My tall chest of drawers towered against the corner next to my hospital bed. A framed photograph of Bob stood at the top along with photos of my four grandchildren.

Robbie visited me frequently and brought me stacks of novels to read. After a while, my ability to concentrate began to fade with the onset of dementia exacerbated by my refusal to be tested for hearing aids. I couldn't stay focused long enough to read and spent my waking hours staring out the window or at the floor or at the wall or at the framed photograph of Bob on the dresser. My pride would not allow me to capitulate to my increasing deafness. I pretended I understood what people were saying to me, but, in reality, I socially isolated myself.

To facilitate communicating with me, Robbie brought in a white board and marker pens to pose simple questions that I could answer. But even my weakening voice was losing its clarity.

Pushing my walker, I would chug along down the hallway three times a day to the communal dining room for bland, uninspired, unappetizing meals. The chef both ignored and didn't understand what constituted a vegetarian diet, even though Robbie had provided a written description and list of representative foods and how to prepare them. Despite what the management told us, their attempts to honor my requests were woefully inadequate. One day, in disgust, I angrily told the young woman waiting on me to "Take this shit away!"

I rapidly lost interest in food and, consequently, lost weight. Like Bob, I hated to look at myself in the mirror and see my sagging wrinkled face. I did not want my picture taken at the last few holiday gatherings at Robbie's house. A resident caregiver had to wash my thin body in the walk-in shower and support me sitting on a plastic stool to prevent me from falling on the wet rubberized floor.

For the most part, I appreciated what the staff women were doing for me. Robbie was paying a lot of money out of my retired teacher's pension and IRAs to support me.

To improve my appearance, I had my hair done weekly in the salon on the main floor.

As my toenails began to curve over like dirty yellow claws, Robbie arranged for a pedicurist to come and trim them. I had always used to cut them myself, but I could no longer bend over to reach them. A caregiver had to help me dress.

Robbie took me to doctors' appointments and to have weekly coumadin checks, since I was taking blood thinners to prevent clots. He would often bring me over to his house for Sunday dinners and his children's birthday parties. Despite my protests, he did take a few photos of me. He said he wanted a record of my ninety-first birthday, the last meal I ate there.

Chapter 46

My Time, My Turn

Growing old is a covert shrinking of my inner self. The physical shrinking is overt. My face maps both geographically.

I remember when my Mum passed away. I was at her bedside. Her last request was for a spoonful of tomato sauce. I held the spoon to her dried lips. She tasted it on her tongue and died.

Something is amiss. Self-induced insomnia is punishment. Where is the luster of living? I need to reach it again, perhaps through remembering. Those Sunday mornings, three pajama clad funny paper readers on all fours, fannies up. Stepping backward into time. No, that's not the answer.

Dominant – I heard that word from my children. I'm that type. I had hoped caring and responsible would have been their assignations.

I love wholly or I withdraw wholly. I fear I'm being pushed toward withdrawal. I do have tendencies toward the hermetic.

Why or how did I contribute to Pam's accusation that I made her a psychological cripple. I don't think she sees me as a person – a self. Did I see her as a person, other than my confused daughter. I've seen her hurt these past years of our lives. Bob and I thought we could economically ease her leaving us. Emotionally, no.

Looking back, much of what I did I might think was extreme. I knew I was difficult, but I was striving to live for the future in the moment. Although I have regrets, I offer up no excuses for my behavior. I am who I am, Just Mary.

About the Author

Author and retired business and management consultant in a wide range of industries throughout the country, Rob resides with his wife in Southern California.

He is a graduate of the University of California, Santa Barbara and of the University of California, Los Angeles with Bachelor's and Masters of Fine Arts Degrees. He is a recipient of the Samuel Goldwyn and Donald Davis Literary Awards and has also worked in advertising, corporate communications, and media production.

An affinity for family and generations pervades his novels.

His works are literary and genre fiction that address the nature and importance of personal integrity.

Readers and Book Club Discussion Topics

Born and raised in 1922 in a coal mining town in the Alleghany Mountains of eastern Pennsylvania, Mary Wenger struggles to escape the influences and stigma of her impoverished immigrant childhood and pursue her goal of becoming a middle-class housewife and mother in pursuit of the American dream.

Emotionally torn between the conflicting historical social forces of feminism and the traditional roles of women in post-World War II society, Mary Wenger struggles with a deep sense of despair that plagues her as she encounters one disappointment after another.

Spanning the continent during the decades of the 1930s, '40s and '50s to the turn of the century, her pathological, compulsive lifelong odyssey in search of an acceptable house in which to realize her personal and economic goals throws her out of balance with her family and her siblings. She is blind to the fact a particular house is not necessarily a home and that her neurotic obsession undermines her ability to find happiness.

1. Both as a child and as an adult what is Mary's typical reaction to social and physical obstacles? Why are rational thinking and problem-solving difficult for her?

2. What are her perception of and attitude about her immigrant parents' superstitions and religious beliefs?

3. What made the beginning of the war a romantic experience for Bob and Mary?

4. What happened during the war that changed Bob's life?

5. What early events as a young family caused Mary's paranoia regarding the health and safety of her children?

6. What are the similarities and differences between post World War II America and American society today? What class and

racial prejudices did women have to overcome then and continue to have to fight against now?

7. What was the expected role of men then and now? How important was masculinity then and now? How did the drive to be successful in business affect Bob Wenger?

8. How would you describe the relationship between Bob and Mary Wenger?

9. When and why did Mary say she refused to lower herself? What did she mean?

10. What was Mary's vision for her family's gracious living? What are the characteristics?

11. Why was the sanctity of her home so important? How did she react when it was violated?

12. Why did the family move to Streator cause her so much emotional stress.

13. What people did Mary care about? Who was important to her?

14. During the 1950s, who created the propaganda to define a woman's role and to suppress women's rights? Through what media did Mary absorb the propaganda?

15. How does an ensemble of oppressed neighbor women and the published feminist writings of a wartime friend, Gwen Gebhardt, ratchet up her intense psychological conflicts and challenge her mental stability in confronting change.

16. Can you identify scenes of subtle humor in Mary's memoir of discovery. Why was her fear of separation from her children so intense? Why does she value her relationship with her children as being more important than with her husband? How does her separation anxiety affect her husband and children, as they mature and independently

react to her attempts to mold them to her vision of how they all should be as a family?

17. In what two locations and in what houses was she satisfied and experienced a sense of personal happiness? What caused those two situations to come to an end? How did Mary react?

18. From Mary's perspective, what was not acceptable about living in California? What was acceptable? What was she able to achieve?

19. What in Bob Wenger's life and in the nature of his personality caused him to have a mental breakdown? How did his wife and children react?

20. Toward the end of her life, why was Mary depressed that she had not achieved her vision of herself as a mother? What was that vision of herself, how she had wanted to be regarded and remembered? What were her successes in terms of her ambitions? Was she insecure about herself or did she take pride in her accomplishments? How would you describe her level of self-esteem? Would you say Mary was a strong individual with an aggressive personality, or would you describe her as being quiet and passive?

21. Why did Mary refer to herself as "just Mary?"

***

www.ingramcontent.com/pod-product-compliance
Lightning Source LLC
Chambersburg PA
CBHW030628310726
48979CB00003B/924
9781952020193